To my good friends

Steve and Pip.

John de Caynoth

Moth Island

By

John de Caynoth

Cover Picture

The Deaths-Head Hawk Moth, Acherontia Lachesis, so called because the yellow marking on the thorax is said to resemble a human skull. There are three species in the genus found mainly in Europe and Asia.

The genus name, Acherontia, is derived from the Greek mythological river Acheron, a tributary of the River Styx.

When threatened the moth emits a loud squeak by drawing air through its epipharynx.

'However, let the cause of the noise be what it may, the effect is to produce the most superstitious..... feelings of awe and terror.'
Edward Newman, C.1850

Cover picture. Copywrite 2018: Claire Ballardie

Dedication

This book is dedicated to my friend and companion, Sammy, the large black poodle dog. He is lying on the floor in front of my table as I write, watching me and hoping that shortly we will go outside a do something exciting.

Acknowledgements

My wife Claire for her encouragements, inspiration and patience correcting my spelling and grammar.

My good friend, Alan Johnson, for reading my draft manuscripts and correcting mistakes.

Finally the Islands and people of the Caribbean which provide the inspiration and background to the stories. The Island of Keata itself does not exist but is inspired by the wonderful Islands of the Eastern Caribbean, some of which I have been lucky enough to visit.

This book is a work of fiction. Names, characters, businesses, organisations, places, events and incidents are the product of the author's imagination or are used fictitiously. Any resemblance to actual persons, living or dead, events or locals is entirely coincidental.

Kaeta Island

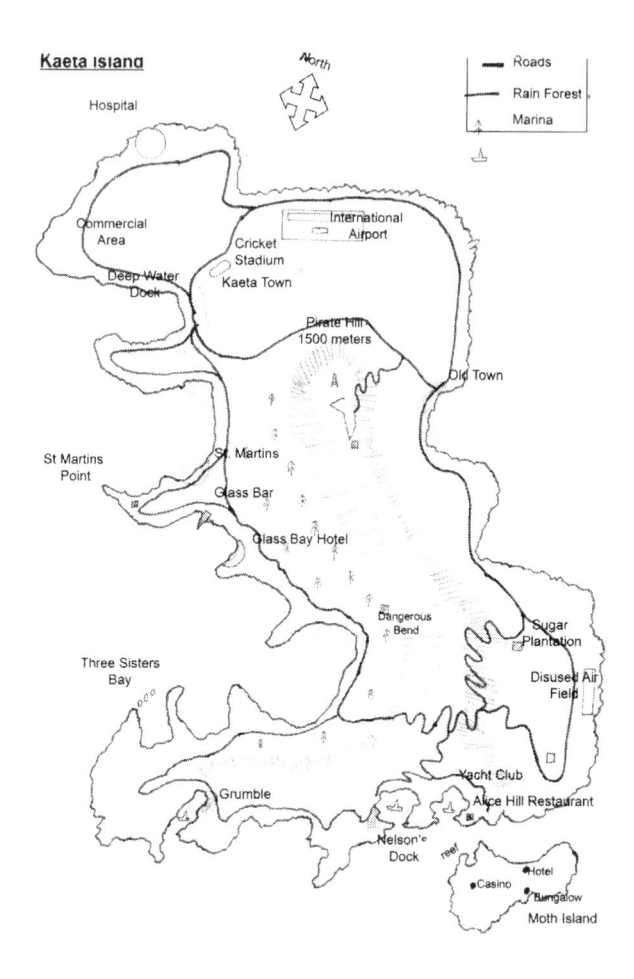

Prologue

The woman was silent as she lay on the beach sunbathing. Douglas, whose thoughts strayed from the point of their discussion, found he was studying her breasts rise with her breathing as he waited for her to speak again.

'The problem is,' Eva whispered, 'in my experience, men who extend a helping hand to me always want something in return.' She turned her head towards Douglas but he could not see her expression through her dark glasses.

He again had an uncomfortable feeling that Eva had just read his thoughts as she lay on her towel asking, 'What is your price Douglas?'

On the other side of the world, another woman, still a girl really, her name was Linda, she was just sixteen years old and she was Welsh, not that that was relevant. She sat in the hotel lobby waiting to be summoned and she was excited, a job in the Caribbean, it was her dream come true. As she waited, day dreaming about long, palm fringed golden sandy beaches, sunshine and azure blue sea, her mind wandered to thoughts of how she came to be sitting in the lobby of the Savoy Hotel.

Linda grew up in Bridgend, she had an older sister who she was constantly reminded had done well, been to university and was now training to be an accountant with one of the big four accountancy firms.

Linda was pretty, with piercing blue eyes and long black hair, but she was a little podgy from a diet of chips and burgers and was not the brightest of girls. At just sixteen she announced she wanted to leave school and travel and that was what had started things.

As usual her father was at the pub and when

she told her mother what she wanted to do. Her mother told her, once again, she should be like her sister, get a job with prospects and good husband, not go gallivanting around. That night Linda decided to leave home and start travelling, initially to Milton Keynes where her sister lived.

She had been staying with her sister for a month, but she had not seen much of her sister who was usually away on audits during the week.

One night, a week ago, her brother-in-law had entered her bedroom, got on the bed beside her and squeezing her breast telling her it was time she earned her keep. She kicked and pushed him away, she had not meant to knee him in groin but that is where one of her kicks landed. He fell off the bed and in anger, fueled by frustration and pain, told Linda to get out of his house.

She did just that, and on her way out took his wallet off the kitchen dresser.

She spent the rest of the night at the bus station catching the first bus in the morning to London. The first couple of nights she spent sleeping rough outside Victoria Coach Station. It was a lot rougher than she imagined, but she was not going home, and certainly not back to Milton Keynes. Fortunately, a bag lady took pity on her and told her how to find a hostel where she could get a meal and possibly a bed for the night.

It was there she had learnt of the interviews for the job in the Caribbean and all she had to do, the following Saturday morning, was present herself at the Savoy Hotel.

A woman appeared in the hotel lobby and beckoned Linda to follow her. She took Linda to a small ground floor room, obviously furnished for business meetings, and invited Linda to tell her about herself and why she wanted to work in the Caribbean. The lady was vague about the location of the job but smilingly told Linda she would work as a waitress and be trained as a croupier. She established Linda had a passport.

'Yes, my dear, I think you will be very suitable, and I am pleased to offer you the job,' the lady declared.

Linda was overjoyed and asked when she could start.

'Report to the BA information desk at six-o-clock next Saturday morning, you will be met and given a travel ticket and documents,' the lady explained. She took Linda's passport, 'So we can book your ticket,' she said. She even gave Linda a £20 note for her train fare to Gatwick.

CONTENTS

Copyright
Chapter 1. Joelle.   1
Chapter 2. Douglas.   14
Chapter 3. Merv.   21
Chapter 3. Brighton   28
Chapter 4. Kaeta.   41
Chapter 5. Moth Island.   49
Chapter 6. Problems   61
Chapter 7. The Kiss   75
Chapter 8. The Day Trip.   84
Chapter 9. Indecisive   95
Chapter 10. The Holiday Resort Company Limited   103
Chapter 11. The Weekend   111
Chapter 12. Moth Island   121
Chapter 13. Douglas's weekend.   130
Chapter 14, Joelle's Saturday.   138

Chapter 15. Joelle's Sunday	149
Chapter 16. Monday	160
Chapter 17. The Ending.	172
Chapter 18. One Step Forward.	183
Chapter 19. A Second Body.	191
Chapter 20. Miserable Weekend	206
Chapter 21. The Casino.	215
Chapter 22. The Project	223
Chapter 23. Linda	235
Chapter 24. Joelle's date	239
Chapter 25. Josh.	249
Chapter 26. Martin Pleasance	257
Chapter 27. The Meeting	265
Chapter 28. Douglas disappears.	274
Chapter 29. Friday afternoon.	281
Chapter 30. Monday	289
Chapter 31. Joelle's Trial	295
Chapter 32. Eva's Lover.	307
Chapter 33, Dinner with Oys.	313
Chapter 34. Lunch with Oys	324
Chapter 35. Oys.	336
Chapter 36. The Casino	341
Chapter 37. One step forward.	348
Chapter 38. Ralph's Claim.	353

Chapter 39. The Inflatable	358
Chapter 40. Terrified	366
Chapter 41. Guilt	374
Chapter 42. The Military.	382
Chapter 43. The Arrests.	390
Chapter 44. The Day After	401
Chapter 46. Break Through.	409
Chapter 48. The Drug Gang	414
Chapter 49. Tears	418
Chapter 50	427

CHAPTER 1. JOELLE

The two Americans were sitting on a bench outside the tourist shopping arcade in Kaeta town. It was approaching mid-morning and it was sunny and hot. There was a small pedestrian square in front of the arcade around which were planters containing small trees to give some shade and benches for the comfort of the tourists. The arcade was newly built of red brick as were the other buildings on that side of the street. The road was one of the main routes through the town and at that time of the morning was busy with an assortment of vehicles from new cars and mini busses through to decrepit old pick-up trucks all revving their engines and honking their horns as they weaved through the parked vehicles and pedestrians on the highway.

A large cruise ship had docked earlier that morning and most of the passengers had finished breakfast and were now disembarking for the 'Kaeta Town Shopping Experience' and streaming the arcade which was strategically placed at

Mr John de Caynoth

the end in the terminal at which the cruise ships docked.

However, the two Americans, teenagers doing the Caribbean before going to college to study for a post-secondary degree, had not arrived on the cruise ship, they had flown to the Island from St Lucia a few days earlier and were discussing what else they wanted to do while on Kaeta.

Josh, he was the larger teenager, nudged Francis, known as Cis, sharply in the ribs.

'Aw man! What did you do that for,' Cis exclaimed, moping spilt Coke from his shorts.

'Look at that,' Josh leered at the police woman standing casually in the shade under the old shops and offices on the other side of the road watching the street touts to make sure they did not overly bother the new visitors to the Island.

'She can arrest me any time she wants,' Josh leered again rubbing his groin suggestively.

'Yea well,' replied Cis, 'you just better put that joint down or she just might.'

They watched the officer move slowly along the pavement and pause at another vantage point.

She was tall, about five foot eleven, and still in her late thirties she was very attractive with a well-proportioned slim athletic figure. That day she was wearing her uniform. Dark blue long cotton trousers, which had been tailored to fit snugly round her hips, showing off her long legs, and a matching blue short sleeved shirt, which again had been cut to fit her slim waist without pulling too tightly across her bust. Her long brown hair was straight with a slight wave and was tied in a pony-tail which flowed out from the back of the blue baseball cap with the Kaeta Island Constabulary shield on the front just above the peak. She preferred the baseball cap to the rather larger and hard flat police caps her colleagues wore.

The teenage boys watched as she walked slowly along the opposite pavement. Her large brown eyes were hidden beneath the peak of her cap and they were too far away to see her smile at the young woman handing out flyers for the Crystal Bay Restaurant. The police woman knew the young lady, she was her daughter, Jasmine, who with her partners, Eva and Douglas now ran the restaurant.

The police woman crossed the road dodging between tourist buses and pick-up trucks in various states of disrepair. She walked up to Jasmine, who with her light olive coloured skin and European features was the image of her mother, both of whom were of mixed parentage. Jasmine, however, a recovering anorexic, was of slighter build and had yet to develop an attractive figure like her mother's.

The police woman stood politely behind her daughter listening to her explain that the restaurant was only a short taxi ride out of town but was certainly worth the visit for lunch as they served the best traditional fish dishes on the Island.

The group of tourists moved on and Jasmine turned to her mother, 'Sorry Joelle', she said. Her mother was Joelle de Nouvelas, a Detective Inspector in the Kaetian Police. 'You asked me to let you know if I picked up any gossip about drugs, but I have heard nothing so far.'

Inspector de Nouvelas was concerned, there had been an explosion in the amount of marijuana and cannabis on the streets in recent weeks. The Islands strict drug laws prohibited recreational drugs and although there was always some marijuana on the Island provided it was kept behind closed doors the police did not get too excited, but recently large amounts of both drugs had appeared, and were being offered to tourists and Joelle wanted to find its source.

Joelle nodded to Jasmine and wishing her luck moved on slowly down the street. She paused in the shade at the entrance by the arcade and one of the American boys blushed as she caught his eye looking at her. She paused, deciding whether or not to go in to the arcade. She did, and enjoyed the cool air conditioned atmosphere of the hall after the outside temperature in the high twenties. She walked through the shops and stalls exchanging greetings with the owners. Then she walked out of the arcade into the sunlight and stopped, sniffing.

Marijuana, she thought as the faint but distinctive smell drifted through the atmosphere. She looked round trying to see from where it emanated and her gaze fell upon the two teenagers sitting on the bench. She knew perfectly well the two boys had not been able to take their eyes of her as she had walked along the other side of the road and she had seen them watch her talking to Jasmine and entering the arcade. She was used to men watching her, and while she did not particularly like it, she was not bothered these days, but with marijuana on her mind she wondered if the teenagers had had a particular reason for watching her movements.

She walked silently up behind the two who were now ogling two local girls in short tight skirts and even tighter tops. She paused behind the two boys and noted that the smell of marijuana was much stronger and that the larger of the two teenagers was smoking. Under other circumstances she might have confiscated the boy's joints and let them off with a warning but this time as she could catch them in possession of drugs and as they had been observing her movements carefully she decided she would arrest them, perhaps they could give her a lead.

'Good morning lads,' Joelle said politely as she moved to stand in front of the boys. 'On holiday in Kaeta are you?' She enquired, watching Jake hurriedly drop his smoke and stamp on it and Cis try to discretely drop a small white packet behind the bench. The two boys looked in horror at each other as Joelle asked, 'And what were you smoking just now?'

'Nothing Officer,' Jake replied nervously.

'Was it marijuana?' Joelle confronted him.

'I don't know Officer, some bloke just offered me a cigarette,' Jake tried to bluff.

'What bloke?' Joelle asked.

'Don't remember,' Jake shook his head.

'I am arresting you for possession.......' Joelle started to caution the boy but he jumped to his feet and tried to run. He lunged at Joelle standing in front of him but she nimbly stepped aside and grabbed his hair as he tried to run past her. The boy yelped in pain and surprise as, holding his hair, Joelle pulled him to the ground and then with one knee on his chest snapped a handcuff on him. Leaving him lying on the ground she cuffed him to bench frame and looked round expecting to find his friend had also run. To her surprise he had not run but had picked up his little white package and was busy trying to hide it in a planter.

'Give that to me,' she ordered him.

He looked like he might run but seeing Joelle pull a small cosh from her bag, changed his mind and handed over the packet. She ordered him to lie on the ground next to Jake and handcuffed the two teenagers together passing the cuffs round the bench frame. She picked up the squashed joint and sniffed it confirming that it was marijuana.

By this time a crowd had gathered round to

watch the excitement.

'Show is over now folks, please move on.' Joelle asked the audience, 'Now!' she added threateningly and they reluctantly started to disburse. She placed the white packet and cigarette in an evidence bag and sitting on the bench used her mobile phone to call for a van to take the boys to the police station.

As she sat on the bench waiting she heard Cis whisper to Jake, 'You got your wish then, you said she could arrest you any time, and she sure did!'

Jake just grunted.

Finding drugs on the two teenagers was not the only thing that Joelle had discovered that morning. She had met one of the receptionists from the Glass Bay Hotel who had told her that the hotel was laying off staff.

'Why would that do that in January, high season?' Joelle asked, and was told that visitor numbers were down and the hotel is only half full. Of course Joelle new that visitors numbers to the Island were down, mainly as a result of recession in America, but this was the first she had heard of the impact it was having on the hotel and this concerned her as she owned the freehold of the Glass Bay Hotel, she had inherited it from her father, and although it was managed by an independent hotel chain, Joelle received an substantial rental income.

She sat on the bench waiting for the police van to arrive to take the two teenagers to the cells and thinking about the implications of the hotel laying off staff she decided to discuss it with Douglas, her fiancé, and see what he thought.

Her thoughts were interrupted by the teenagers who were still lying on the ground handcuffed to the bench leg.

'What are you arresting us for?' Cis asked.

'Possession of illegal drugs,' Joelle answered, her thoughts still on the hotel.

'It's hot and uncomfortable down here,' Cis spoke again, 'couldn't you take these cuffs off?'

'No,' Joelle replied tersely.

She looked down at the two boys squirming uncomfortably on the ground. 'If you promise not to run away again I will let you sit up on the bench.'

'We promise,' Cis replied. Jake just grunted again.

Joelle undid the cuff on Cis, unhooked the chain from the bench leg and replaced it on the boys' wrist, telling them they could get up and sit on the bench, but they would remain handcuffed together until they got to the cells.

'What are your names,' she asked after they had sat on the bench next to her.

'Jake'

'Cis, short for Francis'

Jake started to whine, 'I don't know why you are arresting us, we have not done any drugs or anything.'

Joelle sighed and did not respond, saved from further conversation by the arrival of the van and a constable who escorted the teenagers into the back of the van. Joelle sat in the front with the driver.

When interviewed, separately, later that afternoon both teenagers claimed they were innocent. Jake said he found the cigarette under the bench and had picked up as it smelt funny, while Cis claimed the white packet was lying under the bench, and he just picked it up out of curiosity intending to throw it into a rubbish bin.

Joelle interviewed the boys with her new Detective Constable, Irene Deoyen, she asked them why they had been so interested in her movements, watching her intently as she patrolled the street opposite. Cis shrugged and told Joelle he had not been watching her, and she should ask Jake.

Jake's response was to blush deeply and mumble something incoherently.

'Speak up boy,' Irene told him pointing to the tape recorder.

'I thought she,' he indicated Joelle, 'was very pretty and I said to Cis that she could arrest me any time.'

Joelle snorted and asked why he had run away then when she had arrested him.

'I did not run away, I just stood up to be polite,' Jake claimed and then started to mutter that

Joelle had really hurt him when she had pulled him down by his hair.

Frustrated by the lack of cooperation Joelle had ordered that the teenagers be returned to separate cells.

Cis, who was clearly the more street wise of the two, had said at the end of his interview that he had answered all the questions honestly and was innocent and should be released and that he wanted to speak to the American Ambassador.

'You had better phone the American Consulate and tell them we have two of their nationals here suspected of being in possession of illegal substances,' Joelle told Irene when they got back to the detectives office on the second floor of the police building.

'Where are the boy's ruck sacks, have they been searched yet?' Joelle then asked Irene.

Irene looked blank, 'ruck sacks?' She questioned.

'Yes, they both had ruck sacks, I put them in the back of the van myself,' Joelle told her.

'They must still be there then,' Irene thought.

'Well, would it not be a good idea to get them and search them before we interview the boys again,' Joelle rolled her eyes, and stomped off to her office to phone the Consulate herself.

The American Consulate was only about a five-minute walk from the Police Headquarters in Kaeta Town and a junior official appeared in Joelle's office within the hour just as Joelle and

Irene were finishing their search of the rucksacks.

Joelle went through the first interview with the two teenagers and explained they were both claiming innocence.

The American official sat back in his chair. 'Of course it's up to you to decide, but I don't think you have enough to make a charge of possession stick, I suggest that we inform their parents that they are in trouble and you release them and we put them straight on a plane home.'

'I don't think so,' Joelle smiled at him, producing two plastic bags containing five little white packets and a couple of roll-ups in each. 'I am sure we will find these contain marijuana when we test the contents. The decision for us is whether we simply charge the boys for possession, or possession with intent to deal.'

The Consulate Official, his name was Samuel, sighed, deflated. 'Okay, I will tell the lads they are in deep trouble and they had better cooperate or they will find themselves in a Kaetian prison. We will let their parents know.'

Half an hour later the duty sergeant buzzed Joelle and told her the two Americans wanted to make a statement.

Cis spoke for both teenagers, 'We went on a day trip to Moth Island and got talking to the barman in the beach bar. He asked us if we did cannabis and that sort of stuff back in America. Of course, we told him that it happens at parties,

Mr John de Caynoth

that sort of thing, and then he said if we wanted some he could get it for us, two dollars a packet so we offered him ten dollars and he said as we were nice boys he throw in some extra stuff. We paid him the money and he said he would find us on the beach later and give us the stuff. We only meant to use it while we were on holiday, we weren't going to take any home,' Cis explained looking at Samuel.

The two teenagers were charged with possession and appeared in court three days later accompanied by their parents. They were both fined and their parents told to take them back to America.

That evening, when she got home, Joelle changed into a light summer dress and was sitting on the veranda of her home, a house named Windrush located on a headland overlooking the Caribbean Sea. Sitting with her was her fiancé Douglas and her mother Mary and she was telling them about the two American teenagers.
'I have sent Merv, my sergeant, over to Moth Island to find and interview this barman and sniff around a little.' Joelle was saying.
'Where is Moth Island?' Douglas asked.
'It's about half a mile to the south of Kaeta. It falls within Kaetian jurisdiction but its privately owned,' Joelle explained. 'Its tiny, about two square miles. It's just a horseshoe shaped volcanic rock, but the crater is flooded and

fringed with pink coloured sandy beaches.'

'Why is called Moth Island?' Douglas asked.

'Apparently, long ago, there was a pirate who used it as his base and his ship was called 'The Moth'. Of course it's rumoured he buried chests of gold on the Island,' Joelle explained. 'Over the years there have been expeditions to find them but nothing ever turned up. The whole island is now leased by an Australian hotel chain and they have built a luxury hotel resort and casino there, Moth Island Resort and Retreat.'

'Sound nice,' Douglas commented, 'Merv should enjoy himself.'

'Not too much I hope,' Joelle responded. 'Funny thing is, this is the second-time Moth Island has appeared on the radar in as many days.'

CHAPTER 2. DOUGLAS

The middle-aged man sat alone at a table with a view out across the bay.

Eva, who as usual was working front of house at the restaurant she ran with Jasmine, saw the man sit down as she served another customer. Obviously a tourist, she thought, looking at his floral print shorts and shirt, the buttons of which strained to contain his belly as he sat.

She sighed, she knew what was coming as she walked across to the man. 'Can I get you something Sir,' she asked politely.

Before answering the man looked wolfishly at Eva, who was a very attractive young woman, a brunette, not quite as tall as Joelle, but, like Joelle she had a good figure, and two years in the Caribbean and given her a delicious honey coloured tan. That day she was wearing a fitted white polo shirt, with Glass Bay Restaurant discreetly printed on the left breast, which the man was now studying. She was glad she was wearing a brown apron which hid her shorts and legs.

'You sure could,' the man replied, flirting.

MOTH ISLAND

'Can I get you a drink, a beer or perhaps a glass of champagne,' Eva asked the man.

'Is that all you have to offer?' The man asked, allowing his eye to roam down Eva's body again.

'I'll have a bottle of champagne, perhaps you would like to share it with me,' he invited Eva.

That invitation, however, was going too far. Eva did not mind a bit of harmless fun, it came with the job and she usually managed to get such flirts to spend more money, but she did not like this customer and the way he was coming on to her.

Eva was not the only one who did not like the exchange. Douglas, sitting quietly in his corner, was watching Eva jealously.

Douglas was the third partner in the restaurant enterprise. He put up the money and the two girls ran the business and he regarded the two in a very proprietorial way. Jasmine his step daughter to be when he finally got Joelle to agree to a wedding date, and Eva, five years older than Jasmine; well, he would only ever admit that she was a good friend.

'Douglas,' Eva shook him from his evil thoughts about the customer sitting at the far end of the restaurant, 'please, you take a beer over to that man.'

Douglas, somewhat consoled now Eva had involved him, plonked a beer on the table in front of the man asking, 'can I get you anything else?'

'I thought that nice young lady was serving me.'

'No, she is busy,' Douglas told him dropping a bill

15

for the beer on the table.

After the last lunch customer had gone Douglas and the two girls sat together at a table, sharing a half-drunk bottle of wine left by a customer. Jasmine was complaining that the number of customers were down, 'I don't understand why,' she told the other two, 'look at that food left over from today's lunch.'

Douglas was not really listening, his knee was touching Eva's and today she had not moved her leg away, and he was tingling all over at the touch of her skin.

'Are you going home to Windrush?' Jasmine interrupted his day dream, 'I will give you some fish stew for Mary's lunch,' she was telling him.

Dam, he thought, wishing he had not promised to return to check on Mary He would rather have spent the afternoon with Eva.

Douglas had found Mary and given her the lunch Jasmine had sent and even helped her eat it.

Mary had had a stroke which had left her disabled. She was now recovering but still had difficulty using her right arm and walking which had left her frustrated and sometime bad tempered.

Douglas liked the old lady, but nursing was not his forte and looking after Mary made him irritable. In addition, he was bored, he had enjoyed setting up the restaurant with the two girls but now they were quite capable of running it on their own and while he still visited each day, he frequently found there was nothing for him to do except drink beer.

He idly picked up a copy of the business magazine that was sent every month from the UK and started to flick over the pages. Following his conversation with Joelle when she had mentioned Moth Island he knew he had seen something about that Island in the magazine. He soon found the job advert for a part time Finance Director of the Moth Island Holiday Resort and it started Douglas thinking.

When Joelle came home later that evening, showered and changed and, as was their usual habit, they sat together on the veranda with a glass of wine watching the colours fade from the sky. As nightfall, the vivid colours of the garden faded and a warm inky blackness descended as the sounds of day were replaced by the persistent squeaking of tree frogs searching for a mate.

'Mary is still difficult but she is starting to get more mobile using that walking frame,' Douglas opened the discussion and waited to see how Joelle reacted.

'Yes, a bit, but the doctor says she will improve further although her right side will always be weak,' Joelle responded.

She rose and walked over to the side of the veranda and looked out across the headland watching the lights of a cruise ship head southward to its next island stop. She gave a deep sigh which

Douglas noted and then he too rose and moved across to stand behind her, putting his arms round her waist he nuzzled her neck and asked what she was worrying about.

'Oh, nothing really, we just do not seem to be making any progress with this drug business on the Island and now I have the Commissioner on my back asking when we are going to clear it up. He thinks I should have gone to go Moth Island myself, rather than send Merv.'

Douglas released his hold thinking that Joelle wanted to talk police work.

'No,' she said, 'please hold me.'

Douglas remained standing behind her holding her tightly and nuzzling her neck. She moved slightly to more comfortably feel him pressing against her back.

'I do love you,' Douglas whispered in her ear, but she anticipated his next line.

'No Douglas, I am not ready to fix a marriage date yet, there is still too much going on in my head.'

It was Douglas turn to sigh as he held her, feeling a certain sensual excitement as she wriggled her hips against him.

She turned to face him and giving him a kiss took his hand, 'come,' she whispered, 'I know what we need.' She led him into the garden and a particularly dark corner where she slipped out of her dress and unbuckled his trouser belt.

Later that evening they ate a light supper with

Mary, some of Jasmine's unsold fish fillets with an edible sea weed which Jasmine wanted them to try before putting it on the restaurant menu. After they had eaten they returned to the veranda to finish their wine.

'There is one thing that bothers me,' Joelle confided, now feeling more relaxed, 'I discovered the other day that the Glass Bay Hotel is laying off staff and only half occupied. Rumour has it that the hotel has money problems.'

'Mmm,' Douglas thought. 'That makes some sense, I don't know about money problems, but Jasmine says the number of customer in the restaurant is falling.'

'But the restaurant is okay, isn't it; they are not losing money are they?' Joelle queried.

'No, they have to average half full to break even and at the moment Eva says they are running between sixty and sixty five percent,' Douglas assured Joelle.

Joelle went quite at the mention of Eva. She was most certainly aware of a closeness that had developed between Eva and Douglas, Douglas explained it away as simply that he was helping Eva with her distant learning course work, but it still made Joelle uncomfortable and she did not like it. In fact it was the main reason why she would not discuss a wedding date, she certainly did not want to get married and then discover Douglas was having an affair. She mentally pushed the thoughts away thinking that

Mr John de Caynoth

after what they had done earlier that evening he could not be two timing her. Could he?'

CHAPTER 3. MERV

Joelle was sitting anxiously in her office, Merv had just phoned her to say he was finished on Moth Island and was on his way back to the police station, and Joelle was hoping he found something useful.

Before he arrived however, the Commissioner's PA put her head into Joelle's office, 'The boss wants to see you.'

'What for, this minute?' Joelle asked, cursing under her breath.

'Yes, now and he does not look very happy,' the PA warned Joelle.

She walked into the Commissioner's office,

'Inspector,' The Commissioner greeted her, not inviting her to sit down. Always a bad sign Joelle thought, wondering what she had done.

The Commissioner sat silently looking at a document on his desk before addressing her.

He gave a deep troubled sigh, 'I have here a letter from an American lawyer alleging police brutality and seeking substantial compensation for the victims.'

Joelle looked surprised, 'What brutality, who, where?' She asked.

The Commissioner summarised the letter for Joelle, 'The young man, Jake, that you arrested for possession of drugs. He is claiming he stood up when you arrested him and offered his wrists to you for cuffing but you grabbed his hair, tearing lumps of skin from his skull, pulled him to the ground where you kicked and punched him before humiliating him by chaining him down on the ground.'

'That is a pack of lies Sir,' Joelle responded. He pushed me aside and tried to run away, I just grabbed him to prevent him escaping, and he stumbled and fell. It is all in my report.'

'I know, I have read your report.' The Commissioner returned his attention to the letter. It says here they want the case tried in Boston; I bet they do! We will resist that and settle it under Kaetian law.'

He looked up at Joelle standing before his desk and softened his expression, 'Of course I believe you, but you must more careful dealing with tourists, the last thing we need is for our police force to get a reputation for brutality,' he told Joelle before dismissing her.

She left his office and returned to her desk thinking evil thoughts about the brutality she would like to inflict upon Jake and his companion Cis.

She was still silently fuming about the incident

when Merv walked into her office.

'Well first I interviewed all the staff in the resort and showed the mug shots of the two teenagers, no one even remembers them visiting the Island,' Merv reported, 'I described the bar tender the boys claim sold them drugs but the description was so vague it could have been any one. The photo fit picture was not much better. No one recognised the barman and I did not see anyone who vaguely fitted the description either.'

'Did you get a list of names and addresses of all the staff who might have worked the bar,' Joelle asked.

'Yes,' Merv confirmed, 'and I checked the list against the staff I interviewed. I saw them all except for two who I was told were temporary staff employed through an agency. I will find out who they are and interview them next.'

Joelle nodded, 'so really we are no further on at the moment. No sign of drugs on the Island I suppose?'

'No, nothing,' Merv confirmed, 'but there is one thing which did not feel right.'

Joelle looked up expectantly.

'There seem to be two separate enterprises on the Island. The tourist resort, as you would expect to find, with all the facilities, swimming pool, gym, gift shop, bars all that sort of thing. But there is also a casino, well that's what they called it, it's behind a razor wire fence with a security guard on the gate. I tried to get in but the guard would not let me enter. He said I had to be a member, and I noticed the perimeter was patrolled with dogs.'

'Mmm! Did they give you any explanation?' Joelle asked.

'They said the security was necessary for insurance as there was millions of dollars kept in the casino,' Merv explained.

'Well, I suppose that makes sense,' Joelle surmised. 'Did you interview the casino staff as well?'

'Yes, well, some of them anyway. They would not let me enter the casino, they sent the employees down to the hotel so see me. They assured me I saw everyone but I had no way of checking.'

'So, basically we are no further on with the drug investigation.' Joelle was disappointed. Merv nodded in agreement.

'What about the body found on the beach on Moth Island?' Joelle asked as she pulled the pathologists report from her pile of papers. 'It says here that the body is of a young negro female, but she had been in the water for some time and it's not possible to establish the exact cause of death.'

Merv replied, 'I asked about it but I just confirmed what they told DC Deoyen when she went over to recover the body and escort it back to Kaeta. The remains were found by a tourist out running early one morning. No one on the Island knows the woman and it is supposed she fell overboard from either a cruise ship or maybe a private yacht.'

'Yes,' Joelle confirmed, 'and that is about all we do know. Irene is still trying to identify the woman. She has checked with all the cruise operators and no one has reported any missing persons.

She is now speaking with all the local boatyards but so far nothing and the date for inquest is now set for next week.'

She scratched her head and looked at Merv.

'Not doing very well at the moment are we. Do you think it worth going around all our contacts again and giving them a push?'

'I will give it a go, and if I can find the two temporary employees, that might help,' Merv gave Joelle a lop-sided smile as he left.

As Joelle sat at her desk wondering what else she could do to break open the two investigations, She remembered that Douglas had asked her what she thought about him applying for a job as Finance Director of the Moth Island Resort Company. Initially she had been reluctant asking him why he wanted such a job, fearing that maybe he was getting bored with her, or worse, having an affair. But, she thought, telling herself these fears were unfounded, having someone on the inside on Moth Island could be useful and she also thought, slyly, it would get him away from Eva.

Her ponderings were interrupted by a young man who knocked politely on her open door and asked if he could come in.

She recognised him as one of the attorneys from the Island legal department.

'The Commissioner passed this letter across to us to deal with and I just wanted to confirm your arrest statement,' he started to say.

Joelle groaned guessing what was coming. She went through the incident right from the beginning starting from when she had patrolled along the pavement and noticed that the two teenagers were staring at her, watching her every movement. When she told the attorney that she had heard Cis say to Jake that he had got his wish, arrested by Joelle, and that the teenager, Jake, had confirmed he found her attractive, the attorney looked up interested.

'Did the either of the boys do or say everything else like that.'

'I do not remember them saying anything more,' Joelle paused, 'but I did notice the two of them leering at me and one, Jake, making lewd gestures.'

'What sort of gestures,' The attorney wanted to know.

'Well he was rubbing his groin in a manner that suggested sexual activity,' Joelle blushed.

'And this was directed at you?'

'I think so,' Joelle confirmed.

'Excellent,' the attorney said joyfully, 'I will put in a counter claim for sexual harassment and compensation. That will slow them up, or at the very least put the teenager in a different light.'

CHAPTER 3. BRIGHTON

Douglas opened his emails, as was his habit first thing in the morning, 'Wow!' He shouted with surprise, 'Look at that, I have got an interview,' as he read an email from The Holiday Resort Company.

Jasmine walked into the study to see what Douglas was shouting about. Joelle had already gone to work.

'What interview is that Douglas,' she asked.

'I saw an advert for a Finance Director for the Moth Island Resort so I emailed my CV and look, they have offered me an interview.'

It was a few moments before Jasmine spoke again and when she did, she sounded troubled, 'Does that mean you are leaving us for another job?' She asked nervously.

'No, of course not. If I get the job I may have to

spend some time on Moth Island but this will still be my home.' Douglas assured Jasmine.

'You will still help us with the restaurant', Jasmine worried, but was relieved when Douglas told her he had no intention of stepping back from his involvement, and he explained, 'you and Eva are running the business on a day to day basis perfectly well without me.'

Not wholly satisfied Jasmine pointed out to Douglas that the interview was in the UK.

'Oh!' Douglas exclaimed not having read the email properly in his excitement, 'so it is. Well never mind, I expect that is where their head office is, something like that.'

As he usually did every day, later that morning Douglas went down to the Glass Bay Restaurant thinking he might help in the bar. Eva had told him he did not really need to, the bar was not that busy at lunch times and she could perfectly well serve drinks and wait on table, but Douglas found it a relief from his increasing boredom and, anyway, he enjoyed the two girls company and enthusiasm.

'Jasmine says you are going to London soon?' Eva asked Douglas that lunch time.

'Yes, that's right,' he confirmed. 'I am going for a job interview next week.'

'Have you arranged a flight yet because I was wondering if I could come with you, I left some things with one of the girls at the rehab centre and really should collect them,' Eva asked.

'I don't see why we should not go together, I am going into town this afternoon to arrange a flight, I will see what I can do. It might be difficult, you know how busy flights are at this time of year,' Douglas offered.

Joelle was not happy when she found out that Douglas was travelling to London with Eva and it caused the first serious row they had. Her mood was further inflamed when Douglas told Joelle she was being unreasonable, there was absolutely no reason why he and Eva should not travel together. It ended with Joelle telling him he was spending far too much time with Eva and he was behaving like a dirty old man. Douglas told Joelle she was being utterly ridiculous and when she had calmed down he would accept her apology.

It took Joelle a couple of days to calm down, she never apologised, but did offer to drive Douglas and Eva to the airport to catch their flight.

As Douglas and Eva approached passport control Joelle put her hand on Douglas's arm and, after a quick glare at Eva held him back momentarily so she could give him a hug and kiss. She whispered to him, 'I love you and I am trusting you, please be careful.'

Douglas returned the kiss promising he would be careful and telling Joelle that he loved her as well.

The departure lounge was very crowded, mainly American and British tourists, waiting for their flights home, but Douglas and Eva found a couple of bench seats together and sat down to wait for their flight to be called.

'Have I done something to upset Joelle?' Eva asked.

'No, I think she is just under pressure at work and worrying about me going away,' Douglas assured Eva. But Joelle's comment, 'I am trusting you' was on Douglas mind and he was wondering what she meant, what was she talking about, he was thinking.

The flight was called and the passengers assembled for boarding. Douglas and Eva were split up as Douglas had booked the last two seats on the flight and one was in business class and the other in economy. He had gallantly offered Eva the business class seat, but she had declined telling him that as he had paid for the tickets the least she could do was to let him have the comfortable seat.

They flew into London Gatwick airport, but as Douglas's interview was in Brighton, they were not actually staying in London and Douglas had booked a hotel in Brighton for the two of them. Also, as they had to wait a week before they could get a return flight he had booked a hire car with the intention of driving down to Wiltshire to check on his cottage which he had let when he went out to Kaeta.

Mr John de Caynoth

Douglas was off the plane first and having slept through a large part of the flight was feeling quite bright even though it was only six in the morning. He waited for Eva, who eventually emerged at the end of a long line of passengers looking tired and fraught, explaining that she had been sat next to a woman with a young child who had alternately cried and climbed in and out of her seat and run up and down the aisle all night.

They were booked into the Palace Hotel, but, of course, their rooms were not ready when they arrived early in the morning. They had breakfast and walked along the sea front but spent most of the morning sitting in the hotel guest lounge waiting for their rooms. Eva went to bed for the afternoon, telling Douglas to wake her for dinner if she was still asleep. Douglas lay on the bed quietly reading and thinking about Eva and his interview in a couple of days time.

Two days later Douglas duly presented himself at the Georgian building which had recently been refurbished and turned into offices. He walked up the six steps, over the basement, to the large black front door resplendent with a new, period brass knocker, letter box and large round door handle. He wondered whether to use the knocker but then saw the brass name plate, 'The Holiday Resort Company', with an intercom discreetly set in the wall below. He announced his presence and the door magically swung open revealing a period hall running into the building at the far end of which was a magnificent oak staircase leading up to the floors above.

An attractive young lady sitting at an antique desk beneath the staircase greeted Douglas and enquired after his business.

'I have an appointment with Ms Janice Milicant,' he told the girl.

'I will let her know you are here, please take a seat,' the girl invited him indicating a group of antique seats arranged around a coffee table in one corner.

Douglas declined the proffered coffee and sat looking at his surroundings, admiring the ornate cornices and coving, with the splendid crystal chandelier hanging below the centre ceiling rose.

His pondering upon the cost of such a refurbishment was interrupted by a middle-aged lady, with black hair, purple spectacles and wearing a navy blue trouser suit. She introduced herself as Janice Milicent, the People Director and shaking Douglas's hand invited him into her office on the first floor.

Clearly the same attention to Georgian architecture had not been given to the first-floor offices. Ms Milicent's office was very plain with white walls, a light grey carpet, and leather two seater sofas set in the centre of the room on either side of a coffee table. In one corner was a table on

Mr John de Caynoth

which sat a lap top computer.

Douglas was invited to sit on one of the sofas and Ms Milicent sat opposite him and started the interview, putting Douglas at ease by describing the history of the building before asking him to tell her about his previous experiences and asking him why he wanted the job. She appeared to accept his explanation of why he had not worked for the last few years after being made redundant having negotiated the sale of his previous employer's company.

Half way through the interview a smartly dressed young man, wearing a startling blue open neck shirt under a light grey suit, entered the room and introduced himself as Dick Stump, Money Director. Douglas's expression of surprise at the unusual job titles was noticed by Janice Milicent who explained that their Australian owner was rather unconventional and believed job titles should summarise the holder's responsibilities in a single word, 'hence Dick is the money man, and I am the people lady' she smiled.

Dick Stump started telling Douglas about the job, 'it's only part time, two or three days a week. Each of our resorts is organised as a separate legal entity, helps us organise our liability for taxes efficiently,' he smiled. He explained that while the businesses were primarily running holiday experiences their purpose was to make money and therefore the Australian owner believes that the most important member of the management team was the finance man, 'That is why we are now recruiting a Money Director for the Moth Island Resort.'

Dick picked up Douglas's CV, 'You live on Kaeta, I understand?' He queried.

Douglas's confirmed that he did, 'That's one reason why the role attracted me, Moth Island being so close to Kaeta.'

Dick Stump frowned, 'We had envisaged the job would be based here in England, in our operations building in Horsham.'

Janice Milicent interrupted explaining that the Brighton offices were the head office staff only and they had offices in Horsham where the operational staff for the all the resort companies were located. 'We do run a sales office in the United States for our American clients,' she paused and asked, 'would you be willing to relocate back to the UK.'

'That is not something I have considered,' Douglas replied not wanting to say no, at this stage.

By this point they were coming to the end of the interview and Douglas was asked if he had any last questions.

Only one and he asked, 'I understand that there is a hotel resort and a casino on Moth Island and, so far we have only spoken about the responsibilities for the resort operations. If the job were offered, would the responsibility also include the Casino.'

Mr John de Caynoth

Dick Stump answered, 'Not all the resorts have Casinos, and there are only three Casinos, one on Moth Island and the others at the Pacific Island resorts. They are run as entirely separate businesses owned and run directly from Australia by George Munday our founder.'

Douglas zipped up his fleece as he left the office. It was late afternoon, it was cold but the sun was shining and he decided to walk back to the hotel. One of the first things he and Eva did on arriving in Brighton was to purchase coats as they arrived from the Caribbean not equipped for the English weather.

As he walked he thought about moving back to the UK. The previous evening Eva had mentioned that she had been having thoughts of returning the UK to finish the degree she had dropped after the experience with Ralph Holdswick. Douglas ruefully reflected that if he did take the job and Eva did return to the UK, then she would be his only friend in the country. He smiled as he remembered how she had thanked him the previous night for giving her the confidence to pick up her studies again and reflected that he was really becoming quite fond of Eva.

He also reflected on his life in Kaeta, Joelle, Jasmine and Mary, people he considered were the nearest he had to a family and he sighed as he wished that he could get Joelle to agree to a wedding date.

That night Douglas ate alone, Eva had gone to Bristol to see the girl with whom she had become friendly in the rehab hospital and who was storing her possessions. Douglas was feeling just a little depressed that night. He had convinced himself that he had blown the interview and would not be offered the job and even it was offered he would not accept as he had decided he did not want to move to back to the UK. He was lonely, and being back in England brought back unhappy memories of his divorce and how, when that was all over he had gone for a holiday on Kaeta and met Joelle. He was very much missing her that evening. His thoughts turned to Eva and he wished she had not gone to Bristol, he liked her company and at least she would have cheered him up if she had been with him. His mood lightened slightly when he remembered he was meeting Andrea Spooner the next day and then the following day he was driving down to check his cottage in Wiltshire and then on to Bristol to meet Eva.

It was mid afternoon before Douglas following the Sat Nav in the hired car drove into the suburbs north of Bristol and found Bradley Stoke and the maisonette where Eva was staying with her friend, Jane.

'You must be Douglas,' Jane greeted him, 'Come in, have a cup of tea, Eva is just sorting out the last of her stuff in the bedroom.' She sat Douglas in the open plan living and kitchen area while she made a cup of tea, chatting away telling Douglas how Eva had not stopped talking about him, Joelle and Jasmine.

Eventually Eva appeared carrying a suitcase and pulling a large black plastic rubbish sack behind her. Out of politeness Douglas stood as she walked across the room to give him a hug in greeting asking if he would mind going back to Brighton via the recycling centre so she could dispose of the sack of stuff she no longer wanted. With the traffic on the motorways it took them nearly four hours get back to Brighton and their hotel. During the journey, Douglas told Eva about the interview and asked her how she had got on in Bristol. Her answer was short and to the point, 'OK, it was good to see Jane, and we went into Bristol for some lunch and shopping.' She paused, taking a deep breath, 'actually, I did not enjoy it much, too many bad memories.' That finished the conversation and they spent the rest of the journey more or less in silence.

When they got back to the hotel they went straight into dinner. Douglas tried to make conversation but Eva, who was usually very talkative, appeared preoccupied and unresponsive to Douglas's attempts. After dinner, Douglas decided he needed a beer and invited Eva to go for a walk with him and find a pub.

'I am sorry Douglas, I am very tired, could we just have a drink here in the hotel,' Eva asked.

Again, conversation was difficult, with Eva becoming increasingly tense tearing a bear mat up into little pieces.

'You are very quiet tonight,' Douglas eventually said to Eva, 'What is on your mind?'

Eva did not reply directly, 'Sorry Douglas,' she pushed her glass of tonic water to one side. 'I think I will go up to bed now.'

They retrieved the keys from the reception. 'Mr. Jay, I have a message for you,' and the receptionist handed Douglas an envelope.

'I will walk you up to you room,' Douglas told Eva, putting the envelope in his pocket.

'Are you crying?' He asked as they stepped out of the lift and walked along the corridor to the room. Eva did not reply but hurried ahead of Douglas and reaching her door turned to say goodnight to him.

Her eyes were wet and tears dampening her cheeks. 'Whatever is the matter Eva? Have I upset you somehow? Tell me?'

Now sobbing quietly Eva told Douglas that it was Ralph.

Ralph, Joelle's ex-husband and Jasmines biological father, had been a lecturer at the University and initially appearing to befriend Eva, had taken advantage of her and fed her drugs on which she eventually became addicted. He had also imprisoned Jasmine in an effort to blackmail Joelle and stolen money from a colleague, crimes for which he had been convicted and sent to prison.

Through her tears, Eva told Douglas that she had met some of her old university friends who had told her that Ralph was out of prison and had been looking for her.

'I'm frightened he might appear again,' she admitted

Douglas seeing how distressed she was, put his arms around her in an attempt to comfort her. She responded by holding him tightly and sobbing on his shoulder. Holding her in a close embrace Douglas became very conscious of her soft warm presence against his body and as her tears subsided he kissed her gently on her cheek and tried to step back before he embarrassed himself.

But Eva just tightened her embrace and pulled him closer, 'Please Douglas, don't leave me, I feel safe with you,' she whispered as she turned her face up towards him.

Getting dressed the following morning Douglas remembered the message and reaching for his trousers pulled the crumpled envelope out of his pocket. The message was from the Ms Milicent of the Holiday Resort Company inviting him to a further discussion. It was brief and to the point:

I know you fly back to Kaeta on Saturday, but we have a proposition we would like to discuss with you and we would be grateful if you could meet us on Friday at five-o-clock.

CHAPTER 4. KAETA

J oelle did not believe in coincidences, not now days anyway, and she was looking at a missing person report which, for the third time in as many weeks referred to Moth Island. She put the report to one side and called in Irene Deoyen, her new detective constable.

'Tell me about this missing girl,' Joelle tapped the report sheet on her desk.

'She was reported by her boyfriend,' Irene started, 'they went on a day trip to Moth Island and he says they had a row and the girl friend, Sofia Luka, stomped off in anger. When he had calmed down he went to look for her, but could not find her and expected her to appear to catch the boat back to Kaeta later that afternoon. He said he returned to Kaeta and their hotel to wait for her but she never appeared, although, he assumed she did come back to the hotel and collect her things.'

Joelle frowned, 'If she collected her stuff why does he think she is missing, maybe she just does not want to see him again?'

Mr John de Caynoth

'That's what I thought, but the boyfriend said she just would not leave without telling him, and anyway he has the tickets for her flight home and her passport.' Irene reported.

'Did you check with the hotel that it was Sofia who collected the clothes?' Joelle asked.

'Yes, the receptionist said she asked for a spare key as she left hers in the room.'

'And the receptionist confirmed it was actually Sofia?' Joelle queried.

'Umm! Well no, I suppose not, I did not actually ask.' Irene admitted.

Joelle did not say anything, she just rolled her eyes upwards in disbelief.

'Have you got a picture of the girl?' Joelle asked.

Irene produced her iPhone and showed Joelle a picture of a blond girl in a bikini sitting drinking a glass of champagne. 'The boyfriend sent me this one.' I asked him for a picture Irene said, pleased with herself.

However, Joelle soon wiped the smug look off her face, 'and what good is the picture on your phone, it should be on file. Have you printed it and given copies to all officers and asked them to look for the girl.'

Irene had to admit she had not.

When Irene had gone, Joelle sat thinking that the girl had just got bored with the boyfriend. Probably she has met someone else and gone off with him. We need to confirm it was Sofia who collected the things from the hotel, and being fed up with paper work that day she decided to go and check herself.

She took Irene, who had printed copies of the picture, with her to the hotel and they showed the receptionist the girl's photo. The receptionist admitted she could not really say who had collected the clothes. 'I did not really look at him when I gave over the key, he said he was a friend of Sofia's, paid the outstanding bill and cleared the room.'

Joelle and Irene looked at each other, 'so we know Sofia did not return the hotel and had a man friend, but no clue who he is,' Joelle surmised. She was deep in thought as Irene drove them back to the police building. The Moth Island connection was bothering her.

First there was the body found on the beach, and with no identification or report of any missing person, the coroner had accepted the police explanation that she was probably crewing on a cruise ship or one of the large private yachts that cruise the Caribbean. It was not uncommon for crew members just to jump ship, which would explain why no one had reported her missing and in the absence of any positive evidence the Coroner had returned an open verdict.

Then there were the drugs. The two American teenagers had said they got the drugs on Moth Island, but Merv had drawn a blank there. Of the two temporary employees they had traced, one they had eliminated, the other had taken a job as bar tender on a cruise ship and disappeared, and despite leaning on all their contacts they had so far been unable to trace the source of the drugs.

And now, the third reference to Moth Island, the girl Sofia Luka, apparently missing, last seen on the Island, with an unidentified man friend.

Joelle still doubted she was actually missing and considered it more likely she had just gone off with the man, but the connection with Moth Island still worried her.

It was at this point that a forth connection with Moth Island occurred to her. Douglas, he had applied for a job on the Island. If there was something wrong on Moth Island she did not want Douglas to get involved as she reflected that danger seemed to follow Douglas around.

At the moment he was England, and while he was away they spoke on the phone every evening, he always phoned her as he was going to bed. She smiled at this thought, it was one of the little things he always did which showed he loved her.

He had told her that the interview had not gone well and he had decided he would not accept the job anyway as it was based in England, and as she thought dark thoughts about Moth Island, she was pleased the job was off the table. It still worried her that Douglas had applied for the position as she feared perhaps he was perhaps getting tired of her. Then there was Eva, to whom Douglas seemed to be getting very close.

MOTH ISLAND

Perhaps I should just confront him and ask him if he is having an affair. She considered this idea but was not sure she really wanted to know the answer.

Irene interrupted her brooding by asking what they should do next about the missing girl.

Joelle returned her attention to Island, 'I think we should visit Moth Island and have a dig around. My instinct tells me something is not right there although for the life of me I can't see that there is any connection with recent events.'

Joelle delayed her visit to Moth Island until after the weekend. She wanted to meet Douglas at the airport on his return.

It was Saturday afternoon, she was not on duty, and in anticipation of Douglas's homecoming she took extra care over appearance and dress, wearing her white slacks and black v-neck silk blouse. On a whim, she got the old Austin Princess Limousine out of its garage and decided to drive it to the airport. As the Islands Detective Inspector, she was naturally given preferential parking when she arrived, but suddenly feeling very coy she declined an invitation to wait for Douglas airside, but hid outside the arrivals hall amongst all the other people meeting the flight. It was busy with tour company reps holding up the sign boards for the incoming tourists, porters and touts offering their services, and visitors milling around trying to find their meeting point, and suitcases everywhere, tripping the unwary. It was noisy as well, in the background the whine of incoming jets drifting over the sound of vehicles, whose engines were always left running to work the air conditioning. The more intrusive and urgent blaring vehicle horns overlaid a general cacophony of voices, some excited, others worried or just tired. As Joelle stood waiting, sniffing distastefully at the smell of vehicle exhausts and jet engine kerosene which pervaded the atmosphere, she was wondering how Douglas would be.

She spotted him walking out of the arrivals hall towing his suitcase along. She breathed a sigh of relief, Eva was some distance behind him, one of her worst fears was that he and Eva would emerge arm in arm. She waited, wondering what Douglas would do, she had not told him she would meet him, and she hoped he would look for her anyway; she could take that as a sign of love. He spotted her amongst a group of tour reps and his pace quickened as he hurried towards her, and dropping his bag, he took her in his arms and kissed her. With a surge of affection Joelle returned the kiss and they stood embracing each other joyfully before stepping back, both speaking at the same time asking after each other.

Later that evening they sat together in their favourite place on the veranda of Windrush looking at the sun setting over the Caribbean Sea.

Earlier they had dropped Eva off at the restaurant, from where it was just a short walk along the beach to the chalet that she and Jasmine shared and now Joelle and Douglas were alone and they were catching up with each others news.

Joelle telling Douglas about the missing girl, Sofia Luka who, it was alleged, had disappeared on Moth Island, although she refrained to tell him about her worries regarding Moth Island.

'I am glad you have decided not to take that job,' Joelle told him.

'Ah! I need to tell you about that,' Douglas responded. 'Yesterday, they called me back for a second interview, and they told me that they had changed their mind about the job. Originally it was to be based in England, at their accounting centre in Horsham, but they want to implement a new cloud based real time administration and accounting system and they have decided to trial a new way of working in the Moth Island Resort. As an experiment the Finance Director role will be enlarged to be the Chief Operating Officer of the resort company and will be based in the resort with the resort manager reporting to the COO. Anyway, they have offered me the job, I would be based on Moth Island two or three days a week, and would only have to make the occasional visit to England.'

Douglas looked at Joelle expectantly, 'What do

think.'

'Have you actually accepted the job?' She asked.

'No, not yet, I told them I wanted to think about it.'

What did she think about it, Joelle hesitated before she spoke. She worried that if there was something going on Douglas would inevitably get mixed up in it and end up in danger, but on the other hand, thinking as a police woman, it would be very useful to have someone on the inside.

'It is up to you,' she replied eventually, keeping her thoughts to herself for the time being.

CHAPTER 5. MOTH ISLAND

Joelle and Irene walked along the beach, bare foot and wearing bikinis and light weight beach dresses. Both carried beach shoulder bags containing, hidden under a paperback book and beach towel, their police identification, a cosh and pepper spray and pair of handcuffs. Joelle also carried a small camera and a pair of binoculars.

She had decided that their first visit to Moth Island would be unofficial, arriving as tourists, she told Irene, they might find out more than simply turning up as police asking questions. She had even managed to book a room for a couple of nights so they had three days to explore the Island.

So far they had walked along the beach and done a spot of sun bathing, while Joelle had surreptitiously examined and photographed all the boats and yachts moored off the beach.

'When we get back to the office I want you to

check out each of these boats, who owns them, where they are from, that sort of thing,' Joelle told Irene.

It was nearly lunch time and they were now walking back to one of the resort bars, 'we will just sit here a while and see who comes and goes,' Joelle said selecting a table.

She ordered a glass of lemon squash, Irene a glass of beer, which earned a frown from Joelle, and an instruction to stay on soft drinks. Joelle decided there was nothing remarkable about the other customers in the bar, most were late middle aged overweight couples, the resort had a no children under sixteen policy. At one end of the bar was a marriage party. The two police officers knew that because the group were talking excitedly about the ceremony tomorrow. A group of three single men walked into the bar and joined the marriage party, Joelle watched them for a few moments before her attention switched to the bar and she speculated that the barman might be the one who had provided the two teenagers with the drugs, no use asking him, he will deny it even if it was him, she thought, wondering if there was some way she could expose the dealer.

Irene nudged her, 'Those three blokes over there are watching us,' she whispered, 'do you think they know who we are?'

Joelle's attention returned to the marriage group, 'No, they could not know us, they are probably wondering if we are alone and whether they could chat us up. Come on let's move on, there is nothing interesting here.'

That afternoon they walked slowly round the Island, which although owned by the Resort did have some private villas at one end. Joelle took a photo of each villa and told Irene to note down the name so she could find out who owned the properties when they got back to Kaeta.

They got into conversation with an elderly man who was using a metal detector. 'Looking for pirate treasure,' he told Joelle when she asked him what he was doing. He told them he had owned one of the villas for the last thirty years and spent all his spare time on the island with his metal detector. 'I am covering the ground inch by inch, I know the treasure is here somewhere.' Joelle asked him how much of the Island he had prospected.

'About three quarters' he told her. 'Fortunately I did the ground over there,' he indicated the hill that had been fenced off by the casino, 'before they built that security fence and kept everyone out last year.' He snorted, replaced his ear phones and continued along the beach waving his instrument over the ground.

'I bit eccentric, isn't he,' was Irene's verdict.

They continued round the Island, past the greenhouses where the hotels fresh vegetables and salads were grown and came to the Casino compound entrance.

'Can we come in and look round,' Joelle asked one of the security guards, a large mean looking man with a suspicious bulge under his jacket.

'Are you members,' he asked

'No, we are just curious, we thought we might come back and have a flutter tonight,' Joelle nonchalantly told him.

'Members only.'

'How can we become members?'

'You are either members or you not,' he told them bluntly.

Joelle shrugged and walked off out of earshot. 'Not very helpful, and why does he need to wear a gun,' she asked rhetorically. 'We need to get in there somehow and see what is actually going on,' she said to Irene, who nodded in agreement.

That evening they dressed up. Joelle wore a black cocktail dress discreetly decorated with sequins that showed off her trim figure, while Irene wore a white halter necked smock and tight, deep maroon trousers. Joelle looked disapproving telling Irene she was showing too much cleavage.

They sat in the dining room bar sipping non-alcoholic cocktails, 'We are being watched,' Joelle told Irene, flicking her eyes towards the three men they had seen a lunch time, 'Come on, let's go in for dinner before they move on us.'

After dinner they were not quick enough as they sat at the bar sipping drinks, watching the other guests. Two of the three men moved up silently and took empty bar stools on either side of Joelle and Irene.

'Hi, I noticed you at lunch time, you just arrived?' The man next to Joelle asked.

She turned and looked at him. Late twenties, early thirties, she guessed and looking at his muscular shoulders, decided he was probably quite fit and exercised with weights. She noticed a tattoo just showing below the open collar of his shirt.

She agreed she had just arrived on the Island and decided she did not like the man. He introduced himself as James. The other man had similarly introduced himself to Irene while busy studying her cleavage. Joelle saw Irene preparing to move and placed a restraining hand on her arm, 'Don't go,' she said to Irene, 'We will stay for a few moments and talk to our new friends,' she smiled at James.

Irene was amazed, she had never seen her boss in a mood like this before, flirting with James, even accepting a couple of gins and tonics from him, before she yawned and apologised saying she was very tired and a little tipsy and needed her bed, 'alone tonight,' she smiled at James.

'What on earth are you doing,' Irene asked her as they walked back to their room, 'You are not seriously fancying him are you?'

'No, of course not, he is awful, but I have a plan,' Joelle told her, reverting to her normal behaviour.

Irene looked puzzled.

'Did you not see their eyes, dilated, and notice the slight odour on their breath?' Joelle asked. Irene admitted she had not.

'You wait, we will reel them in tomorrow, just play along with my lead.' Joelle looked pleased.

The following morning Irene wore her bikini expecting another day of the beach.

'I would wear something more substantial than that,' Joelle eyed her critically, 'today we are walking up Pirate Hill and it gets a bit rough towards the top.'

Pirate Hill was the remains of a volcano, extinct for thousands of years and now very eroded and worn down, but it was still over one hundred meters high and Joelle wanted to climb it as it gave a spectacular view over the whole Island, although she was really only interested in looking at the casino complex.

'Now that's what I call a view,' Irene ran her eye round the Island, Joelle agreed as she took in the view as well. They watched a golf buggy pull out of the casino complex and make its way towards the Casino's private landing pier where a motor boat was moored. Joelle took her binoculars and peered at the buggy. 'Damn, the canopy is obscuring the view of the passengers,' she muttered and then, 'it looks like just a single man.' She took her camera and swore to herself again as the telephoto was not powerful enough to take good close-up of the occupant.

Joelle refocused her binoculars on the casino compound and she noted that the whole area was surrounded by two ten-foot high security fences topped with razor wire enclosing a no-man strip. Inside were well laid out manicured gardens leading down to a private beach and the pier. In one corner of the garden under the shade of a tree she could just make out a middle-aged man sitting with a much younger woman. In the centre of the garden was the original plantation house, which had been extended by the addition of a stone built accommodation block. From their vantage point the women could not see the back of the villa but Joelle guessed that the large open sided building, with a tiled roof, housed the casino, bars and dining areas.

'It all looks very peaceful down there,' Irene commented as Joelle used her camera to photograph the complex.

'Umm, it does,' Joelle agreed, 'but why do they need such fortifications, are they keeping people in, or out?' It was a rhetorical question.

The two women took one last look around and then started to descend. They were just over half way down when they saw a security guard puffing his way up the path towards them and when he reached them he stopped.

'What are you women doing up her?' He aggressively accused them.

'Nothing, just looking at the view,' Joelle replied

innocently.

'This area is out of bounds, no one is allowed up here,'

'Why, where does it say that, we were told we could walk anywhere on the Island,' she challenged the guard back.

'I am telling you,' the man was getting increasingly threatening. 'Were you using binoculars and taking photographs up there?'

'Yes, so what.' Joelle answered.

'Let me have the camera,' the man demanded moving to snatch Joelle's bag from her shoulder, but before he could grab it she swung it down and reached inside. The man assumed she was reaching for her camera but instead Joelle produced a pepper spray.

'Back off, or you get a face full,' she threatened. She saw his hand move towards the gun under his jacket. 'If you draw that weapon you will regret it,' she warned him.

Surprised that she knew he had a gun, the security guard looked at Joelle and noticed she appeared taller, standing with her feet apart and shoulders squared, holding the pepper spray in one hand, clearly ready to use it, while the other hand was hanging by her side with the fingers straight and taught, a classic defensive position ready to poke him in the eye he observed. He decided this woman was no ordinary tourist to be easily threatened and backing off said, 'Look I want no trouble. Let me escort you down, it's dangerous this path, that is why we don't like people coming up here.'

Joelle relaxed a bit and they followed the security guard down and all the way back to the Resort buildings.

'We would not want you bitten by a snake, you understand, so please stay away from that end of the Island, it's dangerous,' he said as he left them.

'Snakes, my eye,' Joelle muttered. 'My gut instinct is running overtime, there is something going on in that Casino that they don't want us to find.'

That afternoon she phoned Merv and asked him to get a search warrant for the Casino.

Later the same day Joelle and Irene were again sitting in the bar sipping their non-alcoholic cocktails.

'I am curious Joelle, your plan for those two obnoxious men. It seems to have gone wrong, we've not seen them all day,' Irene commented.

'No, I expect they have been at the wedding, you wait, they will be round after dinner,' Joelle assured Irene confidently.

That evening, the two women wore the same outfits as the previous night, they were the only ones they had with them, and after dinner sat at the same seats by the bar as they had the previous evening.

'Here they come,' Joelle whispered to Irene, 'don't be alarmed, just follow my lead.'

Mr John de Caynoth

'Hi there girls,' James greeted them loudly as he and his friend sat on the bar stools next to them. 'You both look good tonight, can I get you drink,' he asked insincerely.

'Gin,' Joelle muttered under her breath pushing her glass of tonic towards him.

'Sorry we missed you today, we have been at a wedding all day,' James prattled on.

Joelle just grunted and stared sullenly into her glass, now topped up with gin.

Irene looked at Joelle in surprise, she had expected her to behave in the coquettish manner of the previous evening, flirting and leading James on, but tonight she appeared sullen and bad tempered. She mentally shrugged and she did her best to imitate Joelle's behaviour.

After a few minutes of trying to elicit conversation the other man, Alan, gave up, 'What's wrong with you two, you're not annoyed because we have not been round all day, are you?'

Joelle wanted to laugh, which was a good as it made her look even more sullen as she twisted her face to suppress it. Still resisting the urge to giggle, she muttered, almost inaudibly, 'bloody island, I need a fix and I can't get anything here.'

James blinked, not sure if he had heard correctly, 'I might be able to fix you up,' he whispered, 'for a price, of course,'

'Haven't got any money,' Joelle responded still staring into her gin, not wishing to look at James in case he saw the excitement she was suddenly feeling.

'There are other ways of paying,' he explained.

Joelle did not respond.

'I could get you a snort of cocaine and when you feel better we can go back to my room.' James offered.

Joelle grunted and James took that as a sign of agreement, 'Wait here,' he instructed.

As soon as he was out of sight, Joelle nudged Irene, 'I need to go to the toilet,' she announced rising. To her relief, Irene followed her, leaving the other man sitting expectantly at the bar. 'Don't be long girls,' he called as they headed across the room.

Once they were out of sight Joelle pushed Irene, 'Quick, go back to our room and wait for me. I want to follow James and see where he goes.'

Ten minutes later Joelle joined Irene in the room they were sharing.

'Where did he go?' Irene asked, having worked out what Joelle was trying to do.

Joelle looked disappointed. 'Nowhere, he just went to his room and then straight back into the bar. I had hoped he would go to the dealer,' she shrugged.

'Put the lights out and shut the blinds, in case they come to find us,' Joelle advised Irene. They sat in the dark waiting. They heard the sound of someone falling over the outside chairs on the balcony.

'We know you are in there,' a voice called. The

women hardly dared to breath as they sat in silence. The door handle moved as the men tried the door.

'I have a better idea, someone said. Reception will have a spare key.'

The women heard the two men depart.

Irene looked frightened, 'Come Joelle, we had better get out and hide before they come back.'

CHAPTER 6. PROBLEMS

Late afternoon the next day Joelle arrived home absolutely fuming.

'Sorry Douglas,' she apologised for speaking sharply to him.

'What has gone wrong today?' He asked, not taking offence.

'It is that bloody man, Sir Jonah Snifflier-Smyth, the magistrate,' she replied still angry.

Douglas waited for an explanation.

'He is a bigoted racist and should not be a magistrate. Just because his family are white and have lived on the Island for three hundred years he thinks he is some sort of aristocrat and the rest of us are his serfs. His family were only slave traders anyway!' Joelle subsided slightly after her outburst.

Douglas tactfully did not mention that Joelle's father was white and although her mother was coloured the family shared much the same origins. He simply asked what the bloody man in question had done this time.

'I asked Merv to get a search warrant for the Casino on Moth Island. He refused telling Merv I had to report to him and present my evidence in person.'

'But I thought you were on Moth Island today?'

'I was, but Irene and I came back early this morning,' Joelle explained and told Douglas that she had found a possible drug user on the Island who had turned a bit pushy so to avoid trouble they had hidden on the other side of the Island for half the night and got the first boat back that morning. She did not tell Douglas how she had identified the user.

'Anyway,' Joelle continued, 'I was planning to take the search warrant, Merv and couple of uniforms, back to the Island today, arrest the user and search the Casino, but I had to wait until Sir Jonah,' she spat the name out sarcastically, 'deigned to give me an interview, and it was after lunch before I saw him.'

'And did you get a warrant?' Douglas prompted.

'No, he said I had no evidence of any wrong doing at the Casino and all he could do was to give me a warrant to search the room occupied by the user, but he could not do that until he had confirmed he had authority over Moth Island,' Joelle paused for breath, her eyes flashing and body taught with anger.

Douglas decided she looked very sexy when she got angry and had a thought of making love, a thought which he kept to himself, waiting for Joelle to say something else.

She took a deep breath and relaxed a bit, 'Do you know, the old sod had the cheek to tell me off for exceeding my authority in visiting Moth Island without first getting permission!'

Douglas knew there was no love lost between the Sir Jonah and Joelle. The old boy seemed to have a particular resentment of Joelle, Douglas put it down to wealth, of which Joelle had a lot, thanks to her father's foresight, and Sir Jonah had very little.

'What happens now then?' Douglas asked.

'I will send Irene to collect the warrant in the morning, and we will do the search tomorrow.' Joelle told him.

Douglas refrained to comment that sending Irene, a coloured police constable, would probably inflame the old man even more, but then reflected that that was probably why Joelle was sending her.

Still muttering, Joelle went off to have a shower and change, reappearing later in a much calmer mood. As the evening cooled down they went for a walk around the garden while Mary, cooked some supper. Although still suffering after her stroke, Mary insisted she was now sufficiently recovered and did not need to be treated as an invalid any more.

'I hope she does not fall over or burn herself,' Joelle worried.

'She is getting a lot stronger now, let her do something,' Douglas tried to allay Joelle's fears.

They walked on in silence for a bit. Joelle was the first to speak, 'what sort of day have you had?' She asked.

'Big thing today is that I have decided to accept that job,' Douglas told her, 'I rang Janice Milicent, the People Director, this afternoon and told her. She seemed to be quite pleased.'

'Oh!' Joelle exclaimed thoughtfully. It was not that she had forgotten Douglas was considering a job on Moth Island, but more that she had not really considered the implications if he actually took the position.

'You know I have my concerns about that place,' she cautioned him.

'Well, I know you think there may be a drug problem over there, and believe me, if I find anything like that you will be the first to know.'

'Yes, I know, but it is not just the drugs it is also that Casino, something about it does not feel right.'

'You need not worry about that, the Casino is a separate business and I will have no responsibility for it,' Douglas assured her before he changed the subject, 'Did you know Eva is thinking of returning to the UK and her studies.'

'No, really,' Joelle looked interested thinking that it might be a good job if she did, that would remove temptation out of Douglas's way.

'Yes,' he replied, 'but there is a problem, Ralph is out of prison and Eva said that he had been looking for her round Bristol. She was quite frightened and upset while we were England.'

'Yes, I did know about Ralph, I had a begging letter from him, he says he is destitute, living rough, and asking me for money.' Joelle told Douglas and he asked if she had given him any.

'No, I destroyed the letter.'

'I wonder if he has approached Jasmine,' Douglas speculated.

'She has not said anything, but I would not put it past him to ask her as well' Joelle answered.

'Mmm, I think I might go and talk to her tomorrow.' Douglas said quietly, almost to himself.

*****

The next morning Joelle and Douglas left Windrush together. Joelle riding her big Triumph motorcycle to work and Douglas driving his MGB first to the Glass Bay restaurant but then into Kaeta town to book another trip to England.

Although the new job was to be based on Moth Island he had been asked to spend a couple of weeks in the Holiday Resort offices in Horsham to meet the staff and familiarise himself with their way of working.

'Hi Jasmine,' he shouted as he walked into the restaurant.

Jasmine shouted a reply back from the kitchen.

'Busy?' Douglas asked.

'Yes, quite, I am setting up a new menu, and the preparation is taking longer than I thought.'

'Has Eva told you that Ralph is out of prison?' Douglas asked.

'Yes, she did, and she said he was looking for her in Bristol.'

'I was wondering, he has not tried to contact you has he?' Douglas decided the direct approach was the only way to raise the subject.

'Yes, as a matter of fact he has. He wrote to me twice while he was in prison saying how sorry he was for what happened to me but he was out of his mind with stress over the divorce thing. He hoped I would forgive him and we could remain friends.'

Douglas looked horrified, 'What did you do?'

'Nothing, I did not even answer the letters.' Jasmine assured him

'Good, let's hope he got the hint.'

'Well he didn't,' Jasmine shrugged, 'I got an email from him telling me he was out of prison and that he wanted to come and see me make amends and asking if I could send him the money for the airfare as he was broke and living in a hostel.'

'You did not send him money did you?' Douglas worried.

'No, I emailed him back and told him I wanted nothing to do with him. So far he has not replied.' Jasmine started chopping ferociously at a sweet potato.

'I fear we may not have heard the last of Ralph,' Douglas said to himself as he watched Jasmine chopping up her ingredients for the soup she was making.

'Is Eva about,' he asked.

'Yes, she is in the chalet, and Douglas, could you do me a favour?'

'Yes, of course.'

I am too busy to go shopping this morning. Eva has a list of what we need but could you run her into Kaeta town for me." Jasmine asked.

'Be delighted,' Douglas assured her as he walked off towards the chalet where the two girls lived.

'Hi Eva, its Douglas. Can I come in?' He shouted through the open door of the chalet.

'Come through, I am just changing in the bedroom,' Eva called back to him.

He waited in the living room for her and she soon appeared wearing a pair of white shorts and a turquoise tee shirt. He could not help but notice that she was not wearing a bra and that the shape of her breasts was beautifully outlined beneath the tee shirt. He had to physically shake such thought from his head as he offered her a lift into town.

Parking is never easy in Kaeta town centre, the streets are narrow, lined with deep storm gutters with vehicles and people crowding all available space. Douglas headed for the old part of town, where there were fewer people and also some marked parking spaces. He found a spot near the Police Office and Court Building.

Mr John de Caynoth

They got out of the car and Douglas went to the boot to retrieve Eva's shopping bags. He handed her the bags telling her that he had to go to the tourist office to book a ticket and asking if she needed help with the shopping. She said she did not so Douglas told her he would wait for her to return and give her a lift back to the restaurant.
'Thanks Douglas,' she said stepping closer to him to take the bags he was holding out. She took the bags in one hand and placing her other hand on Douglas shoulder leaned towards him and reaching up quickly, kissed his cheek as goodbye.

****

Joelle rode her motorbike into work feeling happier than she had been feeling for some days. She anticipated that the new lead she had found on Moth Island could break the drug problem open and as she rode she was planning a search of the Island as soon as she received the search warrant. She was also more relaxed about Douglas. Since he returned from the UK she felt their relationship had been like it always used to be, they had talked, discussed problems, watched the sunset and made love, and she was thinking that perhaps she was being too sensitive about Douglas and Eva. She was even thinking that it was time they set a date for their wedding.
Her demeanour was only marginally dented when Irene returned from the Court House empty handed and told her that Sir Jonah

wanted to see her in person before signing the warrant.

He kept her waiting for half-an-hour before calling her into his office. She knew he did it deliberately as she glanced through the door when she arrived and saw him reading a newspaper. He gave her another lecture about police procedure telling her that as the Island was privately owned she had exceeded her authority by going there without an invitation from the owners and that as a result any evidence of wrong doing was inadmissible. Joelle was perfectly well aware of police procedures and was about to argue with him but he forestalled her by telling her that he wanted the escalating drug availability on Kaeta dealt with and would under circumstances grant her request for a search warrant.

'And the Casino?' She asked hopefully, but Sir Jonah declined saying there was absolutely no evidence the casino was involved.

It was sheer coincidence that Joelle walked out of the Court House as Douglas drove past in the MGB. Initially she was pleased to see him, but on spotting Eva in the car her pleasure turned sour. Frowning with irritation she watched the car travel about one hundred yards further and pull into a parking place. Probably more out of habit rather than a desire to spy on Douglas she moved up the street a little and half stood concealed in door way where she could watch the vehicle.

She saw Douglas get out of the car and walk round behind it and take an empty bag out of the boot and Eva walk round to take it off Douglas. She watched Eva hold the bag in one hand and step closer to Douglas putting her other hand on his shoulder and in a very intimate manner lean towards him and kiss him.

Joelle was distraught, it was like a brick had landed on her chest, as she tried to draw a breath suffering an emotional reaction, a mix of anger, frustration, disappointment, jealousy. She watched them walk off in separate directions and just stood in the doorway, clutching her search warrant for minutes, completely disoriented by what she had seen.

Eventually she recovered sufficiently to concentrate on the immediate problem, the search on Moth Island. Still in a daze she made her way back to the Police Office where she told Merv to organise transport to Moth Island.

While he did that she went into her office. Her earlier happier mood had evaporated to be replaced by a cool controlled anger. First, she went through the crime reports from the last couple of days: nothing there that needed her immediate attention, so she pulled up on her screen the daily summary from the Commissioner's Office which summarised important event and activities on the Island. Things like, which cruise ships were expected, visiting dignitaries, and visitor numbers. Mostly there was nothing on the list of concerns to her but she looked at it anyway in case there was something that might require special attention and this morning, as her eye scanned the screen, she saw the Glass Bay Hotel mentioned. Out of curiosity pulled up the brief report behind the headline and it told her that due to falling visitor numbers the hotel had been unable to meet its liabilities and had called in the receivers, one of the big international accountancy firms to run the business in administration. She remembered the envelope she had received a couple of days earlier from the management company to whom she had leased the hotel which was still lying on her desk unopened. Her first thought was that she needed to talk to Douglas, he would know what to do. Her second thought was, did she really want to talk to Douglas; after this morning she no longer knew how she felt about him.

However, before she got completely lost in these thoughts, Merv arrived and announced that they were all ready to go as soon as she wanted.

The motor boat Merv had requisitioned pulled up at the mooring key on Moth Island and Joelle, Merv and two uniformed officers stepped on to the jetty and immediately walked across to the reception building and asked to see the Resort Manager. He was not available so they spoke to the Duty Manager.

Joelle showed him the warrant and explained that they wanted to search the room occupied by the wedding guest James. She told him they had reason to believe that there were drugs on the premises.

'That would be James Masters,' The Duty Manager confirmed and assured them that the resort had a zero drugs policy, any staff breaching this would be dismissed and any guest caught indulging in drugs would be asked to desist and leave if they refused.

The house maid was still servicing the room when Joelle and her three officers arrived. They asked her to wait outside while they went through the room looking for concealed drugs. They found nothing but an empty room.

Merv asked the maid if she had thrown anything from the room away.

'Yes, of course, I always empty the rubbish bin,' she sounded slightly offended, but showed Merv the large black plastic rubbish bag.

'How many rooms have you cleaned this morning' Merv asked.

'This is the eighth '

Merv groaned and taking the bag passed it to one of the uniforms and told him to search the bag.

Meanwhile, Joelle returned to reception to find James Masters, the guest.

'I am afraid you have missed him,' the girl on reception apologised, 'the wedding party departed this morning, the hotel boat left before you arrived.'

'Dam and blast,' Joelle swore, 'Do you know where they would have gone?'

'The airport I should think. Hold on, let me check their reservation details, we should have asked for departure information.' The girl turned her attention to a screen and after a few moments, 'yes, here we are, we had to get them to Kaeta International by two for a five-o-clock flight.' She checked her watch, 'It's just after two now so they should have arrived.'

Joelle scratched her head as she thought quickly. Using the hotel phone to ring airport security, she asked them to stop the guest James Masters, search his baggage and detain him.

'Hold on,' the security officer at the airport told her, 'I will check the customs screen, that will tell us if he has gone airside yet,' Joelle waited anxiously. 'Sorry, that information has not uploaded yet, I will go down and check at passport control and ring you back.

'Don't worry, I am on my way to the airport, I will be there as soon as possible.'

She went back to the guest's room to fetch Merv who looked excited and handed her a small white envelope.

'Found it in the rubbish, I'll bet it once held hash,' he enthused.

Joelle looked in the bag and noted a residual sticky substance which she sniffed and nodded in agreement.

'Put it in an evidence bag and bring it with you. Leave those two here. We have to get to the airport quickly, James Masters is on a five-o-clock flight and we must question him before he leaves the Island.'

It took them nearly two hours to get to the airport and on the way Joelle asked if the maid remembered which room the envelope came from. Merv said not, she just tips the waist paper basket into the bin bag.

'That means this evidence is of little use,' Joelle sounded disappointed.

At the airport, they went straight to the security office.

'Sorry,' the man Joelle spoke with on the phone apologised, 'I was too late, James Masters had already passed customs before I got your message. He must be in the departure lounge now.'

Joelle and Merv looked at the CCTV screen and the crowded departure lounge, containing over three hundred people.

Joelle checked her watch, 'we have not got long to find him, the flight will be called soon.'

The security man nodded in agreement, 'the flight is on time, you have about fifteen minutes,' he confirmed.

'I don't suppose you could delay the flight,' she asked.

The security man, remembering the chaos that occurred last time she delayed a flight, gave her a withering look and shook his head.

CHAPTER 7. THE KISS

'Will James Masters please report to air security staff at gate 4.' After a couple of minutes the announcement was repeated. Still James Masters did not appear and Joelle waited anxiously. The security lady at the desk persuaded Joelle and Merv to wait in the interview room telling them their presence, lurking at the boarding gate, might be why James Masters had not shown and the airline agreed to hold the boarding announcement for five minutes and repeated the request for James Masters.

'You!' James Masters stared at Joelle as Merv invited him to sit down at the grey steel table opposite Joelle. A large black security man was standing at the door and apart from the four people, the steel table and four plastic chairs, and a CCTV camera there was nothing else in the grey cell like room.

'Sit,' Merv commanded, and James Masters sat still staring at Joelle.

'I know you, you are the bitch that stood me up

the other night. 'You tried to frame me,' Masters accused Joelle. 'I am saying nothing. You have nothing on me and I have a plane to catch now,' he looked at his watch, and sat silently glaring at Joelle.

She addressed him in a quiet friendly manner. 'Not at all James, you offered me drugs in exchange for sex, my friend Irene heard you. That is soliciting.'

James said nothing so Joelle pushed the white envelope across the table to him, 'I believe this is yours?'

James remained silent.

'No matter,' Joelle told him, 'we will find your finger prints on the envelope and charge you for drug offences as well as soliciting.'

James still said nothing, but did look pointedly at his watch.

Joelle also remained silent watching James become more anxious as the time moved towards 5pm.

'Inspector,' the Security man interrupted, 'the final call for the 5pm flight has just been announced.'

'Thank you,' Joelle responded and turning back to James Masters, 'we can sit hear all night and you will miss your plane, or you can tell me what I want to know and I decide what to charge you with.'

'If I answer your questions will you let me get the plane,' Masters asked.

'Depends what you tell me,' Joelle answered.

James confirmed that he used drugs on the Island, 'but only marijuana, I never used the hard stuff,' he swore.

'Where did you get the drugs,' Joelle asked. 'On the Island or did you bring them in from somewhere else.'

James looked uncomfortable and hedged his answer, 'I can't remember.'

'Oh, come on James, you don't expect me to believe that, do you? Look, I am not really interested in you, I want to know where the drugs came from,' Joelle looked at her watch. 'If you are straight with me now, you can go, you still have time to catch that plane if you talk quickly.'

He took a deep breath and started to speak, 'We are friends of the groom and we all agreed that for his stag we would lie on the beach with some marijuana, perhaps try some coke, and, well just relax and talk. My mate Jim said he knew where he could get the stuff. All I know is he went to meet someone at the Island greenhouse. That's it, all I know.'

'Jim who? Where is he now?' Joelle asked

'Jim Madden, he should be on the plane by now'.

Joelle leapt up, and telling Merv to follow, ran out of the room.

The security guard was taken by surprise at her sudden movement and, uncertain of what he should do with James Masters, told him to remain seated until Joelle returned.

77

Once outside she went to the security office and rang flight control and told them not to let the plane leave the stand as she was about to board it and remove a passenger for questioning.

The flight controller started to argue so Joelle told him she would arrest him for obstruction if he let the plane go.

'Okay, I will hold it for thirty minutes,' the flight controller gave in.

It took Joelle and Merv five minutes to reach the plane and board it, luckily the boarding steps were still in place waiting for the last passenger, James Masters.

'Will Mr Jim Madden please make himself known to the cabin staff.' The head steward announced. Joelle waited anxiously but almost immediately there was a warning buzz from the flight stewards kitchen and red light above a gangway seat in the economy cabin blinked. The flight steward walked down the aircraft and identifying Jim Madden asked him to accompany her.

Joelle politely told Jim she needed his assistance urgently and asked him to leave the aircraft with her. Of course, initially he refused so she told him that if he did not accompany her willingly, she would handcuff him, arrest him and forcibly remove him from the aircraft.

'Don't worry,' she said, 'this will not take long and we will hold the flight until you return.'

They escorted him to the interview room, where, to Joelle's surprise James was still seated, she told him he could go.

'Sorry mate,' he said to Jim as he left the room.

'What is this all about,' Jim asked.

'I won't beat about the bush, we know you procured illegal drugs while on Moth Island and I want to know where and who supplied you.' Joelle told him.

He started to say he did not know what Joelle was talking about, but she stopped him.

'You have about ten minutes to talk and get on the plane, so unless you want to spend the next week in a Kaetian prison on a charge of obstruction, I suggest you tell us what we want to know right now.'

Jim rubbed his chin, now worried he might not get home, 'If I tell you will you let me go?'

'No promises,' Joelle replied.

Jim Madden shrugged, 'One of the waiters told me to go to the greenhouse and ask for the gardener. He told me to find the man trimming the palm trees round the back of the fitness centre. I found him and he said he could get marijuana and cocaine. I paid him some money and he said he would arrange to leave some stuff in my room. When I went to my room after dinner that evening there was a small packet of cocaine and marijuana on the bed. That's all there is,' Jim swore.

'Did you get any names?' Joelle asked.

'No.'

'Can you describe the man that took your

money?'

'He was black, shaved head, not young or old looking and wearing a brown gardeners uniform.'

'How tall was he? Fat or wiry?' Merv asked.

'About my height, and I did not notice his build, about average I suppose.'

Joelle sighed and looked at Merv who shrugged saying he had no further questions.

They let Jim go, and Joelle told the security man to contact flight control and release the plane.

When Joelle and Merv were alone they discussed what they had discovered, 'that confirms the Island is probably the source of the drugs, but we still do not really know who is supplying them.' Joelle concluded.

'Do you want me visit the Island again,' Merv asked.

'I don't know,' Joelle was thinking. 'We have no real lead on who and everyone will just deny any involvement again. We need a more clever approach,' She looked reflectively at Merv.

Back at the Detective's offices later that evening everyone, except Joelle, had gone home. Joelle was sitting at her desk, something was bothering her and she wanted to settle it in her mind before she thought about Douglas and what she had seen that morning. In truth, she was putting off going home because she did not want to see Douglas at the moment.

She pulled her mind back to the missing Dutch girl, Sofia Luka, it was the fact that she appeared to have disappeared on Moth Island which bothered her. Again, she contemplated the body found on Moth Island, the drug connection, and the missing girl and although she could see no connection between the three events, three such events in such a short time was one hell of a coincidence.

She wondered if perhaps both girls were victims of drug abuse, maybe had died, and their bodies thrown in the sea. She dug out the post mortem report on the first body, it told her the body was too decomposed and half eaten by fish for any conclusions to be drawn. However, that still left her hypothesis as a possibility, and the more she thought about it she realised that what she needed was someone on the Island, undercover, ferreting around. Unfortunately no one suitable came to mind. Merv and Irene were known on the Island but perhaps one of the uniformed officers would be suitable. The best person would be her friend Andrea Spooner, a DC with the London Met Police, but asking Andrea would be difficult, she would have to clear it through the Commissioner and the British Police hierarchy and she did not want to ask for help, not yet anyway. Thinking of Andrea brought Douglas back to her mind, and how in the past Andrea had always sorted out her emotional problems, but again she put that thought to one side while she thought how to move forward with the investigation.

She decided that in the morning she would send Irene to the Dutch Consulate and see if Sofia Luka had applied for a replacement passport. If she had, that would indicate she had just run out on her boyfriend and Joelle could close the case. If she had not, then Joelle would send Irene back to Moth Island to show the picture round and see if that produced anything. In the meantime she would see who she could find to send undercover on Moth Island.

Her next problem was that the Crystal Bay Hotel was in administration. She knew they had been having money problems and assumed that meant the hotel had gone bankrupt and as lessor of the hotel buildings and land, the freehold of which she owned, she was unsure of where she now stood and she was worrying that the Administrator may somehow be able to get his hands of her freehold to settle the businesses debts. She wished she could talk to Douglas, he would know.

Finally, she could no longer put off thinking about Eva kissing Douglas, intimately, as she saw it. Over the last few months they had spent a lot time together, they had gone to England together and now she had seen them kissing. Surely, she thought, they must be having an affair. She felt desperate, how could he let her down so, reject her after all they had

MOTH ISLAND

been through together, and for a woman young enough to be his daughter. As her tears formed and insane thoughts flooded her mind she reflected that she had never realised one could be angry and sad at the same time.

As she sat at her desk crying, her mobile rang, she saw it was Douglas and hit the call reject. Eventually Joelle composed herself and decided to get a sandwich and a coffee and looking at the time realised it was late afternoon in the UK and she could phone Andrea.

'Joelle!', Andrea answered the call.

'I need to talk to you,' Joelle said bluntly.

'Is it police business?' Andrea asked.

'No, its personal.'

'Sorry love, I am on duty and a bit tied up at the moment, can I ring you back in a couple of hours when I finish?'

Joelle hung up and put the phone down. She could not turn if off because she was waiting for a call from Andrea but it kept ringing as Douglas called her. She hit the call reject button again. Sod him, she thought.

She did not want to go home, but sat in her office brooding, waiting for Andrea to call, and decided to spend the night in her office, alone.

CHAPTER 8. THE DAY TRIP

Douglas, quite unaware of Joelle's emotional turmoil spent the day planning the start to his new job and preparing to fly out to England the following weekend. In truth, there was not a lot of preparation he could do but he did spend most of the day trawling through the internet finding what information was available on the Holiday Resort Company, and the resorts that it owned, of which there were seven, three in the Caribbean with Moth Island being their latest acquisition. He read the various blogs and customer reviews, especially interesting were the ones on the Moth Island Resort. In general, they were positive, the most commenting the lack of dining choice and menu selection in Moth Island's only restaurant. Douglas was surprised, but not overly concerned, that there was very little, in fact nothing at all on the internet, about the Casino. It was not even mentioned in the list of facilities available to guests on Moth Island. He recalled being told that the Casino was separately owned, run by the Australian founder of the Holiday Resort Company, and he thought no more of its absence from the internet.

The other thing he decided to do if he could organise it was to take a day trip to Moth Island and have a look round. In view of Joelle's interest in the Island he thought to ask her if she would like to come with him if he could persuade her to take a day off. When he mentioned it to Mary she asked if she could come as well and Mary was delighted when he agreed and suggested that he ask Jasmine as well. As Mary said, 'we have not had a proper family day together since I got ill.'

By mid-evening Joelle had still not come home. Douglas was not particularly anxious, it was not unknown for her to get delayed on police business and get home late but that evening he did want to see her and sort out the trip to Moth Island. As the evening stretched on he decided to phone her but her phone just went straight to an answer message. He guessed she might be interviewing so did not leave a message but phoned her again about an hour later but, again, he just got invited to leave a message. Now he was beginning to worry, if she was going to be this late she had always phoned to let him know what was going on. Again, he tried her phone with the same result. Now he was beginning to fret, but Mary told him not to worry.

'You know how she gets involved with something, and anyway if something had happened to her someone would have let us know by now,' she said.

Somewhat comforted Douglas paced around for another hour before going to bed. He spent a sleepless night with every little noise waking him in case it was Joelle returning.

He quite expected to find her in bed the following morning, but seeing her bed was empty rushed down stairs thinking she must have risen early. Mary was in the kitchen alone and when Douglas told her that Joelle had not come home that night, she frowned and commented that that was not like Joelle.

Douglas rang her mobile again, but after a single ring it switched to the answering service. This time he left a message asking her to contact him. He had some breakfast with Mary but after, not having heard from Joelle decided to go into town, the police office, and find her, or at least find out where she was.

'Is Joelle about,' he asked the duty sergeant at the front office.

'Haven't seen her this morning,' the sergeant replied, 'but she may have come in early before I came on duty. You know your way upstairs, go and she if she is in the detectives office.'

There was no one upstairs except Irene, sitting in front of her computer screen.

'Hi Irene,' Douglas greeted her. 'Is Joelle around.'
'You have missed her Douglas. She was in early this morning but left about fifteen minutes ago.'
'Do you know where she has gone,' he asked.
'No, she did not say, but she looked a bit rough, looked like she had been up all night so I guess something big has come up,' Irene told him.

Douglas headed back to Windrush, still worried he could not find, and comforted that at least he knew she was okay, but angry she had not called him. There was no one in the house but he saw Mary in the garden trying to cut some flowers but with some difficulty due to the disability resulting from the stroke. He went out to talk to her but she spoke first.

'Joelle's been home, she had a shower, packed some clothes and went off again in a hurry saying she would be away for a few days and not to worry.'

Douglas looked disappointed. 'Oh! Is that all,' he exclaimed, 'Irene said something big must have come up.'

'She was looking for you, said she needed to talk to you, but when I said you were out, she just said it did not matter,' Mary saw the look of disappointment on Douglas face.

'Did she not say what she wanted to talk to me about?' Douglas queried.

'No,' Mary answered, and then handing him the flowers she had cut, 'take these down to the restaurant for Jasmine will you, and ask her if she

Mr John de Caynoth

wants to come to Moth Island tomorrow.'

It was mid-morning before Douglas arrived at the restaurant and he found both Jasmine and Eva in the kitchen preparing dishes for the day. Douglas watched the girls working and asked what was on the menu, then he went and topped up the bottles in the bar and generally tidied it for the lunch session.

Jasmine called out to him,' We are doing a lot less food today, the numbers have been right down the last few days and we have had to throw a lot away. The freezers are all full.'

'Any reason for the fall in numbers?' Douglas asked.

Eva answered, 'I think it is the hotel, I walked along the beach yesterday to have a look at it and seems to be hardly anyone about. I don't know what is going on.'

Douglas shrugged, 'Joelle was told they were having cash flow problems.' He did not say anything else but did wonder how serious their cash flow problems were.

He changed the subject, 'Jasmine,' he walked into the kitchen to talk to her, 'Mary and I are going over to Moth Island for the day tomorrow, would you like to come?'

'I would love to but I am sorry, I can't, I have a birthday party booking for tomorrow evening and I must prepare for it, but why don't you take Eva, there is not much for to do in the day at the moment and she will be back in time for the evening sitting.'

'Are you sure,' Eva queried.

'Yes, absolutely,' Jasmine replied. 'That is if it is okay with you Douglas.'

'Of course it is,' Douglas was not uncomfortable with the thought of taking Eva but was thinking that Mary would not get her family day out and hoping she would not be too disappointed.

Mary was not at all disappointed, Eva was a kind and sympathetic person and had immediately taken charge of Mary, holding her arm and discreetly supporting her as they walked from the car across to the boat taxi taking them to the Island. Eva had made sure she got aboard safely and now the two of them were sitting at the stern nattering away together.

It surprised Douglas how few people there seemed to be on the island. Unlike the crowded beaches of Kaeta, especially ones adjacent to the hotels, the Moth Island beaches were almost empty and the little group soon found a discreet spot, furnished with beach loungers under the shade of a couple of Palm Trees. Douglas and Eva saw Mary comfortably installed on a lounger, with her book and water bottle in easy reach. Eva asked her if she had brought her swimming costume and would like to change.

'Certainly not,' Mary told her smiling, 'at my age the last thing I would do is to embarrass you and myself with the sight of my naked flesh.'

Mr John de Caynoth

'Would you mind if I slip on my bikini, 'Eva politely asked.

'Not at all love, your body is much prettier than mine,' Mary laughed.

Douglas was sitting quietly on a lounger listening to this exchange and watching Eva slip off her sun dress, lay a towel out in the sun, and stretch out to sun bath. He admired her figure and thought of the first time he had seen Eva sun bathing, when he, Eva and Jasmine had been discussing running the restaurant together. He remembered how she had asked him what his price was for helping her. He looked at Eva lying in the sun for a little longer before announcing that he was going for a walk round the Island.

It was midday before he returned, hot and thirsty. Mary was reading her book and Eva had moved into the shade and was dozing on a lounger. Douglas's return woke her and she announced she was going for a swim to cool off. Douglas, hot after prowling round the Island, decided to join her.

The sea looked very inviting, very clear, very blue, and there being no wind, very smooth with just small waves lapping at the sand. At the water's edge the beach became steeper and within a few feet of the shore line dropped away quite steeply into deeper water.

Eva set off in an energetic crawl, while Douglas swam more gently out from the shore, where on feeling he was far enough out, slipped over in the water and did a lazy back stroke watching the white fluffy clouds attributing animal shapes to them.

Suddenly a deluge of water washed over him and something grabbed his foot and pulled him under. He struggled back up to the surface, coughing and spluttering, and saw Eva floating a couple of meters away, laughing. She shrieked as he gave chase, but happily let him catch her as they splashed water at each other. He dived under and swimming round, surfaced behind her, catching her round her waist in a leg lock and putting his hands on her shoulders said, 'I have you now, what shall I do with you?'

She went limp against his body giggling, 'Pray Sir, I am at your mercy now to do with what you will.'

At that invitation, many thoughts tumbled through Douglas's mind, but he decided that the safest thing would be to release her. As he let her go he pushed her under anyway and swimming away as she surfaced announced he was going to find a beer and some lunch, inviting her to join him.

When they asked Mary to join them she said she was too comfortable to move and that the nice young beach waiter was looking after her and had promised to bring her some lunch when she was ready. 'You two go and explore,' she dismissed them, 'I am quite happy here,'

Douglas cautioned Eva not to let on who he was,

telling her that he just wanted to experience the dining room and bar as a guest, 'see how they work,' he said.

They looked at the dining room's lunch menu. Although it offered a full meal there were only two dishes on it and they both decided they would prefer a bar snack.

The bar was located in a circular open sided room thatched with palm leaves. The bar itself was also circular, but set to one side of the room adjacent to the kitchens with a swing door between the public and service areas.

They sat at the bar both looking around the area with a professional eye.

'If this were mine I would reposition those couches so people can look out over the Island rather than into the kitchen,' Eva commented. 'It also looks too stark, it needs something to soften the atmosphere in here.'

Douglas was looking at the number of customers trying to assess the economics of the bar. He gave up knowing he would see the figures soon enough anyway.

The barman emerged from the kitchen with a tray of food which he took over to a waiting table and returning asked Douglas and Eva how he could help them. All three looked at each other with surprise. Douglas and Eva recognising Sean, who worked part time at the Glass Bay Restaurant and Sean recognising Douglas and Eva as his other employers.

MOTH ISLAND

'What are you doing here?' Douglas asked.

'I do the lunch time shift here now, and the evening bar at the Glass Bay when Jasmine needs me.' Sean told them.

They spent a pleasant couple of hours in the bar talking with Sean between customers and eating the seafood roll he recommended. In view of Douglas's and Eva's interest in the business side of the bar and restaurant Sean took the opportunity to introduce them to the chef who invited them to look round the kitchen. Douglas, knowing he would soon appear as their new boss felt obliged to admit he was soon to start working for Holiday Resort although he did not tell them what he would be doing.

The day after the visit to Moth Island Douglas spent packing and getting up to date in preparation for his trip to England. Although excited, and apprehensive at the thought of the new job, his pleasure was spoilt as Joelle had not been home and had not made contact. He had tried unsuccessfully to phone her and even been to the police station a couple of times to find her but on each occasion had been told she was not in or not available.

The day of his departure Jasmine offered to leave Eva in charge of the restaurant and drive Douglas to the airport. In the car, Jasmine admitted her mother was puzzling her, 'she phoned me yesterday and asked if I had seen you and how you were. I told her you were okay and I asked her where she was. I don't know, she was in a strange mood. She did not tell me what she was doing, just that she would be home soon and asked when you were leaving for England. She asked me to say goodbye to you for her.'

Douglas admitted he had been unsuccessful trying to contact her and secretly hoped that she might be at the airport to say goodbye to him. She was not.

CHAPTER 9. INDECISIVE

Joelle sat miserably in a state of indecision waiting for Andrea to phone her and it was after midnight before they spoke. They had a long conversation in which Joelle admitted she thought Douglas was having an affair with Eva.

Andrea's first reaction was, 'surely not, he is old enough to be her father, and I cannot imagine Douglas as a sugar daddy taking up with someone so young.'

Joelle pointed out she was much younger than Douglas but Andrea dismissed this as irrelevant, telling Joelle she was not that young.

'Oh, thanks for that!' Joelle reacted, but it did bring a smile to her face.

Andrea asked why she thought Douglas was having an affair, 'have you actually caught them, so to speak?' She asked.

Joelle admitted she had not but that Douglas spent a lot of time with Eva, 'he says he is helping her with her studies,' she told Andrea, eventually admitting she had seen them kissing. But when she described the incident Andrea pointed out they were not actually kissing and Eve could have simply been saying good bye, 'After all, as I remember the girl, she was always the touchy-feely type.'

Andrea planted sufficient doubt in Joelle's mind for her to not end the relationship with Douglas immediately.

'Why not just ask him if he has a relationship with Eva?' Andrea asked.

Joelle dismissed that idea saying Douglas would deny it anyway, even if he was. Andrea was not sure of that, but suggested that alternatively they spend some time apart pointing out that Douglas soon would be away for a couple of weeks, and that, after all, they do say absence makes the heart grow fonder, 'calm down, see how you feel when he comes back from England,' was Andreas advice.

Joelle did spend the rest of the night sleeping, unsuccessfully, in her office chair and the following morning decided to return home and confront Douglas and get it over with. However, still consumed with uncertainty, when she found Douglas was not at home she decided to take Andreas advice and not see Douglas while she let her emotions settle down and see how she felt when he returned from England.

She packed a bag and left Windrush, hoping that she would not meet Douglas as she rode her bike back into town and once there she booked into a hotel for the rest of the week.

Joelle did spend that week rather miserably in her own company. She was worried about the lack of progress on the drug investigation and the missing girl, Sofia Luka and was disappointed that there was no one suitable to put under cover on Moth Island.

Irene did make further enquiries at the Dutch Consulate but they had no record of the Sofia ever having visited the Consulate and helpfully checked to see if a replacement passport had ever been issued, confirming that one had not.

By the end of the week Joelle was no further forward with the drug investigation and the Sofia Luka file was still open.

Joelle also missed Douglas and the way they would talk together and she realised how she relied on him to bring some perspective to her thinking but she was determined to take Andrea's advice and not see him for a period, hoping that that would make him come to his senses and realise what he was throwing away.

Just before Douglas went away she nearly weakened but she phoned Jasmine instead and that phone call did trigger another thought in her mind. She needed someone undercover in Moth Island and Douglas already had a job there. At this thought she put her emotional problems to one side and with her police mind working realised this was her best opportunity to get a spy into Moth Island. Of course, this meant she had to remain on talking terms with Douglas, but as she thought, was that not what she really wanted to do anyway? For the sake of the investigation can't be that difficult, she thought.

The other problem Joelle had to deal with that week was that the Crystal Bay Hotel had gone into administration. She really wanted to talk to Douglas about it, realising he would immediately understand the problem and advise her what to do. In fact she knew he would take the problem on board and deal with it on her behalf, but for the moment she had cut herself off from him. She brooded about the problem for a couple of days before deciding to go and speak to David Rail, the attorney in Kaeta Town that she and Douglas had used before.

David confirmed that he had heard the hotel had gone bankrupt and had temporarily laid off some of the staff but not cancelled bookings while they assessed the businesses financial viability. Basically, he advised her the administrator had to decide whether to cut their losses and close the business now, or whether to keep it running and try and sell the hotel as a going concern.

'I own the freehold, land and buildings, although the hotel has done a lot of work improving the buildings and providing additional facilities,' Joelle told David Rail.

'I assume you have a lease and the management company pay you a rent,' David said making a note.

'Yes, but I don't think this year's rent has been paid yet, its due in November at the start of the main season.'

'Hmm, I think you will be lucky to get that paid now,' David surmised, 'I will make sure the administrator has a record of your interest. Can you let me have a copy of the lease?'

'I am thinking of the people who work there, they will find it difficult to find another job on the island. Surely as owner I have some say in what happens?' Joelle asked.

'Your position depends on what is written in the lease, but I rather suspect you will just rank as an ordinary creditor and will have to wait and see what happens.'

The day Douglas left to fly to England Joelle wanted to go to the airport and say goodbye, but fearing Eva also would be at the airport to send him off she decided to keep away. The last thing she wanted was to see Douglas and Eva being intimate with each other.

Her next problem was that she knew Douglas would phone, usually daily unless circumstances prevented for some reason, and now she did not know whether she wanted to speak to him or not. If they were having a separation it would be better not to speak, but Douglas did not know they were having a separation and her heart was telling her she was missing him already.

In the event, it was a couple of days before he did ring her. She was sitting at her desk and, deciding whether to answer the call or not, she just stared at the mobile screen which was announcing dispassionately that Douglas was phoning. Eventually the phone stopped ringing, Joelle continued to stare waiting for the answer service to call with a message.

'Hi Love, just rang to say hello. Finished my first day meeting people and got another day in the Horsham Office tomorrow then they are sending me down to Bristol, (of all places!) to train in the new software. Hope all is good with you. Love and kisses.'

She frowned and then shrugged resisting the urge to cry at the message, thinking miserably if he says he loves me why is he playing around with another woman.

It was while Douglas was away that Joelle received further bad news. A member of the Islands legal-council bounced into her office and happily told her he had news. Joelle looked up at him expectantly thinking she could do with some good news.

'We have got a result, the brutality case,' he started, 'you know, the two backpackers you arrested for drugs,' Joelle nodded, she remembered the two very well.

'Their attorney has agreed that the brutality

case should be heard here on Kaeta and they have applied for a trial date.'

'This is a result? I thought you said they would probably drop the matter,' Joelle commented.

'Uhh, well yes, we did lodge an accusation of sexual harassment, but in agreeing for the trial to go ahead in Kaeta the other side are applying to the court to have that accusation struck out and, as we have no witnesses, we will probably not object' The council looked a little crestfallen.

'Well that's great,' Joelle was getting angry. 'So now I am in the frame for brutality with nothing to back me up.'

'It might not be that bad,' the council responded wilting under Joelle's anger. 'We have requested the medical evidence the other side claim supports the brutality accusation.'

'But basically it is my word against two boys and whatever evidence they can manufacture, 'Joelle challenged the council.

'Well, yes, it looks like that, unless you have a witness to the events,' The Island's legal-council officer looked miserably at Joelle, beginning to realise that perhaps this trial would not be as straight forward as he first thought.

Joelle dismissed him but sat thinking about witnesses. Jasmine might have seen what happened she realised, and then there were the two girls that the boys had been ogling. They looked like local Kaetians and had been flirting, teasing the boys; they might have seen the arrest.

'Merv,' Joelle called out, and as Merv put his head through her office door, 'can you prepare one of those 'did you see the incident' request boards for the arrest of the two American teenagers and put it in the tourist shopping arcade down by the port.'

'What's up boss? They have already been to court, why do we need witnesses?' Merv queried. Joelle explained they were accusing her of brutality when she made the arrest.

'No problem boss,' Merv grinned at her, 'I'll fix up some witnesses for you. Two pretty young girls you think.'

CHAPTER 10. THE HOLIDAY RESORT COMPANY LIMITED

'Good morning,' Douglas greeted the receptionist sitting in the foyer of the steel and glass office building just outside Horsham in England. 'My name is Douglas Jay and I have an appointment with Janice Milicent.'

The receptionist checked on her screen and then handed Douglas a visitor's badge and access card to the inner sanctum of the building and told him to take the lift to the fourth-floor offices of the Holiday Resort Company.

'Douglas, welcome, please come through,' Janice Milicent showed Douglas into an empty meeting room which she was using as an office. 'Just a few formalities to run through then I will take you out and introduce you to Martin Pleasance, he is the Moth Island Resort Manager, and Jason Shaft, the accounting centre manager.'

Martin Pleasance had also usurped an empty

meeting room to use for the day.

'Martin,' Janice interrupted him as he worked on a laptop, 'Let me introduce Douglas, the new Money Director for Moth Island and turning to Douglas, as she left him explaining, 'we are a first names company, friendlier that way,'

Martin invited Douglas to sit down and they started to talk. Martin had been summoned to attend a review meeting the next day.

'They are chaired by Dick Stump and they happen every couple of months, they are hard work and I hate them,' Martin confided.

'Well, I will be joining you tomorrow so let me know if I can help,' Douglas tried to be supportive.

'I have prepared my presentation, we just have to see how it goes tomorrow.' Martin said gloomily. They continued to talk about Moth Island and how it worked and Douglas began to get the impression his appointment was resented by Martin Pleasance, especially when at one point Martin confided that he did not know why the role had been created and what Douglas would do.

'There are a couple of other Money Directors but they each have more than one resort to look after,' he complained.

'They said something about a new operating system for Moth Island,' Douglas said.

Martin shook his head, 'I know nothing of that, what new system?'

Douglas shrugged, 'I will find out soon, apparently, I am to go on a training course later this week.'

After an hour or so Janice retrieved Douglas and took him into a large open plan office with about fifteen people sitting in little cubicles working on computers. It was a light office with windows on two sides, the blinds on the south side pulled half down to shield from the sun, not that there was much sun that February afternoon. The third wall had performance target charts pasted up and looking at the charts as he was escorted through the office Douglas observed that Moth Island was bottom of the league. One corner was occupied by a large desk and tall wood filing cupboards with a balding harassed looking middle aged man sitting behind the desk. Douglas was introduced to Jason Shaft, the Accounting Office manager.

He spent the rest of the morning with Jason who introduced him to all the staff and explained how the accounting was organised.

After lunch, a sandwich with Jason, Douglas was introduced to John Tidy, the Money Manager for the Pacific Resorts. John was quite friendly and explained the job was easy, 'basically it involves monitoring the results and giving the resort manager a rollocking if he fails to meet his targets. Mind you,' he continued, 'You have a bit of a problem, Moth Island is the bad child, it's not in my portfolio, but I know the results are way below target and everyone says Martin is not

Mr John de Caynoth

really up to the job. Good Luck,' he cheerfully wished Douglas.

That night Douglas settled down in his hotel room to read the reports and operational manuals he had been given. It was tedious work but it took his mind off feeling lonely and as a reward for concentrating he promised himself a whisky from the room fridge and a phone conversation with Joelle. When she did not answer, he was disappointed, but he guessed she was still at work and busy, and he contemplated ringing the restaurant to talk with Eva or Jasmine but decided to save that one until later in the week.

He spent the following morning in the review meeting alongside Martin Pleasance. It was a very uncomfortable meeting. Dick Stump was highly critical telling Martin the resorts performance was appalling and the losses unacceptable. Janice too was critical, pointing out that the staff turnover was the worst in the group and that the use of temporary agency staff was costing a fortune. Douglas sat listening with increasing concern as Martin whined at the quality and laziness of the local staff and justified his losses by explaining that he was covering the Casino overheads as well as the resort overheads.

That afternoon Douglas was summoned to a meeting with Dick Stump and was slightly taken back at Stump's aggressiveness, especially when he had appeared so friendly and laid back in the interview.

Dick Stump did not waste words, 'You heard this morning's meeting. You have three months to turn that resort round, I want to see positive moves towards meeting the targets by the next review.'

'Doing that, alongside implementing a new system will not be easy,' Douglas tried to explain.

Dick Stump was not in a mood to be sympathetic, 'Yes,' he agreed, 'I want that system operational as well by the next review.'

That evening Douglas ate dinner and went to the bar feeling miserable, wondering what he had got himself into. He wanted to talk to Joelle and waited until midnight before calling her hoping he would catch her after work. She did not answer her mobile, it just switched to voice message. He rang the Windrush house phone and it was answered by Mary, he asked if Joelle was home and Mary told him to hold on, she would go and find her. He heard her calling Joelle and in a few moments Mary was on the phone again telling him Joelle was in the bath and she would call him when she was dressed.

Douglas went to bed and waited for the call, but it never came.

****

The rest of Douglas time in England was spent in Bristol at the offices of the company that had written the new software and built the resort operating system. He was on an intensive ten-day training course, the first part of which covered the background to the system, the various modules and what they could do, and how to customise the software to meet the needs of the particular hotel or resort. The second part of the training was on the training manuals and how to set up local training to teach staff how to use the system, the different screens and what they were for.

Although the system itself was complicated the user interface was relatively easy to use. All the data was input to the system locally, but all the processing would be done back in the Horsham Accounting System. The system operated in real time and Douglas, as the nominated system manager would have access to and control over all aspects of the system and would set up the various users with limited access to only those modules they would need.

Douglas was not even half way through the ten days before it became obvious to him that to get the system up and working he was going to need a computer literate person to help him. He hoped he would find someone suitable already working on Moth Island.

By the half way point he had given up phoning Joelle daily, she never answered the mobile. He rang the restaurant once, and Eva had answered. She had listened sympathetically as he told her his worries about the new job and he began to feel more cheerful as they talked. She told him they were struggling a bit with customers since the hotel went into administration. This was news to Douglas but Eva did not know the background and could not really tell him much more. He asked if she had seen Joelle but Eva said she had not.

The following evening, he telephoned Mary and explained that he was having trouble getting hold of Joelle, 'she never answers her phone these days.'

'She has been a strange mood ever since you went away Mary confided, 'I do not know what is wrong with her, when I ask she just says work.'

'Could you ask her to telephone me?' Douglas asked.

'No need, she is in the study, I will get her.'

'Douglas, you wanted to talk to me?' Joelle asked rather formally.

'Yes, I have been trying to phone you for ages and left messages, why did you phone me back?'

'Sorry, I have been busy.'

This rather stilted conversation went on for another couple of minutes with Douglas asking about the Glass Bay Hotel and what was happening, and Joelle answering in the briefest possible way. Eventually Douglas gave up, said goodbye and that he would ring her again in another couple of days. He sat for a long time thinking about call. Obviously, something was not right, work related he supposed, although at the back of his mind the argument they had had about

Eva niggled away and he wondered again what Joelle knew, or thought she knew.

He did phone her as promised but she did not answer. He did not bother to leave a message but sighed deeply, knowing things were not right, but thinking he would be home, back in Kaeta in a few days. He put the problem aside until his return concentrating on trying to learn about this new system.

CHAPTER 11. THE WEEKEND

Mid-afternoon on Saturday and Joelle was waiting at the airport outside the arrivals hall. Douglas's plane had just landed and she was looking forward to his return although a little anxious how he would greet her in view of the way she had been avoiding speaking with him while he was away. As usual Andrea's advice had been good and having let her emotions settle down and giving herself time to think things through, she had almost come to the realisation that she might have misinterpreted a series of coincidences and jumped to the wrong conclusion. There was still a little fear at the back of her mind but for now she was going to ignore it and give their relationship a chance.

Douglas saw her standing, scanning the emerging passengers, as soon as he walked out of the baggage hall. As usual a blast of heat hit him as he emerged from the air-conditioned interior of the airport and he had to fight his way through hordes of passengers, tour guides and porters milling round noisily. He too was a little nervous as he approached Joelle but thought it a good sign that she come to the airport to meet him. He tentatively greeted her with a kiss, which as it was returned, gave him the confidence to embrace her, kiss her again and tell her he had missed her.

Joelle breathed a sigh of relief, he was pleased to see her and that she took to be a good sign.

As was their habit together, that evening they sat on the veranda looking out over the Caribbean Sea watching the sun set. As the orange faded through red, burgundy, purple, dark blue and finally inky black they listened to the night sounds, the sea swishing gently against the rocks below the low cliff in front of the house and the tree frogs squeaking round the garden.

Douglas told Joelle about his trip, what he had learnt about Moth Island and that he thought the job was going to be much harder than he originally thought.

'They have given me a really stiff target to turn the resort round, financially, in just three months, and implement a new system as well,' he explained.

'Well, what will they do if you don't turn it round in three months?' Joelle asked

'The worst they can do is to sack me.'

'Would that matter?' Joelle responded

'Not really,' he shrugged.

The discussion turned to the Glass Bay Hotel and Joelle told him that it had gone into administration and that they had defaulted on the last rental payment to her.

'David Rail checked that I am on the list of creditors and luckily as I own the freehold and the main buildings the administrator cannot get his hands on those assets, but he says there may be an issue with something he called leasehold improvements.'

'That is where the Management Company have spent money extending the buildings, but if they liquidate the business as an asset sale I can't see that the leasehold improvements having any value, but I suppose if they sell it as a going concern the buyer may pay something for them.' Douglas speculated.

'David says he was told there is no real value as an asset sale so the administrators are going to keep the hotel running and try and sell it as a going concern.' Joelle explained.

'Well, that will be good for the staff, at least some of them may keep their jobs.' Douglas reflected and then said, 'it also explains Eva's comment that the hotel looked deserted and the restaurant customers have dropped off. I must go down to the restaurant tomorrow and see the girls.'

Joelle bridled at the mention of Eva and had to stop herself thinking, is he really just going

Mr John de Caynoth

down to see Eva.

Next morning, Douglas, Joelle and Mary breakfasted together sitting outside enjoying the relative coolness of the early morning before the sun got up and baked the garden. Douglas announced he was going down to the restaurant after breakfast and unknowingly forestalled Joelle's suspicions by asking her to come with him. Joelle mischievously suggested that they go on her motorcycle,

'Much as I would enjoy sitting behind you with my arms round you I think we will take the MG,' Douglas grinned back.

'We might be able to arrange for you put your arms round me later,' Joelle playfully teased him.

It was actually mid-morning before they arrived at the restaurant and both Jasmine and Eva were busy preparing for the day's opening. The girls interrupted their preparations to sit with Douglas and Joelle for a few moments and enjoy a coffee together. Eventually conversation turned to the Glass Bay Hotel and its bankruptcy and Jasmine admitted that it had had a serious impact on the restaurant.

'Our place servings have fallen by half,' she admitted, 'and our wastage has shot up as it is hard to predict how many customers we will get each day now we are reliant on passing trade.'

'How bad are the figures?' Douglas asked.

MOTH ISLAND

Eva answered, 'I tried to do a set of accounts to see, but I am not sure they are correct as I could not get them to balance.'

'Would you like me to have a look,' Douglas asked.

'Please, but they are on my laptop back at the chalet,' Eva explained.

To Joelle's dismay Douglas said he would walk over to the chalet to look at the accounts and he and Eva set off across the beach together.

'What is the matter Mum?' Jasmine asked her as they worked together in the kitchen, 'you are not talking at all.'

'Oh, nothing really,' she replied, and then added, 'I just sometimes get a bit jealous of Douglas spending so much time alone with Eva.'

'That's silly mum, he does not see Eva, she is with me most of the time.' Jasmine dismissed her mother's fears.

Nevertheless, Joelle decided she would walk along to the chalet and just see what Douglas and Eva were actually up to.

She walked in to the main room, they were not there, she could hear them talking in one of the bedrooms. Some very uncharitable and nasty thoughts went through her mind and she violently pushed the door open expecting to find them naked in bed together.

She gasped as she stood in the door and two of them looked up at her.

'Hello Joelle,' Douglas greeted her, 'Won't be a

minute we are just finishing, if you hang on I will be ready in a tick and we can go home.'

Joelle breathed deeply to control her emotions and let the adrenaline drain from her system before she spoke, but she never got the chance as Douglas rose and walking across to her hitched up his shorts and put his arm round her inviting her to go home with him.

'Do you want drive the car,' he invited.

Later that afternoon Joelle lay on the beach in a state of confusion. After leaving the restaurant, instead of returning to Windrush, she and Douglas had driven out to Joelle's favourite place on the Kaeta, the secluded Three Sisters Bay, a sheltered sandy beach fringed with coconut palms, which could only be accessed by a half mile walk down a rough path.

There they had held each other tightly, kissed and made love.

Douglas was now in the sea swimming gently across the bay and Joelle was lying on the beach watching him convincing herself that she was wrong in believing him to be having an affair with Eva. How could he make love to her so tenderly if he had just made love to Eva, she thought? Joelle was sure she would catch them when she had burst into the chalet, but instead she had found them sitting in the bedroom pouring over a computer screen and printing accounting reports. The bed had been pushed into one corner and a table and some filing cabinets moved into the room which was clearly being used as a study. Joelle had tried to examine the bed to see if it had been used but it was covered in books and papers. Of course, she told herself that she was relieved to find Douglas and Eva had been doing exactly what they said they were doing, checking Eva's accounts, but with her police instincts she was frustrated that the circumstantial evidence pointing to something going on between Douglas and Eva but there was no actual evidence. She knew she would have to sort this out soon as eventually it would destroy their relationship, but for this afternoon she just wanted to enjoy being with Douglas, he would be going away again tomorrow to start his new job on Moth Island.

Douglas did go to Moth Island and he spent the week there, meeting the staff, finding out how the place worked and planning the implementation of the new system, but he also was acutely aware that in addition to his role as 'Money Director' he had another responsibility on the Island.

The day he left to start the new job, he and Joelle lay in bed together talking over a first cup of tea. Joelle had told him that she was convinced that the source of the drug wave on Kaeta was Moth Island but, despite conducting interviews and searches on the Island, she had been unable to find any tangible evidence of drugs or anyone involved. She asked him to be alert and perhaps dig around for her and see if he could find the evidence she needed to close down the drug operation. Initially Douglas had not seen her request as a problem and assured her that if he should find any illegal activities operating on the Island she would be the first person to know.

'It is not just drugs,' Joelle explained, 'there is that missing Dutch girl, Sofia Luka, the last place she was seen was on Moth Island, but now she has completely disappeared. Her belongings were collected from the hotel but, we believe, not by Sofia. She has not been in touch with the Consulate and not been home. We have no idea where she is or what has happened to her.'

'Well, if you could not find her on Moth Island, I don't expect I will be able to,' Douglas reasoned.

'I know, but look out for her anyway,' Joelle had asked as she gave him a copy of the girl's picture. As he planned his work on Moth Island Douglas came to the realisation that what Joelle had asked of him was more than just simply reporting illegal doings if he happened to see something, she had asked him to actively look for evidence and that would be a whole lot more difficult.

It was on the Wednesday morning when Joelle called him. After asking how he was getting on and what he was doing, she told him she had been dressed down by the Commissioner and she asked Douglas if he had made any progress on the drug issues. He had to admit he had not really had time to think about that yet. Joelle then told him she had a possible theory about Sofia Luka's disappearance.

'I am wondering if something happened to her on the Island. Perhaps a fight or something in which got injured. Is there anywhere on the on the Island she could be injured, or even hidden if she is dead.' Again, Douglas had to admit he had no idea.

The call finished with Douglas disappointed he had not been much help, but he shrugged, he could not do everything at once and right now his priority was to prepare for the staff briefing he had called for the next day.

He called most of the staff together mid-morning the next day. This was usually a quiet time between breakfast and lunch and needed only a few staff left on duty to care for the guests. He explained the resorts poor financial situation and that one of his priorities would be to address that. Then he told the assembly that a new administrative system would be introduced which would give much more accurate and up to date information. He finished his briefing by inviting questions. There was much concern about the extra work the new system might require from the reception, housekeeping and kitchen staff and Douglas had to tell them that they would be required to input information to the new system. The briefing concluded with much muttering, some like the head chef were heard to say they were surprised that such a system had not been introduced before while others muttered that had enough to do without some new-fangled way of working being imposed.

However, the real shock for Douglas came later that afternoon when, Martin Pleasance, the Resort Manager came to see him to tell him that the head receptionist and bookkeeper had resigned, saying she was not interested in any new system. This was a blow to Douglas as he had already identified that the Resort Manager and Receptionist/Bookkeeper were the two people key to implementing the changes.

It was shortly after this news that Douglas got the phone call from Eva. She asked when he would next be back on Kaeta and explained that she needed to see him on his return. Despite worrying what he would do having lost a key member of staff, hearing her request sent a tingle through his body, it was something he would only admit to himself but he found her a most attractive woman and secretly looked forward meeting her.

CHAPTER 12. MOTH ISLAND

While Douglas was on Moth Island, Joelle had a busy, and not particularly productive week, which, first thing on Monday, started badly.

She had only just got to her desk and finished her early morning coffee and was about to start the daily briefing meeting with Merv and Irene when she was summoned up to the Commissioner's office.

He handed her a copy of a letter that the Cabinet Member for Tourism had passed to him for attention, and told her to read the second paragraph;

As you will be aware our company operates a strict 'no drugs' policy on board ship and passengers are warned that illegal drugs found in their possession will be confiscated and handed to the police in our home port together with the names and details of the passengers involved.

In recent weeks we have noted a gradual escalation of illegal drug use by our passengers, with most of

Mr John de Caynoth

the incidents occurring after the ship has docked at Keata. We regret that we must inform you that if this situation continues we will have to consider removing Kaeta from our tour itineraries.

'Naturally you will appreciate the seriousness of this situation,' The Commissioner glared at Joelle. 'The Island cannot afford to be removed from the itineraries of the cruise ships,' the Commissioner boomed.

She tried to say something, but the Commissioner warming to this subject stopped her.

'Inspector, you will hear me out before interrupting. As I was saying this is a most serious matter, this epidemic of illegal drugs on Keata has been developing for months now and you appear to have made no progress towards stopping it.'

The Commissioner continued his tirade dressing down Joelle for some minutes more before she was able to speak.

With her fingers crossed she told the Commissioner that she had traced the source of the drugs to Moth Island and now had someone under cover working on the Island to identify the culprits.

'Commissioner, I am confident we will clean this up within the next two or three weeks.' Joelle said with more assurance than she actually felt.

The Commissioner grunted, 'you had better,' and dismissed her curtly, but then remembered another problem.

'There is another thing,' he said, 'I have been contacted by the Rotterdam police about a missing person Sofia Luka. Apparently, her employer contacted the police to report her failure to return to work after her holiday on Kaeta. The Rotterdam police say they have made enquiries and it appears she never returned to her flat, and no one has seen her since her holiday,' The Commissioner looked questioningly at Joelle.

'Yes Sir, we have it as an open case. It appears she disappeared on Moth Island.'

'Well, we don't want an international incident so you had better find her.' The Commissioner dismissed her handing the email from Rotterdam to her to deal with and she left his office praying that Douglas would come up with something soon.

In the briefing that morning Merv confirmed that they were still picking up tourists smoking marijuana.

'As you instructed, we arrest them and bring them in for questioning before releasing them with a warning.' Merv told Joelle.

'Do they say where they obtained the drug?' She asked.

'Most say a friend or fellow passenger, only a few admit they were offered drugs when they visited Moth Island.' Merv answered.

Joelle consulted the weekly port schedule update which showed her which cruise ships were

Mr John de Caynoth

expected to dock in Kaeta.

'This week we only have two ships in and they are just twenty-four hours stop overs but that massive Queen of the Caribbean ship docks on Saturday morning leaving Sunday Evening and then next week we have a three day stop over,' she noted.

'Right you two, don't make any plans for this weekend, with thousands of tourists around the town we are going to be working.'

Merv interrupted her with a groan, 'Joelle, don't forget the fish festival parade is this Saturday as well, so the main streets will be closed off and the town packed.'

Joelle shrugged, 'We are going to be very busy then.'

She rubbed her chin thinking and then turned to Irene, 'I doubt there will be anyone going to Moth Island over the weekend but, Irene, find out if there is a Moth Island excursion next week.' She turned to Merv, 'if there is the three of us, and anyone else available, will invite ourselves to Moth Island and see what is going on.'

She finished that mornings briefing by telling the team that if they found anyone else using marijuana to let her know immediately as she wanted to attend the interview.

When they had finished the briefing, Joelle asked Irene if there had been progress on the Sofia Luka case.

'Not really,' Irene admitted, 'I found the boat

owner who took Sofia and her boyfriend out to Moth Island with a small group of tourists. I showed him her picture and he says he remembers her only because the boyfriend was very worked up that he could not find her and insisted that they wait for her on the return crossing. It just confirms the boyfriends story that she was last seen on Moth Island.'

'This boyfriend,' Joelle speculated, 'Where is he now?'

'I suppose he has gone home,' Irene replied.

Joelle looked at the file. 'Hmm, he is British,' she mused, 'when we questioned him we did not really push him hard about the argument. What if he lost it and killed her, in a fight perhaps, and hid the body somewhere on the Island and then collected her clothes and paid her bill himself.'

Irene looked surprised, 'that is a rather large jump, there is no evidence of that at all and the boyfriend looked genuinely upset that she had disappeared.'

Joelle nodded, 'He might be a good actor and just because we have not found the evidence does not mean it does not exist. Let's just follow it up as a new line of enquiry and see where it takes us.'

Irene agreed, not sure what they could do.

'I will contact, Barbara Green, my old boss when I was seconded to the London Met and see if she can arrange to interview this boyfriend and push him a bit on what actually happened after the argument,' Joelle decided.

Joelle went home frustrated and late that night. Her time was being taken up fiddling around making sure that visitors from the cruise ships were not getting into trouble and she was not making any progress on the two open case files, the drug wave on the Island and the missing person Sofia Luka and now she had the Commissioner on her back looking for results. 'Sod it,' she muttered, 'I forgot to contact the police in Rotterdam.'

It was Wednesday before Joelle got back to dealing with her two open cases and the first thing she did, in the privacy of her office, was to ring Douglas. She did not want anyone knowing she had asked Douglas to be her informer, but, also she just wanted to talk to Douglas and did not want anyone listening. She got through to the hotel reception and was put through to him after a few seconds and he sounded pleased to hear her. She felt a bit guilty unloading her problems on Douglas, but at least she felt better having talked to him. She was disappointed that he had not got any information for her, but realised he had only been on Moth Island for a couple of days so had not had much time. At least she had explained her theory regarding the Sofia Lukas disappearance and Douglas said he would see what he could find.

That conversation buoyed her up for the rest of the day and her mood was further improved by a brief phone call later that afternoon.

'Hi Joelle, its Barbara. I have spoken to my 'oppo' in Reading, that is where Sofia's boyfriend lives and they have agreed to let one of our officers visit the area and interview the young man.'

'That's great, thank you Barbara,' Joelle was relieved that at least something was happening.

'I am going to send Andrea Spooner. No doubt she will contact you soon for the background.'

Joelle was delighted at the thought of working with Andrea again, even if it was at a distance, and the next day she and Andrea had a long phone call where they covered not only the back ground to the Sofia Luka case but also caught up with each other's news. The call ended with Joelle telling Andrea it was about time they got together again and inviting Andrea to come out to Kaeta for a holiday.

Bad news was a letter from a firm of Bristol lawyers advising Joelle that they had been engaged by Ralph Holdswick to investigate a claim that he had been forced under duress to sign a divorce agreement relinquishing any financial claim on her estate and that they intended to appeal the Divorce Court ruling and if necessary would subpoena Ms de Nouvelas, her daughter and Mr Jay to make statements under oath concerning the allegation. Joelle cursed Ralph and threw the letter to one side to deal with later.

It was the end of the week when Joelle got a phone call from Douglas.

Mr John de Caynoth

He told her he had not made any progress regarding the drug investigation but hoped to do something about it soon but that he had spent an afternoon walking round the island. 'It is not very big and I pretty much covered the whole Island except the six private houses, and the Casino complex, but the security is so tight up there that I don't think even a rat could get in without a pass. Anyway, I am afraid I have found no sign of Sofia, I even looked to see if there was any newly dug ground where she might have been buried, but nothing.' They speculated if there was somewhere else she could be hiding, one of the houses perhaps, Joelle suggested, and Douglas remembering the body that had been washed up on the beach, wondered if she have been thrown into the sea.

'Well, if she was, eventually she will wash up somewhere I suppose, but thankfully we have had no more bodies reported,' was Joelle's response.

They finished the conversation realising they would hardly see each other over the weekend. Douglas said he would be working on the Saturday and be home late and Joelle telling him she was also working all weekend and as a big cruise ship was in town.

That evening she finished work early and decided to go to the Glass Bay Restaurant see Jasmine and relax over a glass or two of wine.

When she arrived, Jasmine sat with her for a

few moments. Joelle asked where Eva was and Jasmine told her that as business was very slow at the moment Eva was having the evening off. Joelle commiserated over the lack of customers and spoke a bit about the Hotel going bankrupt. Jasmine admitted to Joelle that while she still enjoyed the cooking the restaurant had not been much fun since the numbers dropped off. Joelle feeling sorry for her daughter decided to eat in the restaurant and let Jasmine take her order and disappear into the kitchen.

Joelle went over to the bar and asked Sean for another glass of wine. She sat at the bar talking to him for a few moments and together they bemoaned the lack of customers.

'Of course, I am lucky,' Sean told Joelle, 'I have another job on Moth Island. I do a lunch time shift in the bar there now Jasmine only needs me in the evenings.'

Joelle pricked up her ears and was about to ask Sean if he had ever come across drugs on Moth Island, but at his next comment she was lost for words.

'Only recently,' he said, 'I saw Douglas and Eva over there, doing a day trip I think they said.'

CHAPTER 13.
DOUGLAS'S WEEKEND

Douglas finally had time on the Saturday to think about the drug problem Joelle had given him. He suspected that whoever was distributing drugs was likely to be in a fairly junior position and the problem as he saw it was that, as the boss, no one was going to confide in him and he certainly could not stroll round the resort as a junior gardener or waiter. It was then he had his best idea of the week, he had already noted that Martin Pleasance was advertising vacancies for gardeners and ground staff and he thought to phone his old friend and private detective Josh Worthington, and see if he would like a job. He dialled Josh's number and was disappointed at the answer phone message informing him that the office was closed for the weekend and inviting him to leave a message.

He had barely finished recording the message when his mobile rang.

'Josh, my friend,' Douglas answered the call reading the name on his mobile screen.

'Hey man, how are you doing?' Josh greeted, 'Sorry about the answer phone.'

Douglas wasted no time on small talk and explained where he was now working and why he needed Josh's help.

'Man, I am sitting here reading the newspapers bored out of my mind, two weeks in the Caribbean sounds like a holiday. 'Course I want to come. I'm on the next flight out.' Josh agreed promising to let Douglas know when he expected to arrive.

Most of the rest of Saturday Douglas spent in reception, partly covering for the receptionist who had resigned and not come to work that day saying she felt ill. This gave him the opportunity to talk to the departing guests, asking if they enjoyed their holiday, what they had done, and reading their feedback forms. He put the picture of Sofia Luca on the reception desk under a note, 'Have you seen this girl', but got no response. He also hoped he might pick up a comment about drugs but again, nothing, except that the Island shop was very expensive and poorly stocked. He made a mental note to inspect the shop himself. The resort maintained limited on site staff accommodation. For the resort manager, on the far side of the Island, away from the resort buildings, was a small bungalow comprising a bedroom, an open plan kitchen come diner and living room and bathroom. Remaining staff were accommodated in two concrete block buildings constructed behind the restaurant, kitchen and main bar. Eack block had fifteen bedrooms, all with on-suit bathrooms and this meant that about a third of the resorts staff number lived on site. The remaining employees, about sixty people, lived on Kaeta and were ferried to and from the Island by boat. There were three such taxi boat services each day. One at about seven in the morning which usually did two or three runs to bring all the employees across, another at about two, after lunch, which took the morning shift back to Kaeta and picked up the afternoon and evening shifts and final boat at about ten in the evening which took all the employees as well as the evening entertainers home when the resort wound down for the night.

Martin Pleasance had reluctantly offered to move out of the chalet, but Douglas declined telling Martin he did not intend to live on the Island and was quite happy to use a spare staff room when he stayed overnight. Martin, grateful not to have move himself, allocated one of the better staff rooms permanently for Douglas's personal use. Unfortunately, this room was used by the receptionist/bookkeeper, who was evicted and moved to a smaller room at the back of the block. Another reason why she had resigned and had only agreed to work out a week's notice as she needed the money.

That Saturday, Douglas caught the evening staff boat back to Kaeta picked up his MGB from its parking place in the yacht club's car park and headed back to Windrush. He contemplated calling at the Glass Bay Restaurant for a drink but decided he was too tired. He got back to Windrush at about eleven and found the house already in darkness. Mary always went to bed early, so he silently crept up to Joelle's bedroom, he paused outside the door and decided that rather than wake her he would sleep in the spare room, not realising that Joelle was not home, she was still working.

He awoke late the next morning and after dozing in bed for a while decided to get up and go and find Joelle and some breakfast but only Mary was in the kitchen, alone.

'Where is Joelle?' He asked.

'You missed her, she went to work early. What with the parade yesterday and that enormous cruise ship, she had a busy night and said she needed to get in early today to sort things out.'

Mary cooked him a couple of eggs and after eating he mooched around the house for a bit and then, remembering the phone call from Eva decided to go down to the restaurant to see her.

He found both Jasmine and Eva in the restaurant, Jasmine cleaning down the kitchen and Eva vacuuming the dining area.

'You wanted to see me,' he approached Eva.

She turned off the vacuum cleaner and invited Douglas to sit at a table with her.

'Jasmine and I have been looking at the restaurants takings and at the moment we think we are running at a loss,' Eva started to explain as Jasmine came out of the kitchen to join them.

'Yes, with the hotel going bankrupt, and we discovered, taking down our adverts and discouraging people from walking along the beach to us, we don't see things getting any better in the immediate future,' Jasmine added.

Douglas drew a deep breath and regarded the two girls looking seriously at him.

'We have decided,' Eva explained, 'that we have to cut costs, and as, at the moment both Jasmine and I are drawing a salary from the business one of our salaries is the obvious first cost to go. Jasmine is essential as she does the cooking but she thinks she could manage most of the time with just a part time waitress and the barman Sean when it is busy.'

All Douglas could think of saying was, 'oh! I suppose that makes some sense.'

Eva gave a lop-sided smile, 'yes it does, so now I am unemployed looking for another job.'

'Does that mean you are leaving Kaeta?' Was Douglas's first question.

'Well, I don't want to, I will see if I can find a job on the Island first. The hotel has lost a lot of people, I might be able to get a temporary job there.' Eva was philosophical, 'I don't want to leave the restaurant, and you all, but if I can't find work locally I suppose I will have to leave eventually.'

'Oh, Eva, you don't have to go,' Jasmine was almost tearful, 'you can stay in the chalet as long as you like, even if you don't have a job.'

Douglas looked thoughtful, 'No of course you don't have to leave us, but I might have an idea.' He paused, thinking hard, it was Eva mentioning the hotel which triggered the thought.

'The receptionist/bookkeeper on Moth Island has resigned and leaves at the end of this week, I think that could be a good job for you Eva, but I must warn you that it will be hard work at first as we are implementing a new system and much of the set-up work will fall on the bookkeeper.'

Eva looked interested. 'What does the job involve?' She asked.

Douglas gave her a brief description but explained that the roll would probably change with the new way of working.

'Would Eva have to live on Moth Island? Jasmine asked.

'Not necessarily,' Douglas considered, 'she may have to spend the occasional night there but the majority of the staff live on Kaeta and we run a staff boat to get them to and from the Island for their shifts.'

The three of them discussed the possibilities further with eventually Eva concluding that as long as she did not have to live on Moth Island

Mr John de Caynoth

she would like the job.

'Good,' Douglas said, relieved. He was confident she would cope, and he knew she could be a great help to him implementing new procedures. Also, he felt isolated on the Island and was pleased he would have a friend with him, especially Eva. He liked her company and was going to enjoy working with her.

'Some practicalities to consider,' he suggested, 'first, how soon can you start? And I suppose you ought to be interviewed by Martin Pleasance, he is the resort manager.'

Eva shrugged and looked at Jasmine for support, 'I guess I can start immediately.' Jasmine nodded agreement.

'Excellent,' Douglas was pleased. 'In that case, you could come over the Moth Island with me tomorrow morning, meet Martin, and have a look round. You would then have a week with the old receptionist to pick up the job before she leaves.'

Eva just nodded, now feeling nervous not knowing what she was letting herself in for. At least I will be with Douglas, she comforted herself.

That afternoon Douglas's other plan started to come together. He received a phone call from Josh who explained he had got a flight for the following day, Monday, and would arrive at Kaeta airport about mid-afternoon.

'That's good Josh,' Douglas thought quickly, 'but

we need to think of a plan. We will blow your cover if I meet you and bring you over to the Island.'

'I thought of that, 'Josh told him, 'I looked on the web site and printed out the vacancies list, I guess I can make my own way to the Island and once there I can say I have come to ask for a job. You are boss so you should be able to fix it so that I get one.'

'Good plan,' Douglas agreed, 'get a taxi from the airport to the Kaeta Yacht Club, and from there you find someone to ferry you over. I will lurk round the reception and intercept you when you arrive.'

Douglas spent the rest of the afternoon and most of the evening reading through the procedure manuals for the new system and waiting for Joelle to come home from work. He tried ringing her mobile to see how long she would be but she did not answer, it just switched to a message. Douglas was puzzled, she always used to answer her mobile when I called but these days it's almost like she does not want to talk to me, he thought.

CHAPTER 14, JOELLE'S SATURDAY

That Friday night Joelle went to bed confused and unhappy. She had more or less concluded that she was being too imaginative thinking Douglas and Eva were having an affair, and then she learns that they spent a sneaky day together on Moth Island. There could be a simple explanation, she thought, after all she knew Douglas had taken the job on the Island, he might have just gone over to see what it was like, but why then take Eva for company? She could think of one reason and she did not like it.

She had a bad night with dark dreams and when she woke up she knew she had to lay the ghost one way or another and confront Douglas.

She went to work tired and irritable not looking forward to the day ahead. She had the whole team, detectives and uniform officers, in for the Saturday to police the fiesta parade and look after the thousands of tourists that would arrive that morning on the cruise ship.

She held a briefing meeting in the morning and by lunch time she and the duty sergeant downstairs were the only ones left in the office, everyone else being out on patrol around the town.

Just after lunch the Commissioner looked into her office and asked about the arrangements for policing the town.

'Let me know if I can be of any help,' he boomed at her, not expecting her to take him seriously. 'We don't want any trouble, or drugs,' he added as an afterthought.

Joelle, in not the best of moods and irritated at being checked up on, devilishly thanked the Commissioner for his offer and suggested that he take a police communicator, wear casual clothes, and help by walking around the town, 'but call for help if you see anything,' she cautioned him. Her challenge backfired, she expected him to back off, but to her surprise and even greater irritation, the Commissioner looked delighted.

'It's ages since I did any real police work,' he said happily as he walked out.

Joelle sat at her desk and swore. The last thing she wanted was to spend the afternoon walking around the town with the Commissioner and she had not planned to spend the whole afternoon walking round the town anyway.

She decided to phone Andrea, but it was early morning in London and Andrea's mobile just went to the answering service.

When the Commissioner reappeared, wearing jeans and a colourful shirt, she spent an hour in the town with him, looking at the preparations for the parade and checking the route was covered.

'My word, there is a lot of people here and it's so noisy. I usually only see these parades from the Governors stand,' The Commissioner commented.

Joelle agreed and added gratefully that, at least for the moment, everything was very good natured and peaceful.

'It is this evening the trouble will start when everyone has a few drinks inside them,' Joelle told him and then suggested that perhaps it would be better if they split up, 'less obvious,' she told him. 'In any case I should go back the office to co-ordinate if anything does kick off.'

As she walked back to the police offices she realised she was feeling happier. At least being busy with the Commissioner had taken her mind off Douglas and Eva, and now she felt more rational, she hoped that at some point over the weekend she would have an opportunity to sort things out with Douglas.

The parade concluded in an orderly fashion and the spectators dispersed, some returning to their ship, others heading for one of the towns bars. By early evening as darkness began to fall coloured lights started to sparkle round the old town centre and fish market and the whole area became a kaleidoscope of colour, and noise. Visitors began to reappear on the streets for an evening's entertainment prowling between the market stalls and eating from the street vendor's steaming bowls of curry, goat stew, and barbecued fish. The whole area was soon crowded, music blaring out from every market stall and the aroma of cooking food pervading the atmosphere.

Joelle knew from experience that this was when the trouble, if any, would start. The pick pockets, bag snatchers and drug pushers would be mingling with the crowds waiting for an opportunity. Joelle decided it was time to desert her desk for a walk round. She wanted to see her officers and check what was going on, in particular if anyone had noticed any drugs.

She found Irene and Merv in the general market.

'Nothing serious to report Boss, a few scuffles we broke up and we arrested a pickpocket, that's all,' they told her.

'Any sign of drugs?' She asked.

'Only the usual marijuana houses, but they are all behind closed doors and minding their own business,' Merv shrugged. The police on the Island were perfectly well aware that they would never completely stop the marijuana habit and so had an unwritten understanding that provided that it was practiced discretely, in private, and did not interfere with the tourists they would turn a blind eye. However, the current situation where someone was deliberately targeting tourists was a quite different matter.

'We did see the Commissioner,' Irene volunteered, 'he's putting himself around in the old town, laughing with the street vendors and shaking hands with anyone he can button hole.'

Joelle looked surprised, 'he said he wanted to help and would go out on patrol for us,' she told the two officers.

'Well, you know why. Its election time soon and he is drumming up support,' Merv guessed.

Joelle nodded knowingly, 'That explains it. I wondered why he was so anxious to help this afternoon. We will leave him to it, he can't do any harm.'

It was much later that evening, after nine-o-clock, when Joelle's communicator crackled into life. At the time, she was sitting in her office starting her report on the day's work and thinking that she only had another hour to go before the streets cleared and the tourists returned to their ships.

The communicator hissed and crackled at her demanding attention. It made her jump, no body used the old communicators, mobile phones were much better, smaller and a much clearer signal.

She fumbled with the communicator and remembered she had to press the receive button.

MOTH ISLAND

'I have cracked the drug operation,' a distorted voice hissed through the device.

Joelle quickly recovered her wits and realised it had to be the Commissioner calling in. 'You have cracked the drug operation,' she exclaimed surprised, and then remembered she had to release the receive button to transmit.

'Yes, I have,' the Commissioner sounded proud of himself.

'Well, how, what,' Joelle demanded, 'no, wait, where are you?'

'I am on Poudre Voie, just where it meets the fish market.' The device hissed and crackled.

'Okay, wait there, I am on my way,' Joelle shouted into the communicator.

In response, the device told her to bring reinforcements, there is more than one person involved.

Joelle ran out of the building, pausing only to tell the duty sergeant on the front desk to send the arrest wagon to St. Peters Square and wait there for her. She decided not to take a car, she would never get it through the crowded streets so she ran down the hill into the old town dodging between the tourists slowing only to call Merv on her phone telling him meet her and the Commissioner.

She found the Commissioner talking smilingly with a group of shopkeepers who had businesses on the Poudre Voie and as she joined them she heard the Commissioner saying that shop lifting would be his top priority if he was re-elected. She wondered how many other top priorities he had promised that day.

'Ah Inspector,' he boomed at Joelle, 'how opportune that you join us. We were just discussing the problem of shoplifting, all these gentleman have lost stock today.'

'Oh dear,' Joelle tried to look sympathetically concerned, 'It is a problem and very difficult to police unless the thief is actually caught in the act.'

'Indeed,' the Commissioner agreed, 'but we must give it more attention, these good ladies and gentleman are losing a lot of money.'

Smiles and handshakes all round as the group dispersed and the Commissioner, taking Joelle by the arm moved her to a quieter doorway.

'Shoplifting Sir?' Joelle looked quizzically at the Commissioner.

'Oh, don't worry about that,' he dismissed the previous conversation. 'Now, drugs. Everyone thinks I have been shaking hands and kissing babies, well I have but I have been watching as well. There is an organised group operating, four people at least. They are working the fish market, Saint-Pierre Rue and Poudre Voie. They target likely looking tourists. I have watched them passing across small white envelopes in exchange for a handful of dollar bills.' He nodded his head to the left, 'Over there, that man, he is one of them.'

MOTH ISLAND

Joelle looked at a nondescript black man, skinny with a shaved head and wearing a brightly coloured shirt and shorts. She did not recognise him, he was not one of the known drug pushers on the Island.

'Where are the other three?' She asked.

'They are operating singly, they will be on the street somewhere,' the Commissioner told her.

At that moment Merv and Irene joined them. Joelle observed the man in the coloured shirt spot Merv and move quickly away.

'Right,' Joelle took charge, 'There should be a wagon waiting for us in St. Peters Square. Will you recognise the culprits?' She asked the Commissioner, who said he would.

'We will walk round together and when the Commissioner points out a suspect we move in for an arrest. They might recognise us and try to run so we need to be quick.'

They set off after the coloured shirt man who they found half way up Poudre Voie innocently looking at a stall selling tourist trinkets. They cornered and arrested him round the back of the stall. Merv cuffed him and took him the arrest van.

They soon spotted another culprit who was also easily arrested and escorted to the waiting van by Irene. Joelle and the Commissioner made their way to St Peters Square and picking up Merv and Irene started to walk down Saint-Pierre Rue. They saw the third suspect actually approaching a couple of young white people. They hung back, hoping the see him execute a deal but he spotted them and took to his heals. Joelle started to chase him and Merv cut through an alley and over the bins between two shops hoping to cut him off. Fortunately, although young, this culprit was heavily built, overweight, and soon started to slow down while Joelle being fit and with long legs soon quickly gained on him. As she caught him she grabbed his shirt and managed to kick him in the back of his knee, causing him to crumple to the ground. She cuffed him and left him on the ground waiting for Irene and the Commissioner. When Merv appeared he and Irene took the arrested man back to the van in St Peters Square.

After that arrest, they all spent the next hour looking for the fourth man, but he had disappeared and by half past ten the streets were emptying and the shops and market stalls clearing up and closing down.

Joelle gave up, 'he has gone, let's get the other three back, process them and get them into cells.'

The Commissioner, very pleased with himself, announced he was calling it a day and going home.

'No, please sir, you must come back to the station and give us a description of the fourth man.'

The Commissioner raised his eyebrows and was about to issue a mild reprimand to Joelle for being presumptive, but she forestalled him by pleading, 'please Sir, you are our only witness.'

It was nearly midnight before Joelle and Merv finished that evening. Earlier she told Irene to go home after she had taken the Commissioner description of the fourth man.

The prisoners were searched, two of them had a single packet each containing a small quantity of marijuana but the second man arrested was clean. Joelle and Merv interviewed the prisoners individually and all three told the same story. They all denied knowing each other and the two caught with the drugs claimed they were for personal use only. The second man arrested claimed he never had any drugs and all three vehemently denied drug dealing. Joelle tried telling the men she had witnesses to their dealing they just laughed. 'No way,' they said.

Eventually, Joelle tired and frustrated, put the three suspects in the cells for the night and she and Merv went home.

Windrush was in darkness and not wanting to wake anyone, Joelle tiptoed upstairs and stopped outside the room she shared with Douglas. She was too tired to have a conversation with him tonight, and more to the point, suddenly was not sure she wanted to share a bed with him anyway. She moved along the corridor and gently opened the spare room door but then stopped in her tracks as she heard a gentle snuffling coming from the bed. She peered into the room, the curtains were not drawn and with the little light that filtered through the window she saw Douglas fast asleep. She shut the door and moved back to the first bedroom.

That night she lay in bed for ages with her mind magnifying her suspicions, was Douglas sleeping alone because he could no longer wanted to sleep with her.

CHAPTER 15. JOELLE'S SUNDAY

Joelle woke early with the sun streaming into the bedroom, she had forgotten to draw the curtains the night before. She got groggily out of bed and went for a shower to freshen up. Surprisingly, this morning her thoughts were not on Douglas's infidelities but on the three prisoners. She needed to talk to the Commissioner again and get a detailed statement from him. The previous night he had only given Irene the barest minimum description of events and Joelle realised that for a prosecution she needed to find someone who had actually bought drugs the previous evening.

Joelle used her Triumph motorbike, a massive 1500cc Thunderbird Commander, to drive round to the Commissioner's home. She arrived just before eight in the morning and she hoped he would be up. She knew she was very early but her plan had to be executed before around ten or it would be too late.

Mr John de Caynoth

She was lucky, the Commissioner opened the door himself and invited her in.

'Inspector, you are about early for a Sunday morning,' the Commissioner greeted her, 'I am just eating my breakfast, would you like a cup of coffee.'

'No thank you, Sir,' we need to hurry.'

The Commissioner looked questioningly at her and she explained that unless they could find witnesses to the prisoners actually selling drugs all they had on two of them was possession and nothing on the third.

'Surely not, is my statement not sufficient for you,' the Commissioner looked accusingly at Joelle.

'Of course, Sir, but I need to get down all the detail you can remember later,' Joelle avoided a direct answer. 'I would like to visit the cruise ship while the passengers are at breakfast, and see if you can recognise anyone who bought drugs from the men yesterday,' Joelle informed the Commissioner.

After a bit of grumbling he agreed and the two of them set off for the docks in the Commissioner's private car.

Out of courtesy they first saw the Captain of the Queen of the Caribbean to explain what they wanted and ask his permission to board is ship. They assured him that they would not arrest anyone should they find drugs, in that event they would leave the Captain to take appropri-

MOTH ISLAND

ate action, they simply wanted a statement of where the drugs were purchased.

The Captain agreed to show them round the ship personally, 'but naturally, we can only visit the public rooms,' he informed them.

They walked through all the restaurants and along all the decks. They inspected the shopping arcades, the libraries and games rooms and the Commissioner began to look more and more dismayed.

'I am sorry Inspector, I thought I would remember but everyone begins to look the same after a while, I am not much help I am afraid,' The Commissioner apologised.

Joelle, who thought it was a long shot anyway, sympathised and told the Commissioner not to worry. They took their leave of the Captain who promised that he would ask his crew to be extra vigilant and if they did discover any drugs he would get a statement from the responsible individuals and let Joelle have a copy.

On returning to the Commissioner's residence Joelle questioned the Commissioner in detail noting everything down and then getting him to sign a statement. It took all morning and it was well after midday before Joelle arrived at the police offices. She was hungry so decided to go straight to the staff rest room and buy a sandwich for lunch while she planned her interviews with the three prisoners.

After eating, back in her office, on her desk she

found a note from Merv to say he had circulated the description of the fourth man to all the officers on duty and that he would be out around the town all day and to call if she needed him. The other note on her desk was from Irene to tell her that the tour company with the cruise ship docking at Kaeta in a couple of days time, had organised a trip to Moth Island for the next Wednesday. She made a note for Mondays briefing.

Before interviewing the prisoners again, she read through the files of information she had on them and noted one had given an address that turned out to be false. The other two were recorded as having no fixed address and she suspected that all three had probably given false names as they had no identification or personal information on them. The only things that had been found when they were searched were the drugs and a handful of US dollars. She noted the man who had no drugs had nearly a hundred dollars in his possession.

Her first interview that afternoon did not go well. She was questioning the second man they arrested, the one on whom no drugs were found and he stuck to his story that he was innocent had never been involved with any drugs and had earned the money doing casual work around the docks, was paid in dollars and, no, he could not name the employer. She spent over an hour quizzing the man but he stuck to his story and eventually in exasperation she sent him back to his cell.

She found Irene waiting for her upstairs, 'Ma'am, you said you wanted to interview any one we caught with drugs,'

Joelle nodded.

'I have arrested a young man, he tried to sell me marijuana!' Irene snorted in disbelief.

'Rather unfortunate for him,' Joelle commented, 'let's go and talk to him,'

The young man sat at the steel table, bolted to the interview room floor, and looked unhappily at the two officers opposite.

No one spoke as Joelle read the arrest sheet.

'It says here you are nineteen years old, and hold a Danish passport,' she peered at the prisoner for confirmation. He nodded.

'Well, young man, we have you bang to rights, offering drugs to a police officer, my detective constable here,' Joelle nodded towards Irene.

The young Dane nodded miserable and agreed he had offered Irene a small envelope of marijuana.

Joelle invited him to make a full statement before being charged.

He told them he had taken a day trip to Moth Island where a bloke, walking along the beach, and 'no, I don't know who he was, I assumed he was a beach vendor,' had asked him if he would like to buy some marijuana, cheap. He said he had bought five packets, used one himself, but then realised he might be searched going through the airport so had decided to sell the other four packets.

Joelle asked him to describe the trinket seller and that is where things got interesting. His description was very similar to the fourth man the Commissioner had seen the previous day, the man they had not found. Joelle suspended the interview and returned to her office to fetch the Commissioners description of the fourth man.

It was while she was upstairs that she received a phone call. It was from Andrea Spooner in the UK.

'I have interviewed the boyfriend of that Sofia Luka,' she started telling Joelle. 'In fact, I invited him to come to the police station and rattled his cage quite hard. He admits they had an argument but flatly denies either of them lost their temper,' Andrea paused and chuckled, 'he says they argued over sex, he wanted them to make love on the beach and she said no, she was not getting covered in sand and told him to go and have a swim and she walked off telling him she would come back when he had cooled down. That is last he saw of her.'

'Pretty much what he told us, not the bit about the sex though, he told us he could not remember what they argued about.' Joelle explained.

'I told him we thought he was lying and that they had had an argument and a fight in which he had killed her and then buried her in the sand.

'What would you say if I told you we have a

body,' Andrea said she asked him.

He looked distraught and started crying and repeated that they did not fight and he did not kill her.'

'Andrea, we never found her body,' Joelle reproached her friend.

'No, I did not say you had, I just told him you had found a body, which you told me you had. Anyway, I believe he is telling the truth, I don't think he harmed the girl,' Andrea concluded.

'Oh well, it was just a possible line of enquiry, could you send me a copy of the interview?' Joelle asked.

'Of course, but I have something far more exciting to ask you,' Andrea changed the subject. 'Last time we spoke we you invited me to Kaeta for a holiday.'

'I did,' Joelle agreed.

'Well, I have done a lot of overtime the last couple of months and Barbara has told me take a week off. Can I take you up on your offer? Jim, my husband, can't get the time off, so I would be on my own.'

'Andrea, that would be wonderful. I will get some time off as well,' Joelle promised.

They finished the phone call with Andrea asking Joelle how her relationship with Douglas was going and Joelle explaining her latest fears. Again, Andrea pointed out that all Joelle's suspicions were based on circumstantial evidence. Nevertheless, she did sympathise with Joelle's fears but challenged her with what would she do if Douglas admitted he was having an affair with Eva. 'You told me you love him. Do you want to leave him or give him a second chance?'

Joelle sat at her desk, Andrea's question was the one she had feared to ask herself, and she did not know the answer. She sighed, she would have to face that later, for the present she had a prisoner downstairs who might be just about to give her a new lead on the drugs case.

She picked up the Commissioner's description of the escaped fourth man and took it downstairs to show the young Danish prisoner. He read the statement and agreed it could describe the beach vendor who had supplied him with drugs.

Joelle told him she would have to charge him with supplying illegal drugs, but that as he had pleaded guilty and helped the police with their investigation he would probably receive a fine, possibly a suspended sentence, and be told to leave the Kaeta immediately.

By now it was late afternoon and Joelle still had two prisoners to interview before she could go home. She sat in her office and closed her eyes for a few moments but was rudely awakened by Merv returning from his patrol.

'That's this weekend all finished, thank God,' he shouted across the office. 'The cruise ship has gone and all is quiet and calm again. I hear you and Irene have had an interesting afternoon.'

Joelle left her desk and walked over to Merv to tell him they might have identified the fourth man as a beach vendor on Moth Island.

'Great,' Merv said, preparing to go off duty.

'Could you stay and help me with the interviews, 'Joelle asked.

Merv looked a little guilty, 'Well, if you really need me.....' he paused, 'but I promised to take my wife out tonight....,' he left the excuse hanging.

'That is okay Merv, you go home, I will be fine,' Joelle tiredly dismissed him.

In the event Irene stayed on to help Joelle with the two interviews.

The first prisoner interviewed stuck to his story, the drugs were for personal use and he had got them from one of the private hashish joints in the town.

When this was stated Joelle suspended the interview and she and Irene drove down to the house and asked if they had supplied the marijuana. The owner of the property, who Joelle knew stuck to the unwritten rules, confirmed he did not know the man and would never have supplied him with any drugs. 'You know all we have is for our personal use,' he told Joelle indignantly.

Back in the interview she confronted the prisoner but he just shrugged dismissing the denial and telling Joelle the man was lying. She asked about Moth Island and the fourth man but the prisoner said he had never heard of Moth Island and denied knowing the fourth man.

Joelle pushed him for over an hour but he just claimed he had made a true statement and had nothing more to say. She asked him if he wanted a solicitor but he said he did not, he had admitted to possession for personal use and had nothing more to say.

She returned him to his cell and asked for the third man, the one who had run away, to be brought up to the interview room.

His story was much the same as the previous prisoner, except he could not remember where he had got the marijuana. Again, Joelle pushed hard but could not shake his story. She told him she had a reliable witness who had seen him selling drugs, but he simply said the witness was mistaken and explained that he had been begging and that the rich visitors had kindly given him money.

By eight thirty both Joelle and Irene were frustrated and exhausted and had given up with the interviews. 'Let's hope that the Captain of the Queen of the Caribbean comes up with something helpful,' Joelle forlornly said to Irene as they packed up to go home.

Joelle pulled the Triumph up outside the front door of Windrush and kicked the side stand down supporting the bike as she dismounted.

She walked into the house and removed her helmet and leathers in the hall dropping them on the floor, too tired to put them away and stood wondering what she was going to say to Douglas and if she really wanted to hear his answer.

In the event she did not have the chance, Douglas heard her arriving home and walked into the hall and put his arms round her kissing her, completely disarming her rehearsed questions. He told her she looked exhausted and he had run her a bath and led her upstairs to their bedroom where he handed her a gin and tonic and told her to relax in the bath and to come down and get something to eat when she was ready.

He left her undressing. She moved to the bathroom and saw he had put her favourite salts into the tub with the hot water. She lay in the bath luxuriating and started to cry, she did not have it in her to confront him that night, she just needed some love.

CHAPTER 16. MONDAY

Douglas pulled the back door shut as silently as he could and looked at his watch.
Six on a Monday morning, still dark, and despite the residual warmth in the tropical pre-dawn, he still shivered, remembering all the cold Monday mornings back in England when he had set out for work. He questioned what he had let himself in for. This Moth Island job, he mused, was supposed to be part time amusement but it was rapidly turning itself into a full time and rather stressful job. 'I must be mad,' he whispered but there was no one around to hear him, 'it's not even as if I needed the money.'

He started the engine of the MGB and for a few moments listened to the deep burble of the V8 engine before slipping the car into gear and allowing it to roll forward crunching across the gravel towards the road and down to the Glass Bay Restaurant.

He saw Eva waiting outside the restaurant. As the cars headlights swept over her he briefly no-

MOTH ISLAND

ticed she was wearing a black skirt and white blouse under a fleece jacket. She looked very vulnerable, huddled into the fleece, the thought made him smile with affection.

They were catching the seven-o-clock staff boat across the Moth Island, Douglas to work and Eva to meet Martin Pleasance and finally to decide if she wanted the receptionist/bookkeeper job.

They sat huddled together on a bench near the bow of the staff boat, glad of each other's company watching the sun breaking over the horizon far away to the east in the Atlantic Ocean.

Eva gently touched Douglas's thigh, 'look at the clouds, even the ones over Kaeta are pink,' she observed. He looked, but was really trying to suppress the sensuous excitement he always felt at her intimate touch.

'What will you be doing this week,' she asked.

'I have to work through the staff procedures manual and rewrite them for the new system,' Douglas replied, 'Next week I have booked a tutor from the software supplier to come out and run the staff training. I need to have the procedures ready for then.'

'That sounds like a big job,' Eva commented sympathetically.

Later that morning Martin Pleasance found Douglas in the office he was using.

'I have spoken with Eva, nice girl, pretty, but rather lacking in experience to run the reception I

Mr John de Caynoth

thought,' he looked to Douglas for a response.

Douglas agreed she had little previous experience but explained that he knew Eva, 'she is a hard worker and follows instructions. I think she will soon pick up the job,' he assured Martin.

Martin shrugged, 'Okay, your decision, on your head be it.'

Douglas finished the instruction he was drafting and then went to find Eva in reception.

'What do think now you have looked round. Happy to take the job?' He asked her.

'I guess so,' Eva confirmed,' but Martin told me the duties are six days a week from eight in the morning till four in the afternoon and that it is a live in post.'

'I don't think it is necessary for you to live in but you do really need to be on duty through the day when reception is busy with guests.' Douglas thought for a few moments. 'If you get the staff boat across in the morning I am sure we can arrange for a boat to take you back to Kaeta in the late afternoon. It often goes across anyway to collect evening shift part timers and entertainers. If you did need to stay overnight any time you could always use my room.'

At this point, Josh walked into reception.

Can I help you, Sir?' Eva politely asked, saving Douglas from upsetting the surveillance plan by greeting Josh as an old friend.

'I have come to see if you have any work going,' Josh stated, playing his part.

MOTH ISLAND

Eva looked at Douglas for support and guidance.
'I will handle this,' Douglas took charge leading Josh into his office.

'Good to see you,' Douglas greeted Josh with a hug when they were alone. He went through what he knew of Joelle's investigation on the drug case and the Sofia Luka disappearance and agreed with Josh that the best role would be the gardener/handyman job, which would allow him to visit anywhere he wanted on the Island. He suggested Josh should stay on the Island but told him there was not a room available until the end of the week when the departing receptionist vacated her room.

'In the meantime, I would suggest you share with me, but that would look very odd,' Douglas apologised.

'No problem man,' Josh assured him, 'I will look after myself. I have been thinking about this drug business and they must be smuggling it on to the Island somehow. A bit of night time surveillance is needed I think.'

Together they returned to reception where Eva was introducing herself, telling the other girl at reception that she did not need a room of her own as Mr Jay had said she could use his room. He interrupted their conversation and asked where he could find Martin Pleasance.

'I think he has gone on a walk about,' Eva told him.

'No matter, I will catch him later,' Douglas

turned to Josh, 'Go and find the head gardener, he will fix you up with a uniform.'

It was not long before Martin Pleasance stormed into the office.

'What is this all about, you hiring a new gardener?' Martin angrily asked.

'No big deal, I am not taking over your job, but you were not around,' Douglas tried to calm Martin down, but he carried on grumbling and, clearly unhappy, left Douglas muttering to himself. Douglas sighed philosophically thinking that the next one to resign would probably be Martin.

After lunch Eva came to see him and suggested they go for a walk round the Island. 'There is no one else to show me round, the receptionist says she can't leave reception and I can't find Mr Pleasance,' she explained. Douglas was immediately more cheerful.

As they walked through the gardens Eva told him she had accepted the job and seen Martin Pleasance to sign a contract.

'I officially start on Wednesday,' she told Douglas.

'Oh, I thought you might start straight away,'

'No, I can't, I want to get back to see Jasmine tell her I can help in the restaurant in the evenings and tomorrow I need to find some transport so I can get across Keata every day. I have arranged to go back on the five-o-clock boat this evening.'

'How will you get across the Island to Glass Bay

MOTH ISLAND

then?' Douglas asked, a bit disappointed as he had expected Eva to stay at least for the time being.

'I suppose I will have to get a taxi, unless Jasmine closes the restaurant for an hour and collects me.' Eva thought out loud.

'I suppose the easiest thing would be for you to take my car, I shan't need it until the end of the week when I go home,' Douglas offered, slightly reluctantly.

That Monday, while Douglas had been organising his affairs on Moth Island, Joelle had also been organising her week. She had heard Douglas leave but decided not to get up and see him off, and then overslept, with the result that she was late in arriving at the police office that morning. She called the team together for a briefing, most of which was taken up discussing the arrangements for the surveillance exercise on Moth Island the coming Wednesday when the cruise excursion took place. She was pleased to note that the search warrant from the previous occasion was worded in sufficiently general terms to give her the authority she needed to visit Moth Island again.

After the briefing her plan was to interview her three prisoners once more. She was pretty certain they were just the sales men and the fourth man, the one who had escaped was the leader. She interviewed the three men separately. She

Mr John de Caynoth

told them all they had been followed all afternoon and had been seen selling drugs to tourists, she asked who the fourth man was and where they supplies came from. It got her nowhere as all three stuck rigidly to their stories. Frustrated she returned the three to their cells while she considered what she could charge them with.

She had barely sat down at her desk to review the weekend activity reports when the Commissioner walked into her office. Such a visit was so rare that the general office fell strangely quiet as the Commissioner walked through, booming a general good morning to the assembled officers.

'Now Joelle, tell me we have cracked the drug ring, and we have arrested the leaders,' he challenged.

'I'm afraid not Sir, of the three men we arrested, two only admit to possession for personal use and the third, on whom we found no drugs, is claiming he is not involved,' Joelle had to admit.

'Ridiculous,' the Commissioner muttered, 'you have interviewed them and told them you have an impeccable witness?'

'I have Sir, three times.'

'I will speak to them,' the Commissioner pompously declared and marched out of the office. Joelle made to follow him.

'No need Inspector, I will see them in their cells,' and he marched off.

Half an hour later The Commissioner returned and handed Joelle a short hand written statement, with an illegible signature scrawled at the end. She looked questioningly at the Commissioner.

'I took down the statement from the third man we arrested,' he proudly told Joelle, 'he was most anxious to talk to me.'

'How so?' Joelle asked, wondering how the statement was extracted and if it was legally admissible.

'I simply advised the young man that the other two prisoners had told us he was the ring leader and they had just bought the drugs off him and if he could not explain himself he would be charged with supplying illegal drugs and spend a long time in the town prison.' The Commissioner grinned smugly, 'I did tell him that he would well cared for there, the other inmates like nothing better than a fat boy to ride all night.'

Joelle raised her eyebrows but said nothing and read the statement. It described the way the pushers operated. The dealer kept in the background and never sold anything himself, just holding the drugs and running a gang of pushers, five of them that afternoon. He would give them a couple of packets to sell, telling them that if they were caught to claim personal use. Once sold they would find the dealer, hand over the money and collect more drugs. They were paid five dollars for each packet sold.'

'This dealer, did the prisoner give you a description or name?' Joelle asked hopefully.

'He said he was dark skinned, possibly tanned, wore a hat and dark glasses. No name. He told me he had been recruited by a friend that morning. He said he does not know the other two men we arrested,' the Commissioner replied.

'Well, this gets somewhere, we now know how they are selling the drugs and we are looking for a white man, but I am not sure this statement will be legally admissible.'

'Of course it will be,' the Commissioner told Joelle as he walked off.

She looked at the statement she was holding in her hand and wondered what to do about it. Clearly it would not be admissible as evidence, whatever the Commissioner thought, and she did not relish being the focus of his anger when he was told it was inadmissible.

'Merv,' she called, 'I need you, we have some interviews to finish.'

She switched on the tape recorder, checked Merv had pen and paper, announced the date, time and name of the suspect and then handed the fat man the statement the Commissioner had noted down and asked him to confirm that the paper he was holding were a true and fair note of a private discussion he had with the Commissioner.

The man, perspiring heavily, looked nervously around the room. 'What's going on?' he asked.

'Just read the document,' Joelle told him.

He started to read.

'No, read it out loud for the tape recorder,' Joelle instructed.

He stumbled through the statement and agreed that it was what he had told the Commissioner.

'And you made this statement freely and were not coerced into this admission in any way,' Joelle prompted.

The fat man asked what coerced meant and on being told by Merv, nodded his agreement.

Joelle then questioned him about the dealer but he could add no further information to that which he had told the Commissioner.

'Do you think he is telling the truth,' Merv asked after the man been returned to his cell.

'Yes, I do, he is scared and I don't think he is clever enough to make up another lie all on his own,' Joelle concluded. 'Lets interview the other two, with this admission we might shake their stories.'

Unfortunately, the other two men were older and more street wise than the fat man and stuck to their stories claiming they did not know each other or the fat man.

By the time they had finished the interviews and Merv had typed the statements and got them signed, it was late afternoon and Joelle announced she had had enough and was going home.

'Joelle, what shall I do with those three prisoners,' the duty sergeant shouted after her as she left the building. 'I must charge them with something or let them go this evening,' he added.

Joelle rubbed her eyes tiredly.

'Charge them with possession and dealing,' she decided, thinking that the prosecutor would not allow a possession charge against the man on whom they had not found drugs and probably would drop all the dealing charges, but at least the Commissioner's ire would be directed at him and not her.

Joelle used her key to open the front door of Windrush and called out to Mary. She still could not get used to Mary being at home in the evenings after all the years she had run the restaurant.

She walked past the hall stand and saw a letter lying there. Her stomach knotted and she experienced a mild sense of anxiety. The letter was post marked Bristol and she recognised the handwriting. His letters were always bad news and her instinct was to screw it up and throw it away unread, but despite herself she wondered what Ralph wanted now.

My dearest Joelle,

She started reading and snorted in disgust as she read the opening paragraph which, in typical Ralph style, described how he missed her, thought of her every day but realised that a reconciliation was no longer possible.

It is another begging letter she decided and

skipped to the last paragraph in which Ralph always set out his demands. She had to plough through his wordy explanation of how hard life was for an ex-convict with no job and no money before she got to the relevant bit.

If you could see your way clear to sending me a small financial gift, I do not want to be greedy and £250,000 would be just about enough to enable me to buy a small house and restart my life alone. My solicitor is confident my appeal against the marriage settlement will be successful and will result in a far larger sum being awarded, but I will happily drop my legal action on receipt of your generosity.
Yours as ever,
Ralph.

Joelle took a deep breath and threw the letter to one side realising she had done nothing about the first letter she had received from Ralph's solicitor advising of his appeal. Her first thought was to talk to Douglas and take his advice, but her second thought was to hesitate. Should she talk to him about Ralph before confronting him with Eva, and if he admits he is having an affair with Eva, what would she do? Then she remembered she had asked him to be her inside man on the Moth Island drug case. Would he still help if she challenged him over Eva?

CHAPTER 17. THE ENDING

Josh was given a brown shirt, trousers, boots, a pair of heavy gloves, a rake and a black rubbish bag and assigned to beach duty and told to start immediately, the day he arrived.

Beach duty involved raking the sand flat and sweeping all the paths first thing in the morning; he started work at eight. With that finished he was then supposed to spend the rest of the day walking the beaches picking up rubbish, leaves and returning used drink glasses to the bar. In the evening his job was to collect beach towels and cushions and stack the sun loungers. It was the most boring duty in the gardens but it suited Josh, it meant he was free to roam along the half mile of sand surrounding the Caribbean coast of the Island, watching. Gardeners worked a long day, they finished work at five but were given a two-hour break at midday.

On his first day Josh used the break to walk around the Island to get his bearings. As he walked he reflected that the drugs had to be smuggled on to the Island and therefore a suitable landing place would be needed. They would not use the Caribbean shore, to near all the hotel buildings, so the obvious place to look was on the Atlantic side of the Island and he soon found a suitably sheltered inlet. On inspection, he could even see marks in the pebbles where a boat had been dragged up the beach.

Another thing he noticed as he walked around the Island was that the hotel had constructed a number picnic spots for the guests taking advantage of the more picturesque locations. Each was furnished with a trestle table, a barbecue and a hammock strung between two eight foothigh poles. Some of the hammocks even had palm leaf roofs as shelter from the sun. A readymade camp site, Josh realised, but obviously the one at the head of the inlet was no good to him so walked on round the Island hoping to find a more concealed spot where he could set up camp and still watch the inlet.

He was in luck, on the headland adjacent to the inlet, but not visible, was another picnic spot selected for its fantastic views across the Island and out over the Atlantic Ocean.

Perfect, Josh thought. He would ask Douglas to get him a sleeping bag, borrow a tarpaulin from the garden store to replace the palm roof which had collapsed, and there was plenty of undergrowth where he could hide his baggage during the day.

He explored the area around the inlet a little further and walked up a well-used track running inland. A couple of hundred meters back from the shore line, set discretely among a group of palm trees, was a small bungalow beside which was an inflatable dingy, with a large Mercury outboard motor, sitting on a launch trolley. After checking there was no one in the bungalow, Josh inspected the dingy and wondered what such a high-powered inflatable would be used for on this side of the Island. Water skiing possibly, or maybe a high-speed tender to meet a much larger ship, he speculated.

The following day, Tuesday, Josh was taken off beach duty and told to assist another gardener to cut down the dying palm fronds and tidy up the trees in the gardens. This gave Josh the opportunity to talk to the man. Most of the conversation was of a general nature but eventually Josh got around to asking what entertainment existed for when they were off duty. The man explained that most staff lived on Kaeta so there not much on Moth Island for the staff's after-hours entertainment. Josh shrugged, and watching carefully for the gardener's reaction, said, 'Oh well, I will have to get some weed and amuse myself.' The other man did not react; Josh had not really expected he would.

****

On Wednesday morning, at the Kaeta Yacht Club quay, which served as a landing pier for the motor boats across to Moth Island, Joelle assembled her small team for the search and observation exercise. Merv, who knew everyone on Kaeta, had arranged with the boat owner, for Joelle and her team to join the cruise ship excursion for the crossing. Merv was not included in the team, 'you are too easy to recognise,' Joelle told him, so the team consisted of Joelle, Irene, and Miranda, normally a uniform patrol officer but who volunteered for the day.

The Plan was for Joelle to stay out of sight in the offices and for Irene and Miranda to mingle with the cruise visitors in the hope of spotting who was selling the marijuana.

When they arrived on Moth Island the two girls wandered off down the beach and set themselves up under a sun lounger from where they had a good view along the beach. They idly watched a gardener walking along the beach with a black rubbish bag, pausing occasionally to pick up scrap of paper or a dead leaf.

'What a boring job,' Miranda commented to Irene.

'Just like being on surveillance,' Irene told her, dismissing the gardener from her thoughts as she watched a man pull a small motor boat up on to the far end of the beach. He hoisted a rucksack over his shoulder and from a plastic bag extracted strings of beads which he hung from his arm. He made his way down the beach offering his wares to the sunbathers.

Irene prodded Miranda, 'when he gets to us show some interest, even buy something, hopefully he is the marijuana dealer.'

The two girls waited with anticipation as the man approached. He stopped in front of them.

'Nice ladies,' his opening greeting, 'would you like some lucky beads,' he stretched out his arm so they could inspect the beads. As they showed some interest he dropped the rucksack and pulled out a couple of chiffon scarves, 'real artificial silk,' he assured the girls.

Miranda examined on the scarves, 'How much?' she asked and after some haggling they agreed a price and she purchased the scarf.

The beach vendor turned to Irene, 'You my dear lady, would you like to buy something?'

'I don't expect you will have any of what I want,' Irene said hoping to prompt a response.

'And what would that be,' the vendor replied.

'I need to find some weed,' Irene looked expectantly at the man.

He shook his head sorrowfully, 'That I do not have,' but misreading the look of disappointment on her face leaned towards her and whispered, 'but sometimes one of the gardeners here can help out.'

He strolled off down the beach still trying to hawk his wares leaving Irene wondering how she was going to identify the particular gardener she wanted.

After some time the gardener with the black plastic bag came wondering back down the beach. Irene waved to catch his attention.

'Yes ma'am,' he said politely.

'I am told it is possible sometimes to purchase a small supply of weed. Would you know who I might approach if I needed any?'

Josh realised this might be a good opportunity to identify a pusher, and so to encourage her, without frightening the her off, replied, 'It might be possible, I will see if I can find someone to help you,' and he wandered off into the gardens to put the word around that someone wanted to buy some weed.

The rest of the day he tried to remain unobtrusively near the two girls hoping the pusher would get the message and approach them.

Meanwhile Joelle had requisitioned an office and was interviewing the staff about illegal drug trading believed to originate from Moth Island and the disappearance of Sofia Luka. She was particularly interested in any light coloured or tanned employees who may have been off duty the previous Saturday morning, but she did not make much progress. The only white employees were Martin Pleasance, the sous chef, and one of the girls on reception, and Saturday was her day off. One of the assistant chefs was of Asian extraction but Joelle dismissed the woman as a suspect as she had been working all day the previous Saturday. She also thought it unlikely the receptionist was her drug dealer suspect but decided she had better interview her anyway.

'You had better be quick then, she leaves at the end of this week, she should be in reception now,' she was told.

Joelle was stunned when she walked out to reception to find the girl. 'Eva, what are you doing here,' she asked an equally surprised looking Eva.

'Working,' Eva replied, 'I have a job here as receptionist, I started this morning.'

Joelle let her breath go with relief. Whatever she thought of Eva she certainly did not want to find she was a drug dealer.'

'Is there another receptionist, the white girl?' Joelle asked.

'Yes, she is not far away, I will ask her to see you when she returns.' Eva offered, trying to be helpful.

A very bitter receptionist met Joelle in the office she was using. She agreed she had been on Kaeta last Saturday looking for another job. She explained with some disgust that Mr Jay, the new hotel manager, had wanted her to take on much more work, and had moved her from her nice apartment, giving her a small room at the back instead. Finally, she spat the words angrily at Joelle, 'he brought in his friend, that Eva out there, to live with him in my apartment,' putting a particular emphasis on the word 'friend'.

Joelle did not immediately appreciate what she had been told, she was thinking that the girl was not her suspect and would probably be of little help to her investigation but as the girl's words sunk into her conscience her jaw dropped open, she had trouble breathing, and she felt like an enormous weight had suddenly fallen on her crushing the very existence out of her.

'What did you say?' she stammered

'I was in Kaeta looking for a job,' the girl started to explain.

'No, about Eva living with Mr Jay.'

'Yes, that's right, she told me, she told me she would be sharing Mr Jay's apartment,' the girl confirmed.

Joelle sat speechless trying to breath. She waved the girl away and just sat trying to take in what had happened and it was all became very clear to her, Douglas had taken the job on Moth Island so he could bring Eva across to live with him. She felt empty, deserted, betrayed and desolate. All the time she had suspected he was having an affair she had not wanted to believe it, she had even come to accept that if he had had some sort of flirtation with Eva she would forgive him and rebuild a life together with him.

But, now this. She cried.

It took her an hour to refocus on what she was on Moth Island for and as lunch time approached she felt she had recovered sufficient composure to get on with her work. She decided to go for a walk around the Island to get her brain working again. That was a pity because, of course, she was immediately recognised and the word soon got around that there was a police presence on the Island. The gardener, who acted as a go between for the drug dealer, immediately shelved any thoughts he might have had to arrange for a drug delivery to Irene.

Irene therefore spent a frustrating afternoon waiting to be contacted while Josh spent an equally frustrating afternoon lurking near Irene and Miranda.

By the end of the afternoon Irene called the surveillance off and went to report to Joelle.

She told Joelle about her conversation with the beach vendor and then she mentioned the gardener, who had behaved very suspiciously and spent most of the day watching them.

'Do you think he could be the drug contact watching you, waiting for an opportunity to talk with you alone?' Joelle asked.

'It's possible,' Irene replied, 'Shall I bring him in and we question him.'

Joelle agreed.

To Irene's irritation Josh could not help laughing when she produced her warrant card and told him to follow her.

'I have never been arrested by a police woman in a bikini before; where do you keep the warrant

MOTH ISLAND

card?' He asked cheekily.

Irene ignored him and as she escorted him into the office Joelle was using, he had a big grin on his face.

Joelle's features went from stern, through surprise to recognition as Josh sat down before her.

'Josh,' Joelle exclaimed, 'what on earth are you doing here?'

It was Irene's turn to look surprised, 'You two know each other?'

'Yes,' Joelle explained, 'Josh is a private detective and we have worked together before.'

'Well,' Irene repeated the question, 'What are you doing here, working as a gardener.'

'Same as you I imagine,' he replied, 'Douglas asked me to come out here to help him track down a suspected drug racket operating from the Island.'

Joelle sighed, 'It was final kick in her stomach to find that Douglas was as good as his word and was actively trying to help her.'

Joelle and Josh exchanged what information they each had. Josh told Joelle his plan was to approach things from the other end by tracking down how the drugs were arriving on the Island while Joelle agreed that the focus of her operation would be to identify the dealers and pushers. She asked Josh to report anything back to her personally.

***

Mr John de Caynoth

It was unfortunate that Douglas chose to stick his head round the door of the office Joelle was using. He had been with the chef all day working out new kitchen procedures and it had been hard going, although the chef claimed to support the new system, he was not particularly open to change his way of working. Douglas had been told Joelle and her team were on Moth Island and so, tired and stressed after a long day with the chef he was looking forward to spending an evening with Joelle.

'I thought we might go to the bar and have dinner together,' he invited her, but was knocked back by the icy, hateful look he got.

'I do not want to drink or eat with you,' Joelle quietly told him. 'In fact, I never want to see you again.'

CHAPTER 18. ONE STEP FORWARD

Josh wondered if his meeting with Joelle had blown his cover. He thought probably not and this was confirmed the day after Joelle's team visited the Island when he was confronted by a couple of the resort workers who wanted to know why he had been questioned by the police. He stuck closely to the truth and told the men that two women on the beach had asked where they could get weed.

'I would not know,' he said he had told the two women, 'I have only just started here. The two women turned out to be police and took me to see their boss who questioned me about where and who was supplying drugs. I told them I had know idea and eventually they let me go.'

The two nodded to each other and dismissed Josh with a single word, 'Good.'

Later, in his break that day, Josh decided to go and explore the Casino. He noted the security fencing enclosing the dog patrol strip and wondered why they needed such security. Definitely suspicious, he considered. He walked to the entrance of the Casino compound and was confronted by a guard who immediately warned him off. Josh tried the friendly approach but the guard was having none of it and told Josh to clear off. Josh walked away with his alarm bells ringing, certain there was more to the Casino than simply high class gambling. He decided he needed to get access somehow and would have inspected the security fencing again looking for a weakness but the guard had summoned support and Josh's movements were being closely watched. He left, thinking he would return later. The next day, after he had finished raking and sweeping he made his way down the beach to the far end supposedly rubbish clearing. Guests rarely went this far as it was a long walk along the sand and involved some wading in the sea in order to get around the rocks. However, when Josh reached the end he considered the hike had been worth the trouble as shoreline terminated against a short headland along the top of which the Casino fence had been constructed. Unfortunately, reaching the fence involved some rock climbing and fighting through the scrubby vegetation growing on the side of the headland. Eventually Josh gave up, the undergrowth was just too thick and thorny, but he did gain sufficient height to look out over the end of the headland. He observed that the security fence stretched right down the headland and into the sea. He speculated that he might be able to swim round the headland and into the bay but on careful inspection he could see rocks stretching out beyond the headland and looking at the broken water just beyond the headland he guessed that there were underwater reefs.

By the end of the week Josh's investigation had taken a further step forward but then one step back again. The positive step was that Josh was returning a handful of drinks glasses to the bar and was called over by the barman who, on checking that they could not be overheard whispered to Josh, that if he was approached by anyone else looking for hash there was a supply on the Island. 'You take their money and arrange a collection point and then you find Dooley in the greenhouses, give him the money and he sorts it out. No questions asked.'

'What do I get out of it?' Josh asked.

'Dooley will see you okay,' was the reply.

'What can he get and where does it come from?' Josh tried to find out.

'I said, no questions,' the barman cautioned Josh. After work that day Josh made his way to the vegetable gardens to find Dooley who, having finished work for the day, was sitting in his greenhouse with his feet up on a box smoking. Dooley, a skinny coloured man of indeterminate age, and greying hair was happily staring at nothing and it took a few moments for Josh to explain who he was and get Dooley's attention.

'I am told you could get me some weed,' Josh stated.

Dooley gave him a bleary-eyed look, 'might be able to, who wants it?'

'Me,'

Dooley rummaged about in his pocket and produced an old tin from which he extracted a thin rolled cigarette which he offered to Josh.

Not unaccustomed to the odd smoke, Josh accepted thinking it might be a good way to pump Dooley for information.

Dooley moved his feet from the box and motioned for Josh to sit as he lit his cigarette. The two men sat in companionable silence dragging on their cigarette for a few minutes. Dooley asked Josh what he was doing on the Island and where he had come from. Josh made up an inoffensive story and asked the old man how long he had been on the Island. Eventually Josh raised the subject of drugs. Dooley confirmed that he did have source but only supplied cannabis derivatives explaining that his brother had died with heroin addiction. Josh asked where the drugs came from but Dooley tapped the side of his nose in a knowing fashion, 'that is my secret, best you don't know.'

Josh pushed a little harder but could see Dooley was getting agitated so dropped the subject planning a return to hopefully glean a little more information.

Josh's curiosity about the Casino was not helped when he was collecting towels near the water sports cabin on the beach. He got into conversation with one of the boat men and on the pretence that he was looking for the best place to see the underwater life asked where he might snorkel. He was directed the beach away from the Casino and told he would find some underwater rocks about twenty meters out from the shore. Josh asked what the swimming was like in the other direction but was told it was dangerous.

'There is a reef that end which stretches out round the southern tip of the Island out into the Atlantic side and in places the rocks are only just below the surface that would rip you open if you got caught. Also, it is where the Caribbean meets the Atlantic and there are very strong eddies where the warm waters of the Caribbean meet the cold Atlantic waters. You don't want to swim round there, it's very dangerous.'

'But there is a little cove just round that headland, I have seen boats going in an out there?' Josh questioned.

'Its private,' the boat man explained, 'It belongs to the Casino and it is all fenced off, they blasted a narrow channel through the reef so they could get a boat in and out but we are forbidden to land there.'

Josh grunted his thanks deciding the only way he was going to get into the Casino was to befriend the guard on the Island gate, and that would be tricky given the guards unfriendly attitude.

With all the beach towels collected Josh wheeled the laundry trolley round the back of the service building and then, having finished for the day decided to go and find Douglas to report what he had discovered. Not bad progress for the first week he was thinking, but it was Friday evening and unfortunately Douglas had already left to return to Kaeta for the weekend. There was nothing he could do his mobile phone had no signal and was not going to risk using a landline.

Douglas had finished his preparation for the following week when the trainer from the software house was flying in to instruct the staff on using the new system and that Friday evening he was anxious to get home to see Joelle.

Her announcement the previous Wednesday, that she never wanted to see him again, had stunned Douglas and he was telling himself that he had caught her at a bad moment when all she wanted to do was get home after a bad day. He hoped that he had misheard her, but in any event, he wanted to see her to smooth things out, so he had arranged to catch the five-o-clock staff boat back to Kaeta.

Eva was also on the boat and as it neared to landing pier on Kaeta Douglas offered her a lift back to the hotel.

She looked at him guiltily, oh, I am sorry Douglas, we have been so busy I have not had chance to tell you.'

'Tell me what?' Douglas asked, 'You have not smashed up my car have you,' he accused, half seriously.

'No, nothing like that. Last Tuesday, Jasmine and I went to see Rusty Rick. You know, he runs the motor bike shop on the Island. I needed my own transport to get across Keane each day to catch the ferry and Rick let me buy one of his old hire scooters and as I did not want to risk damaging your MG, I have left it at the restaurant and been using the scooter for the last couple of days.'

'Oh well, no problem,' Douglas responded, relieved, 'I will get a taxi.'

'You don't need to do that,' Eva invited him, 'the scooter has a pillion seat, I will give you a lift.'

Douglas hesitated, not sure he wanted a motor bike ride across the Island, but then thinking it would be a pain waiting for a taxi, he accepted.

They stood looking at the scooter, it was a 50cc Yamaha, a cross between a moped and motorbike with a step through frame and large wheels. It was cream and black and judging from the dents and scratches had led a hard life. Douglas gave the machine a beady look and noticing the 'L' plate asked, 'you have ridden one of these before?'

'Well no, but I do have a provisional license and it is a simple twist and go so it is quite easy really.' Eva informed him.

She stepped onto the machine and Douglas looked at the small pillion pad mounted high up on the rear mudguard, 'are you sure this thing will carry two people?' He queried.

Eva told him to stop being a wimp and sit behind her.

Once seated Douglas found he was sitting extremely close to Eva and as the pillion seat was set some height above the main saddle he was sitting with his legs round Eva's hips. He decided, sitting in such a position behind Eva was not an unpleasant experience.

She pressed the electric starter and machine purred into life. She snapped the throttle open and the machine lurched forward. It was not a particularly violent lurch but with all Douglas's weight set over the rear wheel it was enough to momentarily lift the front wheel off the ground and Douglas fearing he was about to be tipped of the rear of the machine threw his arms around Eva to steady himself. As they wobbled off down the road he heard Eva shout, 'Douglas, I don't mind you holding my breast but could you let me have my arms back, I can't steer properly.'

CHAPTER 19. A SECOND BODY

If Wednesday was a bad day for Joelle the rest of that week just got worse.

She did not sleep at all on Wednesday night. She realised that her dismissal of Douglas had been more from a gut reaction rather than any considered thought of the future and she lay in bed wondering if she had done the right thing. She spent ages trying to decide if she still loved him but that always ended in feelings of rejection and anger.

She thought, it would be more bearable if he was having an affair with an older woman, but Eva, a girl young enough to be his daughter, she was disgusted and thought, worse still, it puts Douglas in the same league as Ralph. How could I love someone like that?

The one question for which she had no answer.

She arrived at work the following morning tired and irritable only to find a post-it note stuck to her door telling her to report to the Commissioner first thing. She groaned and made her way up to his office. He was furious, ranting at her that he had been told by the Island prosecutor that all charges against one of the drug peddlers he had arrested, had been dropped and the other two were only to be charged with possession.

'It is not my fault Sir,' Joelle started to say, but this just increased the Commissioner's fury and he turned his ire on to Joelle's failure, as he put it, to apprehend this drug gang that were in danger of ruining the tourist visits to the Island.

'Do you realise how serious this matter is, Inspector,' he ranted. 'I am criticised for an ineffective police force, I have the Minister for Tourism on my neck almost daily wanting to know what is going on and why we have not yet arrested anyone, and when I arrest someone you only charge them with possession.' Again, Joelle tried to explain that was not the case but the Commissioner, now incandescent with anger told her he wanted no more excuses and curtly dismissed her.

'On my desk by lunch time, I want a full report of what actions you are taking to rid us of this drug business,' he screamed at her as she dived out of his office before he became violent.

'What is the matter with him this morning?' Joelle asked his PA as she shut the door on the fuming Commissioner.

'He has just heard that Sir Jonah Snifflier-Smyth is also standing against him for Police Commissioner in the elections, and he is furious about it.'

'Not Sniff the magistrate,' Joelle exclaimed.

'Sniff?' The PA asked.

'Oh sorry, that is what we call him downstairs.'

'Well, whatever, yes the magistrate.' The PA handed Joelle Sir Jonah's election manifesto, 'that's what has got the Old Man so upset.'

She pointed at a paragraph and Joelle read;

Under the Commissioner the Island Police have become lax and ineffective and if elected I, Sir Jonah, pledge to correct this shambles and turn the Police and Kaeta's armed forces into an efficient body properly serving this Island's people.

Joelle groaned, 'This is appalling and a down right lie. Jonah as Commissioner! Anyway, if he is elected I am resigning, no way will I work for that bigoted old hypocrite. What does this bit about Kaeta's armed forces mean.'

'You know that after that failed coup and your shoot out in the hills the President decided he needed a proper Army and set up the Kaetain Military in the old Fort.'

Joelle nodded.

The PA continued, 'well, now it is up and running he wants the newly elected commissioner to be his second in command of the Army as well as the Police.'

'Anyway,' she shrugged, 'if Snifflier is elected I will probably resign with you,' and then changing the subject told Joelle, 'by the way the Island Prosecutor's Office is looking for you. They came round yesterday but you were out, I said I would ask you to look into their office on your return.'

'You wanted to talk to me?' Joelle asked the Head Prosecutor, and then added, 'Why did you tell the Commissioner that I dropped the charges against those drug pushers?'

'I did not exactly tell him you did it,' the Prosecutor, a lawyer in his late fifties, prevaricated.

'Well thanks very much, I have just spent thirty minutes being told off for my failure,' Joelle feeling aggrieved glared at him.

'I wanted to see you about this,' he handed Joelle a letter from the US firm of lawyers representing the two boys, Jake and Cis, who Joelle had arrested. The letter stated that, in order to minimise the stress the two boys were suffering which was interfering with their studies they were not prepared to wait for months for a court appearance in Kaeta and had applied to the Boston judiciary for an early hearing of their claim.

Joelle looked questioningly at the Prosecutor.

'Don't worry about that,' he told her, 'we have spoken with the Court officials here and one of the circuit judges has agreed to hear the arguments in two week's time.'

'That is a bit soon isn't it?' Joelle looked worried.

'I think it suits us, we will defend the claim and go ahead with our counter claim for sexual harassment,' The prosecutor smiled.

'I thought you were going to drop that because of lack of evidence?' Joelle looked surprised.

'But we now have four witnesses who not only saw the arrest but also overheard the boys talking in lewd terms about you and other women on the street. Of course, we have to exchange witness statements but we will leave it as long as possible to make it hard for them to counter our case,' the prosecutor looked pleased with himself.

'Who are these witnesses?' Joelle asked.

'Two girls the boys were ogling have come forward and two men, Alvin Sinclaire, and Sticky Morris, say they saw and heard the whole thing,' Joelle was told.

'I know nothing of this?' She queried.

'It was your Sergeant who tracked down the witnesses,' the Prosecutor told her.

When Joelle got back to the Police Offices she cornered Merv and, with some suspicion, asked how he found the witnesses.

'It was that witness board you asked to be put out. Those four came forward and I thought it best for you not to be involved so Irene and I interviewed them and sent their statements over to the Prosecutors office,' Merv looked very pleased with himself.

Joelle now very suspicious, 'Alvin and Sticky, they are you drinking buddy's aren't they.'

'Yes,' Merv said innocently, 'lucky they saw

everything wasn't it.'

Merv looked serious, 'leave that Joelle, we have a much bigger problem.'

Joelle's heart sank as she waited for Merv to explain.

'Some scuba divers have just pulled a body out of the sea. I have called the mortuary but told them not to move the body before we arrive, I was waiting for you.'

They arrived at the Kaeta Yacht club quay to find Irene and a couple of police officers holding back a small crowd gathered round the mortuary ambulance. Moored by the landing stage was the dive boat owned by the Island Scuba School. Joelle and Merv made their way through the crowd and headed past the ambulance to the moored boat.

Irene joined them, 'the body is still on the boat, we have not moved it. It's not a pretty sight.'

'Who found it?' Joelle asked.

Six people stepped forward, still wearing wet suits.

'Please do not move until we have taken statements,' Joelle instructed.

The body was partially covered with a colourful beach towel, 'All we had to hand to hide him,' one of the men in a wet suit explained.

'And you are?' Joelle asked.

'Captain,' he replied.

Merv gingerly pulled the towel aside and the three detectives looked down. Irene turned pale and moved to vomit into the water. She returned and apologised.

'That's okay,' Joelle assured her biting down her own urge to be sick, 'it is the worst I have ever seen.'

They were looking at the severely lacerated, naked body of a young man. One arm had been torn off by the shoulder and one foot was missing. Lumps of flesh had been torn out of his trunk, his remaining arm and his legs, he had no eyes and his face was so badly damaged he had no features left. What really disgusted the three officers was some sort of sea leech crawling from what had been the man's mouth.

Joelle gulped with horror and indicated to Merv to re-cover the body. She told Irene to tell the ambulance crew they could move the body.

Merv speculated that the man had fallen out of a speed boat and got entangled in the propeller, and the fish had done the rest.

'Maybe,' Joelle commented, 'but no one has reported such an incident.' She gazed across the half mile stretch of water between Kaeta and Moth Island thinking, Moth Island again. Is this just another coincidence? But her intuition was telling her it could not be.

She asked who had actually found the body. Three of the divers, one woman and two men stepped forward and explained they were on a diving holiday and exploring the wrecks round the Island.

'We were looking for the wreck of the Moth, it supposed to have sunk out there,' the woman waved her hand in the direction of Moth Island, Joelle nodded, she knew the story of the wrecked pirate ship.

'We were diving in the rocks about five meters deep when we saw the body wedged in some rocks. We tried to free it but it was stuck so we surfaced and got a rope and attached it to the body. They pulled from the dive boat and those two,' she indicated the two men, 'wiggled the body to free it.'

'I am afraid the foot dropped off while we were trying to free the body,' one of the men apologised.

They spoke to the other members of the dive party and all told much the same story. Details were taken and the group told they were free to go but they would be required to attend the police station before they left the Island.

Joelle and Merv walked out along the landing pier and Joelle gazed out towards Moth Island again.

'Have you ever done any scuba diving?' Joelle asked Merv.

'No, I don't like the water.' Merv replied firmly.

'I have done a bit,' Joelle said.

'What are you thinking,' Merv asked, fearing he could guess. He was right, Joelle nibbling her finger nail spoke quietly, 'I think we need to see where they found that body.'

MOTH ISLAND

The Captain of the dive boat agreed he could find the place where they had moored and the two men who had freed the corpse offered to dive with Joelle and show her the spot. The Captain scanned the water, 'It should not take long, we have all the gear on board and the weather is ideal. I can take you now if you like.'

Joelle did like, she borrowed a wet suit and equipped herself with a tank, goggles and weights and an underwater camera and dived with an instructor and the two men.

Merv was waiting anxiously for her when she surfaced.

'Are you okay? What did you find?' He wanted to know.

'Let me get out of this stuff and I will tell you,' she said watching the instructor re-enter the water with a recovery basket.

While Joelle changed, Merv watched as the instructor and the crew pull out of the water a ripped cash bag attached to a chain and bracelet. The Instructor noticing Merv's puzzled look explained, pointing at Joelle striping off the wet suit, 'She found it and told us to recover it.'

It was late afternoon before they finally finished and drove back to the Police Offices. Merv was driving and Joelle was deep in thought but when Merv interrupted her she did tell him she found the foot wedged under a rock.

'What about the cash bag,' he asked.

'That was lying nearby and I thought it curious that a cash bag, the sort used by a security firm, should be lying near where a body was discovered.' She lapsed back into silent thought.

The following morning, Friday, Joelle rode the Triumph to work. She took the long route round the Island as she needed to think. She was expecting Douglas to come home and she still did not know what she wanted to say to him. She had decided she was not going to ask him outright if he was having an affair with Eva. If he denied it she would believe he was lying and if he admitted it she knew it would be yet another dagger in her heart. She almost hoped that he would say he wanted them to get back together again and she gave up worrying how she was going to react and started worrying instead about the mutilated body of a young man found submerged in what she was sure was going to prove to be suspicious circumstances.

When Joelle eventually got to work, the Commissioner walked into her office and shut her door as she was checking her Emails and waiting for the underwater pictures she had taken to be enlarged and printed. She braced herself for another tirade, she had forgotten to let him have the report he asked for, but the Commissioner surprised her by his friendly tone.

'I hear you found a body yesterday.'

She agreed and explained the circumstances.

'And you think it may be suspicious?' He commented, Joelle nodded.

He said nothing more and Joelle thought he almost looked embarrassed.

'I think I owe you an apology,' he eventually muttered.

Joelle surprised, waited to hear what he was apologising for.

'I was a bit hasty yesterday, I have been told it was not you who dropped charges against those gun runners and whatever the circumstances I should not have lost my temper.' Joelle nodded, accepting his apology and told him that his PA had explained he was upset by Snifflier-Smyth's election paper.

'Indeed I am, the man is a buffoon and an idiot, how dare he publicly criticise me and my Officers,' the Commissioner said indignantly.

'He certainly has a bit of cheek, especially as he is the one who obstructs our work more than anyone else,' Joelle agreed.

'How so? Tell me,' The Commissioner asked her.

Joelle explained how he had questioned her investigation on Moth Island and refused to give her a search warrant allowing her to get into the Casino. 'My instinct tells me that Casino operation is dodgy but old Sniff would not give a search warrant.'

'Would he not, that's interesting,' the Commissioner looked pleased.

Later that afternoon Joelle and Merv went to the hospital mortuary to talk to the pathologist

Mr John de Caynoth

doing the autopsy.

He disagreed with Merv's diagnosis that the man had fallen into the propellor of a boat.

He pointed to the wounds on the man's chest and arm, 'These wounds were not made a propellor, or fish, come to that. Look at these marks, these are teeth marks made by an animal with a large jaw and ripping teeth, a large cat or wolf like creature, and as there are no such animals on the Island I would guess a dog, a big dog, or dogs. Also, I think the man was alive when he went into the water, only just alive but there is a little water in his lungs.'

Joelle and Merv looked at each other both thinking, where would such a pack of dogs be found. 'Moth Island,' they said in unison.

'There is more,' the pathologist pointed at the man's leg, the one with the severed foot.

'See the way this leg has been severed. The ankle joint was obviously broken when the body was recovered, but see the way the flesh and tendons have been sawn through by something rubbing and cutting at the leg.'

Joelle mentioned that she found a cash bag with a chain and bracelet near the body.

'Ahh,' the pathologist exclaimed knowingly, 'I am guessing but I think the that bracelet was attached to the man's leg, probably the bag was weighted, and he was dropped in the sea. There is a strong current round Moth Island and through that channel and the weight was just enough to hold him underwater but as the gases build up inside the body the current could have towed him along and the bag dragging along the sea bed would explain the laceration. Pure chance he got caught on the rocks.'

When they got back to the Police Office Joelle told Merv she had had enough that week and was going home. 'I have some personal business to sort out this weekend, we will pick this up Monday morning.'

On her way home, she realised she was grateful that she had been so busy, it had taken her mind off the forthcoming confrontation with Douglas. She mulled things over in her mind as she rode the Triumph. She remembered how she had met Douglas and fallen in love with him. How he had stood by her, even putting himself in danger to help her, how he had been like a father to Jasmine, but that thought brought Eva crashing back into Joelle's confused mind.

Douglas was not home when she arrived at Windrush. She went straight upstairs for a shower and to change so did not hear Douglas' MGB roll into the back yard where he parked the car.

She walked into the kitchen but stopped at the door, she had not expected to find Douglas talking to Mary, she had wanted to have time to compose herself.

'Come and sit down love,' Mary invited her, but she preferred to stand. Nobody said anything and Mary sensing the tension between the two of them and wisely decided she had something to do in the garden.

Alone now and not knowing what to say to precipitate the conversation they had to have, they stared sorrowfully at the floor.

Eventually Douglas spoke, 'Let's get a bottle of wine and go sit outside and talk.'

'No Douglas, we can't just open a bottle of wine and carry on as if nothing has happened.'

He countered, 'Look Joelle, I am really sorry about Wednesday evening, I am sorry if my timing was bad, I know you had a bad day and probably just wanted to get away from Moth Island and home. Truly I am sorry I upset you.'

Dam him, Joelle thought, he always does this, plays the injured party and then apologises for it and I fall for it every time.

But on this occasion, she kept her position, 'No Douglas, it was not that.'

He frowned and looked puzzled, 'what was it then?'

It was Joelle's turn to frown, this was the question, what did she mean, she knew her answer would change their relationship forever, so she hedged her answer.

'What I meant was that I am not sure I want to marry you anymore,' she spoke slowly.

'Why?' Douglas asked, puzzled.

'Oh Douglas, I don't have to spell it out, you must know why.'

'How could I know why, if you wont tell me.'

Joelle detected the edge in his voice and rather than start a pointless argument she said, 'I know you moved to the Island to be with me and this is your home now and, of course, you can stay here, but I think we need a little space between us before we commit ourselves.'

Douglas was silent as he rose from his chair and paced round the kitchen. Joelle waited, watching him fearful of what he might do.

He stopped pacing and with his back to her said, 'You have put off our wedding three times, and now you telling you need space before you can marry me. I can't go on like this Joelle, waiting and being pushed away while you decide what you want.'

He turned to look at her and saw a tear in his eye, 'perhaps you're right,' he said, 'we should just finish it now.'

He walked out of the kitchen.

CHAPTER 20. MISERABLE WEEKEND

Joelle sat in the kitchen, not moving. She heard Douglas upstairs in the room they shared. She heard the stairs creak and then his steps receding across the hall floor. She heard the small squeal as he opened the front door and then heard it bang as he closed it. Then silence. A car door slammed, she heard the rumble of the engine start and then the crunch as the car rolled over the gravel round the house fading into the distance as it moved down the drive. She heard the engine roar as the car accelerated on to the road and away.

She sat numbly listening to the silence.

The following morning, Saturday, she went to work. It was better than sitting at home brooding with miserable thoughts. She felt rejected and now; angry, Douglas had walked out on her! That was not what was supposed to happen. But she also felt philosophical, all her relationships had turned sour in the end, and this latest one just proved a point. It had not helped either when she told Mary that she and Douglas were leaving each other and Mary refused to believe Douglas was having an affair, that made her cross, especially when Mary pointed out it was her fault Douglas had left.

She was driving her old Toyota that morning, she did not trust herself on the motorbike. She sighed and thought, alone again, sad. She wiped away a tear, trouble was, she really had loved Douglas.

She picked up the pathologist's report on the body they had found, she knew that he must have worked the previous night to get the report to her so quickly. She read it, it was brief, factual and to the point and told her nothing more than they had spoken about the previous day. She sat back in her chair and mulled over the pathologist's theory that the body had been weighted, dropped in the sea and then swept by the current to where it was found. She went on to the internet and looked at a map of the sea currents round Kaeta and worked out that the body could have entered the water, somewhere off the southern shore of Moth Island in open water out beyond the reef. She looked at the chart again and observed that the current split when it flowed into the channel between Moth Island and Kaeta. One arm continued round Kaeta into the Caribbean Sea but the other, smaller, arm, curled round towards the beach on Moth Island. She pulled the report on the body of the girl found on the Moth Island beach and sat back thinking, I wonder, could we have been wrong? The girl did not fall overboard, she was thrown in the sea and swept on to the beach by the current.

Moth Island keeps cropping up she was thinking. What the hell is happening on Moth Island. It just can't be a coincidence that Moth Island appears to be the source of the drugs, there are two deaths, both of which seem to come back to Moth Island, the girl, Sofia, was last seen on Moth Island, and now Douglas is working there.

Surely Douglas is not connected as well, is he? He has been there for some time and apparently not found anything. No, I can't believe he could be involved.

But the thought was lodged in her mind now.

She realised the scenario she was imagining was based on circumstantial evidence and supposition and she still had no real proof. She dismissed her thoughtful imaginings for the moment and turned her attention to the more immediate problem of what to do about the latest body, which, she decided, was beginning to look like it might be a murder. She would start on Moth Island. More interviews to check if anyone was missing and if anyone knew the now dead young man. This time she was determined to get into the Casino as well, she still wanted to know why it was so heavily guarded.

She tried to find a telephone number for the Casino to speak to the Manager and make an appointment, but it did not appear in any of the Kaeta directories and she could not even find any web site for the Casino, only the Resort Hotel was listed. She rang that number anyway and asked to be put through to the Casino Manager. The operator apologised and informed her that she had rung the Moth Island Resort Hotel, and no, she did not have a phone number for the Casino. Joelle asked to speak to the Resort Manager thinking he must have a way of contacting the Casino.

She was taken aback when she heard the Manager's voice, she had not expected it to be Douglas. She recovered her composure and asked him if he had a way of contacting the Casino.

'No, I do not,' he told her, 'not at the moment anyway, but I do need to introduce myself and there are some issues I need to sort out with them. I will let them know you are trying to contact them and come back to you.'

'Please do,' Joelle said.

She was about to hang up when Douglas said, 'by the way, I have some information for you, but I don't want to speak over the phone.'

'Another body has turned up, and I need to come over to Moth Island and interview you all about it,' Joelle told Douglas.

'Oh, not everyone is in at the weekends, it would

be best to come next week sometime when all the staff will be here.'

Joelle grunted, not pleased at being put off and hung up.

Douglas placed the phone back into its charger and thought about Joelle again. Actually, she had never been far from his thoughts since he walked out the previous Friday evening. He knew he still loved Joelle and had not wanted to end their relationship, but he thought that perhaps it was wise to have a break from each other, hoping that it would give Joelle time to reflect and he hoped, then they could get back together. He had felt a twinge of excitement when he heard voice on the phone but she sounded very officious and off-hand with him, certainly not phoning to suggest they meet. It brought to mind the small niggling worry that kept prodding him. He had assumed the cause of the break-up was because Joelle was still trying to come to terms with the thought of actually marrying, but her statement, *'she did not have to spell it out, he must know why,'* puzzled him. Why would she say it like that? What was she really thinking?

He shrugged and got on with his analysis of the Resorts running costs. He was mindful he had been charged with restoring the businesses profitability and he was working through old invoices analysing where money was being spent. He needed to speak with Martin Pleasance about the inadequate accounting, there was no analysis of overheads, just a single account called 'Running Expenses.' He decided it was a good thing the previous bookkeeper had left, at least now he could work with Eva and set up a proper set of accounts.

'Dam it, where is the man,' he swore to himself. Martin had disappeared again. That's another thing I need to speak to him about, what does he do all day? He never seems to be around when he is needed. He returned to his stack of invoices and spread sheet, reflecting that at least spending the weekends on the Island would give him more time at work.

When he left Joelle, after she told him she did not want to marry him, Douglas had no real idea of where he was going, he just drove. Without consciously thinking of a destination he had found himself in the car park outside the Glass House Restaurant. He sat in the car, Jasmine would be busy in the kitchen but he could ask Eva if he could stay in the chalet. On reflection, he realised this was not such a good idea, more appropriate to live on Moth Island, it would be lonely but at least he would have a friend there now Eva had accepted the job. He drove to the Yacht Club and caught the last boat when it went over to the Island to collect the evening shift.

He spent all weekend entering invoices into a spread sheet and by Monday morning he thought he had discovered at least one reason why the overheads were so high. The kitchen seemed to use an extraordinary amount of food. The chef had told him that every week he stock-checked the food store but there was no record of the food stock in the accounts, but this did not explain why so much food was being used.

The trainer from the software house had flown in over the weekend and was staying as a guest at the hotel, and Douglas's first task on Monday was to meet her, introduce her to Eva who he had asked to organise the tutorial schedules.

The training started with an introductory meeting involving all the staff. As the meeting finished, Douglas caught Martin Pleasance and asked about the high kitchen costs. Martin told him that he purchased all the food for the Island including the Casino. 'They give me their monthly order and I add it to the Resort order, we get a better price that way and save on shipping costs. Sometimes the Casino chef runs out and raids our kitchen as well,' Martin explained.

'How and where are these kitchen supplies recharged to the Casino?' Douglas asked, as in the accounts he had not seen any invoices to the Casino.

Martin shrugged, 'I don't know, I leave that to the accountants.'

Douglas was furious, he now knew why the food bill was so high, and he was fast coming to the conclusion that he would have to find a new resort manager.

At least Martin kept copies of the Casino food orders and Douglas gave them to Eva and asked her to work out how much should be billed to the Casino.

He then rang Pietor Oys, the South African manager of the Casino, he found his phone number on Martin Pleasance's contact list. Mr Oys sounded a very reasonable person and happily invited Douglas to come up to the Casino to meet him, 'happy to show you round old boy,' Oys invited him, 'but don't come up today, make it tomorrow morning, about ten.'

Douglas remembered he had promised to get a contact number for Joelle and when he mentioned it to Pietor Oys he was invited to bring her as well, 'I'll show you both round.'

Before Douglas could telephone Joelle, he had another telephone call. This was from the Managing Director of the Holiday Resort Company, an affable gentleman who Douglas had met briefly on his introductory visit to England.

After asking Douglas how he was settling in, he confided he was calling about a new opportunity they were considering. He asked Douglas what he knew of the Glass Bay Hotel and explained that they understood that it was up for sale. They knew it had gone bankrupt and they had received a sale circular from the liquidator.

Douglas described what he knew of the hotel and the Managing Director told him that they could be interested in acquiring the business. He told Douglas that the management company that ran Glass Bay also had a hotel in Barbados and, on paper at least, the two hotels looked like they would be a good fit with the Resort Company's existing chain of Caribbean holiday destinations.

'Dick Stump is going to lead the project and he is visiting Kaeta later this week. As you are our man locally, we would like you to meet Dick, join the project team, and show him round.

CHAPTER 21. THE CASINO

'Tell Mr Jay I am here and waiting for him,' Joelle commanded Eva. It was nine forty-five on Tuesday morning and Joelle and Merv had arrived on Moth Island in connection with the now suspected murder. That morning both were in uniform, Joelle carefully dressing in her tailored shirt and trousers.

'He is in the office, go through,' Eva invited Joelle.

'I said, tell him I am here waiting,' Joelle spoke sharply.

Eva said nothing, and wondering what had bitten Joelle, went to find Douglas.

They walked across the Island to the Casino in silence, Douglas glancing at her occasionally reminding himself how attractive she looked when in uniform. At the entrance to the complex a driver and golf buggy were waiting to take them to main buildings where Pietor Oys met them. He was a large, fit looking man, with a ruddy complexion and sandy hair, just beginning to thin. Joelle guessed he was in his mid-forties and immediately dismissed him as the possible drug dealer, he looked nothing like the description, such as it was.

Pietor Oys shook them both firmly by the hand, introduced himself, 'call me Oys,' he said, and invited them to follow him into the main gambling room pointing out the guest lounge, library, fitness centre on the way.

'As you can see we have state of the art guest facilities here,' he boasted.

Joelle told him it looked absolutely delightful, Oys preened himself and putting his arm round her shoulders invited her to look into the kitchens with him, Douglas stood, surprised by Joelle's behaviour, most unlike her he thought. She and Oys emerged from the kitchen clearly flirting with each other, Oys apologising that he could not invite her as a guest, 'we operate a, strict members only policy,' and Joelle telling him if he had time when he next came to Kaeta to look her up.

Douglas did not know whether first to be angry or hurt, he was feeling both emotions and he suspected she was flirting just to upset him, so to break up their little tete-a-tete he commented that there appeared to be no guests around.

Oys explained that the guests never appeared in the mornings, 'we operate strange hours here, breakfast is served between four and six in the morning as the Casino closes. Our guests are usually up all night and asleep most of the day,' and as they walked round the gambling hall Pietor Oys explained that they operated a very exclusive and expensive establishment. 'We do not advertise and our Casino Clubs are only available to members who have to be introduced by two existing members and then approved by the member's committee.'

They adjourned to Oys's office and Joelle haughtily told Douglas to wait outside while she conducted her interview. By now Douglas was very jealous, and also annoyed at the way Joelle was treating him as he suspected she was doing it just to get at him.

Oys summoned a waiter and told him to take Douglas to the lounge and give him a coffee and to Douglas irritation the man remained, watching him. Douglas tried to dismiss the waiter but he refused to leave, explaining Douglas could not be left alone.

Meanwhile Joelle was showing Oys the pictures of both the dead man and Sofia, and asking if he knew anything of them.

'I wish I could assist Joelle, but I am afraid no one here is missing and I have certainly never seen the girl,' Oys apologised

Joelle than asked him about drugs.

'We do not tolerate hard drugs but occasionally a guest may bring in marijuana or stimulants to help them stay awake and as long as it is for personal use only we will turn a blind eye. I am sure you understand the position,' Oys charmed her.

Joelle explained that she believed that Moth Island was the source of an increase in drug dealing on Kaeta involving cannabis sales to tourists. Oys was sympathetic and said he certainly had no knowledge of any such activities.

'I have already asked Mr Jay, the Resort Director, to be aware of my suspicions and to be on the alert for any such illegal activities and report to me. Perhaps I could ask that you do the same.' Oys responded that, of course, he would do all he could to help.

Joelle's final request was to interview the Casino staff. Oys told her he would assemble those who were on duty, but most of the staff also slept during the day. 'Anyway,' he added, 'they never leave the complex so I think it most unlikely they will know anything. Tell you what, I will copy those pictures of yours and show them round later and if anyone knows anything I will let you know.'

Rather uncharacteristically Joelle agreed.

She returned to the Resort, driven all the way in a golf buggy, leaving Douglas with Pietor Oys discussing the financial arrangements between the two businesses.

When Douglas got back to the Resort he found Joelle had taken over his office for interviews and was working her way through all the Resort managers.

He joined Eva in the reception office asked her

how she was getting on with the food orders for the Casino.

'Slowly,' she said,' but I have found an easier way, Martin just writes the Casino order on the bottom of the Resort order which makes it easier to tie up with the invoice and get the prices.'

Douglas told her that he had agreed with the Casino Manager to invoice all the food supplied to the Casino this year and in future to invoice separately for every order, 'When you have worked out the cost we add ten percent on for our trouble,' he added.

'Does Joelle want to see you,' he asked Eva.

'I think so, but I am not looking forward to it, she has been glaring at me all morning and all the ones she has seen say she is practically accusing them of murder and supplying drugs. I don't know what is wrong with her today, she is being very aggressive.'

Douglas shrugged, he was not yet ready to tell Eva, or anyone else, that he and Joelle had split up.

At that point, Martin Pleasance walked into the office.

'Martin,' Eva called him over, 'Inspector deNouvelas wants to see you. Martin went white as a sheet, almost in tears, looking like he had seen a ghost.

'What is wrong Martin?' Eva asked, but he just rushed out of the office waving his hands defensively in front of his face apparently indicating he could not talk

Eva and Douglas looked at each other. 'What's wrong with him,' they said together.

Joelle shouted for Eva to go and fetch the Chef.

'I am not her skivvy,' Eva complained.

'Better do as she says or she will arrest us for obstruction,' Douglas joked.

With Joelle obviously in a mood, Douglas decided to get out of her way and go for a walk around the resort hoping to find Josh.

He did find Josh, in the bar with a tray of drinks. 'Just helping the barman out, delivering drinks along the beach.' Josh winked at him, 'go and walk casually along the back path where we can talk alone.'

Douglas asked Josh how it was going and if he found out any more from Dooley in the greenhouses.

Josh shook his head, 'No, not a squeak. I have nearly been off my head smoking weed with him but he won't say anything. I think he's scared.'

'I will try and see Joelle later and tell her what we have got so far.' Douglas mused, 'do you think it is worth pulling Dooley in and questioning him formally?'

Josh thought about this, 'No, I am sure the way to crack this is to see how they are bringing the drugs in and I think they are using that little cove by the bungalow on the far side of the Island.' He paused for more thought, 'No, I need the time to wait until they have another shipment

MOTH ISLAND

and if Dooley is arrested it will probably blow my cover. If Dooley is so scared of something, this could be a dangerous place, I am not hanging around.'

Douglas warned him that Merv was on Moth Island asking questions. 'Will he recognise you from last time you were here?' Douglas asked.

'He might, he certainly saw me,' Josh replied.

'You better go and hide, say you are running errands for me if anyone asks,' Douglas advised.

Douglas was the last person to be interviewed by Joelle that day.

She was not being friendly, in fact she started the interview telling Douglas that if he thought he was getting special treatment because of their former relationship he was quite wrong.

'I would expect to be treated the same as anyone else. You don't need to be so aggressive.' He replied, but that just made Joelle even more officious.

She would not admit it but she was burning up inside having seen Douglas and Eva together earlier and how easy their relationship appeared.

She challenged him with the pictures and he upset her by reminding her that before they broke up she had shown him the picture of Sofia and he told her he knew nothing. As for the dead man, he apologised that he could not help.

'However, on the drug front, I do have some information,' and he told her that Josh had identified Dooley as the middle man. She was all for rushing off to arrest Dooley but Douglas placed a restraining hand on her arm.

'Think about it,' he cautioned, 'If you arrest Dooley now, you will blow Josh's cover and we will be back to square one, losing the only positive lead we have.' He told her Josh thought Dooley was very scared and would not talk anyway.

The conversation reminded her of the times she and Douglas had discussed a case and he had given her sound advice. She wished that they could return to those times but she would not let herself relax with the picture of Douglas and Eva burning into her mind. As Douglas explained Josh's fears that the Moth Island would be a dangerous place if his cover was blown, she forced herself to agree to let Dooley run for the moment.

She dismissed him curtly with, 'that's all. You can go now.' But then as he moved to the door she called him back. He turned towards her expectantly, hoping that perhaps she was going to offer an olive branch, or at least give some sign of hope for a reconciliation, but she looked expressionless as she handed him an envelope.

CHAPTER 22. THE PROJECT

After that meeting with Joelle, Douglas felt he needed some time on his own. He felt mightily depressed, all along he had hoped that their parting would be temporary but in that meeting, she had given absolutely nothing away, in fact he did not like to admit it, but if anything she looked like she hated being in the same room.

'Oh well,' he was talking to himself, sadly, 'perhaps I had better get over Joelle.'

He was then surprised when he saw Josh bounding down the path towards him.

He had not realised he was on the west side of the Island looking at the small cove Josh thought was the possible landing point for the landing the drugs.

'Hey Douglas,' Josh greeted him. 'Checking things out?'

'Not really, Joelle and I have split up and I was just walking to clear my mind.'

Josh looked sympathetic. 'That's bad,' was all he

said.

They stood in a companionable silence looking out over the Ocean for some minutes before Josh spoke again.

'Come on, no good moping around, that won't help. Come and look up here, there is an inflatable by the bungalow and I am guessing that is what is used to bring the drugs ashore.'

'This must be where Martin Pleasance lives,' Douglas commented as they approached the dwelling.

They inspected the inflatable, 'the outboard looks well maintained,' Josh peered under its cover.

'It's very clean as well,' Douglas commented, 'in fact it looks like it has been recently washed,' he added as he spied a bucket, sponge and bottle of detergent by the trailer wheel.

Douglas spent the evening with Josh at his camp site concealed in the trees and undergrowth on the headland. They cooked some fish on Josh's gas powered barbecue and Douglas bored him reminiscing, mainly about Joelle.

The next day was a busy one for Douglas. He first had to apologise to the instructor running the seminars on the Island because he was unable to stay for the final session as that afternoon he was meeting Dick Stump at Kaeta International Airport. He then needed to sit with Eva and plan the implementation of the new system which was due to go live in ten day's time. Thank God I have Eva, he thought. While she was not very academic she was very practical and willing to take on anything asked of her.

As he and Eva finished their planning she reminded Douglas that Martin Pleasance wanted to talk with him. When she left, he noticed the envelope Joelle had given him. He had been putting the moment off and his hand trembled slightly as he picked the envelope up, forgetting that Martin wanted to see him. He thought it might be from Joelle telling him their relationship was over, as if I need telling again, he thought, but he saw it had a UK stamp and London postmark and was addressed to him at the Windrush. He opened the letter, it was from David Evans of Benson Solicitors. Douglas remembered David Evans, he was the solicitor he and Joelle had used when Joelle was in trouble on secondment to the London Met.

He read the letter. It explained that Benson's had been retained by Miss deNouvelas to defend an action brought by her former husband Ralph Holdswick claiming damages of one million dollars as he was coerced and blackmailed into signing an agreement under which he relinquished any claim on Joelle's assets as a divorce settlement. Douglas was asked to provide his correspondence including emails, related to the divorce and warned that as Ralph had specifically named him as part of a blackmail plot he would be required to provide a witness statement and attend court should the action go that far.

Douglas threw the letter into his briefcase to deal with later. He was in a hurry to get to the pier to catch the hotel motor boat over to Kaeta and meet Dick Stump.

He was standing on the pier, with some returning guests and a couple of the hotel ground staff watching the boat approach when Martin Pleasance appeared asking if he could have a few minutes.

'Got a bit of a problem,' Martin explained.

Douglas looked at the approaching motor boat, 'I don't really have time Martin. Can it wait until I return.'

'Not really,' Martin replied nervously wringing his hands.

Douglas listened impatiently as the boat floated slowly up to the pier and a groundsman grabbed the ropes, holding the boat against the pier.

Martin explained, 'it is about that body the police found in the sea. I have some information, well, in fact I might have been inadvertently involved, and now it has turned into a murder investigation I would not want anyone to think I was anything to do with a killing.'

Douglas, anxious to get away replied, 'Martin, I am sorry, I don't have time now. In any case, if you have information you should inform the police. See Eva, she has Inspector deNouvelas's direct line number. Phone her.'

Martin nodded and watched as Douglas climbed aboard the boat and speed off towards Kaeta.

'Nice car,' Dick commented as he climbed into Douglas's MGB. 'V8 engine?' He asked.

Douglas nodded agreement and related the story of the purchase to Dick as they drove away from the airport.

They soon however got down to business as Dick explained that they saw an opportunity to run large resort style hotel complexes near their existing businesses, 'greater staff flexibility, sharing of overheads, greater purchasing power all that sort of thing. We can also offer multiple destination holidays more easily and cheaply,' he enthused.

Douglas told Dick about the Glass Bay Hotel explaining that it had been run by a hotel group who leased the hotel from the freehold owner.

Dick nodded, 'Yes, we know that and we also know that Miss deNouvelas is the freehold owner. She is your fiancé, isn't she?'

'Was, we have broken up,' Douglas told him.

Again Dick nodded thoughtfully, 'that's good,' but realising what he had just said, 'I mean, not good you have split up but good because it means you can join the project team without any conflicts.'

Douglas just nodded.

'My secretary has planned the trip for us,' Dick

than explained, 'we are booked into the Glass Bay tonight, gives us time for a good look round tomorrow before we leave to catch a flight to Barbados where we stay overnight and next day check out the other hotel we are interested in before I fly back to the UK and you are booked on the late evening flight back to Kaeta.'

Again, Douglas just nodded agreement.

That evening Douglas suggested they walk along the beach to the Crystal Bay Restaurant.

Dick Stump was interested in who owned the beach and land behind.

'All the beaches of Kaeta are public, but the de Nouvelas family own the area between the foreshore and beach along this whole stretch of coastline,' Douglas confirmed.

'That is a lot of land,' Dick mused, 'and the restaurant, is that run by the hotel?'

'No,' Douglas replied, 'the restaurant itself is owned by old Mrs deNouvelas and run by her grand-daughter.'

'I like this restaurant, it has a lot of potential,' Dick commented as they ate.

The next day they were met by a representative from the liquidator who accompanied them round the Glass Bay Hotel. Not much had changed since Douglas had stayed there a few years previously but even he had to admit that it was beginning to look a little tired. Dick Stump looked distinctly unimpressed and when they had finished at the hotel he suggested they drive along to the restaurant for a late lunch before leaving for the airport.

'Pull over here,' he asked Douglas as they drove the short stretch of between the Hotel and the Restaurant. 'This strip of land,' he indicated the area between the road and the Beach, 'This is all owned by the de Nouvelas family?'

'As far as I am aware Joelle owns it all,' Douglas confirmed.

'Dick walked towards the beach through the palm trees and scrubby undergrowth, Douglas sat in the car waiting for him.

'It must be half a mile from here to the beach,' Dick commented as he climbed back into the car.

'At this point probably a bit more,' Douglas confirmed. 'The hotel access road is half a mile long and this road curves round so it's probably about nearly three quarters of a mile at this point.'

Dick nodded knowingly and asked who owned the land running beyond the restaurant. Douglas confirmed that all the land along this stretch of beach was owned by the deNouvleas family.

They ate a light lunch and set of for the flight to Bermuda. They did not say much to each other during the journey. Dick was deep in thought and writing notes.

Douglas was brooding, he had found meeting Jasmine difficult. She obviously did not know he and Joelle had split up and while he had meant to tell her, with Dick Stump accompanying him it had not seemed appropriate. He sat on the plane and realised that telling Jasmine would somehow finalise the separation and deep down he still hoped that he and Joelle would get back together.

That evening Douglas and Dick ate in the hotel. Douglas was curious as he had noted the hotel name was 'The Holiday Resort Company Club, Bermuda', and he took the opportunity to ask Dick about the name.

'This is our hotel,' Dick told him, 'we own this one and the hotel we are interested in is next door, we will see it in the morning.'

This seemed to unlock Dicks silence and he told Douglas they were really, only interested in the Bermuda hotel, as it was next door it offered the opportunity to incorporate the two business into one creating a much larger complex. He explained they would more than double the guest rooms and have more facilities, and acquire a decent stretch of private beach.

'Keep quiet about this,' he whispered to Douglas, 'but by sharing facilities we could make some real cuts in overheads, for example we could completely close one kitchen.'

Dick then went on to say that the problem was that the liquidator was insisting that both hotels be purchased as part of the same deal. 'I am not really interested in the Glass Bay Hotel,' he explained, 'it is too small for us to create a proper holiday complex and it does not have the number of guest rooms we need to make it profitable. There is also the complication that it is leasehold and they are paying a lot of money in ground rent. If the liquidator insists it is included we will knock him down on price and just close the hotel down.'

There was not much Douglas could say to this but he did think that Joelle would not be too pleased if the Glass Bay Hotel was closed down and now he had another problem, should he tell her or just keep quiet.

The following day was uneventful as far as Douglas was concerned. He trailed round after Dick listening to him enthuse about the possibilities and opportunities for merging the two hotels before escaping mid-afternoon when they shared a taxi back to the airport.

While waiting for Dick's flight they had a brief opportunity to discuss what was to happen next.

'We want to get the projects finished by this November so we get the new businesses up and running for next season, so if we go ahead there is some pressure to get a deal agreed. We should target the end of this month to finalise the purchase,' Dick thought out loud.

Douglas raised his eyebrows, 'that's some time scale, the last business sale I did took six months to finalise.'

Dick dismissed that, telling Douglas they had to

get the new resorts open for next season, so if the deal is spun out for months they would just walk away. 'I am meeting the MD over the weekend and we will decide if, and what, we are prepared offer and then I have a meeting in London early next week with the liquidator where we will make it clear that unless he agrees a deal before the end of the week we are walking away. That will give us three weeks to complete due diligence and finalise the purchase. I will want you involved in the due diligence so clear your diary for the rest of the month,' Dick instructed Douglas.

Dick's flight was called, but he had one more instruction for Douglas before he left, 'by the way,' he said, 'I don't need to remind you that all this is secret until the deal is done, so don't tell anyone, even Martin Pleasance.'

Douglas had to wait until nine thirty before his flight back to Kaeta was called. By ten he was in the air and by ten forty-five he was back in Kaeta. Tired, he climbed into the MG and sat thinking what to do. He was too late to get a boat over to Moth Island. The weather was hot and sultry, he sniffed the air deciding a thunder storm was imminent and the thought of sleeping in the car did not appeal and it was not an option to go to Windrush to suffer the indignity of begging for a bed for the night. He thought of Eva and Jasmine, he was sure they would put him up and if he hurried he would just catch them as they closed the

MOTH ISLAND

restaurant.

'I lost my key and the lights were all out at Windrush so I did not want to wake them all up,' Douglas made up the little white lie when Jasmine asked him why he was not going home.

'Of course, you can spend the night here, but it's only the couch in the living room I am afraid,' Jasmine offered without question.

Eva said nothing, just smiled knowingly at Douglas.

By the time they finished clearing up the restaurant the thunder storm was in full swing and the rain slashing down.

'Come on guys, lets run,' Eva shouted excitedly.

'You two go, I will catch up when I have put the food in the fridge and locked up.' Jasmin hung back.

Of course, Eva and Douglas were soaked to the skin by the time they reached the chalet.

'You use the bathroom and strip off, I'll use the bedroom and get you a pillow and some sheets,' Eva invited Douglas.

When he had dried off he returned to the living room to find Eva had already left him bed linen. He laid his wet clothes out to dry and settled himself naked onto the sofa covering himself with the sheet. He had only just done this when Eva walked into the room wearing a very flimsy night dress under an equally flimsy dressing gown.

'In case you get cold,' she handed Douglas a blanket, but did not move, just stood by the bed looking at him.

'Jasmine will be here any minute,' he said.

'No, don't worry, she will be ages yet. She likes to go round by herself and make sure everything is in order before she comes home.' Eva assured him.

She sat on the bed, and laid her hand on his shoulder. 'I know about you and Joelle, it's all round Moth Island.'

'How, I have told no one?' Douglas asked.

You were overheard when Joelle told you it was finished, and when you moved into the flat, well, some of us put two and two together.'

She moved her hand down across his chest and moving towards him kissed him gently on the forehead and whispered, 'I am sorry about you and Joelle and I am a good listener if you want company.'

CHAPTER 23. LINDA

The girl looked at the man lying on the Casino terrace. He was rather overweight and at the wrong end of middle age.

The girl, her name was Linda, had just turned seventeen, she was pretty, with long black hair and having lost her teenage pudginess was now a very attractive young lady, which pleased her employer greatly. But while her age might have qualified her as a girl, her experiences over the last nine months had turned her into a hard-hearted woman.

Unemotionally she watched the pool of blood from the man's head spread out over the wet terrace, diluted by the heavy rain. She had not meant to hurt him, and looking at him bleeding profusely, she feared she might have killed him.

The thunder storm seemed to excite him and he had insisted that she accompany him outside as he wanted to stand in the tropical rain with her and watch the storm pass overhead. Linda had thought that was not a very good idea, but as a Casino hostess her job was to make sure her guest was happy. Her evening dress, which was made from a very light material was soon virtually transparent as it became soaked by the heavy rain. This, in itself, had not bothered Linda, after all the man had seen her naked before, but he soon lost interest in the storm and became fixated, staring at her body. It was when he approached her asking to do something she found physically abhorrent that she had pushed him away. He went to grab her but slipped on the wet floor and fell, hitting his head on the coping stones along the top of the low wall surrounding the terrace.

She watched him bleeding at her feet, she did not feel sorrow for the man, in fact she felt nothing, not even disgust anymore, but it did occur to her that the repercussions of the accident would be severe and directed at her.

That was when she came up with her escape plan.

She had been effectively enslaved at the Casino. She come out expecting to work as a waitress and croupier but the Matron had taken one look at her and told her she would be working as a hostess. The woman was not really a Matron, her job title was Assistant Manager and she was responsible for the team of hosts and hostesses, all of whom were young and good looking.

'Your job,' Matron told Linda, is to keep the guests happy, you do everything and anything they ask, and I mean anything,' Matron repeated threateningly.

After a couple of weeks Linda asked one of the other hostesses when they got paid.

'Paid!' The girl laughed, 'You don't get paid, first they deduct your airfare, then your clothing allowance, board and lodging, food and drinks, you end up owing them money and they will tell you that you can't have your passport back until your debt is paid off. No love, you will never get out of here.'

Standing in the rain, listening to the storm rumble its way over to Kaeta and watching her guest bleed, Linda saw her opportunity, everyone had seen her go outside with the man and no one was going to come looking for them while it was raining. If she could get down to the beach undiscovered she was sure she could swim across the narrow channel, after all, she reasoned, she had been a strong swimmer at school and had even swum the one mile challenge once and it could not be that far across to the Kaeta.

She ran.

Her courage began to fail her as she stood on the beach looking at the sea. It was not the azure blue calm stretch of water she had known while accompanying her guests swimming. Breakers were crashing up the beach driven by the storm and out beyond the headland she could see the white surf as the wind whipped the sea over the reef. She heard the dogs snarling and barking, excited, as they ran down the gardens and guessed the man's body had been found and her absence discovered.

She took a deep breath, she had two choices, stay and be torn apart by the dogs or plunge into the waves and swim.

CHAPTER 24.
JOELLE'S DATE

Linda, Douglas and Eva were not the only ones to get wet the night of the thunder storm. Joelle was similarly soaked but, unlike Douglas and Eva, was not happy about it. She was in Kaeta town, another large cruise ship was visiting and she and her officers were in the town on patrol. Joelle was hoping to trap the drug peddlers but the only miscreants they had come across before the storm hit, were a couple of pick pockets working the markets. Sheet lightning and thunder heralded the arrival of the tropical storm. At first people just stood and watched the light show and accompanying rumbling creating an eerie atmosphere over the town. Suddenly the tropical rain started to lash down, it was as if hundreds of fire hoses had been directed from the sky. Everyone ran for shelter but few made it in time as the tropical storm rolled overhead. Initially some tourists tried to shelter under the awnings and tarpaulin covers of the market stalls but these were quickly overwhelmed and collapsed under the weight of water. Panic started to spread as the now soaked tourists started to run towards the indoor markets, open churches and any other open building that could give shelter, but these were already packed full, and fights broke out as people pushed to reach shelter.

Joelle tried to muster her team of officers to control the crowds and direct the tourists back to their ships, but it was hopeless, she could not find half her officers, and those she could find were simply overwhelmed by the noise, screaming crowds, lashing rain, swirling winds and thunder rumbling in the background.

The rain stopped as suddenly as it had started. In reality, the worst of the storm was over in about fifteen minutes and the thunder and lightning receded out beyond the Island to the west eventually disappearing over the Caribbean Sea.

Calm descended on the town as the soaked tourists started to emerge from their shelters and make their way back to their ships. Joelle did manage to round up most of her officers, and despite being soaked to the skin she insisted they remain on duty.

'There may be injuries we have to attend to,' she observed and pointing to the remains of the market stalls, 'I fear we have to deal with some looting.' Many of the stalls had been swamped by the rain and their contents washed to the ground, and those that had survived the storm had been overturned by the panicking crowds.

Unfortunately, Joelle was right on both counts and the police were kept busy for the next couple of hours dealing with injured tourists, most not serious and quickly patched up so they could return to their ships, but a couple of people had been trampled and ambulances were required. However, the bigger problem for the police was the looting. Some of it was tourists picking up and taking trinkets and other articles spotted lying on the ground but there were some more serious thefts by individuals who appeared with large bags which they systematically filled openly in front of the stall holders who were desperately trying to recover their stock and rescue their stalls.

It was this handful of systematic looters that Joelle and her team arrested and escorted back to the police cells and once they had been processed and locked up for the night they all breathed a sigh of relief.

Finally, they could all go home.

That night was the culmination of a rather hard and unsatisfactory few days Joelle experienced after the day she spent on Moth Island finally breaking up with Douglas.

She had tried to put him out of her mind but, naturally, thoughts of Douglas kept popping into her head. When they did she savagely reminded herself that he had rejected her for another woman, feeding her simmering anger.

Her drug investigation had stalled again, the Commissioner was still pushing her for results and she was beginning to regret that she agreed not to arrest Dooley. Worse, a little devil at the back of her mind kept asking why was Douglas was so insistent that she did not arrest Dooley? Was it really to avoid compromising Josh, or did Douglas have some more personal motive? The only good thing she reflected as she sat at her desk the morning after the storm was that there had been no sign of any drugs the previous evening. But that was probably only because of the storm, she thought morosely.

'Irene,' Joelle summoned her DC, 'have you made any progress with the manacle and cash bag we found in the sea near the body.'

They had had the bag forensically examined. There was nothing on the manacle itself which would link the manacle to the dead body and the examination had concluded from the algae growth on the bag that it been in the water for some time. They had however managed to make out the name of a security firm printed on the bag and Joelle had instructed Irene to contact the firm and see if they could identify to whom the bag had been issued.

'Yes Ma'am,' Irene told Joelle nervously. For the last few days Joelle had been morose and snappy, not her usual self, and dealing with her had been like walking on egg shells. 'I left a report on your desk yesterday, but you were busy.'

Joelle grunted and angrily shuffled through the papers on her desk looking for the report.

'Oh, dam it,' she swore, 'I can't find the report, just tell me.'

'It is a cash collection bag used by their security agents to move money. Could be delivering from businesses to banks, or the other way round, and even between banks. They do not keep records of which bags are issued to whom. The bags are freely issued to their customers as needed,' Irene reported.

'That is a big help,' Joelle was sarcastic.

'Well, they did say that they have customers on Kaeta, there is a list attached to my report,' Irene timidly told Joelle.

Joelle swore under breath again and started to shuffle through papers.

'The Holiday Resort Company on Moth Island, is on the list.' Irene ventured to tell Joelle as she retreated backwards out of the Office.

For the first time that day Joelle looked pleased. 'As soon as you have finished what you are doing get over to Moth Island, take the bag and see what you can find out,' she shouted to the disappearing Irene. It was the following Monday before Irene went to Moth Island, it was too late on Saturday to go and Sunday was her day off. As a result, it was Tuesday before Irene reported back to Joelle.

'I spoke to Mr Jay and Eva,' Irene started her report and Joelle looked up sharply at the mention of Douglas and Eva, but said nothing. 'They had no knowledge of the bags and said they doubted they would need such bags anyway as they rarely needed to bank cash. All holidays are paid in advance and most people settle their local hotel bills by credit card.'

'Did you speak to the manager, Martin Pleasance, 'he has been there since the resort opened and may know more?' Joelle asked.

'No, Eva said she had not seen him for a couple of days. I did go over to the shop, I thought they might use the bags. The shop manager confirmed they had, very occasionally, used collection bags. When they have enough cash to bank they ask for a bag and they take it over to Kaeta and meet a security van who take it to bank for them. But they said they don't keep a stock of the bags they just ask for one when they need it.'

Joelle nodded, 'There is more chance the Casino might use the bags, they must have a lot of cash. Did you get chance to ask?'

'No, I did ask but was told there was no one available from the Casino,' Irene replied.

'No matter,' Joelle told her, 'I am seeing the Casino Manager later this week, I will ask him.'

But before she met Oys, she received a message from her attorney, David Rail, inviting her to his office as he needed to speak with her as a matter of urgency.

He introduced the conversation by reminding Joelle that she had instructed him to care for her interest in the liquidation of the management company running the Glass Bay Hotel.

'I have been contacted by the liquidators who say they have received an offer for the Glass Bay Hotel and its sister business in Bermuda.'

'That's good isn't it,' Joelle interrupted.

'Possibly,' David Rail was cautious, 'but the offer contained certain pre-conditions, one of which concerns you.'

'Oh yes?' Joelle looked interested.

'It appears that the buyer will only proceed with the offer if they can secure the freehold of the Glass Bay Hotel.'

'What!' Joelle exclaimed, 'I don't want to sell the freehold, my father built that hotel, and anyway I need the income from the lease.'

'Hold on, I am afraid there is more,' David continued, 'not only do they want the freehold they want ten hectares of land surrounding the hotel, up to the main road. No listen,' David stopped Joelle interrupting again. 'And they want all the land between the hotel, Mary's restaurant and main road.'

He sat back waiting for Joelle to explode, which she did, 'This is ridiculous, I don't want to sell all that land, it was my father's, and anyway I don't own it all, Mary owns the restaurant and the land round it and that land was acquired by my ancestors after slavery was abolished and is willed in perpetuity to the family.'

David cautioned Joelle to calm down and think about it. 'This is the only offer the liquidator has had for the Glass Bay. They told me that the hotel in Bermuda is larger and easier to sell as they own all the land.'

Joelle asked, 'If I don't sell the land, what are the alternatives?'

David pursed his lips, 'the alternatives for the hotel, I am not sure. The land they want is not used for anything I suppose we could offer to lease it to them.' He frowned thinking, 'I suppose it might depend on what they want the land for.'

Joelle and David looked at each other, each silently seeking answers.

David was the first to speak, 'They have asked for a meeting, the day after tomorrow to discuss the offer.'

'A meeting, with whom and where?' Joelle asked.

'You, and the buyer, meeting probably in Bermuda.'

'Impossible,' Joelle exclaimed, 'for a start I can't spend a day getting to Bermuda, I am too busy here and I certainly want you involved.'

David promised he would see what he could organise and later that day he got back to Joelle telling her the meeting would be on Kaeta at midday in his office. 'Three people from the buyer, you and I will be at the meeting,' David informed her. She wished Douglas would be present as well, as she really would have liked his

MOTH ISLAND

help.

That meeting was to be on the Thursday, but before that Joelle had another meeting to worry about. It was more of a date really and now she was wondering why she had ever accepted the invitation to join Oys for dinner on Wednesday evening, especially as he left a message for her telling her to dress-up, he had booked a table in the exclusive Paradise Hotel and would pick her up from Windrush at seven pm. When she accepted the invitation, she had planned to eat in Jasmine's restaurant where she felt safe. This new arrangement did not suit her at all and she was betting he had booked a room at the hotel for the night as well.

However, she did dress up, and even felt a tingle of excitement at the thought of a date with someone new and told herself it was silly to feel guilty that she was somehow letting Douglas down by going out with another man. She did feel guilty though.

Oys was prompt picking her up at exactly seven. As he opened the taxi door for her she decided he looked very handsome if a little rugged, in his white dinner jacket, waistcoat and dress trousers. She noticed Mary glaring at her through the window as they drove away.

They got to the restaurant and before leaving the taxi she told the driver to be back at eleven to drive them home.

'No need,' Oys dismissed the taxi, 'I have booked

a room for the night.'

'Fine for you, I want the taxi,' Joelle told him, thinking I knew he would try it, and wishing it was Douglas she was with.

In fact, and despite her fears, she had a very good evening. Oys was excellent company, regaling her with stories of South Africa, working on a game reserve with wild animals, 'I got attacked once, that is how I picked up this limp, injured my leg,' he told her. 'After that I worked in a massive casino and hotel complex in Johannesburg. One thing led to another, that's how I ended up here,' he explained. Joelle tried to get him to talk about the Casino on Moth Island but he avoided any direct answer.

When she asked him about the cash bag, he looked puzzled, 'I have no idea how one could have ended up in the sea. Probably a security custodian dropped one sometime. We have a weekly cash collection. We bring four, armed security custodians over to collect our cash for banking in the motor launch and they bring the bags with them.'

No more was said about the room for the night and prompt at eleven Oys took her out to her taxi, kissed her hand, said goodnight, and asked if could take her out again next time he was on Kaeta.

'I would like that,' Joelle smiled at him.

CHAPTER 25. JOSH

Another person who got soaked the night of the tropical storm was Josh and for him that storm heralded the start of a short but uncomfortable week.

When he finished work the afternoon before the storm, as usual, he made his way round the Island to his camp.

He was conscious of a rather eerie atmosphere pervading the Island. It had been building up all afternoon. Late morning it became very humid and this developed into a muggy hot afternoon, the sort of weather where even the slightest physical exertion causes a torrent of perspiration. Then a haze appeared on the eastern horizon which gradually spread across the Island, not exactly blocking the sun but turning it into a strange orange looking ball hanging in the sky shining a weird light on the Island. The wildlife, mainly birds, disappeared and were absolutely silent, and most of the guests retired to their rooms or the bar. The head groundsman prophesied a storm and instructed the outside maintenance team to move everything into cover and tie down that which could not be moved. The sea on the Caribbean side of the Island was strangely flat and weird orangey grey colour. Nobody spoke as they cleared down the resort waiting for the anticipated storm and by late afternoon the Island was absolutely silent, bathed in a strange green grey light.

Josh made his way round the Island wondering if it was wise to remain outside all night. He had never seen weather like this before and it made him feel weird, even a bit frightened. He reached the cove and stopped above the beach looking out over the ocean. Unlike the sea on the western side of the Island the Atlantic on the eastern side looked distinctly threatening. Now, as the light faded it was a dark grey, almost black colour and a big sea was building with evil looking rollers marching towards the Island with military precision and crashing up the beach. What surprised Josh was that he could see the waves and surf washing up the beach but the atmosphere was so heavy that it appeared to be silent. Even stranger he thought was that there was no wind at all.

It was then that he noticed a launch trolley pulled up on the beach. He guessed it was from the inflatable speed boat, cautiously he made his way up to the bungalow to check and sure enough, the boat was gone. He scanned the sea but there was no sign of the boat. Are they taking

MOTH ISLAND

a drug delivery tonight, surely not with a storm imminent, he thought, but it could be the perfect time with nobody about.

Once in his camp he sat watching, occasionally scanning the sea with his binoculars but as night fell he had to give up, it was too dark to see anything. He sat wondering what to do, go down the beach, or stay hidden in the camp, when he thought he heard the sound of an outboard motor rounding the headland below him. In the dark, he made his way down the beach but half way he nearly ran into two men walking up the path towards him. He only knew they were there because they were talking to each other. Josh dived into the undergrowth beside the path and dared not even breath as the two passed him not a meter away from where he was crouching.

'That was rough, I don't want to go out in a sea like that again,' he heard one man say.

'Better that than another carpeting from Pete,' the other added.

'Yer, it did need moving, it was beginning to stink.'

As the men walked on past Josh he heard their conversation fade into the distance.

'Yer, and I hope it does not come back and haunt us, we should have dumped it further out.'

'What in that sea!'

'Your right, but it could drift, it was not weighted.'

Josh wondered what they were talking about,

251

had they taken a delivery of drugs and lost them in the rough sea? What did they mean by weighting, deliberately sinking the shipment conceal it to be recovered when needed? And what did they mean by beginning to stink?

He cautiously walked down the beach. The trolley was gone, and when he checked the inflatable speed boat was back beside the bungalow being tied down by two men. In the light of their torches he recognised one of the men, Josh only knew him by his nick-name, Saws. He crept forward to better hear what the two were saying.

'Shit,' Josh cried out as he hit his shin on the exhaust pipe protruding from the wall of the generator shed that he was creeping round.

'Who's there,' the men shone their torch but Josh had already shrunk back behind the shed and was retreating back, down the track. He made his way back to his camp. The weather was still oppressive, but, he thought, at least it is dark now and that strange eerie light has gone. As he reached his camp he saw, on the horizon out to the east flashes of blue light accompanied by a distant rumbling. He sat, fascinated with a grandstand view of the storm rolling in towards the Moth Island. Soon the Island was illuminated, sometimes for seconds by a fierce blue light as the sheet lightning flashed across the sky. Accompanying thunder became louder and almost continuous, Josh thought it sounded like some fierce ancient battle going on above the

MOTH ISLAND

clouds. As the storm moved over the Island Josh became a little afraid as it occurred to him sitting high up on his headland he would certainly be fried if the lightning struck his camp. He was pondering upon alternative places to shelter when the rain started. Suddenly a torrent of water was tipped on his camp site, and it kept coming for what seemed like hours to Josh, but was actually only about twenty minutes. His camp site was destroyed, his shelter collapsed in the first few minutes and his hammock flapped and cracked in the wind, he tried to hold it down to shelter beneath it but it just filled with water, split and drowned him again. The wind caught his sleeping bag and any other items not anchored down and blew them away. What was not blown away by the wind was washed away by the torrent of water falling on the headland. His clothes, food, everything, was scattered across the headland and soaked.

The rain finished as suddenly as it started as the storm rumbled its way towards Kaeta.

As it passed the temperature dropped and although it was not that cold, Josh sat wet and shivering, emotionally drained and utterly exhausted. He had been like that for about ten minutes when he became conscious of someone sloshing their way up the path guided by a flash light.

'Ah, I thought you might need rescuing.'

Josh looked up and blinked, dazzled by the flash

light.

'It's me, Dooley,' the voice behind the light informed him. 'That was quite some storm, years since I have seen one of those.'

Josh sat in Dooley's greenhouse, recovering, drinking a concoction made from chocolate, liquidised bananas and rum.

'That storm was something,' he said to Dooley, who agreed and pointed out that up on that headland he had taken the brunt of the weather, 'down here, much more sheltered by the hill,' he observed.

They were silent for a few minutes before Josh spoke again.

'Dooley, how did you know I was up on that headland? I have told no one where I was camping.'

'You did not really think you could keep it secret on an Island this small did you,' Dooley squinted at him. 'For the moment, you were doing no harm up there so you were left alone, but now, not a bad idea to move back down to the resort.'

Josh wondered what he meant by that, but let it pass for the moment as he wanted to ask Dooley another question.

'I noticed there was a fast inflatable speed boat near the cover and it was out with some guys today, just before the storm, what on earth would they be doing?'

Dooley's expression changed, he looked around

furtively before replying, 'best you don't know. Those guys, they did not see you, did they?'

'They might have, I cracked my shin and swore, so they knew someone was there.'

Dooley looked very serious, 'My friend, I don't want to see you get hurt, you are not safe on this Island now, get out on the first boat in the morning.'

Josh started to argue and ask why, but all Dooley would say was, 'there are bad men on this Island, and now you have seen too much, I am telling you, they will be looking for you in the morning and if they find you, you will end up feeding the fish. Get out or you will get us both into trouble.'

Josh could see that Dooley was seriously concerned, and on reflection decided that it would be good to heed Dooley's advice, especially now that his camp site was no longer a secret. Anyway, he considered his work on the Island was done. He was pretty certain he knew how the drugs were being smuggled in, and he had identified how they were being distributed to the Island visitors. He also had some contact names. He was not concerned at turning Saws in, so called because he had completed the chain saw training, but he felt a twinge of guilt regarding Dooley, with whom he had become quite friendly over the last couple of weeks. He was also bored stiff walking up and down the beach, definitely time to get back to Miami he thought. So, it was that the following morning he left the greenhouse early, retrieved his damp rucksack which fortunately still contained his credit cards, rather damp passport and open flight ticket back to Miami and was doing his best to conceal himself round the resort buildings while he waited for the morning staff boat to arrive.

Josh had not tried to contact Douglas assuming he would be on Kaeta over the weekend and so he was surprised when he saw him alight from the boat with the morning shift. He hurried across the pier and caught Douglas' attention.

'Got to be quick I need to get on that boat,' he told Douglas as the last passengers climbed on to the pier. 'I have been rumbled and warned to get out, but I was right about how the drugs come in,' and seeing the crew begin to push the boat away from the pier he indicated he wanted to board, 'watch out for the gardener they call Saws,' he called to Douglas as he jumped aboard. He heard Douglas shout back, 'Write down what you got, I will get it to Joelle.'

CHAPTER 26. MARTIN PLEASANCE

Douglas was not thinking when he told Josh to write a report and that he would get it to Joelle. Walking back to his bedroom that morning he debated how to do that as, apparently, Joelle no longer wanted anything to do with him, then after further thought he considered it would be a good opportunity to at least talk with her again. Time might have softened her attitude.

He spent most of that Saturday and the following Sunday supervising the clearing up of the resort after the storm. They had to close the beach bar, it lost part of its roof in the wind and had been flooded by the rain and they had also lost their telephone connection. Apart from that most of the damage was superficial, a bit of water damage here and there and a lot of debris to be cleared from the gardens and beaches.

To his intense irritation, Martin Pleasance did not put in appearance over the whole weekend, a grumble he laid upon Eva when she arrived for work the following Monday morning.

'Now you come to mention it, I have not seen him for over a week,' Eva commented. 'I did not think about it last week as we were busy with the training, but it seems a little strange. I wonder if he is ill.'

They decided they needed to visit Martin's bungalow and check. They walked across the Island together and reaching the bungalow found it to be locked and apparently deserted.

'Do we have a spare key?' Douglas asked Eva.

'I don't know, I suppose we might have.'

An hour later Douglas returned alone, Eva did not come, she needed to cover reception and, also there was a lot of data to be input to the new system before it went live the next weekend. He opened the door and immediately an unpleasant smell hit him. He looked in the kitchen and saw the remains of a meal on the worktop, covered in flies and maggots. The source of the smell he concluded as he threw it into a waste bin. He searched round the house and found it strangely deserted. There were certainly signs Martin had lived there but all his clothes and personal possessions were gone. It was then that Douglas saw the letter lying on a coffee table addressed to him.

It was from Martin and was short and to the point, explaining that Martin felt his job had been usurped and he had no interest in working with the new system so had decided to move on. Please consider this my letter of resignation, he wrote.

Douglas pocketed the letter, swore that Martin had not even tried to work with the new system, locked up the cottage and walked back to the resort buildings.

He showed the letter to Eva, who frowned as she read it, 'either he was drunk when he wrote this or it is not his hand writing,' she declared.

Douglas looked at the note again, 'how do you know?'

'I spent a week going through his hand-written orders. This writing is spidery and child-like, Martin's was much firmer and educated looking.'

'He was probably drunk, I had my suspicions about the man all along.' Douglas said, annoyed that, along with everything else, he was now going to have to pick up the Managers responsibilities and then find a replacement.

He and Eva spent the rest of the morning re-organising duties. Eva showed the new receptionist how to load data into the system and then she and Douglas divided the Resort Managers duties between them.

It was mid-afternoon before Douglas was free again and he was cursing with frustration. He had telephone calls to make and the land line was still down and mobile signal on the Island non-existent.

'Sometimes you get a mobile signal if you walk

up the hill, or why don't you just take the hotel motor boat over to Kaeta and phone from there,' Eva suggested, calming him down. He took the boat and it took him ten minutes to drive the MGB up to Alice Hill where the mobile signal was strong. His first call was to the Kaeta telephone Company to report the fault on Moth Island's land lines. They promised to get an engineer out as soon as possible, 'but we are very busy so it may be a couple of days,' he was told. The best promise he could extract was that someone would attend the problem as a matter of urgency. He frowned irritably, urgency generally did not feature in the Kaetian culture.

His next telephone call was to Janice Milicent, the Resort Company's People Manager to tell her that Martin Pleasance had left and ask if there was anyone available on a temporary basis and find out how he could recruit a replacement. She assured him she would do what she could do.

His final telephone call was to David Evans of Benson's Solicitors to find out what was going on between Ralph and Joelle. David confirmed that Joelle had engaged him to defend a legal action launched by Ralph claiming he had been blackmailed into relinquishing any claim he might have had on Joelle's assets when they divorced and that Douglas was involved as Ralph was claiming that he had delivered the blackmail message. Ralph claims to have a letter from Joelle offering him a substantial amount of money as part of a divorce settlement and we have been instructed to hand over the first draft of the divorce agreement which does includes a substantial financial settlement.

Douglas explained that he Joelle had separated and that he did not see how he could help.

'Your relationship now is immaterial, we need copies of any letters, emails or any other documentation you may have relating to your dealings with Ralph Holdswick,' David explained.

'I don't think I have anything, and if I had its probably been destroyed anyway,' Douglas told him.

'No matter, please look anyway. What we also need from you is your witness statement setting out your relationship with Ralph and in particular the conversation you had with him where he claims you delivered the blackmail threat.'

Douglas said he would write down his recollection of the events and send David a copy.

'No sorry Douglas, it does not work like that, I am afraid we need you to attend our offices here in London so we can interview you and prepare a statement for you to sign.'

'I can't possibly spare the time to come to London,' Douglas excused himself. 'Could I not get our attorney here on Kaeta to take my statement?'

'We thought of that but David Rail is acting for Miss deNouvelas and feels any involvement with you could compromise his position,' David

Evans responded advising Douglas that as the key witness he had no alternative and if he refused to appear the court would simply subpoena him.

Douglas sighed, feeling defeated and agreed he would arrange a visit to London as soon as possible.

David concluded the conversation, 'I am afraid its is rather urgent, we have an evidence review meeting in a couple of weeks with the judge. It is a critical meeting as all Joelle's correspondence with Mr Holdswick has already been produced and his solicitors are seeking to have the letters relating to his conviction disallowed claiming they were part of the criminal case against him for which he has already been punished. We really need your version of events as it is important to our defence that those letters are presented in evidence.'

Douglas returned to Moth Island thinking that having lost his hotel manager and trying to get a new a system up and running there was no way he could afford to take time off to travel to London. Nevertheless, he wanted to do what he could to help Joelle so he decided he would write down his version of the events involving Ralph and post them to Benson's. For now, that would have to do.

However, that was not the way things worked out for him. It was Wednesday lunch time before the land line connection was restored and that

MOTH ISLAND

afternoon he received telephone call.

'Hi Douglas, I have been trying to call you for a couple of days, where have you been?' It was Dick Stump phoning him.

Douglas explained the phones had been down.

'No matter,' Dick enthused, 'We need you come over to the Glass Bay Hotel now, 'I am with our MD, we arrived this morning and I am showing him round the hotel and discussing our plans.'

'What now, immediately,' Douglas fretted.

'Yes, drop everything for a few days, this is important.'

'I can't just drop things here, now, Martin Pleasance has gone and I have no resort manager.' Douglas tried to explain.

Dick was beginning to sound irritable, 'You have that girl, Eva that you speak so highly about, leave her in charge and get over here.'

Douglas pulled a resigned face thinking that if the boss wants you to jump, you jump.

A couple of hours later he arrived at the Glass Bay Hotel and was immediately taken into the library where Dick and the MD were pouring over plans.

'I had these rough plans drawn up when I got back to Brighton,' Dick explained.

'We think we can make a go of this hotel, we build a range of accommodation chalets up the hill and along the edge of the beach, add a couple of new swimming pools, a couple of theme restaurants and bars, but here is the sweetener, we build a golf course in this area behind the beach running up past the restaurant you took me to.'

'But that land is not part of the hotel,' Douglas commented.

'Yes, it is owned by your ex. and it is critical to these plans that we buy the hotel freehold and all the land we need,' the MD spoke for the first time, 'we don't like leases, not when we are spending millions improving the facilities.'

'I see,' Douglas was quiet for a few moments before hesitantly adding, 'I don't know if she will want to sell. Her father originally built the hotel and I know it is very precious to her.'

Dick joined the conversation, 'everyone has their price, we have a valuation for the land of two to two and half million US dollars. We will offer her less than two million as starters but we have done our sums and spoken to the owner in Australia and if really pushed we would go to three million. If we own the freehold we have the liquidator by the short and curlies, he won't be able to sell the hotel to anyone else and we can save half a million by telling him we are only prepared to pay for the Bermuda hotel, we want this one for free.'

Douglas sat back in silence.

Dick looked triumphant. 'We have a meeting scheduled with Miss deNouvelas and her attorney tomorrow to make the deal, we want you there with us in case any matters requiring local knowledge come up.'

CHAPTER 27. THE MEETING

While Josh was waiting on Kaeta for his flight he tried to contact Joelle to tell her what he had discovered but when he arrived at the police station he was told she would not be available until the following Monday morning. Oh well, he thought, I tried, I will do it the Douglas way and write it up.

After Josh left Kaeta he did not get back to Miami until late on the Monday afternoon and went straight round to his girlfriend's flat. While Grace was pleased to see him she also gave him a bit of a hard time for disappearing for a couple of weeks and not telling her where he was going. To placate her he decided it would be wise to spend a couple of days with her before starting work.

When he eventually got to his office he found a stack of mail waiting and a couple of jobs that he had dropped and which, in his absence, had become urgent requiring immediate attention. It therefore was over a week before he got back to the Moth Island case, wrote out his report and emailed it to Douglas. As an after-thought he printed two paper copies of the report, one to send to Douglas with his bill, the other to send to Joelle with a short note explaining that he was sad that she and Douglas had split up and hoped they would get back together soon. He signed Joelle's note and then as an after-thought added

PS - Douglas is one of the best.

PPS- Look for someone called Pete, I think he works the bar.

He put the papers into two large envelops and threw them on his desk to post, but, unfortunately, it was some days later before he found the envelopes again and actually sent them.

At about the same time Josh unlocked his office and pushed open the door against the stack of mail piled up behind it, Joelle walked up the steps to David Rail's offices and pushed his door open announcing her presence to David's receptionist.

'The other party are already here in the meeting room, but David asked me to take you to his office first as he wants a private word,' the receptionist greeted Joelle.

'We need to agree our tactics for the meeting,' David wasted no time as Joelle joined him. 'First question is, are you willing to consider selling the land?'

Joelle looked pained, 'I have discussed it with Mary and if it is the only way to keep the hotel in business and employment for the people, then yes, for the right price, we would sell and grant a long lease on the land held in perpetuity.'

'Good,' David Rail moved on, 'I have spoken with some land agents and been advised that the freehold land the hotel is built on, alone, is worth about two million US dollars, may be a bit more. We do not want to look too anxious to sell.'

Joelle interrupted him, 'We are not anxious to sell.'

'Yes, indeed, so we first offer to lease the land and see how they react.'

They joined the group from the Holiday Resort Company in the meeting room.

Joelle's first emotion was one of surprise, quickly followed by shock, then disappointment and horror. She had spent a sleepless night wishing Douglas would be present in the meeting, but never in her dreams did she imagine him there as an adversary speaking for the buyers in the negotiation.

Douglas, of course, knew Joelle would be in the meeting so he was not surprised to see her, but nevertheless, he was uncomfortable. He knew his loyalties should be with the Holiday Resort Company but he felt for Joelle and wished he could support her. He was trying to imagine, guess even, how she was feeling but after her initial reaction her expression gave nothing away.

Dam it, he thought, she dumped me, why should I feel responsible for her.

The meeting started with polite platitudes and thanks all round for making the time to attend the meeting. Both Joelle and Douglas were silently watching each other.

Dick Stump, opened the conversation by briefly describing their plans for Glass Bay Hotel.

As Joelle listened she became interested and switched her attention from Douglas. She liked the plans Dick was presenting and could see the potential, not only for the hotel, but for Island economy as well, as he described the new jobs they would create and the opportunities for attracting more visitors to Kaeta.

David Rail responded to Dick's opening presentation by offering to discuss extending the hotels lease to include the additional ground.

'Let us be very clear why we are here today,' the MD spoke quietly but with considerable authority, 'we are not interested in leases, our plans involve significant capital expenditure and we will only commit such funds if we own the freeholds of the estate we are creating.'

Dick Stump followed up these comments, 'Tomorrow we are flying to London for more meetings with the liquidator of the two hotel businesses. It is critical to those negations that we know if the deNouvelas family will sell us the freeholds we require. We therefore expect to agree a deal today.'

MOTH ISLAND

'And if we are not in a position to agree anything today?' David Rail asked.

'The Glass Bay Hotel will not be on the agenda for our meeting with the liquidators.' Dick told him.

'So, what will happen to the Glass Bay Hotel?' Joelle asked.

Dick shrugged, 'Not my problem, but I imagine the liquidator will be unable to sell it as it is, so it will just close.'

Douglas was silent, staring at the empty pad of paper on the table in front of him throughout this exchange. He missed the pleading look for support that Joelle threw at him.

The meeting was silent for minutes while all parties considered how to move forward.

David Rail spoke first. 'This puts us in a very difficult position, I need to confer with Miss de Nouvleas,' and he and Joelle left the room.

It was over half an hour before anything happened and that which did happen came as an enormous and not entirely pleasing surprise to Douglas. One of David Rail's paralegals put her head round the door and asked to speak with Douglas privately.

'Mr Rail has instructed me to contact a group of wealthy Kaetians to enquire if they would be prepared to consider joining a consortium which would acquire the Glass Bay Hotel. The intention would be to raise enough money to enlarge the hotel and add new attractions to make it a viable business. You are one of the individuals I have been instructed to approach.'

Douglas stood in the corridor and listened with some concern before replying, 'I am sorry,' he told the woman, 'I am not in a position to even respond to that request, even telling me of such a plan puts me in an impossible position. You realise I shall have to tell my colleagues about this consortium idea.'

The woman nodded and shrugged as she thanked Douglas for listening to her.

That information resulted in a slightly acrimonious conversation between Dick and MD who was cross that Dick had been so explicit about their plans especially as they realised that if this consortium was in a position to make an offer to buy Glass Bay Hotel it would weaken their negotiating positions. The MD was for increasing their initial offer, but Dick resisted this on the grounds that they had approval from the Australian to go up to three million dollars and that gave them plenty of head room. Douglas contributed to the conversation by pointing out that Joelle would be very aware of the value of the land and would reject outright an unreasonably low offer.

It was after lunch (burgers or hot dogs brought in from a local cafe) before the meeting restarted.

Dick immediately asked if there was a consortium expressing interest in purchasing the hotel.

David Rail was non-committal, simply confirming that there were ongoing discussions to form a consortium.

Dick followed this by telling Joelle they were prepared to offer one and half million dollars.

Joelle did not even think about it, she simply said, 'No.'

The rest of the afternoon and into the evening was spent in negotiation. Joelle and David Rail proposing reasons why the offers were inadequate and Dick and his MD playing a double act and looking pained every time they increased their offer.

By seven that evening they hit an impasse. Dick saying their absolute maximum offer was two and half million and Joelle saying she had to consult with her mother and daughter before she could agree anything. They agreed to meet again briefly the following morning to see if there was any common ground.

Douglas found the whole process very uncomfortable. All afternoon he had watched Dick Stump grind Joelle down and, on more than one occasion had bitten his tongue to stop himself joining the arguments and speaking for Joelle. He had done his own calculations for the value of the land and concluded that just the freehold of the hotel and surrounding land was worth two and half million dollars based on the annual rent of the existing lease.

That night Douglas lodged in the same hotel as

Dick Stump and the MD but feigned an excuse to avoid joining them for dinner. He sat in his room uncomfortable that Joelle was being pushed into selling her land at less than he considered to be its real worth. In the end, he sent her a text explaining his basis for valuing the land and telling her that she should push for an offer of three million dollars.

When the meeting reassembled the next morning, Joelle was re-invigorated. She explained that she had spoken with her mother and daughter and they agreed that one of their priorities was that the hotel should remain open and all the existing staff retain their jobs and that if the buyers were prepared to guarantee this then she and her mother would be prepared to sell the necessary land.

Dick and the MD looked smugly across to each other thinking they had secured a deal but

Joelle soon disappointed them by adding, that her price was three million dollars.

'Impossible,' Dick spat at Joelle.

She sat back, 'take it or leave it,' she smiled, silently thanking Douglas.

Dick argued that her valuation was unreasonable as the management company was bankrupt and therefore not paying any rent, but Joelle responded to all the arguments with 'three million, that's our price, take it or leave it.'

After an hour, Dick gave up and agreed to pay three million dollars, but that was not the end of the negotiation as the MD threw in a curved ball. 'For that price, we want the Glass Bay Restaurant, the chalet bungalow and a lease on the land surrounding them.'

Douglas groaned silently, suddenly he was involved but with a foot in both sides.

Joelle and David Rail held a short, whispered conversation. David beckoned Douglas to step outside the meeting for a moment. Douglas knew what was coming and followed into the corridor.

Joelle tells me that you are a one third partner, together with her daughter and Eva in the restaurant business. Obviously, we now need the agreement of all three partners in order to comply with the terms of sale.

It was at this point David's receptionist interrupted them with a message for Joelle. Her sergeant at the police station was on the telephone urgently needing to speak to her.

CHAPTER 28. DOUGLAS DISAPPEARS

'Merv, what is it?' Joelle had stepped out of the meeting to take the call. 'We need you urgently, two bodies have been washed up in Grumble Bay.'

Joelle, her mind still in the meeting, did not immediately register what Merv had said and the mention of dead bodies made her think, Moth Island.

'No Joelle,' he told her when she queried what he had said, 'nothing to do with Moth Island these bodies are on the beach at Grumble Bay.'

'Well, what has happened to them, are they dead, how did they get there?' Joelle asked.

'I don't know, they were reported by some tourists who said they found the bodies lying on the beach. I have sent Irene with a couple of uniform constables over to secure the area, but I thought you should know.' Merv told her.

'Okay, I will finish up here and meet you at the beach as soon as I can.'

Joelle rejoined the meeting and explained she had to leave.

Dick spoke first, 'that is not a problem, we are finished now anyway. I think we have a deal, subject to Mr Jay and his partners in the restaurant business agreeing to include it in the sale.'

They had to wait a further half hour while David Rail drafted a letter of intent which was signed by Joelle and Dick Stump before they left. Dick and his MD for the Airport, Joelle to Grumble Bay and Douglas to Glass Bay to talk with Jasmine.

Joelle looked at the first body, one of a young girl, naked, and covered in grazes and cuts. Joelle noticed her eyes, dull in death but, she imagined, had once been a vivid blue colour. She thought that unusual given the girls long black hair, now tangled and matted.

'She looks as if she has been in the sea for a few days,' Joelle said reflectively. 'Do we know how she died?'

'Difficult to tell with all those cuts and grazes,' Merv answered.

'We need the pathologist, has he been called?' Joelle asked.

'On his way,' Merv confirmed.

'Where is the other body?' Joelle asked. 'Funny but I expected to find them together,' she commented as she and Merv walked the hundred meters along the beach to where the second body was covered by a blanket.

Irene pulled the blanket back and Joelle stared at the dead remains of a middle-aged man.

He was partially clothed and although his garments were tattered Joelle presumed they had protected him from the cuts and abrasions suffered by the woman. However, he had suffered some cranial damage, Joelle did not particularly want to touch him to check how much but she could tell that the back of his skull was broken.

'This one must have been in the sun more than the girl, he smells a bit high,' Merv wrinkled his nose in distaste.

'Not much we can do with these two until the pathologist has gets here and examined them.' Joelle announced throwing the blanket back over the man. 'Who found them?' She asked.

Merv pointed to a small group of people standing with Irene.

A man in a flowered shirt and swimming trunks spoke for the group. 'We are staying at an apartment in Grumble and we drove out to the bay this morning for a picnic and a day on the beach. We saw the two bodies and immediately phoned the police,' he explained.

'Did you see anything else? did you move the bodies?' Joelle asked.

'We did not touch the man, we could see he was dead, but the girl was half in the water so we pulled her out in case she was still alive.'

Joelle nodded, 'and you saw nothing else? No

MOTH ISLAND

clothes or papers or anything?'

The man just shook his head.

Joelle and Merv walked along the beach. 'Are we looking for anything in particular?' He asked.

'No, just looking but there is nothing, lots of footprints, but nothing we could link to those two.' Joelle mused. As they approached the tide line she paused, 'look at this, does it strike you as unusual,' she kicked a long line of sea weed, bits of wood, discarded plastic and other debris piled up along the beach.

'Not particularly,' Merv also kicked the jetsam, 'there is usually all this stuff along this side of the Island carried in by the current.'

'Yes, but there is much more here now than I have seen before,' Joelle took a final look, 'I wonder why?'

They let the subject drop and walked back up the beach to where Irene was holding back a small crowd of curious on-lookers.

'Has anyone here seen anything that might be connected with the two people, lying on the beach.' Joelle questioned the crowd.

'Are they dead?' A small boy asked.

'Yes,' Merv answered

'Murdered?' The boy ghoulishly asked.

'It is too early to say how they died but we treat all such incidents as suspicious until we can establish the circumstances.' Joelle stopped that conversation.

A couple of teenagers stepped forward. 'We were

on the beach the day before the storm and the bodies were not here then,' they told Joelle.

'Are you sure?' She asked.

'Yes,' one of the lads told her, 'we walked all along the tide line beach-combing through all the stuff washed up.'

She asked if anyone else had seen anything but this just got a negative murmuring and shake of heads from the crowd.

By this time an ambulance had arrived with two medical orderlies. They apologised for the pathologist; he was delayed with patients at the hospital.

'Can we recover the bodies,' they asked.

'Yes, when the photographer has finished,' Joelle answered.

She, Merv and the orderlies made their way down the beach.

'I reckon they were together, probably in a speed boat, had an accident, turned too sharply or something like that, fell overboard, the boat ran over them, that would explain the abrasions on the woman. I expect the propellor hit the man's head, that would explain his injuries,' Merv concluded.

'Maybe, but let's wait for the pathologist,' Joelle responded, 'and if your theory is true, where is the speed boat.'

'Sunk,' Merv answered, satisfied he had solved the mystery.

MOTH ISLAND

***

In the meantime, Douglas had been to see Jasmine and returned to Moth Island and was deep in conversation with Eva.

'They want the restaurant and chalet included in the land sale,' he told her. 'I spoke to Jasmine, and she spoke with Joelle and Mary about the future of the restaurant and Mary had pointed out that with the hotel enlarged and with new restaurants it might change the way the our business operates. Jasmine said she did not know whether she wanted to run it under different circumstances and, given the way things were changing would not be too unhappy to let it go.'

'And you, how do you feel?' Eva asked him.

'I am in a difficult position. Obviously, Dick and his MD expect me to persuade you and Jasmine to agree, but it's yours and Jasmine's business so I will go along with your decision.'

Eva decided she needed to talk to Jasmine.

'I have to let Dick know the position this evening,' Douglas reminded her.

Together they phoned Jasmine. Eva explained she did not mind either way, she had another job now anyway, Jasmine repeated she was not unhappy to quit, saying she might try and go back to college and do a tourism course. They concluded the call by agreeing that Douglas should phone Dick and tell him they could have the restaurant and chalet.

'Now,' Eva hung up and turning to Douglas, 'about this new system, we are nearly ready, some data left to load up and the new terminals to install and test, maintenance will help with that on Sunday, but we should be ready to go live on Monday and run in parallel for a few days while we check the new system is working.'

'That's good,' Douglas responded looking at the installation plan. 'Between us we should easily finish the preparations this weekend.'

Eva frowned and hesitantly said, 'If it's okay with you I would like to go back to the chalet this afternoon to see Jasmine. I promise I will be back in the morning and will stay all weekend if necessary.'

Douglas cursed silently, he had wanted to get on loading data and testing the new system, but, realising she had been working hard over the last few days, agreed to let her go, warning that they might have to work late into Saturday night and perhaps next week to catch up.

'If we stay late you can sleep in my room,' he invited her.

'Actually,' Eva told him, 'now Martin has gone I got housekeeping to clean the bungalow and I thought that you might use that, it's got more rooms and is lot more comfortable than your old room, and it means we can get away from the resort when we are not on duty.'

CHAPTER 29. FRIDAY AFTERNOON

Once Eva had gone, Douglas rang Dick Stump's mobile and told him the restaurant and chalet would be included in the sale.

'I will ring David Rail and get him to add an addendum to the letter of intent,' he promised.

'That's great,' Dick was pleased. 'Now, we are ready to move on, I rang the liquidators after you left this morning to confirm Monday's meeting. I told them we had secured the freehold of the Glass Bay Hotel and would be revising our offer. They asked how much we were prepared to offer and when I told them they accepted over the phone; amazing, I never expected that.'

Douglas agreed they must be very anxious to dispose of the businesses.

'Yes, well they told me they are closing Glass Bay, its losing too much money and the Bermuda hotel must also be running at a loss, we have been told they have had a lot of cancellations,' Dick explained and then. 'It works for us, it gives us three weeks to do the due diligence before the completion date. Now, I want you to lead the due diligence team, you will be working with our lawyers and accountants and one of our best resort managers.'

Douglas started to ask where the due diligence would be based but was interrupted by Dick, 'We are spending all day tomorrow with the liquidators and I want to spend the afternoon agreeing the terms for the due diligence. You need to get here for that, hire a private jet if necessary but be here by lunch time.'

'But it will cost thousands to hire a private jet,' Douglas started to remonstrate.

'Look Douglas, this deal is worth millions, we have already saved more than the cost of a jet with the purchase price we have agreed and now time is of the essence if we are to open for next year's season.'

Douglas agreed, but still rang the BA office to see if he could get a seat on a scheduled flight that night. He was offered a stand by ticket.

I had best get to the airport as soon as possible, he decided, thinking that being there in person he could better stress the urgency of the situation.

He packed a bag and made his way to the hotel pier intending to get the hotel launch to ferry him over to Kaeta but there was no launch by

MOTH ISLAND

the pier. He cursed having forgotten that this was the afternoon that the launch did the island sunset cruise for the holiday makers and would not be back until late. He checked his watch and cursed again. Then he remembered that the gardener, Richard Sawyer, sometimes used an inflatable speedboat for waterskiing. Mindful of Josh's warning he was slightly nervous of trusting Richard Sawyer, but reflected that he no choice. He found Sawyer in the garden

'Hey, Saws,' Douglas remembered the man's nickname, 'any chance you could use that speed boat of yours to ferry me over to Kaeta urgently.'

Saws looked up and smiled slyly. He had been waiting for an opportunity to talk privately to Douglas. 'Sure Boss, but we have to walk over to the Atlantic side where the inflatable is beached.'

On the way Saws, trying to be casual, started questioning Douglas. First, he asked about Martin Pleasance, 'we have been looking for him. I wondered if you knew where he was.'

'He has left, resigned,' Douglas said briefly, not really concentrating on the conversation. Saws persisted, 'Did he speak with you before he left?' He asked.

'Yes, he did, something about not wanting to be drawn into a murder,' Douglas replied, his mind not on the conversation.

They walked on in silence for a few paces before Saws commented to Douglas. 'Of course, you know the inflatable speed boat we use.'

Douglas looked surprised, 'I don't think so,' he replied.

'Yes, you must remember, you and that new gardener were having a good look at it only a few days ago, the same day you had a barbecue together up on the headland. Was he a friend?'

Douglas was alarmed, he had no idea he had been seen with Josh and now Josh's warning really was ringing in his ears.

They approached the inflatable in silence, Saws thoughtful, Douglas looking worried.

It was just after lunch and Eva was sitting with Jasmine in an empty restaurant. 'Are you okay with losing this. I thought Douglas was a bit pushy earlier forcing us into a quick decision.'

'He came to see me and talked about it earlier,' Jasmine was philosophical, 'and yes, I am okay with it. It was fun when we were busy, but with the problems at the hotel and with our covers down so much I don't see how we can make it work anymore.'

'We could be okay once the hotel re-opens.' Eva speculated.

'I don't think that is how it will work,' Jasmine explained. 'Mum says the deal is conditional on them buying all the freeholds, with the restaurant thrown in, and if they don't buy the hotel she thinks it will close. Apparently she tried to organise a consortium to buy the hotel and

keep it going but no one would commit, so.....'
Jasmine pulled a miserable face as her explanation trailed off.

Eva took Jasmine's hand to comfort her, 'Never mind love, we can find something else. Tell you what, when this is all over you could come over to Moth Island and stay with me. Now the resort manager's bungalow is empty Douglas has told me I can use it whenever I need it. I am sure he would not mind if we used it, at least until a new resort manager starts.

Jasmine squeezed Eva's hand in thanks for the offer, 'I'd like that,' she said and then after some thought added, 'why don't we close the restaurant now, why wait, I have been told the hotel is closing soon anyway, and it's not much fun now you are not here.'

'Good plan,' Eva agreed, 'We could put up a notice, closing at the end of next week, clear the chalet, and go to Moth Island and think what to do next. I will ring Douglas now and clear it with him.'

Unfortunately, Eva realised in her haste to get the lunch time boat to Kaeta she had left her iPhone on Moth Island.

That same Friday afternoon Joelle drove up to the hospital mortuary to find the pathologist and see what he could tell her about the two bodies that had been recovered from the beach. When she did eventually find him, he was not in the best of moods and bluntly told her to go away, 'I am dealing with the living at the moment, come back on Monday, I might have had time to look at your bodies by then.' He gave her a withering look when she reminded him it was an urgent police investigation.

She decided to come back on Monday.

Joelle returned to her car and with some relief decided she had had enough that week and she was going to go home take the weekend off. She was picking Andrea up at the airport on the Saturday afternoon and she was planning to spend the Sunday with her friend. She doubted she was going to get much time off the following week to entertain Andrea.

Actually, she did not go straight home, she drove out to Carib Point on the northern side of the Island. It was a desolate wind swept headland and suited her bleak mood. She sat on the bench overlooking the Atlantic watching the rollers crash on to the base of the cliff throwing white spume high up the rocky face.

She remembered the occasion when she first met Douglas some years ago when she had driven him on an Island tour. She was supposed to have been gathering evidence to prove he was a drug courier but had fallen in love with him instead. She smiled at the memory, and realised how much she missed him and wondered what he was doing now.

'On Moth Island with that bitch Eva,' she

scowled.

With thoughts of Moth Island and drugs foremost in her mind she pondered on the current cases. Four unidentified bodies recovered in as many weeks. That's one of a hell coincidence, such accidents were virtually unheard of on Kaeta. Maybe three of them could be explained by boating accidents, but the young man found by the scuba divers, that looked very suspicious. The missing girl, Sophia, how could she disappear so completely without any clue as to what had happened to her. At least, she thought, I have some leads on the drug case and she frowned trying to decide when she should bring Dooley in for questioning. I must send Irene to Moth Island next week and see if Josh has turned up anything she decided. She thought it curious that the supply of drugs to tourists seems to have dried up now, we arrested those men approaching the tourists, but we never found the man we believe was the dealer.

She sat for some time with these thoughts rolling round in her head wondering if she had lost her touch. In the past, some inspirational thought would lead her to a new line of enquiry, but at the moment she could see no way forward.

She also wondered if the purchase of Glass Bay was going ahead. She was pretty sure Jasmine would agree to let the restaurant go and Douglas was clearly on side with the purchaser. It's that bitch Eva who could mess things up, she thought nastily.

She began to feel cold, there was no warmth in the sun which had now dropped beneath the hills behind her and the breeze blowing off the sea, which had been pleasantly cooling when she sat down was now quite cold. Reluctantly she went home to a house that felt empty with no Jasmine or Douglas anymore. She was looking forward to Andrea arriving.

CHAPTER 30. MONDAY

'Don't worry love, it is only Monday, we have the rest of the week to do something, I need a rest today and I am quite happy lying in garden sun bathing and relaxing,' Andrea assured Joelle. 'I might walk down and see the girls in the restaurant this afternoon.'

'Tell you what, I will meet you in the restaurant after work, we can have a few drinks and perhaps eat there,' Joelle suggested to Andrea. 'I need to see Jasmine anyway and find out if they decided to let the restaurant go.'

In fact, Joelle found out about the sale rather sooner than that evening. She had only just got to work when she received a phone call from David Rail asking her to come to his offices as soon as she could as the sale, including the restaurant had been agreed and she needed to sign the letter of intent.

She told him she would stop by later that morning on her way to the hospital where, when she arrived she found the pathologist sitting in his little office in front of a computer screen. He apologised if he was rude to her on the previous occasion explaining there had been a bit of an emergency on one of the wards that afternoon.

'Just finishing my report for you, but let's walk down and I will show you what I have found', he invited Joelle.

They looked at the girl first and he explained that she had been in the water for about a week. 'She was alive she went in and would have drowned, her lungs were full of water, but not before she injured herself causing these scrapes and abrasions on her body. My guess is that she was swimming and was washed up against some rocks, the most severe injuries are on her chest, stomach and legs, see here,' he turned her hands over and Joelle saw that the skin had been stripped off her palms, 'she must have tried to push herself of the rocks.'

The pathologist produced a small glass phial at the bottom of which were some tiny fragments of rock. 'If you can identify where these pieces of rock and coral came from you might be able to discover where she was swimming.'

They moved across to the second cadaver.

'Now, although the two bodies were found on the same beach at the same time I doubt there is any connection,' the pathologist pulled back the plastic sheet covering the man. That blows Merv's theory away Joelle murmured.

'What?" The pathologist asked. Joelle waved her

hand dismissively.

'From the decomposition of the organs I can tell you that this unfortunate person has been dead for longer than the girl and also, as there is no water in his lungs, he did not drown, and was almost certainly dead when he entered the water.'

Joelle looked quizzically at the pathologist and pointing to the injuries on his head, suggesting he might have fallen, perhaps from a cliff injuring his head as fell in the water, or perhaps fallen from a boat which then ran over him.

'He might well have fallen from a boat, those injuries on his head are consistent with propellor damage.' The pathologist took Joelle across to a workbench and showed her the man's clothes, 'the tears in these garments were most likely caused by the clothes snagging on an obstruction of some sort, and this mark on the seat of the trousers is a rust stain caused by the body lying against a large metal bar or hook, and,' he returned to the body turning it gently to one side, 'this mark on the buttock matches the stain. My guess is he was lying in a damp place for some days before he entered the water.'

'Can you tell me how he was killed?' Joelle asked.

'Yes, he was strangled,' the pathologist indicated an angry red mark round the man's neck, 'this mark was caused by a ligament, probably a piece of rope, being tightened round his neck breaking his larynx and choking him. The lack of bruising indicates this as the cause of death.'

Joelle stared at the man before speculating on his end, 'So he was strangled, thrown into a damp place, possibly the bottom of a boat, where the body was left for some days, before being taken out to sea and thrown overboard and then run over, perhaps to disguise the cause of death.'
'That explanation would certainly fit with the damage to the cadaver,' the pathologist agreed.
Before leaving, Joelle asked for pictures of the two bodies to be sent to the police station, but the pathologist anticipated her request and handed her an envelope.

Joelle left work early that afternoon to go and meet Andrea and when she arrived at the restaurant Andrea was already there with a large beer talking to Jasmine. In answer to Joelle's question Andrea told her she had a perfect day relaxing in the garden and then walking down to the restaurant early afternoon. 'I have had a swim, then Jasmine let me use the shower in the chalet, so here I am refreshed, agog to hear what you have been up to all day.'
Joelle told her about the two bodies and produced a couple of posters titled 'Can You Identify this Person'.
'The girl looks normal, but what has happened to the bloke?' Andrea squinted at the picture.
'We had to photo shop it to cover up the injuries,' Joelle explained as she asked Jasmine if she could display the posters. 'I want these put up

MOTH ISLAND

all round the Island, someone must know these people.'

This caused Jasmine to explain that not enough people were coming to the restaurant now and in view of the forthcoming sale she and Eva had decided to permanently close early.

Andrea asked where Eva had gone, Jasmine told her Eva was on Moth Island which earned a sour look from Joelle. Nothing more was said.

Eva was indeed on Moth Island and was not enjoying herself. She had had a stressful weekend and was now a worried young lady.

As promised, she had returned to Moth Island on Saturday morning after spending Friday night with Jasmine. At first, she had not been concerned that Douglas had not appeared and had started work in reception and looked at the data still to load onto the new system. Saturday however was the main change over day for guests so she and the assistant receptionist had been kept busy all day processing the departing guests and the new arrivals. She took a break at lunch time and went to look for Douglas but could not find him and by evening she was seriously wondering where he had gone. No one knew, he just seemed to have disappeared.

On Sunday things got even worse, Eva expected Douglas to reappear, but there was no sign of him. She was also on her own working reception all day, it was the assistant's day off, and the duty manager had refused to help her saying he was responsible for the guests and administration was not his problem. The new system went live on Saturday night, and although she had sat up till midnight preparing for the event she had still not got all the set up finished.

By Monday she was panicking, still no Douglas and now she was struggling on her own with the old system and in parallel trying to get the new system working. In the end, she decided to concentrate on keeping the old system up and running, at least that way the hotel admin was still working, and when Douglas reappeared they could decide how to tackle the new system.

But by Monday evening there was still no sign of Douglas and she was now worried wondering where he was.

CHAPTER 31.
JOELLE'S TRIAL

Andrea had greeted Merv and the other officers she knew from the last time she had been on secondment to the Kaetian Police. She had been introduced to Irene and was now studying the incident board in the detective's general office.

It was Wednesday morning, Joelle had taken a sneaky day off and shown Andrea round the Island, but today her sense of duty had dragged Joelle to the office.

Joelle was starting her morning briefing as the Commissioners PA walked into room and offered Joelle an A4 manilla envelope.

'This came for you yesterday,' she said.

'Put on my desk please,' Joelle asked, and turning to the assembling officers, 'Right everyone, pay attention.'

She told them of her meeting with the pathologist and explained her theory concluding that they needed to know where the bodies entered the water. 'The rock and coral samples have been DHL'd to Miami for forensic analysis. If we know the composition of those grains we may be able to identify where the girl drowned.'

She looked at the assembled officers. 'Anyone come forward to identify our bodies?'

No one said anything.

Next Joelle asked if anyone had any further leads in the drug investigation. Again, a general shaking of heads indicated no further progress.

After the briefing Andrea joined Joelle in her office.

'You certainly have some difficult investigations here, four dead bodies, all washed up, a missing person and drug dealer on the loose.' Andrea sympathised.

Joelle agreed, 'Yes, and somehow I can't believe they are all unconnected, but for the life of me I can't find any links. Apart from the last two they all appear to be connected to Moth Island somehow.'

In discussing the cases Joelle pulled out the tide and current map she had obtained and showed Andrea how the current sweeps round Moth Island possibly depositing the bodies there.

Andrea pointed to the chart, 'That current, where it sweeps in from the Atlantic, does it split there?'

'Yes,' Joelle confirmed, 'One arm eddies round Moth Island meeting the Atlantic flow round the other side of the Island and getting pushed up to

MOTH ISLAND

the beach. We think that's how the first two bodies ended up on Moth Island. The other arm,' she indicated the flow, ' moves round the south of Kaeta washing into the Caribbean Sea.'

'Umm,' Andrea mused, 'the last two bodies were found shortly after the big storm you told me about.' Joelle agreed and Andrea continued, 'Perhaps they were caught in that current and washed up on the beach by the storm.' Andrea proposed.

Joelle nodded her head, 'It's possible.'

'Yes, and if that's what happened maybe they entered the water round here somewhere,' she put her finger on the chart next to Moth Island where the current split.

The two women speculated that these last two bodies were also connected with Moth Island and Joelle concluded she needed to talk to Josh and see if he had turned up anything. She also told Andrea about Dooley and how she had not arrested him in order to avoid compromising Josh's cover.

'I have an idea, why don't I go on a day trip to Moth Island. No one knows me and I can have a good poke around.' Andrea got excited at the prospect of a bit of investigatory work.

That afternoon Joelle got a visit from the attorney defending the brutality action. He was a thin, rangy, elderly black Kaetian who worked in the Island Prosecutors office and he reminded

Mr John de Caynoth

her that the Island Magistrate was holding a review of witness statements the following morning prior to the full hearing in the afternoon.

'Do I need to come,' she asked, trying to assess the competence of the upright, grey haired lawyer with twinkly eyes and a broad smile who introduced himself as Harris.

'Not necessarily, I understand the two boys will be represented by their attorney and will not be in court,' Harris advised. She decided to go anyway.

Joelle groaned when she saw the sitting magistrate was Sir Jonah Snifflier-Smyth.

He opened the hearing pompously reminding all that this was a court of law and required only the truth be told, then turning to the attorney repressing the boys he asked if they had any new evidence to add.

'No Sir, we do not but as we only received the defendants witness statements a few days ago we request a postponement while we give them our full consideration,'

Jonah drew himself upright in his chair, ostentatiously straightening his wig and gown.

'He is actually not entitled to wear those but no one has the courage to tell him,' Harris whispered to Joelle.

'Are you able to read?' Jonah cuttingly asked the boy's attorney.

Surprised at the question the attorney agreed he could read.

MOTH ISLAND

'Well then the witness statements are quite clear, what is there to consider further?' Jonah challenged.

The attorney muttered something about due consideration being given to his presentation.

'I can assure you Sir, this court will give full consideration to whatever arguments you may put forward,' Jonah replied. 'I understand that, at your request, this case is being heard as a matter of urgency, at great inconvenience to the Island Judiciary and our Police I might add,' at this point he smiled at Joelle and Harris before addressing the boys' attorney again. 'No Sir, I see no reason to postpone this hearing. Now, I will ask you again if you have any further evidence to present.'

The attorney confirmed he had not.

Jonah posed the same question to Harris. He confirmed he had nothing further to add either.

Jonah purposely took his time shuffling the papers before him before he spoke again.

'As there is nothing apart from the statements in front of me, which I have considered in great depth, is there any objection to me passing my judgement now rather than wasting time after lunch.'

No objections were raised but the boys' attorney asked permission to speak. He started to say how undue force had been used to arrest his clients who were at the time attempting to co-operate fully.... but Jonah interrupted him in full flight.

'Yes, yes, all that is in your written statement, do you wish to add anything new?'

The attorney sat down, deflated.

Jonah continued, 'I have read all the witness statements and while the medical report indicates minor bruising to one of the alleged victims there is no proof that this bruising was a result of the arrest. Furthermore the report notes that the medical examination was carried out some time after the actual event and as the bruise appeared to be recent it is unlikely the injury occurred at the time of the arrest. The only issue therefore is the suffering of some indignity at being arrested in a public place,' Jonah paused to glare round the court.

Joelle groaned, anticipating Jonah was about to support the boys' claim.

Harris placed a cautionary hand on her arm, 'here him out, he always has to have his moment of glory,' he whispered.

Jonah saved his most intense glare for the boys' attorney and continued, 'I find the witnesses for the defence, and their statements of events, compelling. They are all agreed that one of the males ran away and was apprehended in a perfectly reasonable manner in view of his attempt to evade the arresting officer. They also note that it appeared your clients behaviour was truculent and uncooperative when confronted by Inspector deNouvelas. My conclusion is that there is therefore no case to answer. Dismissed.'

The boys' attorney stood angrily telling Jonah he could not summarily dismiss the action.

'I can and I have,' Jonah told him.

The attorney muttered about appealing but before he could walk away Jonah called him to be seated.

'Now,' he said, 'We have to consider the accusation that you clients behaved in a lewd and inappropriate way towards Inspector deNouvelas. How do you plead?'

The attorney was apoplectic, 'Your honour, this is outrageous, this hearing is about the way the Inspector treated my clients. My clients are not on trial. The accusations of sexual harassment should have been struck out.'

His Honour, Jonah shuffled his papers before replying, 'We have just decided Inspector deNouvelas treated your clients in a perfectly satisfactory way, or are you challenging my decision? In the papers before me there is no record of the sexual harassment accusation being struck out and I see no arguments supporting your present assertions, therefore it must stand.'

Harris chuckled, 'Oh dear, the application was to the US court, not us.'

The boys' attorney recovered his composure, 'my apologies your honour, I had no intention of challenging your decision, but I regret I have not had an opportunity to discuss the counter accusation with my clients and I therefore seek an adjournment.'

Jonah asked Harris if he had any objections before glaring at the unfortunate attorney.

'Very well, we will adjourn and reconvene after lunch.'

'Your honour I regret my clients are not present on Kaeta,' the attorney pleaded.

'Not here!" Jonah boomed in an aggrieved tone. 'They accuse our police of brutality and do not have the manners to appear to support their unjust accusations. I suggest, Sir, you contact them, or I will issue a warrant for their arrest.'

In the lunch break Joelle said to Harris, 'what has come over old Sniff, he is usually anti police and hates me?'

'Ah well,' Harris confided, 'it's the elections. He is standing for the police commissioner's office and after your Commissioner publicly accused him of being anti police he is trying to prove he is really your best friend. You wait for this afternoons performance.'

Indeed, it was quite a performance. The boys' attorney pleaded not guilty so Jonah read out loud the statement made by the two girls in graphic detail. Joelle cringed, now absolutely certain Merv had briefed the witnesses to make the most imaginative and lurid description of events.

The boys' attorney was invited to respond but, on behalf of his clients could only deny they had behaved in the manner described.

'Are you accusing our law-abiding citizens of perjuring themselves,' Jonah trapped him pointing out his clients had already been found guilty of a criminal offence.

To no one's surprise after the circus had ended Jonah found the two boys guilty. Joelle said she was not seeking damages so Jonah ordered that the boys make a contribution of $100 each to the Islands orphan fund and pay costs of $1000. Jonah smiled benignly from his bench and the American attorney left the court muttering about kangaroo court justice.

***

While Joelle was in court Andrea was busy on Moth Island. She had arrived with a one day excursion party and had enjoyed a complementary rum punch in the beach bar before discreetly moving to the reception where she found Eva looking harassed. Andrea knew only two well how Ralph had mistreated Eva, she had been in court when Eva gave evidence at Ralph's trial.

'I am on a mission, love. You don't know me,' Andrea whispered.

'Oh, under cover,' Eva winked conspiratorially.

'Yes, I am looking for Josh. He is working here as a gardener and handy man,' Andrea confided.

'Oh! I think he has gone, I haven't seen him around for about a week now, Douglas would know but he is not here either.'

'Where is Douglas then, I thought he was working here?' Andrea asked.

'He is, well supposed to be, but he has disappeared and I don't know where he is either,' Eva responded.

Having drawn a blank with Eva, Andrea decided to go for a walk and headed for the Casino, only to be stopped at the fence security gate.

'This is private property, can I help you,' the security guard asked. Andrea inspected him, smartly dressed in a white shirt and black trousers with police style epaulets on his shirt and leather holstered pistol resting on his hip.

'I thought this was a Casino, I came up to look round,' Andrea smiled sweetly at him.

'It's private, members only,' she was told.

She looked round and peered through the fence, 'I can't even see the buildings, can't I come in and at least have a look,' she tried charming the security man.

He surprised her by asking, 'are you looking for a job?'

Now, that is a funny question she thought, before saying, 'I might be.'

The guard gave her a look which made her feel he was mentally undressing her before replying, 'Sorry, no vacancies. Go away.'

She lurked a little longer hoping to see what was going on beyond the fence.

'Go away,' the guard repeated, unclipping his holster and resting his hand on his pistol.

At that moment, the telephone rang and he

ducked into his guard house to answer the call. Andrea took the opportunity to slip by unnoticed and quickly made off inside the perimeter fence and into the gardens where she was hidden by the bushes. She made her way round the gardens hoping to find a position where she could get a good view of the buildings. She sensed something moving silently behind her, she looked round but could see nothing, she carried on creeping carefully through the gardens using them as cover. Her senses were jangling and she looked round but again could see nothing. She stopped and listened. Nothing, but then she heard a deep throaty and very scary growl and a dog, it looked like a cross between a Rottweiler and German Shepard, emerged round a bush behind her. It approached to within three feet. Andrea, her training kicking in, froze. The dog also froze and its growl dropped a couple of decibels, which made it seem even more fierce. Andrea and dog stood eyeing each other, Andrea not daring to move. The dog handler appeared and called the dog back. Obediently it retreated backwards, watching Andrea all the time, and was placed on its leash.

She was escorted straight back to the perimeter guard house, questioned, accused of trespass, and told off, before being threatened that next time the dog would not be so restrained.

Once out of sight she sat on a rock for ten minutes to calm down and regain some composure after the incident.

Walking back to the resort she passed the greenhouses. I wonder if that's where this Dooley character hangs out, she thought, and entering she saw a skinny, grizzled man with grey hair sitting in a decrepit old arm chair at the back of the building.

'Hello,' she greeted the person, who just stared blearily at her.

Definitely spaced out she decided, I will just try the direct approach, 'I am looking for a friend, he works as a gardener round here, name of Josh.'

At this the man, she later discovered he was Dooley, became very agitated.

'What you want Josh for? He's not here anymore,'
'A friend, just looking for him to say hello,' Andrea assured Dooley.

'Girly, you let no one know you're a friend of that man. He and his friends are in big trouble, know too much,' Dooley pulled the side of his hand across his throat in a theatrical gesture before sinking back into his chair mumbling, 'you tell no one, you not even seen old Dooley.' He lay back in chair chewing something slowly.

CHAPTER 32. EVA'S LOVER

Jasmine answered the restaurant phone hoping, unrealistically, that it would be a big group booking a birthday party. It was not, it was Eva, 'I am at my wits end here, Douglas has disappeared, the duty manager is off for the day and the receptionist is on a go slow,' she complained. 'I am trying to do everything and I just can't cope.'

'Poor you,' Jasmine was sympathetic. 'You need some time off, why don't you come home tonight?'

That evening Eva, Andrea and Joelle all arrived at the restaurant within five minutes of each other. Eva and Andrea had crossed from Moth Island on the same boat but had made their separate ways across Kaeta, Eva on her motor scooter and Andrea, declining the pillion seat, by taxi. Joelle, who arrived last, had arranged to meet Andrea at the restaurant after work and she was not pleased to see Eva, that she made very clear and pointedly ignored her.

Eva feeling uncomfortable joined Jasmine in the kitchen.

'What's wrong with Joelle?' Eva asked Jasmine.

'I don't know, she has been like this ever since Douglas got the job on Moth Island.'

Eva grunted, assuming Jasmine knew Joelle and Douglas had split up.

She looked at the posters pinned up on the wall next to the bain-marie.

'I know that man,' she told Jasmine.

'Do you. You better tell Joelle then, she wants to know who he is.'

Eva took a deep breath and nervously approached Joelle and Andrea.

'Excuse me, could I have a word?' Eva asked politely, earning only a glare from Joelle.

Eva continued, 'the man in the poster, what has happened to him? I think I know who he is.'

'Well, tell me, who is he then?' Joelle queried doubting that Eva could actually identify the man.

'I think he is Martin Pleasance, the Moth Island Resort Manager. He resigned and left almost three weeks ago now,' Eva informed Joelle and then asked, 'what has happened to him?'

When Joelle told her, Eva was stunned, 'I thought that resignation letter he left looked strange,' was all she said.

Joelle asked Eva if she still had the letter and on being told that if had not been destroyed, Douglas would have it, Joelle instructed Eva, rather formally, to ask Douglas to deliver it to the police station for her attention, and did not appear particularly concerned when Eva said she did not know where Douglas had gone.

'Well see if you can find the letter and let me have it.' Joelle dismissed Eva and turned to Andrea asking about her day on Moth Island.

'Hold on Joelle, Eva has just identified one of your bodies, aren't you interested,' Andrea commented on Joelle's offhand attitude.

'She might be just saying that, she also said he wrote a letter of resignation and left the Island. Anyway after what she has done I don't really want anything to do with her.'

'Now you are being unprofessional,' Andrea admonished her and went off to find Eva and ask her about Martin Pleasance.

She returned a few minutes later, 'Eva is quite sure it is Martin Pleasance, and she says that he was very agitated while you were on the Island interviewing about the male body found by the scuba divers and it was shortly after that when he disappeared.'

Joelle thought back to that day,' Mmm,' she reflected, 'that was a bad day. I never did interview Martin Pleasance. You think there was some sort of connection?' She asked Andrea.

'I don't know but it is worth investigating. You are right about Moth Island though,' Andrea agreed with Joelle. 'I got a bad feeling about the place. That Casino, for example, why is it so heavily guarded? Those security men are more like a military force than ordinary security. It is not just the guard on the gate, I also spotted one patrolling the fence with a dog and rifle. Okay, so they have a lot of money there but they must have a safe and anyway it's on a secluded island, who would even try and break in, they would never get away.'

Joelle nodded in agreement as Andrea continued, 'I was told Josh left the Island over a week ago.....' Joelle interrupted her. 'Yes, I know.'

'Why didn't you tell me then?' Andrea asked irritably.

'I only found out today, Josh sent me a copy of the report he wrote for Douglas and I only opened this morning,' Joelle admitted. 'He said his cover was blown and he was told to leave the Island. He believed his life was in danger. He also gave the names of those on the Island be believes are involved with drug dealing. Dooley the old gardener, a maintenance man they call Saws and someone called Pete. Josh thinks he is one of the barmen. Merv is taking a team over in the morning to arrest the three of them.'

Andrea frowned reflecting on her visit, 'I found the one called Dooley, he was out of his head, chewing hash I suspect. He rambled on about bad men being after Josh and his friends because they knew too much,' Andrea told Joelle. She paused in thought, 'I imagine Josh does not scare

MOTH ISLAND

easily so if he left under a threat it must have been pretty serious. What was it he knew, and did Martin Pleasance know the same thing and that is why he was he was killed.'

'Dooley warned Josh and his friends because they knew too much?' Joelle queried.

'That's what he said,' Andrea confirmed. 'Was Martin Pleasance a friend of Josh's?'

I would not have thought so, but does not affect what they might have known,' Joelle replied.

Jasmine appeared joining Joelle and Andrea interrupting the police talk. 'Are you going to eat here tonight?' She asked. The two women looked at each other and agreed that would be nice.

'Good,' Jasmine looked pleased, 'I will close the restaurant and we will join you.'

'We can have a party,' Andrea announced, Joelle scowled but said nothing.

Jasmine appeared not to notice as she told her Mother and Andrea that it would be a celebration of the Glass Bay Restaurant closing. 'Eva and I have decided tonight will be our last night. Now the sale is agreed we are closing permanently and I am going over to Moth Island to help Eva as she is on her own over there.'

'Jasmine,' Joelle looked miserable, 'the three of you have a nice meal together, I am not hungry I think I will just go back to Windrush.'

'Oh, mother, don't spoil things, just join us, we can have fun, you have been so miserable since

Mr John de Caynoth

Douglas started at Moth Island, what's wrong,' Jasmine gave her mother a puzzled look.

'You better tell her,' Andrea prompted.

'Tell me what?' Jasmine asked.

'Douglas and I have split up,' Joelle whispered her small tear forming in the corner of her eye.

'Why,' Jasmine simply asked.

No one spoke and Eva sensing a private family moment retreated silently into the kitchen.

It was Andrea, brash as ever, who broke the silence, 'Joelle thinks Douglas and Eva are having an affair,' she announced.

Jasmine was speechless. First her jaw dropped open, her expressions moved quickly through shock, horror, surprise to disbelief, then she whispered, 'Eva and Douglas having an affair,' before she burst out laughing.

What are you laughing at, it's not funny,' Joelle told her in an aggrieved voice.

'Oh, mother it's hilarious,' she said trying to suppress her giggles, 'for a police woman you are remarkably short sighted sometimes.'

She turned towards Eva, hiding at the back of the kitchen and called her out.

She affectionately put her arm round Eva and said to her mother, 'Eva has got a lover, it's Eva and I who are having the affair.'

CHAPTER 33. DINNER

The next day Joelle was sitting in her office trying to concentrate on unravelling what was happening on Moth Island.

She had phoned Josh that morning and spoken to him about what it was he knew that might get him killed. Josh explained how he had smoked pot with Dooley as a way of encouraging him to talk. He admitted that he found Dooley a likeable character and told Joelle that he did not believe Dooley was the main man, he was just a go between. 'It was after I asked him about the inflatable motor boat and why it had been out the night of the thunder storm that he got agitated and warned me off, so I guess it is something to do with that boat and what they are doing with it.'

Joelle asked him about the three names he had included in his report, 'Merv has gone over to arrest them, but what can you tell me about them,' she asked.

'Dooley, you know about,' Josh replied. 'Saws, it's his nick name so called because he uses the chain saw. He was one of the men who was putting the inflatable away when they returned just before the storm.'

He admitted he had not really seen the other man with Saws as he was hidden behind the inflatable and did not recognise the two men he saw walking away from the beach.

'They said something about the stuff stinking, or I could have misheard and they said sinking, and it was better than being told off by Pete, so he sounds like one of the boss men.'

When Joelle asked, he confirmed he only knew of one Pete, the barman, on Moth Island.

She pushed the note she had made during the phone call to one side and, in an effort to concentrate on the job picked up the report she had received on the rock samples. That report just told her that the grains found in the girl's abrasions were a mix of fragments from volcanic larval rock and dead coral. She was not sure how this helped, there was volcanic rock and coral outcrops all round Kaeta.

She absentmindedly tapped her pencil up and down on the desk and her thoughts turned again to Jasmine's revelation the previous evening and its implications.

Joelle was in a real quandary. She was relieved that Douglas was not having an affair. She had questioned Eva who had explained the kiss was simple friendly gesture, and that Douglas had invited her to share his room but that was when he was not using it himself and if he had been she would have slept on the floor. She assured Joelle that her relationship with Douglas had never ever been more than one of simple friendship and that Douglas had always been a perfect gentleman treating her more like a daughter than anything else.

Despite this, Joelle was still not sure how she now felt about Douglas, having convinced herself that she could not love him anymore. In her tortured mind, she had began to believe that he had rejected her and did not now love her, and the harder she thought about it the more difficult and painful it all became so now she was hesitating to meet Douglas. It had not registered with her than Eva did not know where he had gone and a little devil in her brain kept whispering that what is done is done, and leave things as they are and she would not get hurt anymore.

And then there was the revelation that Jasmine and Eva were lovers and she really did not know what to think about that. She was still coming to terms with her daughter's sexual orientation and how to deal with it, and as for Eva, Joelle shook her head in disbelief and puzzlement, she did not understand the girl at all, and that worried her as she had always thought of herself as an accurate judge of people. She was left wondering if she was a complete failure as a mother.

Fortunately, her maudlin was interrupted by Merv's arrival. 'I have Dooley, Saws, and Pete the barman down stairs in separate interview rooms,' he announced.

She dragged herself off her seat and they went to interview Dooley first.

He admitted he had marijuana for personal use and when asked where he obtained his supply told Joelle that he grew it. He denied any involvement in any drug circle and denied any recollection of the conversation with Josh saying Josh was in shock and rambling after the storm.

Saws, whose real name was Richard Sawyer, also denied any involvement with drugs and Peter the barman vocally claimed his innocence.

'Lock them up,' Joelle said in frustration. Perhaps they will be more cooperative in the morning.

Late that afternoon Andrea came to find Joelle. 'Hello love, how are you doing,' she greeted Joelle.

'Don't know, it feels like one step forward and two back,' Joelle wearily told her. 'The three arrested men are all denying any involvement with drug trading, my daughter's having an affair with another woman and I have chucked my boyfriend for no good reason. How the friggin' hell do you think I am doing!'

'It will work out,' Andrea breezily told her as she picked up the report on the rock fragments.

'Interesting,' she commented, 'traces of coral. Coral grows under the water so she must have been in the sea near rocks when she was injured before she drowned,' Andrea mused. She pulled

MOTH ISLAND

Joelle's chart showing current and tide flows out. 'Here Joelle,' she called, 'these squiggly lines indicate rocks, don't they?'

Joelle looked at the symbols and agreed.

'Well then the only underwater rocks I can see are near Moth Island. The big reef running right round the south side of the Island. Now why would she be in the water there?'

'She might have fallen overboard, or been swimming from Moth Island, but no one recognised her when I showed her picture round Moth Island so that's not likely,' Joelle told Andrea.

'And you have no reports on anyone falling overboard either.' Andrea replied.

The girls looked at each other simultaneously saying, 'Moth Island again.'

'My instinct tells me it's something going on in that Island. I am going to get another search warrant and this time I want one for the Casino as well, that is the only place we have never looked at properly.' Joelle declared.

By sheer coincidence later that afternoon Joelle got a phone call from Pietor Oys. 'Joelle my dear,' he greeted her, 'I find myself in town with a few hours to spare before I have to return to work. I was hoping you would like to join me for a late lunch this afternoon.'

Joelle looked at Andrea before replying, 'Mr Oys,' she replied, 'unfortunately I have a girlfriend staying with me at the moment...'

'No problem,' Oys interrupted, 'bring her along.'

Mr John de Caynoth

What is he like Andrea asked as they walked the short distance from the police offices to the bar and restaurant where they were meeting.

'South African, bit older than me, tall and broad, sandy blond hair and skin that's seen too much sun. Quite attractive really if you like that sort of thing.' Joelle told Andrea who gave her an old-fashioned look.

'Are you dating him then?' Andrea asked in her usual blunt manner.

'I had dinner with him once after Douglas and I split up,' Joelle replied frostily.

'Ah! I see,' Andrea replied knowingly.

'This is Andrea,' Joelle said, and nodding her head towards the man as she introduced him as 'Mr Oys.'

'Pleased to meet you Andrea, ' Oys looked Andrea up and down before taking her hand and touching his lips to the back of it. 'Call me Oys,' he invited her.

That prompted Joelle to comment, 'I assumed Oys was a family name, do you not use a given name?'

'Oys is my family name. I was in the South African army and that's where I picked it up as a nick name, I rarely use my given name,' he explained, as he gave Joelle a bear hug and enthusiastically kissed her on each cheek.

As they ate dinner Oys enquired after Joelle's drug investigation. She told him they had ar-

MOTH ISLAND

rested three suspects who were currently being held for questioning. She also took the opportunity to show him the pictures of the two people most recently found on the beach.

'We think they might have entered the water from Moth Island,' she explained, 'Do you recognise either of them,'

As Oys looked at the pictures Andrea noticed a curious expression, almost a frown of concern, flash across his face before he assumed his usual innocent boyish look.

He first picked up the picture of the man, 'I did not know him well, but this looks a bit like Martin Pleasance, the Moth Island Resort Manager, but it can't be him as I heard he resigned and left the Island.

The girl, no I am afraid I can't help you there, I have never seen her before.' He stared at the picture a little longer before saying, 'pretty girl. Perhaps she was a guest at the Resort. There can be a strong current at the far end of that beach, maybe she got caught and swept out to sea.'

'Maybe,' Joelle thanked him, 'we need to visit Moth Island again and see if anyone recognises her.'

'Good!' Oys looked pleased, 'Perhaps you would like to take lunch with me in the Casino, we have some excellent lobster at the moment. When are you coming?'

'Soon, but I shall be working,' Joelle said noncommittally.

Oys turned to Andrea, 'Of course, my dear, you are invited as well,' he smiled.
'Why Sir, I should be delighted,' Andrea replied coquettishly, 'If I have not gone home, I leave at the end of this week.'

They left the restaurant early, Oys explained he had to get back to the Casino to oversee the nights gambling.
'Why did you accept his lunch invitation,' Joelle asked Andrea irritably.
Andrea teased her, 'I thought you would pleased, you are obviously taken with him.'
'I am not!' Joelle replied indignantly, thinking of Douglas, 'I went out with him once on the rebound.'
'And are you still rebounding?' Andrea asked pointedly.
'Shut-up, I don't want to talk about it.' Joelle said crossly, still uncertain of her own feelings.

***

It was Friday morning. Joelle had left Andrea at Windrush: she had only two days left and explained she wanted to spend the day sunbathing. 'Got to go home with a proper tan,' she laughed as she waved Joelle off the work.
On Joelle's mind as she rode the Triumph motor cycle to work were two jobs for the day. First, she wanted to interview the three prisoners and get them to talk, and second, she needed to see

MOTH ISLAND

the magistrate to get another search warrant for Moth Island this time including the Casino.

Her first task did not go well. She and Merv interviewed, Dooley, Saws, and Pete again, but all three stuck rigidly to their stories.

'You know,' Joelle said to Merv, 'I am inclined to believe that Pete is telling the truth, he is too open and positive in the way he behaves, but the other two, I am sure they are hiding something.'

Merv nodded, frowning, 'I think Dooley and Saws are afraid, that is why they are not talking.'

After the interviews, Joelle spoke with Harris in the prosecutor's office and he advised that she release Pete as she had no evidence. 'Dooley, we could probably make a possession charge stick,' he thought, 'but the one you call Saws, you only have Josh's statement, you could charge him, but I don't think the Boss would prosecute.'

She told Merv who suggested that he and Irene interview the prisoners again, one last time.

Joelle agreed, she was due to see the magistrate anyway.

Sir Jonah Snifflier Smyth, the sitting magistrate that week, affected a rather false smile of welcome as Joelle entered his rooms.

My dear girl, do come in and sit down,' he beamed insincerely at her. 'I do hope we can get on now that horrid little brutality charge against you has been dealt with. A very satisfactory conclusion, don't you agree.'

Joelle mumbled, not trusting this expression of

friendship at all.

'Now,' Jonah continued, 'What can I do for you. You know I am most anxious to assist the police in every way possible.'

Joelle, reflecting that his friendliness was only because the elections for the new Commissioner were to be held soon, asked for a search warrant covering Moth Island, and specifically the Casino. On this occasion Jonah did not hesitate, he signed the warrant in front of Joelle and handed it to her inviting her to let everyone know how helpful he was being.

She got back to the Police Offices and met the present Commissioner's PA in the corridor. 'Two faced old bastard,' she muttered to the PA, 'I still won't work for him if he gets elected.'

In the general office Merv came bouncing up to her.

'We saw Dooley and Saws again,' he gleefully explained, 'I told them we were releasing them and telling everyone how helpful they had been. Dooley begged us to arrest him and admitted to supplying hash if anyone on the Island wanted some, but he still maintained he grows the marijuana himself. Saws admitted he had sold some hash to visitors and said he got it from Dooley.'

'Releasing them?' Joelle queried, 'where did that come from?'

'Well, I figured if they were frightened of something the last thing they would want would be to be released back to Moth Island. Anyway, it worked.' Merv defended his methods.

Joelle grudgingly congratulated him but remained concerned at his unorthodox interrogation techniques.

'But I think they are still not telling us everything. They are afraid of something and were desperate not to go back to the Moth Island,' Merv added.

Joelle agreed, 'You are probably right, and I don't believe Dooley is the source of the hash, he could not possibly grow enough to supply the volume we have seen here on Kaeta'

CHAPTER 34. LUNCH

'I am definitely not missing out on the chance of a lobster and a champagne lunch on my last day,' Andrea glared at Joelle who was trying to persuade her not join the small team of police going to Moth Island armed with search warrants.

'And, has it occurred to you that getting Oys relaxed over a meal could be a very good way of pumping him for information,' Andrea added.

Saturday, it was one of those sparkling Caribbean mornings, clear blue sky, turquoise blue sea, temperature building towards the high twenty degrees with a gentle breeze blowing off the sea ruffling it's surface and cooling the air just enough for comfort.

Joelle, Andrea and the small team of officers stood on the floating jetty belonging to the Keata Yacht Club waiting for the motor launch Merv had commandeered to ferry the search team over to Moth Island.

'I am on duty, how does it look if I just bunk off and have a good time,' Joelle winged.

MOTH ISLAND

'How does it look if you don't take every opportunity to find out what is going on on Moth Island. Think of it as undercover work,' Andrea retorted.

Joelle snorted but was saved from further discussion by the arrival of Merv and the motor launch.

The team split up, Merv leading one group with instructions to question every one they could find about the two latest bodies and to search the maintenance sheds, bars and Dooley's greenhouses.

Joelle, accompanied by an excited Andrea, Irene and two uniformed officers headed for the Casino.

'You lead the search team when we get in,' Joelle instructed Irene, 'Andrea and I are going to entertain Mr Oys and keep him out of your way. Last time I was here I did not have the warrant and he was very careful to only allow me to look where he wanted.'

They arrived at the perimeter gate and were confronted by the guard who drew his weapon threateningly and tried to deny them access. Joelle ignored his threats and told him they had a warrant and he would be arrested if he prevented their entry. He decided to contact Oys for instructions.

A few moments later a golf cart driven my Oys appeared. He exuded charm saying there was no need for the all the drama and Joelle and her colleagues were welcome to go where ever they wished.

Irene and her team walked to the main Casino buildings checking the grounds as they went. Joelle and Andrea joined Oys in the buggy and drove to the Casino. Joelle showed Oys the warrant but he dismissed it as unnecessary, 'you can look wherever you wish, we have nothing to hide,' he told Joelle, 'but, now, to more important business, I assume you will be joining me for lunch. I have told the cook that we wish to eat at 2.00pm. That gives you plenty of time to look round.'

Before Joelle could speak Andrea stepped in and told Oys they were looking forward to the lunch. Oys beamed with pleasure and excused himself with the excuse he had work to finish before he could relax and eat with them.

'Please ladies, go anywhere you want,' he said leaving Joelle and Andrea standing alone in the main gambling room.

'Come on Andrea, I want to walk down to that little beach and have a good look round,' Joelle pulled Andrea away from a roulette table which she was absent-mindedly spinning. She resisted, inviting Joelle to look under the table.

'There,' she pointed, 'I have seen these before, see that rod there, it operates a brake under the spinning bit. The croupier can press that panel there and slow the rotation controlling where the ball eventually settles. Neat and illegal,'

MOTH ISLAND

she grinned, demonstrating the dodgy table to Joelle.

'Leave it for the moment, Irene and her team can search the house more thoroughly than we can, I want to see the beach.' Joelle moved towards the open French doors leading out on the terrace and path down to the beach. Andrea followed, disappointed that Joelle had not shown more interest in her discovery.

Joelle stood for ages on the beach staring out across the small bay. She watched Andrea walk along the sand dipping her toes into the sea. 'This water is beautifully warm,' Andrea commented as she walked past Joelle towards the landing pier. Joelle appeared not to hear, seemingly with her attention focused on the line of breakers just beyond the headland surrounding the small bay. Andrea walked out to the end of landing pier and looked down into the crystal-clear water.

'Joelle,' she called out, 'come and look.' This prompted Joelle to give her head a slight shake apparently clearing whatever it was that she had been brooding about. She walked out along the landing stage and joined Andrea peering into the water. She was expecting Andrea had found some vital piece of evidence, but all she saw were small fish swimming round the posts supporting the pier.

'You called just to look at fish?' Joelle said disappointed.

'Yes, but aren't they pretty,' Andrea replied.

Joelle snorted and looked more carefully at the pier. She noted that the water here was deep and the sea bed rocky. She also noticed a long line of old car tyres affixed to the side of the pier as a rubbing defender against which boats could be moored.

She pointed this out to Andrea, 'They must have a large boat,' she commented.

'Or two smaller ones,' Andrea supposed.

'I remember coming here as a kid with my father.' Joelle reminisced, 'He called it the secret cove, it was impossible to get a boat in as the reef completely blocked the entrance. We walked over that headland to get here. I remember the cove was always calm, protected by the reef, but was horrible for bathing as the beach head was rocky and stoney. Dad reckoned the pirates treasure, if it ever existed, was lying at the bottom of this cove as it was on that reef that the pirates ship, the Moth, was supposed to have been wrecked.'

'How do they get a boat in now if the reef lies across the entrance?' Andrea asked.

'Apparently, they dynamited a passage through rocks,' Joelle told her. 'All the local preservationists were really up in arms about it. They also brought in tons of sand from somewhere to create that beach,' she added.

The two women sat on the pier with their legs dangling over the edge.

'You know what I am thinking, 'Joelle spoke,

'that girl, the one who drowned with all the abrasions. I wonder if she was swimming off this beach, went too far out, and got caught on that reef and drowned.'

'It's a theory, but Oys said he did not recognise her. If your theory is right she must have been a guest, or staff, here and surely Oys would have recognised her.' Andrea commented.

'Maybe,' Joelle sort of agreed, but not quite prepared to dismiss her theory yet, 'or Oys is hiding something'.

'Well you will get chance to ask him over lunch,' Andrea told her.

After a few moments Andrea added, 'If that theory is correct it would be a hell of a coincidence, given the number of unidentified bodies you have floating about.'

'Yes, it would.' Joelle lapsed back into silence.

After a while Joelle shared her thoughts with Andrea, 'What am I going to say to Douglas? I am bound to meet him when we go across to the resort this afternoon.'

'Is that what you have been brooding about?' Andrea queried.

'I guess. You know he said to me that he could not go on with our relationship with me putting things off all the time and it was best to finish things. I don't know how he is going to feel towards me now. At least, probably very cross seeing as how I treated him. I am afraid that after what I have done he might not want to ever see me again.'

'Or perhaps he loves you enough to forgive you and will be only too pleased to get you back,' Andrea said.

'I try to think how I would feel if it was the other way round and he dumped me. I would be pretty angry, under the circumstances and very hurt that he did not trust me. I certainly would not just give him a hug and say let's forget all about it.'

'No, you would sulk for days punishing him.' Andrea told Joelle. She smiled, grateful Andrea had a way of lightening her brooding moods.

'Anyway,' Andrea reminded her,' 'Eva told us Douglas had gone missing, so you might not have the problem at all this afternoon.'

A look of shock briefly flashed across Joelle's face, 'Oh, she did, didn't she, I had had forgotten that. Anyway, that was days ago, I expect he is back by now, unless he has disappeared to avoid me.' She sunk back into her misery.

'Well, its nearly lunch time, you can think what to say over a glass of champagne,' Andrea said looking at her watch. 'Come on let's go and find that hunk, Oys.'

As they walked up the path from the beach and across the manicured lawn to the terrace the first surprise for Joelle and Andrea was Irene and the two officers with her. They were sitting on the terrace around a table stacked with sandwiches, picnic delicacies, wine and beer.

MOTH ISLAND

'Irene,' looking only slightly guilty explained, 'Mr Oys had this picnic basket prepared for us, he said he had some lunch for you two inside.'

Joelle wisely decided to say nothing, she could hardly tell Irene off as she was about to indulge in a champagne lunch herself. Instead she sat down and asked Irene how the search had gone.

'Fine, well maybe not so fine, we found nothing suspicious at all. We looked in all the rooms, searched the staff rooms and store rooms like you said but found nothing, no drugs or anything.' Irene reported.

'You were quick then, you did look everywhere?' Joelle asked suspiciously.

'Yes, Mr Oys got a couple of staff members to show us around and open all the doors. They emptied cupboards and draws for us and cleared up behind us.'

'They could not have hidden anything from you?'

'No,' Irene confirmed, 'we were with them all the time and we chose where and what to look at. Actually, it's not a very big place at all. Only twelve guest rooms, kitchens and public rooms in the main house and staff housing and store rooms in that building over there. We go and search that this afternoon.'

Joelle nodded, 'Okay, but be thorough.'

'One thing though,' Irene said, 'the place seems deserted, there are no guests and very few staff here, but there is stuff in all the rooms so there must be guests somewhere.'

Joelle and Andrea went to join Oys who was standing in the open French windows listening to the conversation.

'Occasionally, we organise a boat trip round the islands for our guests,' he explained. 'Most of the staff accompany the trip to care for the guests. They take a picnic lunch with them,' he nodded towards the food Irene's search team was enjoying. 'Happily, we had some surplus food we could share.'

Oys escorted the two women into one of the side rooms. A circular dining table was laid in the middle of the room. Silver cutlery, gold rimmed fine white china and crystal champagne and wine glasses beautifully set out on a starched white table cloth set off by a simple table decoration, a crystal vase with flowers, gracing the centre of the table.

Andrea gasped with pleasure as she looked at the table, 'this is fabulous,' she thanked Oys.

'I am delighted you two ladies were able to join me,' Oys thanked Andrea in return.

With a pop, he opened the bottle of champagne standing ready in a cooler bucket.

'To cooperation,' he proposed the toast before inviting the two women to sit down.

Andrea nudged Joelle, 'look, little menu cards,' she read one, 'peppered mushrooms with a cream sauce, butternut squash soup, baby leaf salad with the chef's secret dressing, followed by

MOTH ISLAND

lobster tails and a choice of wines. How good is that!'

'I know, I can read,' Joelle responded. She was suspicious, why was Oys laying on this sumptuous table for two comparative strangers. He wants something she thought distrustfully.

Joelle was uncomfortable through the meal. She tried to question Oys but to her increasing frustration he skillfully evaded giving her any answers. In turn with equal skill she realised he was pumping them for information about the investigation. Unfortunately, Andrea, enjoying herself and with too many glasses of wine, was becoming a little indiscreet, twice Joelle had to kick her under the table to stop her saying too much. Joelle tried to caution her to ease back on the wine but rather tetchily she told Joelle she was not on duty and was enjoying herself.

Towards the end of the meal Joelle produced pictures of all four dead and the missing girl Sofia.

Oys appeared to study them carefully, 'I wish I could help you, but the only one I recognise is the man there. I am ninety nine percent sure he is Martin Pleasance, but I have no idea how he got himself killed.'

Joelle tapped the picture of the girl with the abrasions and explained her theory that she had swum off the Casino beach and the injuries were caused when she got into trouble over the reef.

Oys nodded in agreement, 'That is certainly possible, but I do not recognise her, she is, was, not a guest and never worked here.'

'How could she have got on to your beach then?' Joelle asked.

'Quite possibly she slipped in through the front gate and made her way down to the beach without being noticed,' Oys explained, giving Andrea a meaningful look.

Joelle shrugged, frustrated at getting no further forward.

The meal finished and coffee served. Oys dragged his chair back and said to Joelle, 'My dear, now we have finished there is a small matter of business I need to discuss with you. Come with me.'

Joelle and Andrea left the table.

Oys looked at Andrea, 'No need for you to join us my dear, you are on holiday. Why don't you take one of the loungers in the garden and relax while I show Joelle something she will find interesting.'

As they walked out through the games room Joelle paused, 'Thank you Mr Oys for that delicious lunch, but there is something I must report to the Kaeta gaming authority. We noticed you have some roulette tables that have been tampered with.' I am sorry to be churlish after you have been so helpful and kind but it is my duty to report it.

Oys looked horrified, but quickly recovered and started laughing.

'I don't think you should do that,' he said to

Joelle.

CHAPTER 35. OYS

'Merv,' Joelle found him with his search team going through the staff rooms of the resort complex. 'How is the search going?' She asked

'Nearly finished,' he replied looking tired. 'We have looked everywhere but found nothing.'

The day was moving on and it was late afternoon by the time Joelle caught up with Merv.

'Leave that now and get up to the Casino,' she told him. 'Their perimeter fence is covered by a CCTV system and they have just shown me a recording of Saws. He can just be seen walking up the path and disappearing empty handed into the undergrowth, emerging a few minutes later with a package in his hand.'

'Did he know, how did they find that?' Merv responded.

Joelle continued, 'Oys the manager showed me. He heard we had made some arrests and says he put two and two together thinking it might be helpful. He also showed me an old electrical relay box installed when the Casino buildings

MOTH ISLAND

used the Island electrical supply, it not used now as the Casino has its own generator, but it is right in the bushes where Saws disappeared and its clearly been used for storage recently.'

'Used as drop box for the drugs?' Merv speculated.

'That's my guess,' Joelle replied, get up there and see what you can find in the box and collect a copy of the CCTV pictures. Oys said they would download the relevant recordings for us.'

The next person Joelle saw as she walked back to the resort reception buildings was Andrea strolling down the path towards her.

'Hello love, I have had the best afternoon ever, waited on hand and foot, drinking Champagne by the bucket full.' Andrea greeted her.

'Don't you love me,' Joelle responded angrily, 'I've never been so embarrassed before.'

Andrea looked crestfallen, 'I'm sorry, but I did not know you were going to formally caution him.'

'Well, what did you expect me to do, you told me they were using dodgy roulette tables.' Joelle accused her

Andrea defended herself, 'You should have checked before you waded in.'

'When Oys started laughing and showed us the big bold brass plate on the front of that table, *museum piece, not to be used for gambling*, I have never been so embarrassed before,' Joelle fumed.

'I have said I am sorry, anyway no harm was

done. Oys thought it was funny.' Andrea tried to console the angry Joelle.

'By the way,' Andrea tried to change the subject, 'Did you notice Oys full name. It was on the license board over the front door.'

'No,' said Joelle still fuming.

'Pietor Jan Oys,' Andrea told her, 'Interesting, don't you think?'

Joelle did not think, she stalked off, still angry.

As she walked back to the reception she calmed herself down. She was due to meet the team there for a debrief before returning to Kaeta. Her thoughts turned to Douglas, she had spent most of the day in the Casino and had yet not seen him. She still did not know what she was going to say to him but knew it would get harder the longer she left it.

However, the first person she saw as she neared the reception building was Eva. Joelle felt uncomfortable but she knew she had to face Eva as well.

'Hello Eva,' she said, 'I think I owe you an apology.'

Eva regarded her with a quizzical look which made Joelle feel even more uncomfortable.

'Douglas,' Joelle muttered. ' Well, you and Douglas, I got it completely wrong and perhaps was not very nice to you, I am sorry.'

She was not sure how she expected Eva to react, probably angry or critical and was surprised when Eva simply thanked her.

MOTH ISLAND

The reception telephone started ringing, 'Excuse me, I must answer that,' Eva excused herself. She turned to walk away but then turned back to Joelle,

'I think you should speak to Jasmine. You know that she looks upon Douglas as a father and is very upset at what has happened,' and with that she went to answer the phone.

'Hello, Moth Island resort, how may I help you?' Eva said on picking up the hand piece, but she greeted by a continuous buzzing. They will phone back if it is urgent she thought replacing the hand set thinking no more about the call.

***

'What did you mean yesterday when you said Oys's full name was interesting?' Joelle asked Andrea as she drove her to the airport on Sunday afternoon.

Joelle and Andrea were now friends again. Joelle had got over her irritation at the roulette table incident, had apologised to Andrea and to make up they sat on terrace at Windrush after they got back from Moth Island the previous day. They opened a bottle of wine, drank it, and opened another bottle. The more wine she drank the more Joelle bored Andrea telling her about Douglas, how they used to sit on the terrace and talk for hours and how much missed him now.

Andrea listened patiently letting Joelle get it off her chest until she had had enough, 'For God's sake Joelle, ring him up, tell him you love him and want him back.'

'I don't know where he is. Eva says he has disappeared and no one has heard from him' Joelle told Andrea tearfully.

It was midnight before Andrea persuaded her to make the call, but Douglas phone was switched off. In the car on the way to the airport, Joelle repeated her question. 'What about Oys's name?'

'Pietor Jan Oys, don't you see?' Andrea told her.

'See what?'

'Joelle, you really have to make up with Douglas, you are losing the plot at the moment. What has happened to the old deNouvelas intuition.' Andrea chastised her but explained,

'Josh referred to the two men he saw walking up the beach naming a man, he assumed they meant Pete. Suppose those men were not talking about Pete, the bar man, but PIET,' Andrea spelt the name out.

'Do you really think those men could have been referring to Oys,' Joelle puzzled.

'I don't know,' Andrea thought, then said, 'but I can't help wondering why he is being so friendly and helpful all the time. I mean that lunch he gave us. It really was a bit over the top considering we are strangers that he has only met once before. No, I think he is up to something but I don't know what. You just watch your step with him.'

CHAPTER 36. THE CASINO

Monday morning and Joelle was sitting in her office thinking about Pietor Oys. She decided to speak to Josh to confirm what he actually heard.

'Yes,' he told her, 'they definitely said something like, it's better than crossing Pete.'

'Did you know they meant Pete the bar man. Did you find anything else that would implicate him,' questioned Joelle.

'No, nothing else. I assumed they meant the barman because he was the only one on the Island I knew as Pete. I suppose they could have meant Piet, spelt PIET. They were not that specific at the time.'

Joelle thanked Josh and finished the call still puzzling over Pietor Oys. She thought about Andrea's comment and warning and Joelle guessed why he was being so friendly, she had probably given him a little too much encouragement after she and Douglas had split. He had already told her he wanted to take her to dinner again as soon as she had a free evening. He is polite and just pushy enough to let me know he is interested in me, and she had to admit, handsome in a rugged sort of way, but then, she considered, there is a hint of danger about him, and I can bet I know what he is after Joelle thought cynically.

At this point, Douglas crashed into her thought again and she immediately felt guilty, but then thought, *if he won't have me back, what then?*

'Only one thing for it,' she said out loud to an empty office, 'I will have to go and interview Mr Pietor Oys again.'

'Merv,' she called her sergeant, 'have we got any results from that electric box yet?'

'No Ma'am, they are working on them now, promised for later today.'

***

'Jasmine,' Joelle was surprised to see her daughter at the reception desk on Moth Island. 'What are you doing here?'

'Helping Eva out, she is effectively resort manager while Douglas is not here so I am helping cover reception, keeping the customer accounts up to date, invoices, that sort of thing.' Jasmine reminded her mother. 'Actually, I am quite enjoying it, now the restaurant has closed, it's a change from cooking all the time.'

Joelle nodded, not sure she was entirely happy

with Jasmine working on Moth Island in view of her suspicions that something was going on. She settled for just warning her daughter to be careful, and in answer to Jasmine's question, 'what are you doing here?' she replied that she needed to check some details up at the Casino.

'Oh, you will probably meet Eva then, she is at the Casino at the moment, sorting out food purchase invoices for lobsters apparently,' Jasmine winked knowingly at her mother.

As Joelle and Merv walked up to the Casino they met Eva walking down. They stopped for a brief conversation.

Merv looked at Eva, 'You have a bounce in your step today young lady, have you come into money?' He joked.

'Sort of, but not quite,' Eva replied, 'Mr Oys has offered me a job, more money and a clothing allowance.'

'Doing what?' Joelle asked.

'A croupier and hostess,' Eva replied and then frowned slightly, 'funny sort of interview though, he was not interested in my work experience and whether I have ever done anything like that before, he just wanted to know about my family and if anyone would miss me if I lived at the Casino. He also said he assumed I would be looking for somewhere new to live now I have fallen out with you over Douglas.'

Now it was Joelle's turn to frown, 'How on earth does he think he knows you and I have fallen

Mr John de Caynoth

out? I have only told him Douglas and I had separated.' She shook her head dismissing the puzzle and asked Eva if she was going to take the job.
'No, I told him I would think about it, I have enough on my plate at the hotel at the moment.'

As usual Joelle and Merv were challenged by the guard on the gate to the Casino compound. They were asked if they had an appointment to which they replied, 'No.'
'Wait here,' they were instructed while the guard phoned down to the main house.
A few moment later a golf buggy appeared driven by a fierce looking middle aged woman. Joelle had not seen the woman before and found herself staring at the prominent mole on her chin from which long grey hairs sprouted.
'Mr Oys is very busy this morning but asks if you would not mind waiting he will see you shortly.' The woman invited them to climb into the buggy with her.
They expected to be driven down to the main house but the woman made no attempt to move the buggy.
'Is there anything wrong?' Merv asked.
'No, just waiting for Mr Oys to let me know he is free,' the woman replied.
Joelle and Merv exchanged a surprised look and the three people sat, without speaking in the buggy for fifteen minutes. Eventually a shortwave radio crackled announcing that Mr Oys

would see the visitors now.

'My dear Joelle,' Oys greeted her as ebullient as ever, 'this is a most pleasant surprise, what can I do for you today. I regret I am unable to offer you lunch as I have guests to attend to in a few minutes.'

'That is fine, we will only take a few minutes of your time,' Joelle assured him.

She told him that they had taken samples from the electric relay box, but had not been able to identify anything in those samples and asked if he knew what Saws had been retrieving.

'As you have him under arrest for drug offences I imagine he was using the box to store his drugs,' Oys told her.

'Do you have any evidence,' she asked

'No, only the CCTV of which you now have a copy,' he replied.

Merv then told him that when they examined the CCTV carefully they could just see that he was carrying the bag when he entered the undergrowth, but it was obscured as it was shielded from the camera by his body. 'When we asked him what he was doing he said he had been told the path was blocked, he cleared it and only went into the bushes for a pee.'

Oys shrugged and commented, 'he would not admit he was collecting drugs would he.'

Oys then reminded Joelle that she had specifically asked him to look out for anything strange, 'just trying to be helpful,' he said.

Mr John de Caynoth

'By the way,' he then asked, 'I know you asked Douglas to be on the lookout as well. Has he come up with anything?'

Joelle avoided a direct answer, not wanting to admit she did not know where Douglas was and moved on to a different subject by asking Oys why he used his surname rather than his given name.

He replied, now defensive, 'I told you, I picked it up in the army.'

Joelle's follow up question was, 'Do you ever use you given name, Pietor or shorten it to Piet.'

Now wary of this line of questioning he replied, 'No I never us those names, but of course, people who do not know me might call me that.'

The two detectives asked about the inflatable motor boat, but Oys just responded he did not even know there was such an inflatable on the Island.

Joelle's final request was that they would like to look at the CCTV recordings for some fifteen to twenty-one days ago. She was disappointed when Oys replied that the hard disk they used had a capacity of only about fourteen days and that, on a daily basis, the system just overwrote the oldest recordings. We have no need to keep the history he explained.

When Joelle and Merv got back to Kaeta they reviewed their interview with Oys.

'He did not like you asking about his name,' Merv

commented.

'No, he was sensitive wasn't he,' Joelle agreed beginning to believe that perhaps the two men were referring to Oys as the Piet they spoke about.

Another thing Joelle said, 'Why did that woman hold us at the entrance gate waiting for Oys to see us. Why not take us straight down the Casino? Also, did you notice it seemed deserted, there was no one about, neither staff of guests. Every time I have been there it has seemed deserted.'

Merv shrugged, 'Perhaps they are all in bed still, you did say he told you they are up most of the night gambling and go bed in the day.'

Merv was silent for a few seconds, thinking, 'suddenly finding that CCTV was a bit of a coincidence as well, it almost looked like he was trying to make sure we had evidence to support a case against Saws.' Merv reflected.

But Joelle was not listening. She was thinking about Douglas again.

CHAPTER 37. ONE STEP FORWARD

Joelle was having a frustrating week and by the end of it she felt she was taking one step forward but two backwards. She had reviewed the CCTV pictures of Saws apparently collecting something from the old electric relay box with the Kaeta's Head Prosecutor but they had concluded the CCTV added nothing to their evidence.

She had seen the Commissioner and he was pleased that arrests had been made and that the wave of illegal drugs being pushed to tourists seemed to have ceased. However, Joelle had to dissuade him from writing to the cruise ship operators telling them that the police had arrested those responsible for the sale of illegal drugs and that Kaeta was now clean again. She had to tell the Commissioner that she thought Dooley and Saws were just on the fringe of a much bigger drug scam and remind him that they had still not found the man who had controlled the pushers they had arrested.

Joelle also discussed her conviction that something was not right on Moth Island and particularly the Casino. She explained that she had no real proof of anything it was just a series of coincidences that raised her suspicions. The Commissioner agreed with her that the four deaths and missing girl Sofia appeared to be connected with Moth Island, but he cautioned her to tread carefully pointing out that the Casino was a significant contributor the Islands Tax Revenues and that they would both be very unpopular if an unnecessary police action disturbed that position.

The Commissioner did make one helpful suggestion when he asked Joelle if she had shown the identity pictures to the people they had arrested.

'Merv,' Joelle shouted as she returned to her office. 'I want you go and find those two men we arrested for peddling drugs, you remember, the ones we arrested and charged only with possession in the end. Bring them in I want to ask them some questions.'

In the mean-time she interviewed Dooley and Saws showing them the pictures of the four dead and the missing girl. Both identified Martin Pleasance, but she had expected that as they had worked for him, but they denied knowing the other four.

It was the next day when Martin brought the

younger fat boy they had arrested in to see her. Initially he was unhelpful, aggressive even claiming he done nothing wrong, he had paid his fine and been released. Joelle explained that she needed his help and showed him the five identity pictures. Three of the dead and the missing girl he said he had never seen before but he paused at the picture of the dead man found washed up on the beach in Kaeta.

Joelle studied his reaction carefully thinking she saw a flash of recognition but he just pushed the picture away saying he did not know the person. Merv accused him of lying and threatening an obstruction charge.

Joelle thumped the table and told him she was losing her patience and in the end he caved in.

'Yes,' he said, 'I think I recognise this man but if I tell you who he is I am afraid he might come after me. He threatened to kill me.'

'You need not worry about that,' Merv told him, 'he is dead, so now tell us who he is.'

'I don't know his name, but he is the man who was supplying us with the drugs we were selling that day,' the fat man admitted.

'Martin Pleasance,' Joelle and Merv looked at each other as they both uttered his name.

***

That same afternoon, back on Moth Island, the bar was quiet, most of the guests having either returned to their sun loungers for a bit more sun, or retired to their rooms for an afternoon nap.

'Pete, you okay if I slip away for a few minutes?' The assistant bar man asked not waiting for an answer.

He picked up his gardener mate and together they walked silently across Moth Island to the bungalow.

'I have just had the message, we are on for tonight,' the two men looked at each other.

'Better check the inflatable and get it ready.'

'Yea, and move it. Those two girls have moved into the bungalow. We don't want to disturb their beauty sleep!' The two men laughed.

'It's all clear at the moment, I checked, the girls are in reception,' the gardener told the barman.

They produced a key, unlocked the shed door and took a can of petrol, a rope and grappling iron, and a couple of paddles. 'For emergencies,' the gardener grinned.

The barman fuelled the outboard motor and returned the can to the shed, locking it behind him. The two men then started to drag the inflatable down to the beach, it was quite heavy and they were soon puffing with the exertion as they pulled it down the rough track.

'Now Martin has gone, we will have to find somewhere better to keep this, I am not doing this every time we need the boat.' His mate agreed.

They pulled the inflatable across the grassy area behind the beach and down the makeshift slip way. They then manoeuvred the vessel up behind a couple of sea grape bushes growing on the edge of the beach.

'Should be okay there for a few hours, it's out of sight of anyone walking along the path,' the barman commented.

The gardener jumped into the boat. He primed the outboard motor and on the third pull of the starter rope it exploded into life with a roar and much smoke. He let it settle down in run for a few minutes to clear the smoke before announcing that it should be okay and stopping it, replacing its cover.

After a final look round the two men walked back across the Island to resume their day time jobs.

CHAPTER 38. RALPH'S CLAIM

By the Friday evening Joelle was sitting at home, in the kitchen with Mary. She was only half listening to Mary who was babbling on about how quiet it was in the house now Douglas, Jasmine and Eva had gone.

'You know, I really miss Jasmine,' Mary was saying. 'I know she is grown up now but she's still my little girl. It was not too bad when she was down on the beach in the restaurant. I could pop down and see her, but now she is on that funny little island, well she could be a million miles away.'

Joelle mumbled an appropriate response and turned the letter in hand over again. It had arrived that morning from London and she could see it was from the solicitors handling her defence of Ralph's claim.

Mary prattled on, 'I don't know why she had to go with Eva. She is a nice girl that Eva, but it is like she and Jasmine are joined at the hip these days. Where one goes the other follows.'

Mary gave a big sigh. 'Are you even listening to me Joelle,' she demanded, jerking Joelle's attention away from the envelope.

'Yes mother, Joelle and Eva are joined at the hip. I expect it is just a teenage thing; Jasmine will grow out of it.' Joelle had not told Mary that Jasmine and Eva were lovers. She could hardly come to terms with it herself and she knew Mary would never understand it. Mary was very old fashioned like that, men were men, women had their place, and anything in between was at best rather strange, definitely to be discouraged.

'That's as maybe,' Mary was warming to the subject, 'but neither of those two girls are teenagers any more. They should have grown out of girly crushes by now. If you ask me it's not right, you should say something Joelle. If Douglas was here I am sure he would agree.'

That was too much for Joelle, 'Mary, Douglas is not here and you don't know what you are talking about.'

As Mary smarted from the rebuke Joelle turned the letter over one last time and taking a knife from the drawer neatly slit the envelope open. She still hesitated to extract the letter, she was really not sure she could cope with Ralph's demands and another trial alongside everything else that seemed to be going wrong in her life.

'Are you going to read that letter, or just stare at it,' Mary prompted.

Joelle read the letter, and then looking very serious she read it again more slowly.

'What does it say?' Mary was impatient to know. Joelle waved her hand to silence her mother as she finished reading.

'It says that in the recent evidential review the judge ruled that all the correspondence between Ralph and I, and the statement made by Douglas about his discussions with Ralph prior to the criminal trial, are relevant to the defence and may be submitted as evidence in any court action.'

'Is that good?' Mary asked.

'Yes, listen,' Joelle replied. 'It goes on the say that Ralph's solicitor has reviewed all the evidence and has concluded that his application for legal aid, on the grounds of abuse and blackmail, is unlikely to be granted, and that his case has less than a fifty percent chance of succeeding. Ralph has indicated he is unable to fund legal costs from his own resources and has agreed that if the parties agree to pay their legal costs to date he will not pursue any further claims.'

Mary looked puzzled.

'It means I am off the hook, there will be no court hearing,' Joelle explained to Mary.

'Mind you, I do not expect Ralph has gone away, you wait, I will get another begging letter from him soon,' she concluded, happy the court action was finished but philosophical about Ralph.

Her improved mood lasted over the weekend and she went into work on the Monday morning in a good frame of mind. Merv sensing her improved temper took the opportunity to catch her in her office for a chat.

'I have been thinking over the weekend,' he started. 'I think we could put this drug business to bed now. We have evidence Martin Pleasance was the dealer, and had set up a ring of people to push the drugs and now he is dead the drugs have disappeared. I think he was the ring leader who organised the whole thing and now he is gone it has all collapsed.'

He looked at Joelle expectantly.

'You might be right about him being the ringleader,' Joelle said thoughtfully, 'but there are two things that bother me. First, where did he get his drugs from and second why was he murdered and by whom.'

'Ah,' said Merv realising that perhaps it would be premature to close the investigation down too early.

'Where, then do we go now Boss? Our main lead, the white dealer we now know, but he's dead, a dead end you might say!' Merv chuckled.

Joelle suppressed a smile at Merv's humour and suggested, 'we need another look at that inflatable. It is stored outside Pleasance's bungalow and Josh's theory is that it was used to smuggle drugs on to the Island. We might be lucky and

find some clues there.'
She paused thinking, 'go and put your theory to Dooley and Saws. Tell them we know Martin Pleasance was involved and see what you can get out of them.' Again, she paused and pulled one of Irene's reports from her pile. 'Irene refers to a beach vendor, and that Danish boy we arrested, he said a beach vendor told him where to get drugs. Let's find the beach vendor and lean on him a bit and see what he knows.'
After Merv had gone Joelle got a phone call from the public desk downstairs.
'There are two women down here demanding to see you. I have told them you are busy and they should make an appointment, but they seem very upset and are insisting they need to speak to you now.'

CHAPTER 39. THE INFLATABLE

Two days previously, at half past five on Saturday afternoon, Eva logged out of the old hotel administration system breathing a sigh of relief. On the shelf behind her she placed the lever arch files into which she had systematically put all the invoices and other documents as she had entered their details on to the administration and accounting system. She rose and walked from the office to reception where Jasmine was briefing the young man who was taking over reception duties for evening shift.

'All done,' Eva said to Jasmine when she finished the hand over. 'All the books are up to date and everything is filed away, we can go home more or less on time today.'

Home that day was the manager's bungalow which Eva and Jasmine had temporarily moved into.

They went to the hotel kitchen and collected

MOTH ISLAND

some food for their supper, and a bottle of wine from the bar and linking arms walked across the Island to the bungalow.

'I have just not had time to start using this new system,' Eva was saying to Jasmine. 'It will have to wait until Douglas is back.'

'Where is Douglas?' Jasmine asked.

'I don't know,' Eva replied, 'he just disappeared and actually I am a bit worried in case something has happened to him. I am surprised he left no message. I hope he has not had an accident or something. Do you think we ought to report him as a missing person?'

'I wonder,' Jasmine mused thinking of the occasion some time ago when a previous drug investigation had turned nasty and the gang had tried to kill Joelle and threatened Douglas. She frowned, looking troubled, 'it's the sort of thing he might do,' she murmured to herself.

Eva looked questioningly.

'I expect he was very hurt when Mother dumped him,' Jasmine explained, 'I wonder if he has just disappeared on purpose, perhaps he needed space to decide what to do with life.'

They reached the bungalow. Eva stopped questioningly, looking round, 'something has changed,' she said, not immediately realising what. But Jasmine saw, 'the inflatable has gone,' she pointed to the empty space.

They looked round deciding someone must have moved it.

'Look,' Jasmine said studying the tracks in the sandy soil. 'It looks like someone has dragged it down the path to the beach.'

They followed the path and stood on the grassy picnic area in front of the beach but could not see the inflatable. Eva walked down the slipway, 'Look here, Jasmine. It's been hidden behind the bushes.'

The two girls walked up to the boat. Jasmine sniffed, 'petrol,' she exclaimed looking round the inflatable expecting to see a petrol can. Eva sniffed as well and pulled the cover off the outboard. She pointed to the petrol oozing out of the tank, 'someone has overfilled the tank,' she observed.

'I bet someone has filled it up today and the sun has warmed it up causing it to overflow,' Jasmine guessed.

'Now why would they do that and drag the inflatable down the beach and try to hide it behind the bushes,' Eva speculated.

'Because they are planning to use it tonight,' the girls said in unison.

'Shush, did you hear that?' Eva poked Jasmine as they lay in bed. 'I think someone is outside.'

They both listened and heard a voice saying that the others must have moved the inflatable.

'Did you lock the door,' Jasmine asked.

'I think so,' Eva replied.

They lay in bed hugging each other, a little

MOTH ISLAND

frightened.

'I think they have gone,' Jasmine said after a while, not hearing voices any more.

'Should we go and see what they are doing? I bet they are using the inflatable,' Eva decided.

'Don't wear white,' Jasmine whispered to Eva as they dressed.

They crept out of the bungalow and looked up at the half moon floating upside down behind them. 'That's good and bad,' Jasmine whispered, good we can see them but bad, they can see us as well.'

They crept down the path to the beach, sticking to the shadows as far a possible. As they neared the beach they heard the noise of the inflatable being dragged across the pebbles and the men giving each other instructions. They hid in the undergrowth, they could not see what the men were doing but could hear splashing noises so they guessed the inflatable was being launched. The girls dare not move in case they were seen so they just waited. The sudden noise of the outboard motor starting made them jump. They stayed hidden, tense as the motor settled into a steady tick over. They wondered what was happening but dared not move to look. Eventually they heard the motor rev and as the noise faded into the distance the girls relaxed anticipating that the inflatable was heading away out to sea.

They crept out of their hiding place and peered through the sea grape bushes. In the middle-distance they could see the phosphorous wake the propellor was churning up, clearly silhouetted lit by the pale moonlight, and the inflatable bouncing and splashing its way out to sea.

'Well, there they go then, let's go back to bed,' Eva said.

'No, they are going out to sea for something and I bet it's not fishing.' Jasmine held Eva back. She looked round the beach and then up towards the side of the beach leading up to the low headland, the same one Josh had camped on days earlier. 'Let's go up there, she proposed, pointing. 'We can see further out to sea and they won't spot us up on the headland. I want to see what they are up to.'

Eva grumbled but followed Jasmine anyway.

They perched on the headland peering out across the bay. 'I can't see anything, can you?' Eva asked.

'No, I think they are too far out and the moon has clouded over now,' Jasmine replied.

Then putting her hand on Eva's arm she pointed. 'There, did you see that, a flashing white light, right out there. I wish I had brought some binoculars'

The girls peered out to sea until their eyes began to ache as they strained to see something. They both saw the white light flashing and then a minute or so later it was repeated.

'I bet that is a signal for the inflatable and they are meeting another boat out there,' Jasmine

MOTH ISLAND

surmised now getting excited.

Eva however wanted to go back to the bungalow fearing they might be discovered but Jasmine persuaded her to remain telling her they were quite safe up on the headland and she wanted to wait for the inflatable to return. 'We need to find out what they are doing out there. Whatever it is I bet its illegal.'

They sat on the headland for over an hour waiting, then in the distance they heard the faint scream of a two-stroke engine revving hard. The light was patchy as the moon was obscured by passing clouds and at first the girls could not see the inflatable. As it neared the bay they first saw the phosphorous wake but the inflatable itself, being a dark grey colour was barely visible against the black of the sea. As it headed into the bay the inflatable became clearer and the girls could make out three men sitting down low inside the vessel with one man in the stern with the outboard. The two stroke scream suddenly silenced as the revs were cut. The wake subsided and the inflatable became nearly invisible as a cloud obscured the moon. The only sound was the gentle putting of the outboard as the inflatable slowly approached the beach.

As the vessel neared the beach the cloud cleared and in the pale moonlight the girls saw two of the men jump out nearly up to their waists in the water. The outboard was cut and lifted inboard as the two in the water pulled it up on to the beach. One man, rather more heavily built than the other two stepped nimbly from the boat without getting his feet wet. He stood to one side as one of the men ran up the beach to fetch the launch trailer. The other two pushed the inflatable out into the water enough to float it on to the trailer. Once the inflatable was clear of the water, the heavily built man stepped up and pulled a large rucksack from the boat slinging one of the straps round his shoulder.

At this point, Jasmine pulled out a camera and tried to take a picture. Unfortunately, the flash fired and one of the men, the one who was facing towards the headland exclaimed 'what was that?', pointing up to the cliff.

The girls sank into the undergrowth, 'You fool, what did you do that for?' Eva whispered.

'I wanted a picture to show Joelle,' Jasmine whispered back.

The three men, who had had their backs to the flash whirled round.

'What did you see?' The well built man asked.

'A blue flash, up there, I think there is someone watching.'

All four men stared up at the headland, and at this point the moon peeked out momentarily from behind a cloud illuminating the beach.

'That big man, the one with the rucksack, he is white!' Jasmine exclaimed, surprised.

'Shut up, or they will hear us,' Eva prodded Jasmine to quieten her.

'Someone is up there' the big white man said. 'You,' he pointed to one of the men, 'go up and look. You two pull that boat up the beach and hide it again. Then go and check if those two women are in the bungalow. I am going back to the Casino.'

'Boss, what do we do if they are not there,' the white man was asked.

'If they are not in the bungalow it will be them up there, spying on us. Find them before they get off the Island. You know what to do with them.' He pulled the rucksack up on to his back and marched off up the track to the towards the Casino.

The man who had been told to check the headland pulled an AK47 machine gun from the inflatable and started to walk through the undergrowth up towards the headland.

Jasmine and Eva clung to each other, terrified.

CHAPTER 40. TERRIFIED

Monday morning and Joelle's attention was diverted from the two women by David Rail, the attorney handling the sale of the Glass Bay Hotel.
'Joelle,' he phoned her, 'Can you come to my office. Apparently, there is a problem with the sale of the hotel and the negotiating team in London have asked for conference call to sort it out, now, this morning.'
Joelle silently cursed and told David she would join him as soon as she could get away.
'Merv,' she stopped at his desk on her way out. 'There is a couple of women downstairs asking to speak with a detective. Pop down and see what they want, I have to go out for a few minutes.'
When she arrived at David Rail's office the conference call was in full swing. She introduced herself and sat back to hear the problem.
It appeared that the purchasers were questioning the valuation the liquidators had placed on the assets of the hotel. She listened while the

MOTH ISLAND

solicitor in London leading the purchasers team said that as his client would be demolishing a number of the existing hotel buildings, including Jasmine's restaurant and the beach chalet where they intended to build a golf club house and landing pier. In addition, they would not be reusing many of the furnishings and fittings and they were maintaining those assets were of no value and they wanted a commensurate reduction in the purchase price.

'How much,' asked David Rail.

'Five hundred thousand dollars,' was the reply.

David scrabbled through his papers before responding, 'That is a very large reduction you are seeking and it is considerable more than the assets in question have been valued at.'

'Yes, indeed,' the London solicitor smoothly replied, 'the difference is due to my client's assessment of the risk attaching to their redevelopment plans due to some of the covenants they have discovered in the original deeds to some of the land holdings.'

Joelle sat silently through this exchange and it was some moments before she whispered something to David Rail. She then spoke for the first time addressing the conference call telephone on the table.

'When the price was agreed, your clients must have been aware of the risks they were taking and were certainly aware of the liquidators valuations of the business and anyway, that is of no concern to me, they are not my assets. Therefore, I see no reason why I should agree to a reduction in the purchase price of my freehold,'

As Joelle stood, David Rail announced, 'Joelle de Nouvelas is leaving the conference.'

'Wait, we must be able to negotiate an acceptable value,' the solicitor in London sounded anxious.

Joelle paused and turned.

'Was I not clear,' she stated, 'the price of my land in not negotiable. Now I have more important matters to attend to,' and she walked out.

The solicitor rejoined the main meeting with the liquidators, Dick Stump, his Managing Director. All looked at him expectantly as he sat down.

'Well,' asked Dick, 'did she agree or did you have to give some money away?'

With some trepidation the solicitor relied, 'she walked out of the meeting saying, the price was not negotiable.'

Dick was furious and muttered words to the effect that he would not be treated like that by some coconut on a pokey little Island. He turned on the solicitor and told him to talk to Joelle and make her see sense.

'No point, I told you she would not budge on the price,' he told Dick, who he did not particularly like, finding him to be ruthless and arrogant.

The MD intervened calming the atmosphere.

'Did Miss deNouvelas's attorney contribute anything useful?'

'Not really,' was the reply, 'after she left he told us that he understood she had an alternative plan for the hotel if the sale fell through.'

The MD pursed his lips decisively. 'Okay, phone her attorney and tell him the sale is on, we will pay the three million. Now,' he turned to the liquidators, 'let's get on with the rest of the negotiation.'

***

Merv was waiting for Joelle when she got back to the Police Station. He was looking very serious.

'What is the matter Merv, you look like you have just received a death threat,' Joelle asked him, feeling quite pleased with herself after the conference call.

'Those two women, you better go down and talk to them yourself,' he replied.

Joelle gasped with horror as she entered the interview room. Sat at the table in front of her she saw Jasmine and Eva.

'What on earth has happened,' she exclaimed as she looked at her daughter and her partner. Their faces were covered in grime, hair tangled, arms and legs bare, dirty, scratched and bleeding, their clothes torn and mud stained.

Jasmine and Eva took it turns to explain what they had seen on the previous Saturday night. How they discovered the inflatable, seen it pull out to sea and presumably meet another vessel, how they had seen it return and how one of the gang had retrieved a large ruck sack.

'How did you know he was white?' Joelle asked.

'It was like, more that he was not black,' Jasmine replied, Eva agreed.

Joelle nodded, not saying anything immediately, then asking, 'you said the white man recovered a rucksack from the inflatable and said he was going back to the Casino?'

'That's right,' Eva confirmed and Jasmine added, 'it was quite a big ruck sack and it looked heavy.'

Joelle frowning, thinking and concentrating, 'Did you see the rucksack before they put out to sea?'

'No,' Eva replied and Jasmine added, 'but we were hiding and could not really see what they were doing, we just heard them at that point.'

It was then Joelle noticed that both girls had rough bandages round their hands.

'We cut our hands and knees crawling through the undergrowth.'

'Go on,' Joelle instructed them and they explained that after Jasmine's camera flash had fired, one of the men had retrieved a gun and come looking for them.

'Eva suggested that we move from where we had been hiding, so we crawled along the path and hid in the undergrowth again before the man climbed up on to the headland.' Jasmine said.

'Yes, and when he got to where we had originally

hidden he started just shooting into the undergrowth,' Eva took over. 'We were terrified and crawled deeper into the scrub, scrambled down the cliff face and hid amongst the rocks. The man walked up and down the path occasionally shooting.' Eva took a deep breath obviously still very upset.

Jasmine continued, 'he gave up after an hour or so and disappeared in the direction of the Casino. From his clothes, he looked like he was one of the security men there.

Anyway, when it got light we guessed they would come back looking for us so we swam across to the beach. We stopped at the bungalow and tore up a tee shirt to bandage our hands and knees, they had started bleeding again. We dare not stay in the bungalow so we hid on the Island intending to get the early morning boat from the hotel back to Kaeta.'

Joelle had to fight to stop herself bursting into tears. 'Stop there' she said, 'I need to get you to hospital but I want to get someone in to make a note of what you are telling me.' She called up to the detectives office for Irene to join her.

Between them, they went over the girls' story again for the benefit of Irene's notes. They got to the point where the girls intended to get the early morning hotel boat back to Kaeta.

Eva feeling calmer, took over the story.

'We hid near the hotel pier waiting for the morning boat when we saw one of the Casino security men, with a gun, standing near the pier, watching. We dare not get that boat back, he would be sure to see us and after being shot at we did not know what he would do, so we crept back into the Island and hid for the day deciding to go for the evening boat hoping he would have gone. We had to keep moving during the day because there were three security men patrolling the Island, obviously looking for us.'

'We never caught the boat that evening the security guard was still there,' Jasmine took over from Eva.

'Was Douglas on the Island?' Joelle asked curiously.

'No, he was not there on the Saturday and there was no sign of him on the Sunday, I hope he is okay,' Eva replied and continued with their story of their escape.

'It was Jasmine's suggestion to steal the inflatable. We waited until about midnight and managed to launch it. It was hard work pushing that trailer across the stones so in the end we pulled the inflatable off it and down the beach. We paddled out of the cove before we started the outboard and then, praying there was enough petrol we drove it round to the dock here in the town, tied up to the coastguard's pier and walked to the police station to find you.'

Joelle sat silently as Eva finished the story in such a matter of fact way, imagining how terrified the two girls must have been, but she sneakily admitting to herself, very proud of them for their resourcefulness and courage.

It was while they were winding up the interview that Merv appeared and excused himself for interrupting.

'Thought you should know, Joelle. There are two men, standing across the road watching the police station. They have been there for a couple of hours. And by the way, the coastguard is downstairs jumping up and down because someone has tied an inflatable up to his pier and he is insisting we find the culprit and get the inflatable moved,' he grinned.

'Tell him not to touch that boat, to guard it with his life, its police evidence.' Joelle snarled.

She then put her mind to the more urgent task of getting the two girls to the hospital without the two men outside seeing them.

CHAPTER 41. GUILT

They smuggled the girls out of the back door of the Police station into a waiting police car in which Merv drove them to the hospital.

Joelle meanwhile asked to see the Commissioner.

'I need to get a proper statement from the girls when they are cleaned up and recovered, but these notes tell you all you need to know for the moment,' Joelle explained.

The Commissioner read them with an increasingly worried expression crossing his face. Dropping his usual bonhomie formality, he asked Joelle what she thought was going on.

'I think we have found the source of the drug epidemic. Josh Worthington, when he was working undercover on the Island was convinced that the inflatable was part of a drug smuggling operation. Unfortunately, he was exposed, threatened and had to leave the Island in a hurry before he could prove his theory.'

'And this well-built white man your daughter

refers to?' The Commissioner speculated, 'could he be the dealer spoken of by those men I arrested?'

'No, I don't think so. We believe that the man was Martin Pleasance, he was identified by one of those we arrested,' Joelle told the Commissioner and forestalled his next question by explaining that they had not yet got an identification for the man seen by Jasmine.

The Commissioner stroked his chin speculatively, 'You know Joelle, what is most upsetting about this whole business is the use of guns. The indiscriminate use of such weapons against two young girls. We cannot allow this to go unpunished. Those men must be caught and face justice.'

Joelle silently agreed, then thinking out loud, 'What I do not understand, Sir, is why? Why does the Casino wish to smuggle drugs and then sell them to tourists. By all accounts it is a successful business and by their own admission they are dealing with millions of dollars, why jeopardise that by engaging in relatively small time drug smuggling and selling?'

The Commissioner thought about that, 'Perhaps it is not small time, maybe that are simply a staging point for smuggling on to a final destination somewhere.'

Joelle was doubtful, 'possibly, but we have not picked up any hint that such an operation is occurring, and again if that is what they are doing why risk getting caught through some small-time racket on Kaeta.'

The Commissioner had no answers and began to shuffle in his chair clearly wishing to conclude the meeting. He asked Joelle what she was planning to do.

Without too much thought she told him 'We need to raid the Island and that Casino again and find that rucksack and its contents.'

'And how will you do that? We know they have guns and are prepared to use them.' The Commissioner stated, adding that Joelle was the only officer trained to use a gun, 'and that is only a pistol, not much use against a battery of AK47s,' he pointed out and told her that he did not want another shoot out fiasco like the one in the mountains when Merv and his cohorts were armed with machine guns.

Joelle was silent, expecting that the Commissioner had a solution. This was his way of impressing his audience, raise the apparently unsolvable problem and then offer the solution.

He did not disappoint her. 'I will speak with Colonel Macfarlane and request a platoon of men to accompany you on your raid.'

Colonel Macfarlane was a native Kaetian, a tall broad shouldered man who ran ten miles every morning. He had risen to the rank of Warrant Officer in the British Army before returning to Kaeta to take command of the military force that the President of Kaeta had set up after an unsuccessful coup which had threatened the Kaeta' stability.

'Will you also arrange the necessary warrants sir?' Joelle asked, not relishing another interview with Jonah Snifflier-Smythe.

Joelle left the Commissioner and returned to her office.

She was worrying about something but could not immediately put her finger on what it was. She started to think about the four dead people and began to speculate again if they could be connected with whatever was going on Moth Island. She pulled out a blank sheet of paper and started to make notes. So far, they had only identified one of the bodies, Martin Pleasance and he it appeared had been murdered, and presumably dumped out at sea. Unfortunate for whoever killed him, that he had been washed ashore. She wrote his name and circumstances at the head of the page. The other identification they had was for the missing woman, Sofia Luke, but no body. Joelle was now assuming she was dead somewhere, probably dumped at sea. But the connection here was Moth Island. She wrote that down. Then the young woman's body that had washed up on Kaeta with Martin Pleasance, no identification, but from the injuries she sustained it was possible she was caught on the Moth Island reef. She briefly considered if this could be the body of Sofia Luka but decided not, Sofia was blond this poor girl was a brunette. She noted down the first body found, again a young woman washed up on the beach at Moth Island. That could not be Sofia, she was still alive when that body was found. Finally, she wrote down, *young male, found by divers, injuries consistent with savaging by animals, dead before entering water.*

She stared at her sheet of paper, drew a tentative line connecting the young male with Moth Island, and started at the sheet again.

All it told her was that somehow, all the bodies she had were very likely connected to Moth Island. *But I suspected that anyway*, she cursed in frustration.

'Any problems?' Joelle asked the police officer sitting outside hospital room.

'No Ma'am, nothing.'

She knocked on the door and walked in. Jasmine and Eva were looking much cleaner and apart from bandages on their hands and knees, more or less normal sitting on their beds talking.

'How are you two?' Joelle enquired.

'Okay,' Jasmine replied, 'but they are keeping us in overnight just to make sure. We have been dosed up with antibiotics in case there is any infection from these cuts.'

Joelle sympathised and then told the girls, 'we will have to find you somewhere safe when you are discharged. There are still a couple of men watching the police station. I think we will ar-

MOTH ISLAND

rest them for loitering and find out what they up to.'

'Probably looking for us,' Eva feared.

Joelle agreed and then said to Eva, 'Are you up to answering some questions?'

Eva nodded.

'Do you remember when Martin Pleasance disappeared?'

'Not the exact date, but it was about three weeks ago, maybe a few days more.'

'Did he say anything, or was he behaving in an unusual way?'

Eva thought back, 'Yes, now I think about it, something upset him that day you were on Moth Island questioning us about that young man.'

Joelle nodded, 'Yes I never did find him and question him that day.'

'It was shortly after that he came and asked me for your phone number. He seemed nervous, even frightened, he told me he had spoken to Douglas who had told him he must speak to you.' Eva remembered.

'He never did,' Joelle said thoughtfully, 'was that the last time you saw him?'

'Yes, I think it was,' Eva replied.

Joelle turned to Jasmine asking about the man she had seen on the beach that she believed was white.

Jasmine frowned, 'I honestly can't be sure, I suppose I assumed he was white because he had a lighter skin than the other men, but I suppose it even may have been a trick of the light. I only glimpsed him but he was standing in the full moon light, the others either had their backs to me or were in the shadows.'

'You said he was well built,' Joelle asked.

'Yes. He was a big man.'

'If I showed you some pictures would you be able to identify him?'

Jasmine screwed up her face trying to remember the man and promised, 'I will try, but I am not sure, I just got an impression, I did not really see him.'

Joelle left the girls making a mental note to get someone to take pictures of all the staff at the Casino when they carried out the raid.

She sat in the car thinking that perhaps the mists were beginning to lift. She felt uncomfortable about one aspect though, if Jasmin was right about the big man being white she could think of someone that might apply to, Pieter Oys, and she was uncomfortable that she might have misjudged him and reprimanded herself for accepting his hospitality.

She wished she could talk it through with Douglas, he had a knack of feeding her facts back to her in a way that revealed answers.

Douglas.... The thought hit her like a battering ram. Why has she not seen it before, he had been missing now for over two weeks. She stopped the car and sat struggling to rationalise the thoughts suddenly tumbling into her brain.

Douglas was missing. Martin Pleasance had obviously said something to him which was important enough for Douglas to tell him to speak to her. Martin Pleasance disappeared after that and was subsequently found dead, murdered.

The worst thought of all then hit her. Her guilt was overwhelming. Not only had she dumped Douglas for no reason but she had set him up as well. She had told Oys that Douglas was on Moth Island, undercover, helping her with the investigation.

It was then she panicked, convinced that Douglas's body was floating about in the sea somewhere, or possibly even at this moment lying on a deserted beach, bleached by the sun with the birds pecking his eyes and flesh away.

CHAPTER 42. THE MILITARY

Joelle stood, along with a group of police officers, including Merv, and Irene. She shivered slightly, it was six-o-clock in the morning and dawn was just breaking, evidenced by a distinct lightening in the eastern sky. She pulled her fleece more tightly around her and huddled into her uniform seeking some protection from the early morning chill. Joelle and all the officers were wearing their uniforms that morning.

She shivered again, not just from the cold but also from a sense of expectation about what was coming. She felt icily calm, anticipating with some pleasure what was about to unfold. Strangely, all the mush that had been fogging her brain ever since she believed Douglas was having an affair had gone. As she had sat in the car two days previously, overwhelmed by her feelings of loss and guilt believing Douglas to be dead, she had frozen those emotions to the loving side of her being. Now she wanted revenge and was coldly and calmly planning her actions.

She stood amongst the group of police officers, no one spoke, they had been briefed earlier that morning and had picked up Joelle's new mood. There was no need to talk, they knew exactly what was expected of them.

Joelle's thoughts wondered inconsequentially for a moment as she tried to decide exactly at what point night gave way to day. She looked at the trees, still black, silhouetted against the lightening sky, and the grass and undergrowth still a monotonous grey colour. She decided the turning point was when the grass turned from grey to green.

She noticed that the soldier, a corporal, carrying the field communicator was talking into his microphone but she could not hear what he said. He whispered something to the Sergeant in command of Delta squad waiting at the marshalling point with the police.

'Alpha squad is in position now outside the main entrance and the landing craft with Beta squad is standing off the reef waiting for the command to enter the bay and secure the beach head,' the Sergeant whispered to Joelle. He looked at the sky, 'should not be long now, they are just waiting for enough light for the landing craft to navigate the channel through the reef.'

Joelle thanked him and thought back to the previous afternoon in the Commissioner's office when she had met Colonel Macfarlane.

He had been delighted at the prospect of supporting the police with a raid on Moth Island. 'A real military operation,' he had said enthusiastically.

Joelle explained that all the evidence pointed to the Casino as the principle location of whatever was going on and that she wanted to concentrate the raid on the Casino complex.

Colonel Macfarlane took charge and unfolding a map of Moth Island across the Commissioners meeting table, planned a military operation to capture the target, as he called the Casino. After a little thought outlined his plan to Joelle and the Commissioner.

'We will use a full platoon split into three groups of ten men. Beta squad will use the landing craft to secure the beach head and then move up the grounds to surround the main buildings from the rear. Alpha squad will secure the land entrance and will then move to surround the front of the buildings. You, Inspector, and your officers will remain here, the marshalling point, with Delta squad,' he pointed to the position on the map. 'Once the front gate is secured Delta platoon will move up and join Alpha to secure the buildings. The police will remain at the marshalling point until my men have secured, and made safe, the grounds and buildings of the target.'

He looked to Joelle and the Commissioner for

agreement.

He explained that Lieutenant James would be in command and would give the authorisation for the police to enter the Casino. He asked Joelle what her plan was when the target was handed over to her.

'We will wish to interview the persons found, search the premises and I anticipate making some arrests, but until we gain access and discover what is going on it is not possible for me say what we will find and what actions will be required.' Joelle explained.

'Very well,' the Colonel understood.' Lieutenant James will be in sole command of the operation until the target is secured and you enter the premises. At that point, he will take instruction for you. Is that understood?'

Joelle nodded agreement. They arranged that she and her officers would meet with Colonel Macfarlane and Lieutenant James and the platoon at 3.00am the following morning for a final briefing before setting off for Moth Island.

Oh dam, she thought, it's got light and I missed the grass turning green.

The sergeant whispered to her, 'we have picked up a message, the landing craft is safely through the reef and has secured the beach head.'

Joelle contained her frustrating at having to stand in the side lines waiting to be admitted to the Casino while someone else ran the first phase

Mr John de Caynoth

of the operation,

'Inspector, the target is now secure and Lieutenant James authorises you and your officers to enter the compound,' the soldier, who had run down the path to the marshalling point, told Joelle.

As the police officers approached the Casino buildings they observed it was surrounded by soldiers, machine pistols at the ready. They walked into the main gambling hall where Lieutenant James had gathered all the people found in and around the buildings, some forty-five in all. There were two soldiers on each door threatening to shoot in the leg anyone who tried to leave. Everywhere was confusion and noise. Lieutenant James was being harangued by two overweight grey haired men while he tried vainly to direct his troops. Three security guards were looking speculatively out of a window contemplating an escape but were deterred by a soldier patrolling the back of the building.

As soon as the police walked into the hall they were surrounded by another group of men demanding to know what was going on. Joelle ignored them, looked round for Pietor Oys but could not see him anywhere. She pushed her way up to the raised dais on which the 'not-to-be-used' roulette table stood and taking a pistol from one of the soldiers shot a round into the air bringing down a small storm of ceiling plaster.

MOTH ISLAND

It had the desired effect, the room fell silent and Joelle invited Lieutenant James to join her on the dais.

Joelle asked the Lieutenant if there had been any problems or casualties.

'No Ma'am, but the dog handlers released two dogs in the grounds and we had shoot the dogs, but that is all.'

Joelle nodded and then asked, 'Lieutenant, if you would please, sort out the guests, staff and others. Guests in that corner, staff there, security men in that corner where there are no windows, and anyone else, hold in the centre of the building.'

She addressed the now expectant crowd of people standing silently below her.

'My officers will interview you one by one and we will decide what then will be done,' she told them.

A voice from below shouted belligerently, 'Do you know who I am. A Senator of the Unites States, and this is monstrous. I demand to be released immediately.'

'All in good time Sir, please be patient,' Joelle politely told him.

He started to argue but she ignored him.

Other voices joined in, wanting to know why they were being detained and demanding to be released and before long the clamour was becoming uncontrollable.

Joelle fired the pistol again, but this time over

the heads of the crowd below, releasing another small hail of ceiling plaster.

Silence fell a second time and this time Joelle threatened to arrest anyone who started another disturbance.

The Senator repeated his demand to be released.

'Lieutenant, arrest that man and hold him under an armed guard until I have time to deal with him.' Joelle instructed. The Senator was marched out of the room at gun point, still muttering objections as Lieutenant James ordered his two sergeants and a corporal to start organising the detained into groups as directed by Joelle.

'Lieutenant, as soon you have everyone sorted out perhaps you could assign your men to work with my officers to interview everyone and take down their statements'.

Joelle and Lieutenant James remained on the dais for a few moments watching the soldiers move individuals to their assigned groups.

'If you would be so kind, Lieutenant, I need to search the building and find Mr Oys, please would you be good enough to accompany me.' Joelle asked James when it was clear the crowd below were cooperating.

It did not take them long to find Oys's office, but the door was locked although they thought they could hear voices inside.

'Unlock this door,' Joelle demanded kicking it with her boot. There was no response.

'If you don't unlock the door immediately we will force the lock,' Joelle demanded again, impatiently. Still no response.

'Lieutenant, shoot the lock out please.'

'Delighted,' said James as he fired his machine pistol at the door obliterating the lock in splinters of wood.

Oys was sitting at his desk holding a satellite phone,

'Joelle,' he said, 'you don't know how relieved I am to see you. I assume you have come to arrest this band of villains who have besieged us.'

CHAPTER 43. THE ARRESTS

'Put the phone down Oys,' Joelle instructed him as she presented him with her authority to search the Casino and arrest individuals as she saw fit.

Oys looked questioningly at her.

'These villains,' Joelle indicated Lieutenant James standing behind her, 'are the Kaetian Army. They have the Casino surrounded and are at the moment under my instruction holding all your staff and guests for questioning while we search the complex.'

Joelle pulled out some latex gloves and picked up a large rucksack she noticed lying in a corner. It was empty. 'Is this yours?' She asked Oys.

He shrugged, 'never seen it before.'

'Lieutenant, please could ask one of your men to find a large plastic sack, I want this rucksack as evidence.'

Oys stared threateningly at Joelle his eyes hooded and cold. He said nothing and Joelle was glad that she had the comforting bulk of the big black Lieutenant standing behind her, casually pointing his machine pistol at Oys's chest.

'Please open the safe,' Joelle instructed.

'I don't have the combination,' Oys countered.

'Oh, come on Oys, of course you know the combination.'

Oys sat staring malevolently at her making no effort to open the safe but Lieutenant James tapped Joelle's arm and pointed to a group of post-it notes stuck to a notice board, 'That one, it has a series of numbers written on it, might be the combination.'

Joelle noted a concerned look flicker across Oys's face.

A soldier was summoned to attempt to open the safe using the numbers on the post-it note which Oys had tried but failed to grab. Lieutenant James made him stand against the wall with his hands on his head while the private tried the combination.

The first attempt was unsuccessful.

'Try the numbers in reverse,' Joelle said but that did not work either.

Joelle looked at the numbers. 'This one at the end of the series, the number three, is circled. Try the safe again but this time add three to any number lower than five and deduct three from any number greater than five.'

The safe opened and they peered inside. Not unexpectedly there were a number of large bundles of US dollar notes but, disappointingly, nothing else. They pulled all the notes out and stacked them on the desk.

'How much his here?' Joelle asked.

Oys shrugged again, 'Millions, what else did you expect to find?'

Joelle looked at the notes and out of curiosity picked up a bundle of new twenty dollar bills remembering the case a while back when the discredited American FBI detective Tony Choizi had tried to destabilise the Kaetain economy by flooding it with forged twenty dollar bills.

'They could not be, not again,' she whispered to herself, rubbing one of the notes between her fingers. She tested the paper by feeling another note, a fifty-dollar bill, it felt different. She pulled some notes out of the stack and spread them on the table.

Lieutenant James watched her curiously, Oys watched nervously.

The first five notes all had different serial numbers, but the next five notes repeated the same sequence.

'Please call DC Deoyen,' she shouted to the soldiers on guard outside the door, and then to Lieutenant James, 'Please arrest Mr Oys and put him under armed guard.'

Irene arrived and was told to bag up the money and seal the bags and take them to the Bank of Kaeta to be counted and held in their strong room.

'Tell them the notes are police evidence and I believe the new twenty dollar bills are forgeries,' Joelle instructed Irene and turning to Lieutenant James asked him to arrange transport and a guard to escort Irene to the bank.

Joelle and Lieutenant James then set about searching Oys's office. Joelle started with his desk while James went across to a three-drawer grey steel cabinet. It was locked but Joelle threw him a bundle of keys she found in the desk. There was a bottle of rum in the bottom drawer of the desk, guest lists, a cash book and other paraphernalia normally found in a desk, but the cabinet, when James got it open, was far more interesting. The top drawer was empty except for a cardboard box containing unmarked bags of pills, powders and blocks of brownish resin.

'Well, I think we have found the drugs,' Lieutenant James stated. Joelle replied, 'maybe, but there is hardly enough here for a full-scale supply operation, and certainly not enough to make smuggling worthwhile.'

They opened the middle drawer and it was full of personal records neatly filed in alphabetical order, each file named and containing an employment contract, cash sheet, passport, and sometimes a photograph, contact address, and next of kin. Joelle quickly flicked through the files. She noted that most of the individuals were young, most under twenty-five, predominately female and a mix of races, Caucasian, Negro and Asian and most had no recorded next of kin or contact address details.

What really got Joelle's interest though was that one of the personal files was for Sofia Luca.

Suddenly the sound of gunfire exploded in the garden. The Lieutenant ran from Oys's office shouting to his troops to hold their stations.

Joelle returned to the gambling hall where everyone was gathered into their separate groups. A sergeant was calling to everyone to calm down and the minor panic caused by the gunfire was subsided with the exception of the most troublesome group of eleven middle aged and elderly men, all guests, and Joelle could see that one of the corporals was having trouble containing them.

Joelle walked across to the group and told them to calm down, that she would attend to them as soon as possible.

Their spokesman responded that she clearly did not know with whom she was dealing. 'We are all influential people with connections in the highest places. We have informed this man,' he indicated the Corporal, 'that we are leaving and he is threatening to shoot us. We already intend to make sure your actions here are reported to the highest of authorities but if one of our party is injured there will be the most serious of repercussions,'

Joelle, still icily calm, simply responded, 'The

Corporal is quite correct, his orders are that if you make any attempt to leave this building before I release you, you will be shot. Is that clear.'

She turned to the Corporal, 'Please take down the name, address, nationality, and so called important status of these gentlemen. I will then interview them one by one.'

Lieutenant James reappeared and Joelle looked questioningly at him.

'No problem,' he said, 'My men were searching the grounds and found three security men hiding in the dog kennels. They refused to give themselves up and threatened to release the dogs so my men fired some warning shots.'

Joelle stepped up to the dais again and called out, 'Sofia Lucca, please make yourself known.' A young woman stepped forward from a group of other women huddled behind the staff group.

Once in Oys's office, and accompanied by Lieutenant James, Joelle invited Sofia to sit down and explained that they had been looking for her ever since she left her boyfriend.

Sofia burst into tears and it was some minutes before Joelle could elicit her story.

After the row with her boyfriend she walked off in anger and found herself outside the Casino where she had got into conversation with a security man. She told Joelle that when she explained to the security guard she had run away from her boyfriend his attitude had changed and he invited her into the guard hut while he rang the main building. She was invited down to the Casino and offered a job. 'I was a bit doubtful, but he was told I could have a week's trial and I thought, why not, it will teach Rich, my boyfriend, not to take me for granted. I only ever meant to stay a few days but once I accepted they took my phone and made me sign a contract to be a hostess. I told them I wanted to leave but they just laughed and said the trial was for them not me.'

From Sofia, Joelle established that there were twelve young women and three young men working as so called hostesses and hosts and that effectively they were prisoners in the Casino. She told Joelle that some were, like her, more or less tricked into working. 'Our job she explained is to circulate round the gambling hall, being friendly with the men, making them spend money and gamble. 'If the men wanted more we are told to do what they want,' she whispered. 'When we do they said, we would get paid more. I think some of the girls and boys were professional prostitutes, that is what they told me, and they said they were earning a lot of money and we would get paid when we leave.'

Joelle asked Sofia about the drugs and she told her that Oys supplied drugs to the guests if they asked, and that she thought some of the girls were addicts as well.

Joelle was beginning to build up a picture now. She suspected The Casino was a front for money

MOTH ISLAND

laundering and a brothel, with the drugs for Casino use only.

She began to wonder about the guests, believing that they were not all they claimed to be. She looked at the list of names and details the Sergeant had given her and noted they described themselves as politicians, business men and some even just millionaires.

She looked at the list, thinking hard, and then picked up Oys's satellite phone. She dialed Jeff Conway's number at the FBI offices in Florida. Jeff was a senior detective in the FBI and Joelle had worked with him before and they had become friends.

'Joelle, long time no hear, how are you,' Jeff greeted her.

She explained where she was and what she had uncovered, Jeff was silent as he listened.

'Wow, sounds like you have real mess on your hands,' Jeff was sympathetic. 'How can I help?'

Joelle read him the list of names.

'You have got some serious stuff there. One of those men is a gang land boss who we would seriously like to talk to, another a politician, we have a file on him, and two of the so called business men are of interest to us as well. I don't recognise the other names but I will circulate them and let you know what comes up. What are you going to do with them? Don't let them go until we know more about them.'

Joelle turned to the Lieutenant, 'I am going the

Mr John de Caynoth

detain all the guests, there is not room for them in the cells at the Police office, would you be able to accommodate them somewhere for a few days?' Lieutenant James said he needed to speak to the Colonel

The rest of the day was spent interviewing. Some people were cooperative and some were not but the information Joelle collected confirmed what Sofia had already told her. In addition, she learnt that most of the security guards were okay, but the head security man and a couple of others were pretty unpleasant thugs.

Merv interviewed the security guards and reported to her that all except one had refused to say anything. The exception invited Joelle to join the interview, telling her he was the only native Kaetian, 'He has already been in prison once and I know his mother, he was frightened of her and has offered to talk if we don't tell her what he has been doing.'

'No promises,' Joelle reminded Merv, 'but let's see what he has to say.'

He told them Oys used the security men like his own private Army. 'I never did anything, just took my guard duties on the front gate and patrols round the grounds. We were instructed to make sure none of the girls and boys got out of the grounds. I did not see it but one of the boys once tried to escape and they set the dogs on him. I never asked what happened to him. Another time I was in the garden and I over-

MOTH ISLAND

heard the boss talking to Oys. He said that the resort manager was going to talk to the police but it was okay, they had fixed him'. His next statement filled Joelle with dread, 'Oys was worried about that and asked them who else he had spoken to. That's all I heard as they walked away.'

Merv asked him if there was anything else.

'Not really, I know they had a boat, they used to disappear at night sometimes and go out in it, I know that because they came back the night of the storm, grumbling, soaked, complaining that Oys had sent them out in bad weather.'

Merv told the young man he would be arrested while they checked out his story. Then man begged Merv not to put him in cell with the other security men.

Joelle tried to question Oys, but he would not cooperate or say anything. She did ask him if he knew where Douglas was, but he just laughed. She passed his name to Jeff for further enquiries.

They received one surprise when they searched the building and first aid room. They had to break the lock to enter the room and then hiding in a cupboard they discovered the woman with the hairy mole on her chin.

At first, she denied everything, but when threatened with being charged with running a brothel, Joelle could not stop her talking. She was employed as matron and house keeper, she said, and was responsible for organising the young women and men. She allowed them to sleep in the mornings and in the afternoons made them clean and service the guest rooms while at night they were on duty in the gambling hall. Joelle decided to add slavery to the list of crimes.

By late afternoon both the police and military were exhausted.

The twelve guests had been escorted back to the barracks in Kaeta town and were lodged, under guard, in the Old Fort. Oys, the old woman, three croupiers and all the security guards had been arrested, sent back to Kaeta and detained, some in the police cells and others in the old fort. The remaining people, the young women and men, cooks and remaining casino staff were told they were not yet under arrest but would remain under guard in the Casino for the time being.

A fresh military squad arrived to relieve Lieutenant James and his men. Colonel Macfarlane had agreed to provide a guard at the Casino complex for as long as needed.

At the end of the day Joelle and her officers returned to Kaeta accompanied by bundles of evidence which was to be sifted through over the coming few days.

CHAPTER 44. THE DAY AFTER

Wednesday morning and Joelle was getting up early. She too had not slept well as her mind kept churning through the problems of the previous day and when she did manage to sleep she was woken by a nightmare, the same one every time, Douglas chained underwater calling to her for help.

She walked round the bedroom, it seemed very empty to her now and she wished Douglas had not cleared all his clothes and trinkets, she desperately wanted to touch something of his but she fought back her tears telling herself she had a lot to sort out that day.

She dressed in old jeans and a white blouse, drank a coffee thinking how silent the house was.

There, lying on the kitchen counter top was her engagement ring, where she had thrown it. She picked it up, kissed it, whispered, 'I am so sorry,' and put it on her finger. The house felt cold and silent, no Douglas to talk to and no Jasmine and Eva chattering noisily together, just Mary snoring gently in the down stairs bedroom she now used since her stroke.

Thinking of Jasmine and Eva she decided it was probably safe for them to return to Windrush. Initially she had put them in a hotel with a police guard, but, with the two men watching the police station in custody and the Moth Island Casino suspects arrested, the danger to the girls was past.

She donned her leathers and wheeled the Triumph out. Six-o-clock, she checked her watch, started the motorbike and headed for the police office.

Joelle was first in the detectives' office that morning and she used the couple of hours on her own to read through the statements from the previous day and examine the documents and other evidence they had removed.

The first thing that struck her was that there were more personnel files than people. She registered that thought, planning to ask Sofia when she saw her later.

Sofia had been taken to the hospital for a checkup and being declared fit had spent the night in a hotel, the same one as Jasmine and Eva.

Joelle read the statements again, thoughtfully. One thing she could not yet get her mind round was the drug operation. They had statements confirming that the drugs found in Oys's office were for Casino use. Anyway, they did not find enough drugs to support the scale of the peddling they had seen on Kaeta, and so Joelle was thinking, where were the drugs, that had been sold to tourists, coming from, where did Martin Pleasance fit in, and finally, the two men Jasmine and Eva thought had returned to the hotel, who were they?

Joelle's thoughts turned to the dead bodies, three of which still remained unidentified, and, Joelle, realised could only be linked circumstantially to Moth Island. It was while she was pondering on this thinking of ways to progress the case that Merv walked into her office.

She looked at him questioningly.

'Things have been happening overnight,' he reported. 'We told the German Consulate we had found Sofia and they informed her parents. Her father is his coming out to collect her as soon as he can get a flight, in the meantime the Consulate have said she can stay with them."

'That is good,' Joelle said, thinking of her budget, at least the police would not have to pay for her accommodation.

Merv continued, 'the owner of the Casino, the Australian, contacted us last night to find out what was going on. Apparently Oys telephoned him yesterday and told him the Casino was being raided. The desk sergeant said you would phone him this morning.' Merv handed her a phone number.

Mr John de Caynoth

Joelle tapped her pen on the table while she thought, deciding to telephone the Australian immediately. Merv picked up the linked phone so could hear the conversation.

The Australian answered promptly and Joelle explained that they believed the Casino was being run as a brothel and a front for money laundering, possibly drug smuggling and that a number of arrests had been made.

The Australian was horrified, explained how devastated he felt that such criminal activities could have been going on in his establishment and promised he would instruct his nearest representative to travel to Kaeta immediately to assist the police, take care of the staff and close down the Casino.

'What did you make of that,' Joelle asked Merv.

'He sounded genuine, but....' Merv shrugged.

'You know what I am thinking,' Joelle looked worried, 'That forged currency, we have seen it before. I bet it's come from the same source as the stuff Tony Choizi was using when he tried to set up a coup on Kaeta, and Tony has never been found, he is somewhere in the world with another identity.'

'The Australian, you're are thinking,' Merv read her thoughts.

'Precisely,' Joelle said.

Shortly after this conversation Joelle was telephoned by David Rail. He told her that he had just been advised that contracts had been ex-

MOTH ISLAND

changed and the sale of the hotels completed the previous evening.

'I was asked to tell you that Leanna Truscott, the manager of the Glass Bay Hotel, was contacted this morning and formally offered the managership of the new two centre Resort Island complex on Kaeta and Moth Island and she will be visiting Moth Island within a couple of days to brief the staff about the new arrangements.'

Joelle thanked him, pleased that at least Leanna had been given a job.

However, her mind was on other matters and later that morning she took a police car and went to the hotel to collect Jasmine, Eva and Sofia. She brought all three girls to the police station.

Irene was told to show Sofia the personnel files and see if she could identify those related to the missing people.

Merv was instructed to clear the yard behind the police station lock it down, ' I want you to take Oys and his security men out to the yard for a ten-minute exercise session. Get as many officers as you can find to guard them.'

Merv looked puzzled, Joelle explained, 'I want to see who he talks to, I am betting that he will talk to those men involved with him in criminal activities. I will be at the window with Jasmine and Eva, hopefully they will identify the men they saw go out with the inflatable.

'That's him,' Jasmine pointed to Oys. 'He is the white man I saw.'

'Are you sure?' Joelle queried.

'Absolutely, look, he is much bigger than the others and walks with a slight limp,' Jasmine was certain.

'And that man he is talking to,' Eva contributed. 'He is the one who came searching for us on the headland.'

Joelle nodded satisfied, she had a starting point now.

The next success was with Irene and Sofia. Irene called Joelle to join them in the detectives meeting room. She pushed a personnel file across to Joelle.

Joelle read the name on the file, Linda Jones, and looked questioningly a Sofia.

'Linda and I became friends, she was Welsh, from Bridgend she told me. One day, the day we had the big storm, a guest chose Linda, he was a horrible man, an animal, none of the girls wanted to go with him because of what he makes them do. He took Linda outside in that thunder storm. I don't know exactly what happened, but we found the guest bleeding and unconscious on the terrace and Linda gone. The security said she had run away and escaped by swimming out from the cove.'

Joelle showed Sofia a picture of the dead woman they had found on the beach with Martin Pleasance.

'That is Linda, what happened to her?' Sofia asked sorrowfully.

Joelle showed Sofia the pictures of the remaining two unidentified bodies.

'I don't recognise the woman, but I think the man is Rodriguez,' Sofia pulled out his file to show Joelle. 'He hated that place, I think the boys were treated much worse than us girls. Anyway, one afternoon he tried to run away, he just ran past the security man on the gate but they set the dogs on him. We never saw him again.'

Joelle, Merv and Irene spent the rest of day questioning Oys and his security men. Oys continued to refuse to answer any questions, if fact he refused to say anything at all. Gradually by questioning the security men they built up a picture of what was going on in the Casino and who was involved.

Their biggest break through was while questioning the man identified by Eva.

Merv told him he had been identified and would be charged with Rodriguez's murder. At that point, he gave in and pleaded that he was only following orders

'Whose orders,' Joelle demanded.

'Oys's.'

He told them the head security man did all the dirty work, 'It was him who did for Rodriguez, I only got involved because he trusted me, we worked together before,' he admitted. 'He never trusted the other men, even though some of them wanted to get involved, we got paid extra for the jobs see. He always said the fewer people that know what is going on the better. He only ever used the others to guard the compound and stop people getting in and out.'

With that information, Joelle and Merv re-questioned the head of security. Eventually he also claimed that he had just been following Oys's orders.

He was asked about the inflatable boat and confirmed that once a month Oys would take it out at night and meet a big yacht off shore. 'I have no idea what for, he never told me.'

'Did you go with him?' Joelle asked.

'No, he had his own crew, he liked me to stay in the Casino when he was away.'

Towards the end of the day Merv and Joelle sat putting together what they had discovered.

'Do you think we have enough to charge Oys with something,' Merv asked Joelle.

'I don't know, I will sleep on it and we will make a decision tomorrow,' she replied.

CHAPTER 46. BREAK THROUGH

The next day they did charge four people, Oys, the woman with the hairy mole, the head of security and his trusted sidekick. Joelle threw the book at them, murder, slavery, false imprisonment, money laundering, drugs and anything else she could think of. Oys just laughed and challenged Joelle to prove it all. The other three started to shout their innocence. The remaining security men were charged with false imprisonment.

No sooner had they finished this when Joelle received an email from Jeff Conway with background information on the twelve guests still detained under military guard in the old fort. There was nothing particularly criminal on eight of the twelve but the other four Jeff asked Joelle to arrest, as, with her permission, the FBI would like to send some agents to Kaeta to escort them back to the USA to assist with enquiries.

Mr John de Caynoth

'Merv,' Joelle called her sergeant into the office. She gave him the list from Jeff's email and told him to go to the Old Fort and release the eight men and detain the remaining four.

It was while she was briefing Merv that an American attorney asked to speak to Joelle.

He explained that he was the Australian owner's representative and had been instructed to assist the Police with their enquiries, to offer the guests every assistance to return home, dismiss the staff and close down the Casino. 'I am instructed to ensure the staff, especially the unfortunate individuals inveigled into the more unsavoury activities,' he shook his head sadly at this point, 'receive a generous payment.'

Joelle was extremely grateful the attorney had turned up, she was beginning to worry about what to do with all the people still held in the Casino.

'We will have to question everyone again, but after that I see no reason why we should detain them any longer,' she told the attorney, promising to take him over to Moth Island as soon as she was free.

Freedom took a little longer than she expected as when she returned to the detectives' room one of the officers who had been examining the inflatable was waiting to see her.

'We have had a development,' he told her, very pleased with himself. 'There was not much we could use in the inflatable itself but there were

MOTH ISLAND

a couple of paddles which had some very clear finger prints. We eliminated your daughter's and her friend's and then did a search on the rest. Look, we have a match for one set, one of the Farthing brothers.

The Farthings were an old Kaetian family who lived on the fringe of the law and most of the brothers had been arrested at some time or another.

Joelle pulled out her list of employees on Moth Island. 'I thought I had seen that name,' she said stabbing the list with her finger. 'There, Robert Farthing, a gardener in the hotel grounds.'

'We can match one other set with one of the men you charged this morning, but these prints, we don't know.'

Joelle thanked him for the information and as soon as Merv returned she told him to round up Irene and Miranda, 'We are going to Moth Island to make some more arrests,' she told Merv gleefully.

Leanna Truscott was standing on the Moth Island hotel landing pier, waiting for Joelle to alight from the boat.

'Leanna, I was not expecting to see you here so soon?' Joelle greeted her.

'Am I glad to see you,' Leanna exclaimed. 'We saw you coming over and I must talk to you. I have no idea what I have walked into here. The Island is crawling with soldiers, the Casino end of the Island is out of bounds, the guests are upset, some threatening to leave, and I was told to meet Douglas Jay here but he has disappeared, as has the receptionist, Eva.'

Joelle explained and calmed the woman down. She told Merv and the two police women to go and find Farthing and arrest him, 'handcuff him to something heavy, and then finger print all the male staff here,' she told him.

On her own, she then walked out along the landing pier and looked sadly at the water. Leanne's mention of Douglas had pulled him from the back of her mind and into sharp focus, she was telling herself not to lose control again, all she could do now was to find him and find out what had happened to him.

She was interrupted by the attorney who had crossed to Moth Island with the detectives. He was waiting for Joelle to take him up to the Casino. She pulled herself together, she knew what she had to do about Douglas but it would have to wait until she got back to Kaeta.

The Casino end of the Island was indeed under guard but Joelle was recognised and allowed to pass with a salute as she and the attorney walked up to the Casino. Once there they called all everyone together. Joelle apologised that she had had to detain them. She introduced the attorney and then asked the assembled people to patient as the Police would like to question them all again and take a statement but then they would be free to leave.

MOTH ISLAND

While the attorney then went through his plan Joelle went to find Lieutenant James to thank him and tell him his presence was no longer necessary and he and his men could return to Kaeta.

It was some time before she got back to the hotel, it seemed like everyone in the Casino needed to speak with her before she could get away, but when she did reappear at the hotel Merv and the two police women had finished taking finger prints.

'I am afraid that we found no match for the prints on the paddle,' Merv reported, to Joelle's disappointment, 'but here is a curious thing, we have two people apparently with identical prints.'

Joelle looked at the prints and then asked, 'can we identify any staff members whose prints we have missed.'

Merv went off the check the staff list against the list of people they had finger printed. He returned after a few minutes. 'We appear to have finger printed everyone, but,' he produced the prints again,' this set is from one of the bar men, I took them and I recognised the man so I know they are his, but this set, he produced the identical prints were taken by Miranda and apparently are from another barman.'

'Then we have our man,' Joelle was pleased. 'Go and arrest both barmen.'

CHAPTER 48. THE DRUG GANG

That evening Robert and the two barmen had been brought back to the police station and locked in the cells. All three had been questioned and had denied any involvement, pleading their innocence.

'Lock them up, we will try again in the morning, I have better things to do than listen to this winging,' Joelle had said losing her patience with Robert Farthing. Those better things were that she wanted to speak with the head of the local Coast Guard Service, but by the time she got down to the port it was late and the Coast Guards had finished for the day.

The next morning Joelle was at her desk early again. She wanted to finish questioning the three prisoners quickly so she could get down to the Coast Guard.

The first man questioned, the one who had been finger printed twice, admitted he had covered for his colleague but claimed he knew nothing about drug smuggling or anything else. 'He said he was busy and asked me to cover for him when the police woman came asking for his finger prints so I gave her mine instead,' was his excuse. Joelle released him with a caution.

The other barman claimed he knew nothing and nobody had asked for his prints. Joelle was exasperated when she discovered that, even since his arrest, no one had taken his finger prints to match them with those on the paddles.

Robert Farthing was still claiming he was innocent, it was then that Joelle lost her patience and told him she had evidence he was involved. She instructed the officer escorting him to return him to the cells and charge him with murder, drug smuggling and money laundering. 'And for being so uncooperative we will make sure you get a life sentence,' she told him as he was taken away.

That done, she rushed out of the Police Offices. She did not bother with leathers or a helmet, she kicked the Triumph into life and shot through the town to the port scattering terrified tourists as she rode through the narrow streets at high speed.

She sat with the Senior Coast Guard looking at tide tables, charts and studying current and tide flows.

'It all depends where the body was put into the sea.' The Coast Guard explained. 'The bodies found so far must have entered the water not

Mr John de Caynoth

more than a mile off shore to have been washed in by the current. Further out the currents are much stronger and could drift a cadaver right pass the Island. Are you sure Mr Jay has been murdered and dumped at sea,' he asked.

'Well his body has not been found on Moth Island and no bodies reported on Kaeta and in view of the four bodies we have found so far washed up on the beaches it seems most probable,' she explained.

In the end, they agreed that Joelle would organise another search on Moth Island, looking especially for any newly dug dirt that might be a grave. The Coast Guard would organise one of their boats to cruise round both islands, inspect all the beaches, especially the difficult to reach ones which are not visited often.

'We will start in the morning,' he told Joelle.

'Can I come?' she asked.

She returned to the police station looking for Merv but was told he and Irene were questioning Robert Farthing again. That annoyed her, she had wanted to get Merv to start another search of Moth Island, so in a rather morose mood she glared at her ever growing in tray and started snatching the papers there-in to read. About an hour later Merv appeared and handed her a statement which Robert Farthing had just made. She started reading. Robert admitted he and the other barman had been involved in a drug gang led by Martin Pleasance.

Our role was spot likely guests who might buy drugs and to direct them to Saws who would arrange delivery. I also crewed on the inflatable sometimes. It was Martin's inflatable and he used it to meet a large yacht every so often where he would collect a packet of cannabis which he would split up and sell. He was very careful never to get involved in the sales himself, he always got someone to front it. It started to get serious when the Casino opened and the manager there, Mr Oys, got involved with his security heavies. He started going out with Martin and collecting his own package. I never knew what was in his package. Drugs I supposed, but it was always much bigger then Martin's. Martin discovered they were using the inflatable to dump dead bodies out at sea and when Inspector deNouvels started asking questions he got cold feet, saying he was not involved in murder, and was going to finish things. He disappeared shortly after that.'

'What did you tell him to get him to make this statement?' Joelle asked Merv suspiciously.

'Nothing,' Merv said innocently. 'He asked to make a statement after you threatened him with life imprisonment. All I said was that if he told us everything we would put in a good word for him.'

'Hmm,' Joelle murmured unconvinced,' I don't suppose he gave you a name for this large yacht?'

'No, he said he never saw one, all the names on the hull had been painted out.'

'Difficult to trace then,' was Joelle's conclusion.

CHAPTER 49. TEARS

Eight-o-clock in the morning and Joelle was waiting impatiently on the quay side at the Keata Town docks. She watched as the Coast Guards orange inflatable motored slowly across the bay from its boat house to pick her up.

There were two crew on the boat and the one Joelle assumed to be in charge, the dock's pilot, handed her a flotation vest and asked where she would like to start looking.

'Can we head south as close inshore as possible scanning the foreshore and then across to Moth Island.'

'We can but we only have this boat for two days,' he warned Joelle.

They cruised slowly along the coast and at first Joelle had a pair of binoculars stuck to her eyes as she scanned the beaches and rocky foreshores. After a while her eyes began to ache and she started to feel seasick. The seaman crewing saw her going green and offered to take over for a while. She gratefully accepted his offer and promptly vomited over the side of the inflatable. Nothing was said as the crewman pulled up a bucket of sea water to wash down the side of the boat.

Recovering Joelle assumed her watching again, although this time she did not use the binoculars as much realising that she could see more without them and only needed them to zoom in on anything suspicious.

They spent all morning floating down Kaeta's foreshore and along the south side of the Island. Joelle felt very sad as they cruised into Three Sisters Bay, this was where Douglas had proposed to her, and rather irrationally she had thought she might find him there, but the bay and beach was empty.

They moved rather faster across the stretch of water between Kaeta and Moth Island. The powerful outboard drove the inflatable's stern deep into the water and bow lifted as the boat skimmed across the waves. The wind blew a refreshing spray across the boat and it would have been an exhilarating ride under other circumstances but Joelle did not notice, she was concentrating on watching the water just in case she spotted something.

They reached Moth Island, the pilot refused to take the inflatable across the reef so they had to stand out to sea while they went around the reef. Both Joelle and the crewman scanned the foreshore but saw nothing. As they reached the Atlantic side of Moth Island they moved further in shore and scanned the beaches carefully. At one point Joelle called for the boat to be taken right on to the beach. She had spotted something suspicious but as the got nearer it was only a large lump of wood with a piece of sacking attached and tangled up in some sea weed.

She waved to Merv and the two policemen walking around the Island looking for a grave. They moved into the shore within hailing distance and Merv shouted that he had found nothing. The search continued.

That afternoon Joelle completed the search of Moth Island and crossed back to Kaeta and started to look up the east facing shore line. The pilot told Joelle that he thought they were wasting their time saying that as they headed further north the sea current came straight in from the Atlantic and it was unlikely that the body would be picked up by this flow but Joelle insisted that they complete the searching round the full Island.

'We will do that tomorrow,' she was told as the pilot opened the throttle and headed back to Kaeta town. It took under an hour to get back to the dock side.

The next day was more or less a repeat of the first day except they finished looking up the east, Atlantic coast and then headed across the top of Kaeta and round back down the Caribbean shoreline finishing at Kaeta docks.

Joelle was not sure whether she was disappointed or glad they had not found Douglas. She expected that by this time he would be dead but in her heart she resisted believing her conviction until she could find his body. The two seamen could see she was depressed and did their best to cheer her up, but in reality there was little they could say. They did however dissuade her from borrowing Scuba diving equipment and going out to look for Douglas's body possibly trapped under water by pointing out that there was a lot sea out there and she had no idea where to start looking.

She did decide to re-question the prisoners again this time specifically asking for information about Douglas. The two people, Oys and his head of security, she suspected may have some knowledge of what had happened to Douglas were both unhelpful. Oys continued to maintain his silence and the head of security denied any knowledge of Douglas, as did the rest of the prisoners she questioned.

She had initially suspected the Australian owner had been involved with Oys, even wondering if this was Tony Choizi's latest persona. But the enquiries she had made had been returned with no hint of any impropriety associated with the Australian. He was a reclusive millionaire owning a variety of business and highly regarded as a local benefactor.

She had, of course, enquired into Oys background and it turned out he had criminal record in South Africa for violence and extortion. This together with the evidence that Oys had been utterly ruthless in protecting the secrecy of his activities in the Casino led Joelle to believe that Douglas must have discovered what was going on, possibly from Martin Pleasance and this had resulted in Douglas's disappearance and probable murder.

She had therefore spent four days convinced Douglas was dead and discussing what further steps they could take to try to find his body. Merv was doubtful about this, pointing out that apart from Joelle's suspicions they had no proof that Douglas was actually dead.

'Surely it is worth doing a search at the airport and port authorities to see if he just slipped out of the country, and we have not even looked for his car yet.' Merv proposed.

Joelle was shocked at this suggestion as it dawned on her that she had been so focused on assuming Douglas was dead that she had not even made the elementary enquiries she should have made for any missing person.

Merv depressed her even further when he pointed out that following her break up with Douglas he might have got fed up and just decided to leave and start a new life somewhere.

'He would have told me if he was going to do that,' Joelle reflected.

MOTH ISLAND

'Why,' Merv countered, 'after all you were not even speaking to him back then.'

Joelle felt awful but agreed that they should check to see if Douglas had left Kaeta either by plane or by sea. They also circulated a description of his car to see if turned up anywhere.

It was not long before they had a call from the airport to say that the MGB had been found in the car park. The search of departure records however was not so promising. All Joelle could tell them was that Douglas had probably left sometime over the last four weeks and they had run a computer search of departures with no success. However, the border security clerk told Joelle that they were two to three weeks behind in computerising the departure counterfoils and that if Douglas's departure was in a batch not yet loaded it would not show up on the search.

'Can't you look through the counterfoils then? 'Joelle asked. The clerk told her that could take days, it would be quicker to wait until the counterfoils were processed and then repeat the search.

Joelle groaned, but in the end, she did not have to wait that long for news of Douglas. The next day, Wednesday, late in the afternoon as she was packing up to go home, she received a telephone call from Border Security.

'Miss deNouvelas, that person, Mr Douglas Jay, that you asked us to search our records for. I think you need to get down to the airport. We have a development.'

'What development,' Joelle was curious.

'We have just detained a man claiming to be Douglas Jay attempting to enter the country.'

Joelle gasped, her mouth dropped open, her mind in a whirl and for seconds she sat apparently paralysed, in her chair. Suddenly she came to life, she shot out of the police office without uttering a word and ran to her motor cycle. Her hands were trembling as she fumbled to start the Triumph. She sped out of the yard, forgetting her helmet and leathers in her haste. She made it to the airport in record time, all the way thinking that it could not really be Douglas, someone must have stolen his passport.

The first time she saw Douglas was when she was summoned to the airport to interview a man, Douglas, suspected of drug smuggling. On that occasion she first looked at the suspect, detained in the bare grey interview room, on a CCTV screen in passport control. This time she felt an acute sense of deja vu as she used the same CCTV to inspect the suspect sitting at the same metal table in the same cold grey interview room. She did not recognise the old man sitting at the table. Although the picture was in black and white the man looked old and broken, pale, tired and thin and the camera from its position in the ceiling highlighted the man's thinning, grey streaked hair and balding patch.

Joelle shook her head, he certainly was not Douglas she knew.

Fearfully she went down the interview room, not knowing what to expect. She braced herself as she knocked on the door and entered the room. The man was sitting opposite her at the table, his head bowed staring at the floor obscuring his features, apparently ignoring her entrance.

'I am Inspector deNouvelas of the Kaetain Police......,' she started to say, but was interrupted.

The man looked up, 'Last time you said that to me was when you thought I was drug smuggling.'

Joelle blinked, uncertain. 'Douglas, it is you,' she whispered, aghast at his appearance.

'Of course, it's me, who else were you expecting?' He asked testily, not quite sure what was going on, why he had been detained and was apparently about to be interviewed by his ex-fiancé.

'I am so sorry,' was all Joelle could whisper as she started to sob partly with relief that she had found him alive, and partly from guilt due to his old and broken appearance.

'Sorry?' Douglas queried thinking that perhaps something had happened to Jasmine or Mary, 'why, what has happened?'

He got no answer, Joelle fell back against the wall sobbing uncontrollable, overcome by tears. Douglas stood up and moved tentatively towards her, not sure why she was crying, nor how his advance would be received. As he watched her sobbing her eyes out he could not help himself. At that moment he knew he still loved her and he could not bear to see her crying so. He stretched his arms out and gently pulling her towards him, she fell into his embrace and he kissed the top of her head whispered, 'Shsss, please don't cry my love.'

She lifted her head from his shoulder and smiling through her tears whispered to him, 'Thank you for coming back, I love you so much.'

CHAPTER 50.
RECONCILED

The airport security guard swung his machine pistol into a firing position by his waist and rushed through the door in arrivals marked private, the door slammed behind him.

The twenty or so passengers who had just arrived on the island flight from Barbados via St Lucia froze in shock expecting to hear the sound of gunfire but all they heard was silence as the shrieking and whooping from behind the door ceased as suddenly as it started. The security guard, minus his pistol emerged through the door and whispered to the lady on the immigration desk. She whispered to the younger woman sitting in the same booth manning the immigration desk opposite and both women closed their desks and followed the guard through the private door.

The bewildered passengers stood silently at first but began to get impatient after a few moments.

Mr John de Caynoth

One of the immigration officers appeared and asked them to please be patient for a few more moments, 'there are some VIPs about to pass through,' she told them and disappeared back behind the door marked private.

That door led to the immigration office in which were a selection of old desks and chairs and equally old computer terminals, a kettle, and most importantly at that moment, four CCTV screens, three of which focused on the arrivals and luggage halls, but the fourth covered the camera in the ceiling of the interview room and had been swung round to observe Douglas holding the sobbing Joelle. While there was no sound it was clear to the audience that a happy and passionate reunion was in progress as they gathered round the CCTV screen watching. Eventually Douglas stepped back and tenderly took a handkerchief from his pocket and started to dab the tears and streaked mascara from Joelle's cheeks, he said something to her and took her hand. That was their signal and they all rushed from the office into the arrivals hall just in time to clap and cheer as Douglas and Joelle emerged hand in hand.

The passengers, now totally mystified just stared. Some were holiday makers travelling between islands but the majority were Kaetain nationals and most recognised Joelle, some even Douglas. One woman, standing near the front observed Joelle's tear streaked cheeks and red

MOTH ISLAND

swollen eyes and asked, 'has he been beaten up, is he under arrest?'

'No love,' the immigration official replied happily, 'but I think she is giving him a life sentence.'

Far into the night Joelle and Douglas sat together on the veranda of Windrush with a bottle of wine, although they were too busy talking to drink much wine.

Of course, Joelle had explained her suspicions that had resulted in her telling Douglas they were finished. She had apologised so profusely and tearfully that Douglas had said enough. Although he never admonished her for thinking he was having an affair with Eva he was surprised that she had not realised how close Jasmine and Eva had become and observed that they had both been victims of Ralph's cruelty and that relationship together was probably an enormously important factor in their recovery.

'I had not thought of it like that before,' Joelle reflected, beginning to see that she had been so engrossed in her work that she had failed to see some of the issues and pressures affecting those close to her.

'That reminds me, she remembered, 'Ralph has dropped his law suit but I then got another begging letter from him asking if I could let his have some money as he was destitute.'

'Are you going to?' Douglas asked.

'I don't know,' She replied, 'I might if it would get

Mr John de Caynoth

rid of him, but somehow I think he would just be back for more.'

Naturally Douglas had to explain his disappearance.

'It was all down to the sale of the Glass Bay Hotel. When the sale was agreed, I was summoned to London to lead the due diligence team and I had to rush off that day to catch a flight. The only way I could get to the airport in time was get that Saws, the gardener to ferry me over in the inflatable speed boat he sometimes used. I must admit he made me very uncomfortable but he got me there in time,' Douglas added.

'I am not surprised,' Joelle commented, and told him they had arrested Saws, 'he was one of the gang involved with Martin Pleasance's drug operation and he later became involved in the Oys's activities in the Casino. I found out you had left the Island with him, one of the other groundsmen saw you. That was one of the reasons I feared you had been murdered.' She paused before asking, 'why did you not let anyone know where you were?'

'I did try. I phoned you once but you did not answer, I tried to phone Jasmine and Eva but their phones were off. I had to be careful because I was under strict instructions from Dick Stump to keep the due diligence exercise secret. He did not want anyone to know they were buying the hotels, especially the Bermudian one which was still open. He did not want to lose any bookings.'

Joelle nodded and told him how she had stuck to her price for the Glass Bay freeholds.

'Yes, I know,' Douglas told her, 'Dick was really cross at that, but the MD overrode him on that.' He went on the explain how the due diligence had to be finished in a couple of weeks and they had been working a sixteen to twenty hours a day to get everything finished in time. 'It was so intense I hardly had time to think of anything else and by the time we finished I was utterly exhausted so I took a few days off to rest and try to sort myself out.'

He alarmed Joelle when he told her that at one point he decided he would not return to Kaeta, 'without you I felt there was nothing here for me,' he added, 'but in the end I decided to come back and try to talk with you and see if there was some way we could work things out and get back together.'

A tear rolled down Joelle's cheek and she took his hand before whispering, 'I am glad you did, I really do love you, you know.'

Epilogue

All the arrested prisoners from the Casino were tried and convicted and, except for Oys, are serving time in Kaeta's prison. Following his conviction Oys was extradited to South Africa where he was wanted for fraud and theft offences.

The Australian owner was investigated by the

Mr John de Caynoth

authorities but there was no evidence he was involved with the illegal activities of the Moth Island Casino. The other Casino's he owned were similarly investigated but nothing illegal came to light and the case was closed with the conclusion that it was an isolated crime run entirely by Oys. One outcome of the affair was that the Australian passed his remaining casinos to the Island Resort Company to manage.

The mysterious yacht was never found and Joelle still believes that Tony Choizi was involved and that the yacht was his contact point. The forged twenty dollar bills, with a total face value approaching half a million dollars were returned to the Unites States for destruction. As for the remaining millions, in legitimate currency, recovered by Joelle, the court case to decide its future has still to be heard.

The Moth Island Casino was closed but was then reopened as part of a new Holiday Resort Complex incorporating the Moth Island Hotel and when completed the Glass Bay Hotel, the refurbishment of which is taking much longer than Dick Stump wanted.

With Eva's assistance Douglas installed the new administration system and got it working properly before he resigned and returned to live with Joelle at Windrush.

Leanna Truscott accepted the job as manager of the new resort.

Mary never quite recovered from her stroke and

MOTH ISLAND

became rather reclusive, sitting alone in her garden or retiring to her bedroom.

So, it was that one Sunday morning the family, without Mary were sitting together on the Windrush veranda eating breakfast. Douglas had just commented that work was progressing on the Glass Bay Hotel, 'They have diggers in and are tearing up huge stretches of the gardens, lake and grounds at the moment,' but he was interrupted by Joelle's mobile.

She excused herself and answered it.

Douglas looked questioningly at her when she had finished.

'Only the office,' she said, 'They wanted me to go in, apparently some of the men doing the ground work are refusing to dig out an old swamp. Some Obeah woman has turned up and told them it is sacred ground and haunted. I told them I was off duty and to get someone else to go and sort it out.'

Douglas and Jasmine looked relieved, this was the first evidence that Joelle really meant to take seriously her promise to not let work dominate her life any more.

Douglas took the opportunity to raise a new subject, 'Jasmine and I have been thinking about your new found millions,' he announced.

'Oh, and what have you two been plotting,' Joelle smiled.

'That old plantation house that your ex-boss Bernie Strong once owned, it's never been sold and the girls and I have had an idea,' Douglas was interrupted by an excited Jasmine.

'We would like you to come and look at it with us,' Jasmine enthused. 'We think we could buy it and turn it into a luxury holiday hotel. Eva and I could run it and you and Douglas could be sleeping partners.'

THE END

OTHER BOOKS BY JOHN De CAYNOTH

The Kaeta Series

The Coconut Affair
The Mango Mystery
The Sea Grape

Coming soon
The Obeah Woman

Other fiction by John De Caynoth

Coming soon
The Lacemaker
The Actress

Printed in Great Britain
by Amazon